Beyond the Rose

Books by Sharon Allen Gilder

The Rose Beyond
Beyond the Rose

Praise for ***The Rose Beyond***…"Gilder has matched her Whartonesque setting with a Whartonesque narrative tone that she manages to carry off almost to perfection. Old family secrets are laid bare and all the Hargrove generations must deal with a series of revelations Gilder deploys with a good deal of narrative skill. She layers her story with such lush period color and unabashed emotion that readers will be swept away." *The Historical Novel Society*

"All truths are easy to understand once they are discovered;
the point is to discover them."
Galileo Galilei

Beyond the Rose

A sequel to *The Rose Beyond*

Sharon Allen Gilder

warren press
Maryland

Warren Press, January 2017

Library of Congress Control Number: 2016920660

ISBN – 13: 9780692821312
ISBN – 10: 0692821317

Printed in the United States of America

Dedicated to the memory of
Henry Frank Marraffa, Jr.

For Mark, with love

Acknowledgments

The characters in *Beyond the Rose* have kept me company for many months and I hope they continue their journeys in your imagination and bring you pleasure. I also hope that the joy of reading and escaping to another world never fades as you let literature inform, transform and inspire you.

There are so many wonderful family and friends who continue to inspire and encourage me more than they will ever know. It is impossible to list everyone – you know who you are and hopefully I've thanked you along the way. You are very important to me! To you, my readers, I say a huge "thank you!" Your support of my writing means the world to me. Much gratitude also goes to the editors who publish my work and the booksellers and retailers who promote my books and keep them "top shelf."

Many thanks to my earliest readers: Mark Gilder and Sue Thorpe. Also, thanks to my daughter, Jacqueline Gilder Brentzel, for the light you and your family bring to my life, to my brother, Tom, for cheering me on, and to my mom, Reid Fussell Allen, who gave me my roots and my wings! Special remembrances and thanks to my late father, Warren Collins Allen and my late uncle, James Elbert Allen, Sr. for helping me imagine and give life to my dreams.

The words of teachers who said, "Keep writing," continue to echo in my mind today, and I thank them for their encouragement. But most of all, I thank my wonderful husband Mark, for everything.

This book is dedicated to the memory of Henry Frank Marraffa, Jr. – a wonderful man and terrific friend who is greatly missed.

Poem, "Love's Embrace" ©Sharon Allen Gilder

Special credit and thanks to these talented individuals

Cover photo: Susan Murfin Cardaro

Author's photo: Stone Photography, Bethesda, Maryland

Publisher's logo: Mark Brodsky dba Graphic Squirrel

'Tis The Last Rose of Summer

by Thomas Moore

'Tis the last rose of summer,
Left blooming alone;
All her lovely companions
Are faded and gone;
No flow'r of her kindred,
No rosebud is nigh,
To reflect back her blushes,
Or give sigh for sigh!

I'll not leave thee, thou lone one!
To pine on the stem;
Since the lovely are sleeping,
Go, sleep thou with them.
Thus kindly I scatter,
Thy leaves o'er the bed,
Where thy mates of the garden
Lie scentless and dead.

So soon may I follow,
When friendships decay,
And from Love's shining circle
The gems drop away.
When true hearts lie wither'd,
And fond ones are flown,
Oh! who would inhabit
This bleak world alone?

Prologue

August 2, 1868
England

Her knowledge of him was quite limited. It seemed like only a fleeting moment that she felt his presence from beyond her womb. The turmoil that held her body captive for nay nine long months had ceased, and for that she was glad. She could now be allowed to move forward, to discard the remnants of her past and n'er visit them again. How she had allowed herself to be compromised and placed in such a position she could not easily justify, but rectify her reputation she would.

A wee baby boy. The midwife held him before her. She gazed at her issue and then closed her eyes tight to block him from her field of vision. He cried out and, as he did, tears welled in her eyes and began their journey downward, along her cheekbones, onto her neck, then onto her chest as though the teardrops were messengers with a roadmap to her heart.

There clearly was no turning back. She had cast her fate and his. Their bond would now part, be severed at the quick and, with any luck, no soul would ever be the wiser. He would thrive in a world unknown to her and she would begin a process of not grieving a loss, but of letting go, of denying he ever existed in her universe. This was the way it must be. Denial offered a safe impasse that seemed most appropriate now. Only time would tell if something pushed into the recesses of the mind would ever come calling again.

Chapter One

May 1898
Washington, District of Columbia

"Geese are the spawn of the Devil. They are nasty!" Alexandra's harsh words fell on deaf ears as Arielle pondered the scene before her. A gaggle of the adult fowl had met their fate at the hooves of a team of Morgans. Their driver, shaking his head as he stepped from his wagon, appeared distraught to have so cruelly ended the lives of the creatures passively promenading along the thoroughfare, unaware it would be their final crossing. He shook his head as he observed the carnage. Broken necks and bodies smashed straight through the middle rested among a bed of flayed feathers, some firmly pressed into the macadam.

Arielle turned her eyes away and at once regretted the decision to walk the last blocks to their destination rather than remain in Alexandra's carriage. The sight of any living creature suffering and meeting an untimely end was wont to remain on her mind. She wanted to shake the vision from her memory, to clear her thoughts, as though she had not been privy to the incident. "Aw," was all she uttered as she bowed her head and said a silent prayer for the loss of life, feeling some comfort that no goslings were in sight to be missing their parents.

Alexandra observed Arielle's demeanor. *Always the weakling,* she thought to herself. *What William sees in her is beyond me! She presumably pities every ant scampering on the pavement that meets its final fate from the footfalls of a pedestrian's boot.*

"Oh, gather your wits. Your lips have met the cooked remains of chickens larger than the fowl before us. It is best we be on our way before you plan a proper burial for the winged vermin."

"Alexandra, please show some respect, or at the very least a whimper of care," Arielle said as she glanced back one last time hoping to view a different sight. She shuddered at the unchanged scene. Alexandra glanced back as well most assuredly to gawk at the gore for, in her heart of hearts, she was devoid of compassion for the loss of animal life.

Why, oh why, did I agree to accompany Alexandra today? Time and again I place myself in this position, thinking she will see the error of her ways. But it is all to no avail. William urged me to keep my distance, saying that she was his charge and should never be of my concern. He is so protective of me, and for that I love him dearly but, if she must be part of his life's concern, then she must remain part of mine. Arielle stepped along quickly, all the while trying to conjure ways she could ease the burden of Alexandra from William's duties.

William Clay, a successful lawyer and always the grand gentleman, kept his word to Alexandra's father, Andrew Whitaker, that upon the patriarch's death, he would watch over Alexandra's interests. William knew he would never coddle her in the manner her father had. His catering to her every whim was much to Alexandra's disadvantage for her persistent personality left her bereft of companionship, both male and female. William was quite sure Andrew's offspring would someday meet her comeuppance despite the provisions he had left in place for her well-being. She was not only self-absorbed, but also keenly fixated on William. Her father's death only magnified her bent to have him solely as her own. Her struggle to pull him her direction was often met with fits of pleading and dramatic displays of wont and desire.

Arielle had witnessed more than her fair share of Alexandra's fits and outbursts. She thought that by accepting her invitation to visit a newfound friend before their planned visit to William's aunt, Emma Clay Willard, their relationship would find a new path, one that would prove agreeable to both. However, their personalities were like oil and water, suspended in time with no chance of emulsifying into a cohesive relationship. She had hoped Alexandra would banish her dark side and that her feelings about her relationship with William would have plateaued however, it seemed her resolve to turn William's affections her direction only reached new heights.

Arielle was confident that his heart was hers, while Alexandra was determined to nullify his affections for Arielle. Their courtship was the bane of her existence. If she could only turn William against Arielle and find him jealous of her relationship with a new beau, Alexandra felt full well that his attentions would solely be hers and Arielle would become no more than a distant memory.

The day had begun as so many. Fiona had prepared Arielle's toilette and laid out a lovely dress crafted in a deep, rosy red infused brocade. Burgundy velvet trim accented the garment's petite waistline and its leg o'mutton sleeves. She felt fresh and revived from her night's sleep and ready to face the new day until the doorknocker sounded at the Hargrove's residence and Alexandra's presence was announced.

A tinge of dread passed through Arielle's veins. *What could she possibly want of me? A visit to Emma's should be sufficient to show my willingness to be in her company. I wonder to what she attributes the importance of her new friend whom she so desires me to meet?*

She was brought back to the moment at hand by a sudden waft of the sweet aroma of honeysuckle. It heightened her senses as she looked for the source of the pleasant smell. It was just the balm she needed to draw her away from thoughts of Alexandra's motives and the morbid street scene that began their outing. A lush vine, resplendent with tubular white blossoms, wove along and through-out a picket fence fronting the walkway to a modest residence.

"Here we are," announced Alexandra.

"Where?"

"Why, where I have intended for us to be," came Alexandra's terse retort.

"Why must you speak in riddles? I have asked a simple question and it requires no less than a simple, and, I might add, respectful response."

"Oh, good grief. Why I trouble myself with you is beyond me. I could have gone on this mission alone but, oh no, I took it upon myself to include you. Do not make me regret my decision."

"I must say that I do find myself regretting my decision to ac-company you. Why the mystery? We could have met at Emma's."

"You will see soon enough. Just allow me to proceed." Alexandra lifted her gown to provide her feet the freedom to gracefully ma-neuver the steps leading to the main portal of the residence. "Come along, Arielle. My goodness you are, as they say in the South, 'slower than molasses in January.'"

"Pardon me if I remind you that in Nantymoel, where you know full well I was born, there is no such expression. If you speak of the southern states, they are as unfamiliar to me as my native Wales is to you, that is, of course, unless you have taken it upon yourself to go on another unsolicited and unauthorized journey to snoop into the business of others."

"Will you not let that go? How long must you harp on the same topic? I have put that time behind me and so you must as well if we are to remain friends."

"Friends? My, my, Alexandra, you must be suffering from an extreme case of denial if you imagine we are friends. You, I fear, tolerate me as much as I tolerate you. William is our common de-nominator. It is for his good name and for his ultimate benefit that we show restricted courtesies to one another. It would seem that I must forever have reservations about your intentions."

"William has made it perfectly, or might I say, *crystal* clear that I am no more to him than a ward to whom he is obligated to oversee. His debt to my father supersedes any, shall I say, romantic interests that might ever have been cast my way. I am rather the 'cast-off' and you the chosen one."

Arielle wanted to believe that Alexandra had finally resolved herself to the fact that William would never take her as his lover, however her actions repeatedly boded otherwise. With an abundance of confidence, Alexandra sounded the doorknocker and awaited a response from the other side. Within moments, the door opened revealing a very handsome man with a wavy brown mane of hair just shy of his shoulders. Upon seeing Alexandra, he smiled, revealing a sole dimple on his left cheek. He looked beyond her as his vision captured Arielle, much to Alexandra's chagrin. She thought she would hold his rapt attention and not find him distracted to gaze upon her companion. *I am beginning to see the error of my ways,* fumed Alexandra to herself. *Why I thought it best to bring her along is beyond me. Good grief. I should have waited until I had him caught up in my snare. How will I ever fool William into thinking someone else views me as his object of affection when his eyes are roving Arielle's direction? I must put a stop to this at once if my plan is to work to my advantage.*

"My dear Sully. I have come calling and thought it most appropriate, or proper as some might suggest, to arrive with the benefit of a friend, for you know how the tongues are oft to wag in this city." Alexandra smiled her most demure smile as though the breath of innocence had suddenly blown itself her way. She would exercise everything in her power to deflect Sully's interest in Arielle. *Perhaps she is just a curiosity since they have not previously set their eyes upon one another.*

"Oh, my. Where are my manners? Let me make the proper introductions. Miss Arielle Hargrove, meet Mr. Bernard Sullivan."

"Good morning, Miss Hargrove. I see Alexandra has found a new way to brighten my day."

"Mr. Sullivan," Arielle said as she returned his salutation with a polite nod, though she felt her face flush at his words.

Alexandra was not best pleased. Her plan was taking the wrong course. *I must find a way to redirect Sully's attention from Arielle.*

"Oh, please call me Sully as does Miss Whitaker."

Arielle's ears held closely the intonations in his voice and the sounds reflected from his words. The familiarity of his accent transcended her an ocean away to the dust covered fields and the colliery she knew so well. His was not the crisply executed accent of the United Kingdom as was hers, but the more colloquial tones of the people who made up the lifeblood of the streets of her birthplace. *Nantymoel,* she thought to herself as she looked to his eyes. She had never seen him before this day, yet his eyes held a familiarity as clear as his accent.

"Sir, do pardon my reluctance. It may take some time before I feel that level of comfort. Please do not find me at fault for my caution. Find it a matter of my upbringing or my course of habit."

Alexandra felt a snarl starting to form on her face. *Oh, it is just like her to act mightier than thou and draw more interest with her evasive ways. Sully will be attracted to her if she continues to display this aloof air. Think, think, Alexandra!* She garnered a grip on her facial expression. *Now, settle yourself. You have a new plan, albeit a challenging one at that. I must make it appear to William that Arielle is flirting with my new beau. He must find her behavior deplorable. I will certainly see to that!* Alexandra smiled a big Cheshire cat grin as she looked directly into Sully's eyes. She took her right hand and offered it to him as an assist through the doorway of the brownstone. He took her proffered hand then lent his other arm to Arielle as his skin felt the piercing scratch of Alexandra's splayed claws.

"Why, thank you, Sully," Alexandra smiled sweetly as she gazed into his eyes thinking her wily ways could be dismissed with a smile.

The threesome proceeded to the parlor where the heady scent of spent cigars lingered in the carpet and upholstery. The room was sparse, devoid of accessories or artifacts that would define the inhabitant's interests or roots. Dark browns and greens in the fabrics covering the cushions on four chairs and one divan lent a drab mood to the space only enlivened with buttercream tinted plastered walls. Arielle tried to imagine the room with a livelier motif, one that would invite gaiety and envelope guests in comfort, but her concentration was interrupted by Alexandra's bold voice.

"Come, Arielle, sit. I am certain that Sully would welcome us to make ourselves properly at ease."

"By all means, miladies, make yourselves at home."

"Mr. Sullivan, I must say that I, at first hearing, noted the similarity of your speaking voice to mine. Are you originally from England or thereabouts?"

"You have a keen ear, Miss Hargrove and, as I note from your perusal of this room, a discerning eye as well."

Arielle blushed to think he had witnessed her scrutiny of the parlor. *He is indeed observant, but he is no gentleman to embarrass me so. And, 'miladies', she had not heard that term since her first encounter with William so many months ago when he whisked her from the pavement after she fled her father's manse. I have held a great fondness for the term ever since Will uttered it, however, Mr. Sullivan's use of the word is laced with a tone of sarcasm. I wonder how he and Alexandra came to find one another? At first impression, theirs is a perfect match!*

"I apologize sir, if I have behaved inappropriately. I can say that I am curious about your friendship with Alexandra. If you do not think me too bold, I wonder where you are originally from and how it is that you two have come to know one another? Have you been in the States for a long while?"

"I see you are quite the inquisitive one. Alexandra said you were not docile and I find that an admirable trait in a bird such as yourself."

"Bird? If you are going to be slinging British slang at me, should I now reference you as a bloke?"

"My, my, you two. Let's cease the sparring and save that for the boxing ring. I say we make a fresh start. Sully, please answer Arielle's questions and play nicely with one another for I was so in hopes you would find a common bond." As Alexandra spoke, she let out a deep breath of exasperation.

"Well, excuse my poor manners. Mine was not a royal upbringing, but I do know how to conduct myself in a civil way. To answer your first inquiry, I was born in England but spent the better part of my youth in the Rhondda. I understand from Alexandra that we share a familiar bond to the region."

"I see. Are you saying you have knowledge of the coal mining business?"

"I would be hard-pressed to say I have no knowledge of coal mining for I lived among some of the most prosperous resources for the 'black gold' as the colliery owners so affectionately reference it. But, I was referring to our link to Wales. You, I understand, have quite a history in Nantymoel."

Arielle was unaccustomed to being spoken to in such a bold way. *How brash can he be! And, what on earth has Alexandra shared with him? I have a mind to leave his presence forthwith. My first intuition upon rising this morn was to remain at home. I should never have accompanied Alexandra on her outing. Had I remained true to my instincts I would not now be suffering under this brute's callous insinuations.*

"Oh, I believe you misunderstand. Please, do not think me unkind. I feel we have gotten off on the wrong foot so to speak. I am aware of your father, Sir Ian Hargrove. His reputation as a consummate leader in the coal industry goes without saying. I spent my formative years in Treorchy. The town, as you know, lies in the Rhondda Fawr valley. Though I never worked the mines, when I was of age, I assisted my father as a sawyer on the farm he tended. The coal industry did much to change the look of the land. I am afraid the coal dust put a blight on the meadowlands."

Sully knew at this juncture that he was decidedly not going to mention any details of Arielle's birth, and the revelations about her father and his philandering so deliciously told to him by Alexandra. He would wait until they became more fully acquainted. He felt a great attraction to her history when it fell upon his ears and now, meeting her and witnessing first hand her great beauty, he was all the more intrigued to learn everything he could about her and her sister, Arianna Smithfield. *Yes, I will have to be in her audience on many more occasions.*

"I see. Pardon me for the conclusion I so hastily seized," Arielle said as she glanced at Alexandra with a wary eye. "I have been to Treorchy. It is a beautiful town, undergoing enormous growth and becoming quite congested I believe."

"That it is. I could always find a way to escape through a trip to Bwlch y Clawdd Pass and, of course music."

"Music? I know there are magnificent choirs there."

"That is of what I speak. I was a member of the male choir and enjoyed not only the music but the camaraderie."

"How wonderful to have such talent. Perhaps you will favor us with a tune on some occasion. Without appearing a bit too inquisitive, how is it that you and Alexandra came to be in one another's company? Where did you meet?"

Alexandra was tiring of Arielle's cross-examination of her friend. *Certainly it is no business of hers as to how Sully and I met. I have been unaware of her evil little jealous side until this moment. Perhaps she desires Sully for her own purposes. Hmmm, that might be just the fine turn of events I need to persuade William to see her true colors and have him drop her sorry bones!* Alexandra drew in a calming breath and sat back to hear Sully's explanation.

"We met quite by accident actually. I was in New York City having disembarked the ship from England hours earlier and in my free moments of time, I stepped into a bookstore on Fifth Avenue, Brentano's I believe, to find some reading matter for the final leg of my journey to the District of Columbia. Alexandra had dropped a small treasure, a picture frame as I recall, and I retrieved it for her. We had a brief chat about our destinations and she invited me to visit her once I became settled in the nation's capital."

"Oh, I see. And when was this, what month I mean."

Sully looked at Alexandra to fix the date in his mind and watch her expression to see if she concurred.

"It was this same time of year, in May, I believe, toward the end of the month, isn't that quite right, Alexandra?"

Arielle watched Alexandra's expression change from being at the ready to pounce on Sully's every word to a very placid countenance that overcame her as though she had been stilled like tranquil waters. Arielle remembered very well being brought up to date about Alexandra's shenanigans while she lay in a hospital bed trying to find her way back to her family after the horrific carriage accident in April the year past. For months she was the victim of mistaken identity and thought to be Olivia Smithfield. And, the picture frame. The mention of it brought forward all too recent visions of her father being questioned by a jury of his peers for his indiscretions, and Alexandra's outburst that included hurling a frame with her sister, Arianna's image – a frame she had stolen from Olivia's bedchamber as she lay dying in England. *Most decidedly the frame she dropped at Sully's feet in New York was one and the same. Yes, Alexandra should maintain her composure for she will soon lose Sully as an ally if she sports her true self. That is, of course, unless he is of the same ilk as she. I find it most interesting that luck, or provenance, would have them meet in such a fashion. I shall give him the benefit of the doubt. Heaven knows Alexandra could use a friend in her pocket.*

"Oh, yes, I would imagine that the timing you mention would be quite right if the frame is the one that immediately comes to my mind for it remains a vivid memory. Isn't that right, Alexandra?"

"Oh, now Arielle, let's not dwell on past experiences for they will only serve to muddle our minds. Sully, why don't you share news of your work. I think Arielle will find it of far more importance than I. I am so bored with talk of industry and corporations, however, Arielle seems to have had some 'tomboy' genes rub off on her for she is always dipping into conversations that are typically of interest to the male gender."

"I know my eyes do not deceive me. If I may be so bold, there is nothing unfeminine about you, Miss Hargrove, and I find it quite appealing to meet a woman whose interests travel beyond the usual finds in her Lady's Book or any crafts at hand."

Arielle felt the intense need to draw the conversation away from herself, but Sully kept bringing the focus on her. She wondered if he lived alone in the home and what his business was in the District of Columbia.

"So, you have been on this side of the pond for one year and this is the first I have learned of you?" Arielle found this to be very curious but decided that was a topic she could take up later with Alexandra. "If I may make another inquiry, are you here alone? I mean is the home occupied solely by you?"

Sully smiled as Alexandra made a faint huffing sound and rubbed the shoe on her right foot into the carpet like a racehorse ready to flee. She gathered her composure when Sully looked at her with a raised brow. *I am not so sure that I want Arielle to know about his fellow boarder. He makes me uncomfortable and she will certainly balk at being in his presence, which will ruin my plans to have her around Sully more often. With any luck he is not about.*

"You *are* the curious one are you not? I am renting a room here with another gentleman. His name is Calvin Layton."

"Oh, I see."

"Now, now, it is not what you think, Arielle, and I might add Sully that that is a loose use of the term 'gentleman.' I know you have had some reservations about your boarding mate. Is he about this morning?"

"I should say he is. Would you like for me to call him to join us?"

"Oh, I don't imagine that will be necessary," Alexandra said just as she heard a scampering sound on the staircase. *I would welcome the sight of a big rat right now rather than have that Cal character show his face.*

The threesome turned to see a rather scruffy man enter the parlor. He was unshaven, his hair disheveled, and his clothing rumpled. *Well, it seems I have gotten my wish, for he does quite resemble a big rat this morning*, thought Alexandra.

"Well, what do we have here? What a fine, fine gathering. Why, Sully you have outdone yourself with the lady folk this time. How about some introductions, or at least one introduction, for you, my charming Alexandra, I regret to say are no stranger."

My goodness, thought Arielle. *There appears to be no end to the coarseness being emitted from these two. I must say I am inclined to defend Alexandra with this one. Why on earth has she taken to be in their company?*

"Cal, I am pleased to introduce Miss Arielle Hargrove. She, as luck would have it, is very associated with my homeland and I am sure we will become great friends due to that coincidence."

Cal looked at Arielle and then toward Alexandra. "Well, she is a fine specimen of a woman, she is."

Arielle suddenly felt unnerved. Cal looked at her as though she were standing in the nude. She felt unwashed and sleazy in his presence. This visit was not boding well and she was ready to take her leave when Sully spoke up.

"You know, Miss Hargrove was asking about my growing up years in England and Wales. In addition to being adept with a pit saw, I became interested in the business end of the timber my father cut and sold. He was quite a successful purveyor of timber, or what is called lumber in America. I saw the potential for expanding the family business overseas and came to Washington to explore the options here, in what is often called the land of opportunity. Many a millionaire has been made on these shores, so I thought I might try my hand at that too."

"You sound like you have quite an entrepreneurial spirit. I find that fascinating." Arielle was pleased to hear Sully carry the conversation and squelch Cal's brash tongue.

Sully's expression showed great pleasure. He and Alexandra were not in each other's company very often but when the occasion arose, she rarely wanted him to discuss the business side of his life. Rather, she was wont to meet him at a restaurant in the heart of the city and enjoy a glass or two of claret and a fine dinner where she could tell him of her trials and tribulations dealing with all the people who were unkind to her.

"Business is usually not the world of choice for those of your gender," Sully said as he gave a nod toward Alexandra who scrunched her nose at him. "Your parents made you privy to the dealings of the coal mine?"

"I would not say my parents, but I would say my father. He knew of my interest and has many times kept me apprised of the workings of the mine from both the needs of the management and the employees."

"There is certainly plenty of money to be made, as you are well aware, but it's a dangerous livelihood for the workers and devastating for the owners if a disaster occurs."

"My father has always instructed me that we cannot live day-to-day worrying about what has not occurred. We must always focus on the well-being of the workers to ensure the pits are as safe as they can possibly be on a daily basis."

"Very wise, indeed. I should think I would like to meet your father. As I said, his reputation in the coal industry is beyond reproach."

Alexandra chuckled as she mumbled under her breath, "More than one can say for his personal shenanigans."

"What's that, Alexandra?"

"Oh, nothing, Sully. Something just struck me funny in what you said. It does always amaze me how one can be placed on such a high pedestal without fear of falling. Yet, fall many do, right Arielle?"

Arielle was finding the morning spiraling downward. Alexandra was in her usual poor fetish, Sully was an unknown to whom she was finding it difficult to warm, and Cal was best hidden under the rock from which he seemed to have crawled. It was a motley crew and she was more than ready to cease her time with them. She stood and signaled Alexandra who rose to join her.

"Alexandra, perhaps we should take our leave and let these gentlemen go about their day. Emma is expecting our visit. Perhaps our paths will cross again, Mr. Sullivan," Arielle said as she turned to approach the foyer entrance, feeling awkward with her failure to address Calvin Layton. She hoped not to make his acquaintance again and wondered what purpose their visit served. *What does Alexandra have up her sleeve?*

The two said their goodbyes and took their exit to make their next stop at Emma Willard's home, Chestnut Heights. As they walked along the pavement to their carriage, Arielle turned to

Alexandra feeling the need to address their purpose for visiting Mr. Sullivan.

"Alexandra, I must ask, why did you really want me to accompany you and meet Mr. Sullivan?"

"Oh, quite the contrary. And, I must add, there you go thinking I have some master plan to work some mischief. If the truth be known, when Sully learned that you and I were umm, close, he asked for me to introduce him to you."

"What? Close? Have you led him astray? I should say that is not an accurate statement. Are you using my name for some evil purpose that will in some way benefit you?"

"Well, I am not surprised that your first thought of me is that I am up to something ill-willed. I am shocked that you continue to think I would not have your best interests at heart." Alexandra smiled as she looked at Arielle who was having a difficult time imagining Alexandra with a heart.

"So, Mr. Sullivan wanted to meet me? Did he express why?"

"No, just that he had heard of your father and wanted to know him better. Maybe it is something to do with his business. Your father is successful and maybe Sully thinks he can glean something from him. Maybe he feels a kinship with him."

Arielle was confused. Why would Mr. Sullivan never have approached her father at the colliery and why had he not contacted him in the year he had been in Washington? She felt a sense of unrest. *I cannot put my finger on it, but there is more to know.* There was something there, something about him that drew her curiosity. *Why does he want to know my father? As distasteful as the thought may be, I will have to spend more time with him, get to know him, and learn his true reason for leaving Wales. Indeed, something tells me that Bernard Sullivan's sole purpose here is not what he purports it to be.*

Chapter Two

Thomas found the man whom he let through the portal to be a bit peculiar. He wore an odd shaped hat over his wiry gray hair and a wrinkled, lightweight brown frock coat over his shirt and trousers. He carried a pipe in his left hand and a sizeable satchel in his right. Emma had informed Thomas that a new boarder was on his way, and she had alerted the household staff to ready a room next to the upper library for him. No name or other identifying details had been given. Before Thomas could point the man in the direction of the staircase, the man's satchel was thrust in front of him almost knocking him to the ground.

"I say, old chap, you'd best be minding your reflexes. It's abundantly important that one have his wits about him and be alert to the nuances of the moment in order to be prepared for the game of the day!"

The man's demeanor took Thomas aback, but he had been well-trained by the home's mistress and her late husband, Horace, to never insult a guest at Chestnut Heights. His duty was to make each visitor feel welcome within the mansion's walls. One thing that he knew was in abundance was the man's audacity. *No, my mama would have whooped me to dinnertime if I ever acted like this one. Whew,* Thomas said under his breath as he shook off his immediate reaction and maintained his statuesque calm.

"Oh, come along chap. Show me where a man can rest his weary bones. I've had a long journey and can't wait another minute to settle in for the remainder of the day."

"Yez, sir. Comes right this way. Your room's up the staircase and down the hallway to the right. I'll lead you the way."

Thomas reached to lift the satchel that bore more than the weight of clothing and footwear. The man smiled as he observed Thomas struggle with his baggage, but made nary a move to assist him. As the two approached the first landing, Thomas grasped the newel post for extra leverage to aid his ascent of the stairs. The shuffling sound of a crinoline and quick footsteps emanating from the back of the house announced Emma's approach as she appeared in the foyer.

"Ah, you have arrived. Very well. I see Thomas has welcomed you and all is in order for your stay. When word came from the station about your arrival and your need for housing, the messenger failed to get your name. Let me introduce myself. I am Emma Willard and you have met Thomas. My home runs smoothly thanks to his many efforts. And you are?"

"I am tired. I have been traveling for days and days it seems. I am thankful you had a room to spare and, I must say, the accommodations do not appear to be too shabby."

"My, my, we are getting off to a confusing start. I meant, what is your name? We treat one another like family here, so it is important that I have your name."

"Now, I am the one who must say, *my, my* for, if I am to be treated like family in the way my family treated me, then it would be best for me to abandon the premises forthwith before I am flogged and sent to bed without my porridge."

Thomas was finding some pleasure in imagining this odd character under the influence of a switch and suffering the consequences of his bad behavior, although he was not pleased to have Mrs. Willard become the brunt of his poor manners. He decided to intervene in a delicate way that would hopefully move the man up the stairs to his room. *With any luck, he'll be so tired that he'll remain in his room until sunup and,* Thomas smiled to himself, *miss his porridge.*

"Miz Willard, I was jest gwoin to take this gentleman's bag up the stairs. Is there anythin' else I ken do for you sir?"

"Yes, there is. You can quit calling me sir and call me by my given name. What's the matter with you people? You haven't given me a moment to catch my breath," he looked nervously about him before he spoke his next words, "I am Alistair Whitfield Drake. You will best know me as a writer of mysteries and thus my hesitation to say my name aloud. There is no need in my present state to be beseeched by the adoring fans of my work. I simply must get some rest before the public onslaught."

Emma tilted her chin down holding back a wry grimace. *My,* she thought to herself. *This Alistair Whitfield Drake certainly has a high opinion of himself.* As well read as Emma was, she had not heard of the man or his work. If she could find a way to soften the edges of his personality, and if he was as important as he thought himself to be, he would make an interesting addition to one of her grand dinner parties.

———

Arielle was looking forward to visiting with William's Aunt Emma. She always brightened her day, but curiosity about Bernard Sullivan continued to plague her. *Why did he want to meet my father? Could it really be to expand his business? Why would he not discuss such matters with my father in Wales? Has he followed him to America? What is his purpose?* As she and Alexandra approached the portal to Chestnut Heights, she turned to ask a few more questions before knocking on the door.

"Alexandra, I must ask how you have come to know Bernard Sullivan for a full year and never have mentioned him to me until now."

"Well, my, my, my, must I share my every waking move with you? We see each other on occasion and that is quite all. I found him amusing when we first met and he retrieved the picture frame I dropped. He thought it quite careless of me and he startled at my reaction when I insisted he give it back to me that instant. I think I may have even stomped my foot."

"Imagine that!" said Arielle as the memory of Alexandra admitting to stealing a framed daguerreotype from Olivia Smithfield's home crossed over her with a shudder. *Poor Miss Smithfield, on her deathbed and who does she have to see? The flaxen-haired angel of death.* "So, please answer my question."

"Well, let me see. Sully was busy establishing himself here and I never thought to bring him up. As I said, he asked that I introduce him to you and I have simply honored his request."

"I see. It is just very curious to me that he would want to meet me first before my father."

"It could be that he thinks if he builds a relationship with you, he will have more success with your father."

"Perhaps."

⟜

Thomas and Alistair Drake proceeded up the staircase with Thomas enduring the burden of Drake's satchel. They were midway to their destination when the doorknocker sounded again.

"No need to worry, Thomas. I am well able to attend to the door. Go on your way with Mr. Drake. This is very likely to be Miss Hargrove and Miss Whitaker for I have been expecting them to visit."

"Oh, my, hurry along now, man. I cannot be having these women consuming my time. Once they see me, there may be no stopping their admiration."

Emma rolled her eyes. *This one is certainly going to be a testament to my patience!* She proceeded to open the large mahogany door and to her delight, Arielle stood before her with Alexandra quickly coming up behind. She leaned forward to greet Arielle and kiss her on the cheek only to find Alexandra pressing her way past Arielle and presenting her cheek for Emma's affection.

"Well, excuse me Alexandra. Had I known you were in such a hurry to arrive, I would have stood aside rather than be nearly run down by your enthusiasm!"

"Oh, now Arielle, let's not get off to a bad start for we have just arrived. I am certain Mrs. Willard does not want to be in the middle of a fray of your creation," Alexandra smiled as she stepped through the portal and swung the skirt of her dress around as though marking her territory.

Emma ignored her behavior and greeted Arielle. "I am so grateful for your visit! It is always refreshing to have two beautiful young women grace the rooms of my home. Come, let's sit in the parlor and visit. Cook just made the most delicious cookies to accompany our tea. She said she wanted to test a new recipe she found in the recent issue of Ladies' Home Journal. Sarah Tyson Rorer, who became the publication's food editor last year, suggested it. However, you know Cook, she likes to experiment on occasion, so she has adapted the recipe to her own liking. I am certain you will find them a delicious confection! So tell me, to what do I owe this pleasure?"

"Alexandra and I thought it would be appropriate to extend an olive branch, so to speak, to one another, and to do so in a neutral place. Chestnut Heights seemed the perfect spot. I know I have always felt comforted here by you and your wonderful friendship."

Alexandra felt ready to hurl as she listened to Arielle's words. *Why must she make everything sound so sweet like the syrup made from the drips of a maple tree! She exudes sap! Spending more time in her presence is definitely going to tap my inner fortitude!*

Cook appeared carrying a large silver tray with three china cups and saucers and a pot of tea covered with a cosy. It was accompanied with a tiered porcelain stand filled with aromatic cookies. Arielle recognized the china from her first visit to Chestnut Heights last March. William had rescued her during her rain-swept flight from her home and kindly transported her to his aunt's beautiful residence. *Ah, yes, the first time we met,* Arielle mused with pleasure.

She was prompted to flee her home and seek refuge elsewhere for the night after an incident with her father. His inappropriate behavior toward her was sparked by a letter he received from Olivia Smithfield claiming to have revelations about Arielle's birth. *How that seems like ages ago and yet as fresh as yesterday*, she pondered. *Thanks to God and much prayer, forgiveness and healing have prevailed. And, that evening was also my first introduction to Alexandra. There she sat in the shadows of William's carriage like a nasty wildcat ready to ponce. I should have known then that she would likely never change her ways.*

Arielle reflected on the china and its floral pattern with vibrant tones of forest green, gold, and aubergine that mimicked the colors in the tapestry fabric that upholstered the benches in the nook where she had enjoyed her breakfast the next morning overlooking one of the property's large gardens. Remembering the image of Emma's landscape architect, Simon Peabody, just beyond the bay window overseeing his plantings, brought a smile to her face. She thought of him fondly and hoped to see him today. He was a dear little sprite of a man and was forever fascinated with her eyes. 'Iris freckles' he called the gold flecks surrounding her pupils. Her thoughts had no sooner turned from him than he appeared at the parlor's entrance.

"Oh, oh, oh. I say oh, I'm sorry to interrupt Miss Emma. I hadn't realized that company was in our midst. I mean to say, oh, oh, oh, I mean to say, of course, Miss Hargrove, not to imply that you are not most welcome as family in Miss Emma's home, and, if my intuition is at its most accurate self, it may soon be official that you are indeed family!" Simon could barely contain his glee as he lifted himself up on his toes and back down again like a marionette whose puppeteer had skillfully controlled him with a string.

Arielle smiled and welcomed him with a nod. "It is indeed wonderful to see you Mr. Peabody. I was hoping you would be about the house today."

Alexandra on the other hand was seething. The very mention that Arielle would become part of Emma Willard's family made her skin crawl with angered jealousy. She was less than fond of Simon

20

Peabody. It seemed that he was forever crossing her path while on the heels of protecting Arielle. *How dare he insult me while complimenting her! He knows my association with William and should consider me family well before he starts dragging sweetie sweet Arielle, who was a perfect stranger until last year, into the fold.* She tried to hold her tongue but her jealousy got the best of her.

"Well, Mr. Peabody, are you not the kind one to ignore my presence. Maybe it is time to get those spectacles of yours updated. It seems your shortsightedness and your limited stature go hand in hand."

In an effort to diffuse the moment, Emma lifted the tiered server and offered a cookie to the trio. Ignoring Alexandra was at times the only way to knock her off course. Simon waited until the ladies had partaken of the sweet treat before taking a cookie for himself.

"These are scrumptious! Delectably scrumptious! Yes, scrumptious! Do they have a name? I mean the recipe, of course," Simon asked, joyful that he did not have to exchange further conversation with Miss Whitaker.

"Yes, Simon. Cook said she calls them Oatmeal Crisps. They taste so sinfully good yet, with the oats, how could they not be healthy?" Emma laughed as she selected one more cookie to enjoy.

"If you will excuse me ladies, yes, excuse me, I am going to the kitchen to congratulate Cook on yet another success in her baking efforts!"

Soon after Simon withdrew to the kitchen, a knock came to the front door. Thomas, having completed his duties of delivering Mr. Drake to his room, opened the door to find three unfamiliar faces.

"Good afternoon, we are here to see Mrs. Willard. We have a delivery for her."

Emma heard the voice and knew at once who had come calling. "Excuse me a moment, let me see to my guest."

As Emma rounded the corner, she saw that not one, but three guests stood in her foyer. "Why, Miss Pennybacker, Miss Fielding, and hello to you too, Peepers! What a lovely surprise. You are welcome on any occasion, but what brings you here today? Is there a mystery about of which I am unaware?"

"Mystery? Did I hear mystery?" Alistair Drake's voice came booming from the upper staircase as he cascaded along the balustrade, down the steps and into the foyer.

"Mr., umm, is it acceptable with you for me to introduce you to my guests with your proper name? As you mentioned earlier, I would hate to create a stampede."

"Right you are for asking. At first glance, these guests seem refined enough, especially the tall one here. She appears very discerning indeed!"

"Very well then. Miss Morgan Pennybacker and Miss Agnes Fielding, let me introduce Mr. Alistair Whitfield Drake. Mr. Drake tells me that he is a writer of mysteries. He arrived today for an extended holiday. Mr. Drake, I might add that Miss Pennybacker shares your passion for intrigue and has established quite a reputation for finding the truths that bring cases to a successful conclusion. Miss Fielding is her assistant."

"And what of the bird? A parakeet, I suspect, or budgie, as some would say?"

"Oh, his name is Peepers and he accompanies Miss Pennybacker and Miss Fielding on all of their outings. And, yes he is indeed a parakeet."

"Whoa boy, whoa boy. That's the truth, that's the truth," came Peepers' refrain from his cage.

"I must say, what an interesting character idea. Who knows, old boy, you might just end up in a novel some day!" Alistair threw his head back and boldly laughed at his own suggestion.

"It is my pleasure to meet you, Mr. Drake. In point of fact, I know of and admire your work. When we were last in England, I saw one of your novels in the window of a bookstore and stopped in to make its purchase. 'The Widow's Wicked Web' was the title. The widow was quite a charmer, so much so that she landed several husbands who subsequently landed in their graves. It was very clever how she dodged the authorities until her final marriage to a retired constable who would not be parted from the small pension he had collected. Quite an interesting twist when it is revealed that the constable was the assassin the wife had never met, but hired to eliminate all of her previous spouses. He was happy to help her meet her final demise. The book certainly kept my attention. Oh, but perhaps I am saying too much and ruining the story for others."

"No, Miss Pennybacker, not at all. I am pleased to hear that the book kept you enthralled, for that is my mission when I begin another tome. I want to keep you reading by day, and then have you think of the story before you drop off to sleep, if you dare!"

The entourage laughed with an acknowledging grimace that Alistair Whitfield Drake's works were haunting indeed. Emma was not surprised that Morgan knew who Alistair was. It made perfect sense that she would be attracted to mysteries. Emma's reading repertoire focused on history and the arts with an adequate dose of romance novels for her guilty pleasure.

"This is such a wonderful surprise to have you call today. Miss Hargrove and Miss Whitaker are in the parlor and I would be most delighted if you would join us."

"Thank you, however, we have come by to deliver the Aida cloth and the findings for the needlepoint bell pull you have been working. We have other stops and must be on our way."

"You see, Mr. Drake, I failed to mention that Miss Pennybacker is a businesswoman as well, and quite an accomplished equestrian. In fact, her talents on horseback carry over into her exquisite equine etchings that are on display in her office. She is the proprietor of Pennybacker's Stitchery on F Street. The store is a wealth of fine needlework, finishings, and findings. In fact, the findings portion of her business, is rather a pleasant double entendre, since she is very adept at finding answers for her clients who seek the truth about their pasts."

"Thank you, Mrs. Willard. I do my best. You mentioned Miss Hargrove. We would like to say hello before leaving."

"Well, I dare say, Miss Pennybacker. Before you retreat to the parlor, I am rather looking forward to hearing more about your escapades. The processes of deduction, intermingled with facts and logic, play a significant role in your work, isn't that quite so?"

"Yes, Mr. Drake, you are quite right. I should be glad to carve some time in my schedule to talk with you. Perhaps we can meet the week next. Here is my calling card. You may stop by my shop and make arrangements with Miss Fielding."

"Very well then. I am anxious to know more about my surroundings. Oh, certainly I am not referring to this boarding house, but the greater area. I have a feeling that what I find could be very fruitful to fill the pages of my book. As you, I am sure, are very aware, things are rarely what they seem!" Alistair beamed as he felt a sudden kinship with Morgan and he delighted in what he deemed a snappy repartee.

Emma led Morgan, Agnes and Peepers into the parlor with Alistair Drake fast on their heels. She was not sure if it was his recently fed ego wanting for more admiration or the lure of the smell of cookies wafting through the downstairs that spurred him on.

Arielle stood as Morgan entered the room. The parlor at Chestnut Heights was a grand salon with several groupings of upholstered pieces forming comfortable vignettes for more intimate conversation. It served Emma's needs well, allowing for ample space to accommodate guests at her large parties and numerous smaller groupings for personal tête-à-têtes.

"Well, what have we here? I did not know we had arrived for the cavalcade."

"Who may I inquire is the snarly one?" Alistair stared at Alexandra as he took a cookie and began its consumption.

"I beg your pardon? Who are you to make such a statement?"

"Curiously, asking me who I am seems to be the theme of the day. The only astute person I have encountered thus far is Miss Pennybacker here, but that is not to rule you out, Mrs. Willard. If Miss Pennybacker were a man, I would say she is quite a dandy. And, begging for my pardon would make me your judge and jury, young woman. I must say we have not been in one another's company long enough for me to decide if you are worthy of a pardon.

To date, your crime is the possession of a flawed personality, which is a shame I might add with your fine features and golden locks. I guess one cannot have it all."

Emma was not sure if Drake was reprimanding Alexandra, trying to incite her further, or creating prose for his next work. Whatever his intent, the madness in his method needed to cease. They were both guests in her home and would have to behave accordingly. Arielle observed Emma as she addressed them. She admired Emma's ability to put one at ease very quickly.

"Alexandra, Arielle, this is Mr. Alistair Whitfield Drake. He is a writer and will be boarding here. Mr. Drake, without casting undue embarrassment toward you, we must treat everyone with respect within these walls. At the very minimum, I find it best for one to say nothing if he or she cannot say anything pleasant. I appreciate your respecting my request."

"Right you are, Mrs. Willard. I apologize for my repartee. It would seem introductions are in order now that the young ladies have heard my identity."

"May I introduce Miss Whitaker, whom you have already acknowledged, and Miss Hargrove."

"I am certainly the lucky one to have chosen this boarding house with two lovely boarders such as yourselves."

"You stupid fool, we are not boarders. We are family paying a visit. Maybe it is best that you find your way to your room before you commit another blunder," Alexandra had no patience for Mr. Drake's demeanor. "Mrs. Willard, I do apologize for calling this stupid man, stupid." She held her focus on Mr. Drake. A small smile formed across her mouth as she took satisfaction in the manner in which she expressed regret for her name-calling.

Peepers broke the uncomfortable silence. "Uh, oh! Uh, oh! Remain calm, remain calm!"

"That's quite a bird. Does he always have such keen intuition about his surroundings?" Alistair inquired.

"I would say he surely does," Agnes said as she blew him a kiss and looked on him with pride.

"I think it best that I return to my room. I am in the throws of my next novel and have already allowed too many distractions to dissuade me from writing. Good day, ladies, and Miss Whitaker."

Alexandra felt ready to boil. *That man so gets under my skin! I would never read a page of his excretable words! What a waste of an inked page!*

"So, Miss Pennybacker! How wonderful to see you and Miss Fielding! And I see Peepers is thriving. What brings you to Emma's? Not another truth-finding mission, I hope."

"No, Miss Hargrove, nothing of the sort. The day was perfect for garnering some fresh air, so Agnes and I decided to make several deliveries."

"Actually, there is someone who recently gained my interest. It is only an instinct at this time, but I may want your opinion on the matter in the future."

"I look forward to that. You know where to find me." Morgan turned to Emma. "Thank you for seeing us and for your business. It appears that you will have your hands full with your newest boarder. I had heard that he had his eccentricities. I suppose all of the solitude required of a writer can mold some into less than proper social beings."

It would certainly appear so, thought Emma.

After Morgan, Agnes and Peepers took their leave, Alexandra, feigning a headache, soon followed. A thought occurred to her as she traveled home. *Hmm. Sully is uncomfortable residing with Cal and I need to have Sully in closer proximity to Arielle. I need him in a place where William might encounter them together and see the attraction they are forming for one another. All I need is for William to think Arielle has eyes for another. Hmm. That's it! Chestnut Heights! There is plenty of room there for one more, especially if that incorrigible Drake man takes his leave, and Sully will be in favor of my idea because he wants to get closer to Arielle and her father. Yes! This is the perfect plan! I will soon suggest to Sully that he visit William's aunt and make arrangements to reside in her home! Alexandra you are brilliant!*

Emma offered to have her carriage transport Arielle home so they could enjoy a longer visit. Emma was also curious about Arielle's final comment to Morgan.

"You mentioned something to Miss Pennybacker that peaked my interest. I hope I am not overstepping our friendship to ask to know more."

"Oh, my goodness, Emma, no. I am always grateful for your counsel. It is just that I think I need more time to sort through the feelings that came across me today when I met a friend of Alexandra's. His name is Bernard Sullivan and he is from Wales. He goes by the nickname, Sully. She said she had known him since last May and that they had met in New York City in a bookstore before they made their way here. I was surprised that Alexandra had never mentioned him in all these months. She said he had wanted to meet me and he asked a few questions about my father. It was just odd I guess. I felt he had an agenda that was not being revealed. And the most uncomfortable part of my morning with Alexandra was Mr. Sullivan's roommate, Calvin Layton. There was something rather creepy about him. He did not fit with Mr. Sullivan. It was just very unusual."

"I would say that I have always found you to be an excellent judge of character, my dear. Maybe we should have Alexandra bring Mr. Sullivan around so I can meet him and extract my impressions of him."

"That is very kind of you, but I would rather enjoy leaving Alexandra out of the equation. Mr. Sullivan wants to meet my father, so perhaps we should meet at my home."

"Discuss this with your father and see if such an arrangement is agreeable with him."

"You know my father's ego. He will be in his glory to espouse his principles and viewpoints to another. He is at his happiest when he thinks he is molding someone into his business acumen. It will indeed be most interesting to learn more about this man who calls himself, Sully."

Chapter Three

*W*ell, Sully thought, *Alexandra was true to her word. She promised to bring Arielle Hargrove to meet me. Now, it is her father that I must see.* A sense of turbulence had remained with him since his eyes rested on the unusual passage in his late mother's diary. After much thought, he decided to visit the Big House, the name the locals gave to the colliery owner's mansion in Wales, to make inquiries about Sir Ian Hargrove and to arrange a meeting with him. He learned from the household staff that he had traveled for an extended stay to America's east coast and the center of the country's government and power, Washington, District of Columbia. If he were to try to unravel his mother's message and meet with the man from the Big House, it would have to begin in America. He set his sights on his business and the opportunities for expansion in other markets, all the while determined to pursue his quest to explain his mother's words and put to bed unanswered questions. With any luck, he hoped the answers would bring him calm rather than ignite a firestorm of repercussions.

His thoughts turned to his mother's words. He was making himself crazy with imagined outcomes that suggested that in some way he was related to Sir Ian Hargrove. After he met Alexandra and learned that one of her acquaintances was Arielle Hargrove, she had filled his mind with many details of what at first were thought to be rumors about the Hargrove family but ultimately became fact. Alexandra asserted that Sir Ian Hargrove was a philanderer whose tryst, on at least one occasion, had resulted in the birth of twin daughters. *Could my mum have betrayed my father? Could it be that Hargrove sired me? Could it be that I, in fact, have half-sisters? Who am I?* He was tormenting himself with unanswered questions that arose from his dead mother's writings. *Will I ever know the meaning of her words?*

He decided to take his time in America, establish himself and his business before meeting with Ian Hargrove. He would admit that the idea of meeting with the man intimidated him to some degree. He thought it best to bide his time. Then, the idea of first meeting with his daughter, Arielle, came to him. It seemed like a less formal place to start, so he suggested to Alexandra that she make the proper arrangements for their introduction. The meeting had gone well enough, though there was a sense of uneasiness in her manner. *Maybe that was her way,* he thought, *or perhaps she did not take a liking to me.* He would need to further pursue their relationship, especially if their bloodlines were intertwined. And, as for her sister Arianna, it might behoove him to meet her as well.

He looked at the diary lying beside him. He picked it up and held it securely in his hands. He closed his eyes in quiet meditation and rubbed his left hand up and down its spine. He shifted his right hand to its worn leather cover, pressed it tightly, and brought the book up against his chest. He could feel his heart beating through its pages though his body remained still. Only his chest moved as he took in deep breaths and let them out evenly and slowly. One, two, three, four. He counted them, though all the while his eyes were in darkness as he kept his lids tightly closed, imagining what his mother's written words could possibly mean. Here, within his departed mother's diary, lay a message so cryptic he wondered if it were a fantasy, something she had created in her mind that held no truths. *What could her written words mean?*

His thoughts turned to the day she passed away, only months after his father's death. He remembered thinking sadly that he had now joined the ranks of the millions who were called orphans with no parents to comfort or cheer them. Tears began to well in his eyes, but he stopped them with a swipe of his shirt's cuff across his face. He would not let all that had been good in his life be scorched by the flames of what were possibly the delusional ramblings of a sick woman whose best days had long since passed. His mother had not been the same after his father's death. She became reclusive and seemed forgetful. Her pinpoint sharpness had dulled and the joy she was so known for exhibiting had waned. But, questions burned in his mind and they would not let him rest.

The book, the diary, was amid her belongings placed in boxes by well-meaning neighbors wanting to help organize her home and ease the work for him while he tended to the other matters of death. Had everything been left in its place, he might have found the diary, the personal journal of his mother's life, sooner. He had not been aware of its existence, so it was quite a surprise to find it among her personal effects wrapped in a large white embroidered handkerchief. At first, he thought of disposing of the diary. What interest could it possibly hold for him? But, instead, he placed it in the drawer of his bedside table and there it rested for several months next to the Bible that his mother said had belonged to his grandparents.

It was late one evening, months earlier, when he opened the drawer and, rather than reading scripture, he picked up the diary and hesitantly lifted its unlocked latch. These were confidential words, like a secret garden, a private, hidden space only to be inhabited or viewed by its creator. He felt uneasy entering his mother's confidential realm. Carefully, he flipped through the pages seeing words documenting events that had held importance for her. Family gatherings, a favorite book read, a visit with a friend. Some pages possessed very few words and were seemingly a collection of random thoughts, or a quote or two that must have held some importance. He read one aloud that she attributed to Lord Byron, "The beginning of atonement is the sense of its necessity." He shook his head in thought, wondering why she felt any association with the connotation of the poet's words.

There were pages and pages, far too many to read and absorb in one reading. He silently queried, *Could it be that perhaps these pages are not for me to peruse? Perhaps they are best left to remain idle and collecting dust, or perhaps I should discard the diary by burying it so it can be returned to the earth like my parents. What to do?*

The word 'atonement' hung with him. *Of all the narratives of Lord Byron's, why would this be one of Mum's selections? Was there something for which she felt she needed to atone? And then again, who among us was free of never having committed any wrongdoing? No, that cannot be the reason and, with her gone, I will never know the true reason for her having recorded this quotation.* He closed the diary and laid it on top of the bedside table. A few moments passed as he sat and reflected on his parents and the many happy times they had as a family. He missed them so. It was his father that gave him his start in the timber business, having groomed him as a sawyer and then he elevated him to the position of overseer of the other workers and liaison with the mills that refined the timber for sale. He had excelled at his craft and, armed with his knowledge of the industry, he had become well respected and had built a very comfortable livelihood for himself.

Then, he looked back at the diary. Something was drawing him to it. It was by all means a remaining link to his mother, a testament to her thoughts, her life. He would preserve it for now. He picked it up and began to gently fan the pages. As his right thumb came near the end of the final pages, a flattened flower kept the page from laying flat against its predecessor. *A pansy*, he thought to himself, *the flower of thoughtfulness, love, and remembrance.* Its purple, yellow, and white petals, though faded, held their hues. *It seems a most appropriate botanical for inclusion in a tome such as this. But, why this page?* And that is when the words that so intrigued and confused him came before his eyes.

It appeared to be a passage written soon before her death. As she met her decline, her fingers became less adept at properly holding a writing implement. The nature of her writing left jagged pen marks like chicken scratches across the page making the text difficult to read. He focused hard to decipher each word in the paragraph.

> My son must know. He must. Soon, I will not be on this earth to honor the opinion of another who swayed me from that which I felt rightfully was his to know. His father is dead now, or is he? My mind is muddled. Forgive me. He must know how much I love him and have loved him since the first day he came into my life. But, he must know more. He must seek the truth here in Wales. He must know about family. The truth is with the head of the Big House. Go, find him, find himself. Tell him to do this.

This makes such little sense to me. What is she saying? What truth? And, the Big House in Wales? What connection could Mum have had with the family that lives there? This is very bizarre. Why would Mum think someone would look at her diary? These words might have gone unread had my curiosity not gotten the best of me. Had she not marked the page with a flower, I might never have been drawn to it. And, was she so disoriented that she forgot my father had passed before her? I absolutely do not understand.

He reread the passage again and again, sorting through the words, dissecting them, trying to make sense of her message. *Could she mean the Hargrove family? The only property called the Big House by the locals is the home of Sir Ian Hargrove, owner of Hargrove Colliery. What could he possibly have to do with me? How did Mum know him? Oh, if she were only here to give credence to her words.* Questions continued to circulate in his mind. He knew his mother had never mentioned Sir Ian Hargrove in his presence. *Why is his name surfacing now?* Confusion continued to plague him until he determined himself to pursue his mother's directive for him to visit the master of the Big House. *But, why am I going, what will I ask, and what will I find there?*

Chapter Four

Mid-May 1898

William cleared his throat as he knocked on the portal of the Hargrove residence. Although he felt a certain level of comfort in Sir Ian's presence after having been present at the end of September for the elder Hargrove's revelations about his assignation with Annie Hollingsworth, one of his workers at the coal mine, a tinge of intimidation still remained. The man was a highly regarded and successful colliery owner and he was making a legendary name for himself in his position on the Trade Council at the Capitol. His opinions about commerce and business management were respected and sought out by many in power who were drafting the rules and regulations that governed trade within and without the United States. The purpose of William's visit greatly contributed to his momentary hesitation. He had an important task at hand and anticipated the best of outcomes. With great fervor to accomplish his goal, he reached up and gave a heavy rap with the doorknocker.

Fiona answered the knock. When she opened the door, she was at once so taken with the handsome visitor in the vestibule that she could not speak. She nearly swooned as she pulled the door full wide for him to enter.

"Well, good day to you, Miss Fiona," William smiled as he stepped forward into the foyer. He was enjoying her silence and the impact his presence had upon her. "You look radiant. I would say the spring weather is the perfect balm for you."

Fiona, still unable to utter a word, held onto the door's knob for support. William Clay never failed to have the repeated effect on her. *Ah, what a balm he is. Havin' him cross me threshold is worth bein' in service for Sir Ian's family.* With his thick, wavy brown hair, sea blue eyes, and prominent stature, he was her Adonis. Words began to form in her throat as she regained her composure and closed the front door. She took a deep breath and tried to avoid panting as she finally spoke.

"Mr. Clay, it is a pleasure to see ye, sir. I don't want to be disappointin' ye none, but Miss Arielle is not home at the moment. I ken leave a message from you fer her if ye like."

"Why, Miss Fiona, that is most kind, however, I am not here to see Arielle. It is her father's audience that I seek."

"Oh, my. I see, I do. I knew ye were a brave man. He was workin' in his study. Let me jest check and see what he is about and let him know ye is wantin' to see him."

"Very well, thank you. I will await your direction," William said as he gave a slight bow and nodded his head in agreement.

As Fiona turned to find her employer, her legs were nearly her undoing. William's presence had made her knees weak and she almost toppled over as she spun around to proceed to Ian's study. She fell back toward William who quickly put his arms out to break her fall. Fiona looked up into his eyes and all about her went silent. Even the cacophony of Ian's extensive clock collection simultaneously sounding their noon chimes fell on her deaf ears. *It must be a dream I'm havin' for sure. Oh, let me never wake up from this one,* Fiona thought, not wanting the vision to end that swirled in her head of herself and William Clay.

"Are you all right? That was a close call," William said as he helped Fiona back into a standing position.

"Oh, it's embarrassed I am, sir. Ye must think me a silly twit. It's sorry I am, sir, so sorry. I'll be on me way."

William said no more. He knew Fiona was prone to become flustered in his company and it was best to let her go about her assignment at hand. Within a few moments, Fiona appeared outside the doorway of Ian's study and ushered William in.

"William Clay, to what do I owe this pleasure?" Ian said as he stood and walked around his desk to greet his visitor. "And, Fiona, that will be all. Close the door behind you as you take your leave."

Fiona hated to be dismissed in such a curt fashion, but she knew Sir Ian Hargrove's manner toward her would never find a new path. Neither was fond of the other. He found her to be irritating on her best days and she found him to be a tyrant on most days. She walked quietly across the plush carpet as William and Ian greeted one another. As she exited the study, they were unaware that she pulled the doors closed carefully leaving a notch of open space.

"How good to see you! As I was saying, to what do I owe this pleasure? Please, here, have a seat."

"Thank you, it is a pleasure to see you as well. I am glad that I caught you in and I understand from Miss Fiona that Arielle is not at home. Is that correct?"

"Yes, that numbskull got that right. Arielle should be returning soon. In the meantime, what prompts your visit?"

"Actually, it is your daughter that prompts my visit. I guess I should be more specific since Arianna is your daughter as well. So, to be clear, my visit relates to Arielle."

"Well, cut to the chase, man. You have my undivided attention. What about Arielle? She hasn't fallen victim to another accident has she?" Ian was becoming agitated with the thought of a recurrence of last spring's ordeal when Arielle was trampled by a team of horses, hospitalized at Providence Hospital, and misidentified as Olivia Smithfield.

"Oh no, absolutely not, Sir Ian. I guess I should just blurt this out. I have come to ask for Arielle's hand in marriage. I will tell you straightforwardly that I adore her. She makes my life joyful and I hope to continually enrich her life so she will never want for anything. You know that I am well able to provide for her financially and, emotionally, I will always love and cherish her. So, sir, I hope you will find this in agreement and that we will have your blessing."

Ian remained silent for a few moments that seemed like an eternity to William. He moved to the silver salver atop the buffet in his study where several lead crystal glasses awaited among decanters filled with a variety of libations. He poured a healthy portion of Scotch into one of the glasses and paused with the decanter still in hand. William wondered if his request so unnerved Ian that before responding he felt the need to fortify himself with liquor. Ian turned and looked at William, enjoying the worried look on his face as he filled a second glass with the heady amber liquid. He returned the decanter to its serving tray, picked-up the filled glasses, and as he walked to face William he handed him a beverage.

"Mr. William Clay, I can think of nothing more appropriate or right in this world at this moment than for you and our Arielle to become engaged. You are a fine young man and I know you will do well by her and she by you. She thinks the world of you and has been exceedingly happy since you have come into her life. And, I, sir, will be proud to call you 'son.' Here, let's drink to this occasion, shall we?"

Ian clicked his glass against William's in a cheerful toast to their new relationship. William kept an inward cringe hidden from Ian's sights as he imagined ever calling him 'Father.' That thought had not occurred to him until Ian had mentioned the word 'son.' *Perhaps he will be fine maintaining our first name basis. 'Father' seems a bit awkward to me. But, I will not dwell on that now. We can sort that out as time goes on.* William took a deep sip of the Scotch, looked at Ian and smiled.

"You have made me a very happy man. Now, I can only hope that when I ask Arielle to marry me she says 'yes!' You mentioned that she should be returning home shortly. May I remain to see her?"

"Of course! I would have it no other way! This is an exciting day! Remain here, and refill your glass if you wish. I will go and share the news with her mother. Elsbeth will be filled with delight!"

In a flurry, Fiona scurried away from her listening post just before Ian exited his study. She had become quite adept at finding ways to mill about and appear busy while lingering where she was uninvited. Eavesdropping had become her forte. She was most interested in subjects that were none of her concern and became quite elated when the topic of a private conversation spurred her curiosity. With a feather duster in her hand, she began running its plumes along the wainscoting below the chair rail moulding and looked away to avoid eye contact with Sir Ian.

"Have you nothing better to do than wave that thing around and spread dust throughout the air that we breathe?" Even William's good news was not enough to fully dissuade Ian from finding fault with Fiona. He was a keen example of the phrase, 'old habits die hard.' He caught himself and thought better of his behavior. "Forget the dusting for now. I need you to have Lady Hargrove join me in the conservatory. I believe she is in the upper quarters. Get about this quickly, girl."

Fiona looked about for a place to stow the duster and settled on the nearby pot of the large palm. She forced its handle into the dirt. The plumes flayed against the palm's lower fronds adding an extra enhancement to the greenery. Ian rolled his eyes as he watched her ridiculous behavior.

"You are a unique soul, Fiona. When God was giving out the brains, you must have been in the other room getting your good looks. Now, please go about finding Lady Hargrove. I have something of importance to share with her."

"Oh, thank ye sir fer what ye jest said about me looks." Fiona did a half curtsy and blushed as she went in search of the lady of the house, not understanding the insult that had just been passed her way.

Chapter Five

Arielle stood and looked at herself in the tall cheval mirror in her bedroom. She could hardly believe her eyes as she looked at the ring finger of her left hand, moved it back and forth, and watched the sparkling refractions bouncing from the edges of the large emerald cut diamond William had placed on her hand hours earlier. Tingling sensations ran throughout her body as she relived the moment he proposed. She was so surprised to find him at her home when she returned from her shopping expedition. When she left her purchases in the foyer for Fiona to attend to, she found the girl acting a bit more oddly than usual. She dismissed the thought for there was no guessing what was running through Fiona's mind at any moment. Then, William stepped from her father's study with a handsome, welcoming smile. She felt like she could melt in his arms and remain there forever. He took her hand and with all due propriety asked her to join him in the garden.

May was one of her favorite months only rivaled by October's temperatures and rich colors. With the threat of frost behind the city, she loved the flowers that filled so many gardens after the first week of the month. Azaleas were in bloom and pansies with their velvety tricolor petals lent a colorful air, one of remembrance that someone was thinking about you. William knew of her love of the garden, of outdoor spaces in general, and the restorative effect they had on one's mental attitude and overall health. Arielle and her mother often made Wardian cases, small terrariums filled with greenery planted in layers of dirt. They would take them on visits to sick friends and leave them at their bedsides to give them a healing view of botanicals as they recovered from a malady.

So, it was most appropriate that on a beautiful May afternoon she and William would stroll through her parent's garden and find a familiar spot near a stone wall. The lush canopy of a large October Glory red maple protected them from the day's sun as they found their seating on a weathered bench, the same bench William had stood upon in late September when he viewed a solitary rose growing beyond the wall. William's pensive manner stirred her curiosity. She wondered what he wished to tell her and hoped it was not that his law practice would be taking him away for a period of time. They sat side-by-side and then William took her hands in his.

"Arielle, what I have to say will come, I am sure, as no surprise to you. Our affections for one another have only grown stronger this past year. You are my light and my heart. I can think of nothing I could ever want more than to have you become my wife. I have spoken with your father and he has given us his blessing. I want to build the rest of my life together with you. I have no greater want or desire," William kept his hold on Arielle's hands as he moved from the bench to place one of his knees on the ground. "So, here I am, kneeling before you with much joy and anticipation and I ask you, will you marry me?"

"Yes, yes, oh, absolutely YES!" Arielle answered without a moment of hesitation. Her glee was evident in her voice and every iris freckle in her eyes that glistened with happiness.

William stood and drew her to a standing position. He released her hands and placed a persuasive arm around her waist to draw her closer. She put her arms around his neck as she looked up into his eyes swept with the ocean's most brilliant blue hue. He cupped her chin and leaned down, planting his lips on hers in a slow and caring kiss that swam through her veins. As he released the comb holding her hair in a loose chignon, her raven locks spilled across her décolletage. He whispered in her ear, "I love you," his breath warm against her neck. The rapture of the moment had them both in a distant realm where time and space held no meaning.

"I love you," Arielle echoed back to him as she leaned in for more of his warm, moist kisses.

The sounding of the nearby church bell broke the magic of their garden rendezvous and brought them back into the realm of reality. Arielle released her sensuous curves from William's very capable lean form as they continued to gaze into one another's eyes.

"I am afraid that I forgot where I was for the moment. You have quite a way with me, Mr. Clay."

"And you, milady, with me."

"Perhaps we should return to the manse. Father and Mum may be looking for us and one never knows where Fiona might be lurking about. She might have an ear to the other side of this stone wall," Arielle mused as she brought her hair back up into a twist and secured it with her tortoise shell comb.

"As you wish but, before we go, there is more."

"More? I think I shall faint if there is more or pass out from pure pleasure and desire."

"No, my dear. When the time comes, I want you fully awake and aware of all the pleasures ahead."

"Then of what do you speak?" Arielle queried as William reached into his jacket pocket and revealed a hinged black velvet box.

Arielle's eyes went wide with anticipation. William was quite enough for her without the trappings of jewelry or other refinements, but a piece of jewelry to mark the occasion would be a treasure she would gladly accept. He held the box in the palm of his hand and presented it to her. She looked from the box to his eyes as he nodded for her to proceed. Arielle took the box and looked up before she opened the lid.

"Go ahead, my dear, it will not bite you."

Slowly, she raised the lid and saw the most beautiful diamond ring. Her jaw dropped as the sun's rays captured the stone's facets and sent shards of light bouncing off the sizeable precious stone.

"Oh my goodness, Will, it is absolutely exquisite! But, how did you know I would say 'yes?'"

"My heart told me you would, though nothing is ever certain in this life. I wanted to be prepared for your affirmative response, so during my last trip to New York, I went to Tiffany's to select this engagement ring for you. Having held your hand on several occasions, I guessed at the size so we shall see how accurate I was."

"Will, this is beyond anything I could have ever expected! My goodness, it must be three carats, at least!"

"Four is what the jeweler told me and I have the appraisal for insurance purposes. I hoped you would be pleased with my selection," William smiled, delighted with his choice in spouse and ring.

"Pleased? I am so thrilled and I just cannot wait to show everyone! And, Arianna will be so happy for us! We are so lucky to have her in our lives. We have so much time to make up for having missed a score of years together. My head still spins sometimes when I think that we were separated at birth and that it is only thanks to the fine investigative work of Morgan Pennybacker that the truth was unveiled. But, this is certainly no time to dwell on the past. Today is the beginning of all good things!"

"It is indeed. Arielle, you know I am a patient man, however I would like to set a date for our wedding. I imagine your parents would like some time to put plans in motion and I know Aunt Emma will desire some involvement in the arrangements, if that is agreeable to you."

"I would not think of excluding Emma from all the fun of wedding planning! You might be the one that wants to step aside from the frenzy that I understand accompanies putting a wedding together!"

"As far as I am concerned, you have free rein to plan as your heart desires, colors, flowers, location, food…you can count on my being there!"

"We will need some time, but not an extraordinary amount. I am just thinking. You know we first said, 'I love you' in the fall in this very garden. Fall is my favorite season. I so enjoy the change of colors and the thought of the coming harvest and Thanksgiving. So, I am thinking about mid-week in October. We can see what venue is available and select the date. How do you feel about that?"

"I am thinking that this is May and October seems a long way before us, but if a wedding in the fall is your wish then we shall make it so. Aunt Emma might offer Chestnut Heights for the wedding and reception. You know how she loves to host lavish parties."

"Chestnut Heights is beautiful and Emma is such a dear. If she is accepting of the idea I think her home would be a lovely choice for the reception, but I would like our vows to be said and heard in a place of worship. Perhaps Emma could talk with the vicar at St. John's."

"The vicar? I find it so charming when your English roots show themselves. I am sure she will be happy to speak with the rector who I believe is Reverend MacKay-Smith. I have heard Aunt Emma mention his name on occasion in relation to the Woman's Home Missionary Society."

"Oh, yes, the work she performs to aid those less fortunate in the settlement houses at Purdy's Court. Poor Alexandra had a 'less fortunate' experience there. Fortunately, Thomas came to her rescue. Speaking of Alexandra, I wonder how she will take the news of our engagement?"

"As well as can be expected, I assure you. She is not one to hold back her tongue. I am sure I am in for quite a lashing from her. Pray for me, will you?"

"Let me know if you want my support, though it is probably best that you break the news to her. When I was with her the other day, before we went to visit with your aunt, she introduced me to a new friend of hers. Perhaps she has mentioned him to you, a Bernard Sullivan. They met last year in New York when Alexandra was traveling back from her misadventures at Olivia Smithfield's. There was something curious about him."

"She did mention meeting someone in New York and that he was going to be settling in Washington for a period of time. Alexandra is so full of drama at times that I quite frankly did not want to pursue the topic of Mr. Sullivan with her. I guess it conveniently slipped my mind."

"Well, at first I thought he was her secret beau but, as our visit continued, she seemed to encourage his conversation with me."

"With you? For what purpose?"

"It seems Mr. Sullivan is interested in meeting my father."

"Well, that is curious, though your father is quite an esteemed man. I wonder how this Mr. Sullivan came to know of him?"

"According to Alexandra, he is a successful businessman from Wales in the timber trade. She suspects that he wants to discuss business tactics with my father. I just find it odd that he has traveled all the way to America for that purpose and that he has resided here for nearly one year before he decided to reveal himself to my family."

"You make a good point. Perhaps it is time that I meet Mr. Bernard Sullivan. You have a keen intuitive sense. If he has garnered your curiosity and Alexandra has kept her friendship with him from us then I think it is time for me to learn more. When I meet with her to share the news of our engagement, I will pursue the topic of Mr. Sullivan and see what that yields. With Alexandra in the mix there is no telling where things may lead."

Chapter Six

Sully was nervous as he approached the main entrance of Emma Willard's grand estate. Its massive Italianate façade spoke volumes about the wealth within its walls. Several days earlier, he had met Alexandra at the Vienna Dining Room at 19th and F Streets for lunch. She was quite fond of the restaurant's delicious fare and enjoyed being in the company of its high-profile clientele. She was certain, and it gave her great pleasure to think, that the eyes of the gentlemen diners were fixed on her as she made her promenade around the tables. As Alexandra and Sully dined, she suggested that he change his lodging and consider boarding at Chestnut Heights. He had no idea what she had up her sleeve but, he knew something about Cal made him uncomfortable and he had grown less and less fond of his company. He could not quite place the awkward feelings Cal emanated, but he was indeed ready for a change and wondered if Emma Willard would welcome him into her home.

So, here he was, at Alexandra's suggestion, preparing to meet with the mistress of the manse. He had sent a message to her inquiring about a vacancy and had received a very pleasant reply that she would first like to meet with him before offering him accommodations. He stood before the large portal and raised his hand to knock as the door swung open. Simon Peabody jumped back, surprised that he would find someone on the other side. Sully was equally alarmed. Both he and Simon drew back before speaking.

"My, my, my, oh yes, my, my, my. I do apologize, yes I do," said Simon as he gathered his wits.

"And I apologize if I startled you," said Sully. A smile came over his face as he watched Simon fiddle with his eyeglasses that had slipped down the bridge of his nose. As he aligned them to his liking, Simon backed up and swept his left hand to the side to invite Sully to step within.

"Is Mrs. Willard expecting you, sir?"

"Yes. We have been in communication with one another and she was expecting my visit today."

"Oh then, very well, very well indeed. Come this way and I will inform her that you have arrived. Oh, yes, oh, who is it that I should say is here?"

"Thank you. Bernard Sullivan is my name."

Earlier in the morning, Emma had informed Thomas that another potential guest would be arriving. She had instructed him to prepare the other room adjoining the upper library in anticipation that her interview with him would go well. She did not typically interview boarders. Most of them came to her from referrals upon arrival at the train station. But, this one was different. When she saw his name on the message he sent to her it rang a bell in her memory. Arielle had mentioned him and wanted to know more about him. Perhaps having him at Chestnut Heights under her scrutiny would aid Arielle's mission.

"Thomas, I think that room should suffice nicely. My goodness gracious, we are nearing full capacity. I understand this is another gentleman, which will make his accommodations acceptable with Mr. Drake's proximity to the library."

"Yez, Miz Willard. I'll see to his arrival," assured Thomas as he thought about the man who claimed to be a famous writer. *I sure hope the next gentleman is a fan of the mighty peculiar, yez indeed because that one sure fits the bill for bein' strange. Well, we'll be seein' soon. Like the monkey said when they cut off his tail, won't be long now.* Thomas laughed to himself and shook his head.

Simon escorted Sully to the parlor where Emma sat working on a needlework project. She looked up to see a handsome young man, perhaps in his late twenties, who immediately offered a warm smile and friendly greeting.

"Good morning, Mrs. Willard I presume. I am pleased to make your acquaintance. I am Sul, um excuse me, I am Bernard Sullivan. Miss Whitaker, as I mentioned in my letter to you, referred me."

"Yes, she certainly did. So, Mr. Sullivan, please explain the nature of your visit."

"Of course. My previous accommodations have served me well for the past year however, I feel it is time for a change and your home comes very highly recommended."

Sully's handsome face and deportment reminded her of her nephew. *This one is sure to be a pleasure,* Emma mused to herself as she thought of the young women who would be certain to want to make his introduction. She wondered what Arielle found so curious about him. As he spoke, she could hear the familiar accent to which she had grown so accustomed in Arielle's presence.

"Very nice to meet you Mr. Sullivan."

"We welcome you to Chestnut Heights," Emma said with a broad smile. "I am Emma Willard, and I see you have met Simon. Simon is my landscape engineer, so to speak. He keeps everything on the grounds in tip-top shape."

"Indeed. I was admiring your gardens as my carriage made its way along your lane."

Thomas entered the opening to the parlor and Emma signaled him to step forward. "This is Thomas. If you and I should decide that Chestnut Heights is a good fit, then Thomas will see to your accommodations and help to make your stay within the walls of my home as comfortable as possible."

"Oh, yez sir, I's Thomas and I'll be seein' you to your room when the time comes," Thomas assured.

"I heard earlier in your voice a hesitation. I am not suggesting a stutter but a slight reluctance. Perhaps the cause is an unfamiliarity with the English spoken on this side of the pond, so to speak," Emma inquired with a smile, not wanting to make her visitor feel ill at ease. "Forgive me if I am being too bold, but I am correct am I not, that you hail from the United Kingdom?"

"I have spent some time in England but most of my roots are in Wales. And, yes, you are quite right. I apologize if I appeared hesitant. The use of my formal name is unusual for me. Most of my chums these days call me Sully. You may do so as well if it so pleases you."

"Then, Sully it is," said Emma, still sensing there was more to be learned. "And, you may call me Emma. Have you had a long journey?" She queried as she made light conversation before trying to ascertain more about the man before her.

"Not at all. My temporary residence is several blocks away. Too far by foot but close just the same. Very unlike my arrival last year where my journey began on a ship and ended on a train. It was actually during my stopover in New York City that I met Miss Whitaker, and now she has led me to you."

"Again, if I may be so bold, what brings you to America? Do you have family here, or is it the pursuit of work that has landed you on our shores?"

There was a moment of reflection before he uttered any words. "I am in pursuit of, well, let me just say that there are matters that I wish to make more clear and I hope this will suffice to say for the time being. Thank you for welcoming me into your home, it is quite grand and I look forward to meeting your other guests."

At that moment, Alistair Whitfield Drake rounded the corner with a dramatic sweep provided by the tweed cape he held about his shoulders. He came to a sudden halt as he viewed the gathering, ducked his chin down and looked at each of the parlor's occupants with a questioning glare.

"Ah, hah! I should have known this would be the case!" Drake exclaimed. "Forgive me for overhearing, but I am forever hounded by cryptic turns of phrase! You sir," he said as he pointed accusingly at Sully, "are keeping your raison d'être from us! But, have no fear, as Galileo Galilei said, 'All truths are easy to understand once they are discovered; the point is to discover them.'"

Sully wanted to laugh out loud. *I wonder if he is to be believed? He appears to have stepped from the pages of one of Doyle's works. The poor soul must be daft. Probably best to humor him lest he imagine I am the Watson to his Holmes!* Sully hesitated, an action to which he had become quite adept of late, then looked to Emma for an introduction.

"Now, now, Mr. Drake, or Alistair, if I may. Let me take the liberty of introducing you to another of our guests. This is Bernard Sullivan. Sully, he prefers. He will be residing here with us, that is, I believe that is the decision he has made. I think it best to reserve any and all judgments. I would ask him to extend the same courtesy in your direction. Sully, Alistair is a mystery writer and it sounds as though you share the benefit of the Queen's English. Tell us, Alistair, if you will, where are your roots?"

Alistair shook his head and exhibited a dumbfounded face. "Here I am in this country for a short period of time and I am already subjected to peasants who know nothing about me or my fame! All one must do is read my biography to know from whence I came. I certainly should not have to utter a word that direction and rightly so!"

Thomas stood patiently in the doorway awaiting the signal from the mistress of the house to see their latest guest to his room. He held his usual quiet as he listened to the banter from the one called Drake. Emma held her tongue for the moment as she thought about her response to this fellow she found to be obnoxious at the very least. Difficult personalities, although not her favorite, offered her a challenge. The vast repertoire of artistic types who had crossed her threshold, some invited to her lavish parties, had given her ample opportunity to stroke egos and subdue the ruffled feathers of the most peculiar of the flock at her gatherings.

Sully hoped he could keep his distance from the odd man. There was an air about him that made him uncomfortable. *Yes, if*

I can keep away from him, it will be in my best interest, he reasoned to himself. *And, a mystery writer at that, what are the odds?* Sully knew his mission would take some time. There was no room for stumbling blocks like Drake. He needed a clear path without Drake's shadow questioning his every move.

"Oh, do forgive me, Alistair. Without burdening you with the events at Chestnut Heights in the past year, I must confess that pleasure reading was put on the back shelf while we worked through some very trying times. I will make it a priority to purchase your latest work from Brentano's the next time I venture downtown. It may equally alarm you when I ask the book's title, but I ask that you please do not take this personally. I am certain it will make for a good read. As I recall, Miss Pennybacker mentioned one of your novels, *The Widow's Wicked Web*. Perhaps that is the one I should read?" Emma inquired with a calming smile and expression showing great interest in her boarder.

Alistair started to bristle, then let the sensations melt away. Emma's compliment had served to allay his indignation. He was a stranger in their midst and, as such, he determined himself to rally his forces, at least for the time being, to his softer, kinder side. He smiled and dipped his head to Emma, still casting a look of scrutiny toward Sully.

"Ah, the title. Yes, it took me quite some time to develop the story. On occasion, a title is the last to enter my mind, but in this case, I had a title but no story. I had to create a story that would fit."

"I see," said Emma. "Do you find outlining your work a helpful resource?"

"I do not find outlining to be anything but rubbish. Oh, do not get me wrong, there are times when I sketch out a series of events, but the characters take me places I would never have imagined, so I find an outline to be quite for naught."

Emma feared asking any additional questions about Alistair's writing process. He seemed determined to waft back and forth, but she decided to ask once more about the title of his latest work.

"How interesting. I am just thinking that I should soon have a dinner party with you as our special guest, only if an event of such undertaking would please you, of course. I will purchase several copies of your latest novel to give as gifts and perhaps you would be willing to autograph some of them? I am certain my friends would like to make your acquaintance. Now, what is that title?"

Emma's repartee was working its wonders on Alistair's disposition. He paused as he took in the idea of being the focus of a social gathering. Suddenly, his apprehension about being noticed by adoring fans seemed to dissipate as he likened to the idea.

"Well, is that not a fine and lovely idea? Why, yes and oh, the title. The latest book I have penned is, *The Cabbie's Curse*. Without revealing too much detail, it's a rather macabre story about a cabbie a decade ago who befriends women in London's Whitechapel district. The chap has a rather sad run of bad luck, for it seems the women he is most attracted to meet a grisly and untimely end. The story is not for the faint of heart I assure you."

"Oh, my. I am not so sure I would be able to sleep at night after reading a chapter or two."

"As I declared to your visitor, that Miss Pennybacker you just mentioned, you may drift off to sleep only if you dare!"

Sully was beginning to question his decision to take Alexandra's direction to find lodging at Emma Willard's. Emma seemed unduly curious about him and Alistair Drake seemed a raging force to bear. He hoped he had not made a dreadful mistake. Time would be the barometer to measure the veracity of his decision.

Chapter Seven

The new millinery parlor in the Palais Royal department store at 11th and G Streets had become a favorite destination of society's female elite so, naturally, it had drawn Alexandra's attention. She quite enjoyed having a new hat to perch upon her head and coordinate with the fine, tailor-made frocks the store offered from imported fabrics comprised of rich silks, gabardines, moirés, velvets, and supple wools. Parasols, Hermsdorf Fast Black hosiery, corsets, jewelry, and veils were among the numerous wares available for purchase in the well-appointed shop. Alexandra was enraptured with a particularly frilly hat. She ran her fingers along its ruffled edges and studied its botanical adornments of three large, deep pink chrysanthemums, which she nearly plucked from their bases when a familiar voice startled her and spoke her name.

"Aye, if it's not Miss Whitaker. I thought it was ye that I spied from across the room."

Alexandra knew the face and the voice. The Irish accent sent a tingling irritation across her skin. *What on earth is this Bridget doing in Palais Royal? Perhaps they have her scrubbing the floors. I certainly do not need to be bothered by the likes of her while I am about the pleasures of my day!*

"Surprised to see me here are ye? Don't think I'm good enough for these parts, do ye?"

Hesitant to strike up a conversation with Fiona, who was feeling particularly bold, Alexandra's curiosity got the better of her. "Why must you cast such aspersions my way? I have said nothing of the sort. In fact, I have said nothing. But, now that you ask, what *are* you doing here?"

"Just as I thought, ye would be wantin' to know. I'm doin' an errand for Miss Arielle. Her new gown is ready, so she sent me to be retrievin' it fer her."

"How sweet. Retrieve is a good word for you, like a faithful dog."

Although Fiona had experienced several unfortunate encounters with Alexandra, she never felt quite prepared for her next onslaught. *I wish I had been born with a tougher skin*, thought Fiona. *She can't be havin' the best of me. There must be somethin' I ken say to ruin her lovely day.* And then, it came to her like a bolt of lightning. She knew exactly what she could and would say.

"Well, soon I may be retrievin' somethin' very special for Miss Arielle," Fiona said as she smiled, pursed her lips, and moved her head about as she rolled her eyes.

"Oh, please. Let me go about this store in peace without your silly babbling tainting my ears."

"Well, it's jest fine with me if ye don't want to be privy to exciting news!"

"Exciting? What could possibly be exciting in Arielle Hargrove's life?"

"Her weddin'. Now, I would call that excitin' wouldn't ye?"

"What wedding? What are you talking about?"

"Well, that handsome Mr. Clay had an audience he did with me master, Sir Ian Hargrove, and he asked for Miss Arielle's hand in marriage, yes, he certainly did."

"You are absolutely vile to spread such a ridiculous rumor. Why, I would know if Mr. Clay had such intentions. He would make me aware, of that I am certain."

"Hmm, ye might be wantin' to check on that 'certain' part. I knows what I heard with me very own ears. Fer all I know, Mr. Clay has already proposed to Miss Arielle. Looks like ye are bein' left in the dust by your friend, Mr. Clay."

Alexandra felt the blood rising in her veins. *How can I let the words out of the mouth of a common housemaid take such a toll on my nerves? She must have misunderstood. She has to have misunderstood. Good lord, this cannot be true!* Fiona could see the color drain from Alexandra's face as she processed what she had just heard. She took great pleasure in the impact of her words. *It's high time, it is, that this one gets a taste of her own medicine!*

"How would you, of all people, know such a thing?"

"Oh, I 'ave me ways."

"You are mistaken."

"I ken't mistake what me ears be hearin' clear as the ringin' of a church bell."

"Speak up then and tell me what you think you have heard!"

"Oh, I've peaked yer interest, I 'ave," Fiona's smile was so wide it nearly spread the freckles about on her cheeks.

"You are testing my patience. What did you hear?"

"Well, Mr. Clay came to have an audience with me master, ye know, Sir Ian Hargrove, and he asked for Miss Arielle's hand in marriage. Now I would be thinkin' that means they will soon be married and Miss Arielle will be Mrs. Clay. What do ye think of that?"

Alexandra sensed her blood boiling as it coursed through her veins. As dim-witted as she deemed Fiona, she knew she was more privy to the matters in the Hargrove household than herself. *I think I shall scream! Oh, my god! How can William have betrayed me so? He knows how I feel! He knows full well my intentions! If he would only hear me out and give me the time to show him that I am the one most suited for him. Arielle can never give him what he truly desires. She appears demure, but she is a snake in disguise! She will ensnare him and make him miserable! What am I to do? What am I to do?*

Fiona was feeling quite pleased with herself. She could see the color rise in Alexandra's face and the fury wash across her expression. As proud as she felt for having so disturbed her, she was suddenly aware that Alexandra could lash out at her at a moment's notice. It was time to take her leave whether she had Arielle's gown in hand or not. As she began to back away from Alexandra, the shop's clerk came to her with the package she had been sent to secure. Feeling that the perfect timing of the clerk had saved her, she turned to Alexandra, looked at her parcel and smiled.

"Well it seems it be best that I be leavin'. Me work's done here. Good day, Miss Whitaker."

Fiona's near sneer did nothing to placate Alexandra. She was more incited than ever. She had lost all interest in shopping and wanted to flee, to find comfort amongst a friend, to be welcomed into accepting arms. *Sully, I must go to Sully. He will console me. He will counsel me though I cannot yet let him know that he is not the one I want. Oh, I am becoming so confused. I must have him find a greater interest in Arielle. If Fiona is to be believed, I must devise a plan to get William back. He must see that he is meant to be mine.* Alexandra departed the shop with the express mission to visit Sully and encourage him to change his living arrangements. *He must move into Chestnut Heights!* As she stepped out onto the street, her anxiety directed her to make a stop before she boarded a streetcar to visit Sully. *I need to bolster myself. I am feeling at my wits end. Surely a glass of claret will settle my nerves.* She walked to the northeast corner of 12th Street N.W. where it met Pennsylvania Avenue and stepped into The Raleigh Hotel. *I will be safe here. I will be able to think things through more clearly.*

⟨⟩

Alexandra was feeling quite light-headed as she walked up the steps to Sully's front door. She was barely able to lift the hem of her gown and she stepped on it more than once as she stumbled along her way to knock on the door. Her one libation at The Raleigh Hotel had extended into two. Her morning meal had been essentially non-existent, leaving her vulnerable to the effects of the claret that calmed her nerves but distorted her senses. The fact that she was without a chaperone did not deter her from pursuing her mission. She knocked on the door for what seemed like an eternity. *Where on God's green earth can he be?* She knocked again with more gusto than her previous attempts. Finally, the door opened to reveal Cal. She was supremely disappointed to see him, hoping for the betterment of society that his whereabouts were unknown.

"Well, lookie who we have here. Isn't it just my good luck to have a fair maiden at my door? To what do I owe this unexpected visit?"

"Oh, let me by you silly twit. I am here to see Sully and I need to see him now."

"Well, you know, you cannot always get what you think you want. Guess I'll have to do for now. Come on in and wait if you like. Sully should be back soon."

"Back soon? Where has he gone?"

"Oh, was it my turn to watch him? You know, last time I checked I was not his social secretary. But I invite you to come into the parlor and have a seat until he returns."

Alexandra was hesitant to accept Cal's offer, but feeling a bit off balance and in need of resting her legs she stepped through the portal and selected a spot on the long settee to settle herself. Cal walked to a cabinet and removed a bottle of bourbon and two glasses.

"It looks like you could use a drink while you wait. Here, join me in a glass of this fine bourbon won't you?"

Alexandra was wary to take the drink that Cal proffered, but the glasses of claret at The Raleigh Hotel had put her mind in a comfortable fog that she hoped to continue to grasp. With her senses muddled, she took the glass from Cal as she thought about the news Fiona had shared with her. Fiona's words seared through her. She was dismayed and overwhelmed. She needed something more to cut the pain, to ease the heartache. She held the glass in her unsteady hand, put it to her lips and downed its contents. Cal watched her with delight as he finished consuming his pour.

"That's a mighty impressive thirst you have! Let's have another for old times' sake!"

Alexandra was feeling quite relaxed, more so than she had been in days. She held her glass forward and let Cal replenish the liquor. Again, she emptied its contents in one swallow. Cal watched her expression as her eyes floated up and then side-to-side. He stepped closer and then sat next to her on the settee. She looked into his eyes as her mind became numb to her surroundings and her eyelids closed. Cal moved closer and twisted a tendril of her hair around his finger. Alexandra began to move her head away but succumbed to his proximity and rested her head on his shoulder. She began to drift in and out of consciousness as Cal stroked her face. She moved her chin up, aware of his touch but unable to bring herself fully awake. Cal nestled his nose into her neck savoring the sweet nectar of her scent and rubbed his unshaven cheek up and down the length of her neck. His hand began to fondle her breasts as his passion ignited. He met no resistance from Alexandra and began kissing her chest as he released her breasts from the security of her bodice and suckled one then the other. Alexandra softly writhed at each uninvited touch of his lips on her upper body. She was in a far away dream with no grasp on reality as Cal's hands moved downward along her torso to the folds of her gown. Slowly, he pulled the multiple layers of her dress upward revealing her chemise. The white undergarment was edged in soft folds of lace. He fondled each fold as he tore her chemise open to reveal her bare abdomen. His fingers deftly traveled to the soft opening between her legs and teased their way into her inner depths. Alexandra remained dazed by her circumstances with her eyes closed as her body began responding to the sensations being stirred by Cal's advances.

As her body twisted under his powers, Cal became increasingly aroused as a searing need rose in him. He leaned over her and found his way into the wet warmth between her legs. Alexandra groaned as he thrust himself deeper, lifting out and back in, out and back in, again and again, in a rhythmic plunge until he met his climax and, breathing deeply, fully released himself into her. He lay upon her for several moments as he kissed her lips then moved his mouth to her taut nipples that he teased with his tongue. *It's untouched territory I have here,* Cal thought out loud, quite pleased with himself to have penetrated the loins of a virgin. He became newly aroused as he stroked the contours of her curves and once again his hardness entered the core of her body. Alexandra writhed against his weight but was defenseless against him. She was in a drunken stupor, in a realm that made her feel far removed from the present. Cal once again released himself within her then, feeling fully spent, withdrew himself.

He hastened to restore her clothing to its original fashion and tried his best to tidy her hair. Alexandra rolled from side-to-side nearly thrusting herself from the cushions of the settee. She moaned and reached out to swat Cal's hands away as he refastened the buttons on her bodice. She fell back against the settee and laid her head on a decorative pillow. Her head was spinning. She felt nauseous, but did all within her power to make the sensation retreat, to keep the vile remnants of her consumption from rising forth. Soft moans were all that were emitted from her as Cal lifted her legs and placed them on the settee. With renewed lust he ran his hands up and down her gown.

"My, you're a fine one aren't you? You'll have to come visiting more often. We'll just have to see to it that Sully is no where to be found."

As Sully's name left Cal's lips, he was brought back to the reality of the present. *I have to find a way to get her out of here before Sully returns. He can't know what I've done. Or, I could leave her here to rest. If Sully comes back soon, I can tell him that she insisted on waiting for him, that she needed to talk with him. That's it, I'll tell him that she was very upset and I offered her a drink to help calm her nerves, then she fell asleep and I made her comfortable in the parlor. That should suit Sully just fine, or perhaps not. I need to get her home and with any luck, this fair maiden will have no memory of the pleasure she gave me.* That thought actually gave Cal pause for he was accustomed to the girls he bedded wanting more. He took great sport in their tales of their times with him and found himself wanting Alexandra to remember their encounter. For now, she was in a deep sleep. Only time would tell if any evidence of their dalliance would be revealed.

Chapter Eight

Late May 1898
Washington, District of Columbia

Arielle felt as though she were floating on air. Hardly a day went by when she did not look at her hand to admire the diamond engagement ring William had presented to her. She felt like a queen and could not wait for him to be her king. She reflected on the story he shared about going to his Aunt Emma to seek her approval for his decision to propose. She wondered if he thought there would be any resistance on his aunt's part for they had developed a lovely friendship of which she was most proud. William said that he could barely get his aunt to let go of him when he told her his intentions. She was so excited about Arielle becoming part of her family that she clung and clung to him as though letting him go would alter what she had just heard. It was a dream come true for Emma and she wanted to hold on to it and not let it dissipate as she knew so many dreams did upon awakening. A tap on her bedroom door broke Arielle's focus.

"Yes, who is it?"

"Arielle, I need to discuss something with you. It shall not take long."

"Please, come in Father. Fiona has gone and I am dressed for the morning."

Ian opened the door and reveled in the beauty before him. His daughter was not only easy on the eye, but he knew her to have a strong business mind. Her savvy and interest in an arena typically dominated by men impressed him. He had kept her very well versed in the operations of his colliery and she had always chosen to hear the latest news about the workers and the revenue generated by Hargrove Colliery's output. He was gratified by its success and worked diligently to keep it in top working condition without diminished returns. He needed to prepare her for the latest word he had received from Paul Nesbitt, the colliery's overman. Known to the locals as Paul the Overman, Ian typically referred to him by his surname.

"You are looking quite fit today, Arielle. I would wonder if that gift of jewelry from Mr. Clay has anything to do with the glowing aura about you."

Arielle smiled as a rosy blush found its way across her cheeks. She held her hand up and looked again at the beautiful diamond. She imagined seeing William's reflection in its brilliance and smiled anew.

"Thank you, Father. I am filled with joy. I can not imagine myself happier."

"I am thankful for that and so is your mother. She is anxious to begin wedding plans with you. In fact, Elsbeth and I spoke this morning and wondered if you and Mr. Clay have set a date for your nuptials?"

"We are looking at the fall, September or October. As you know, besides spring, that is my favorite time of year. The colors in nature are so vivid and the temperatures are generally more tepid in Washington. I am not a fan of extreme temperatures whether they be hot or cold. We thought about marrying in England or Wales, but there is much to be said for remaining here where we have begun to establish ourselves, and I am certain that William's Aunt Emma will want to be included in our preparations."

"Very well, then. With that said, I can move to the business at hand. I have come to speak with you about the colliery. The latest post from Nesbitt indicates an uprising of sorts from the workers. The men are being influenced by the formation of regional and local unions in other areas of the Rhondda to represent the workers and negotiate their wages and working conditions. We have avoided a full-blown strike and I am striving to keep the status quo. However, I feel it will soon be necessary for me to return to the colliery and meet with the men who are very active in the Ogmore Miner's Association. Arielle, I share this knowledge with you because of your keen awareness of my work. You have always shown an interest and, more importantly, you have been very adept at understanding the business world. I mention this today, because should I have to venture to Wales, I would like you to accompany me."

"Father, I am complimented and surprised. You are not ill are you? You should have many good years ahead of you to keep the cogs moving in the wheels of the coal mine."

"Oh, no, my dear. Have no fear. This has nothing to do with my health at this time, but I like to plan for the future and, as I see it, you are the only member of our family who has shown a sincere interest in the work I do. I would be most honored to have you join me, meet with the men, and glean what you will from our meetings. I can imagine that all of the workers will be represented from the hewers to the putters, trammers, timbermen, and firemen. The only ones whom I can assure will not be present will be the pit ponies."

Ian chuckled as he thought of the ponies attending a meeting. Their use had been implemented in his mine for more than a decade. The equines were saving young lads and women from the task of pulling heavy metal tubs of coal. Sacks were placed over the heads of the ponies to protect their eyes before they exited the mine into the daylight. As he envisioned the ponies seated at the meeting, their images changed to jackasses. He smiled as he wondered if his vision bespoke the tone that might undermine the successful outcome of the meeting for the colliery. He knew many of the older men who had been with the mine nearly all their lives were feeling like slaves of their work. They were growing weary of the routines and mandated hours that kept them in early morning and late afternoon queues with their fellow workers walking to and from the pit. He looked to Arielle hoping she would be amenable to his suggestion.

"But, I have to ask. Do you think I am well prepared?'

"My dear, Arielle, I have every confidence in you and I always have. It seems, almost ironically, that you have been a child of the mine since conception." Ian reflected on Arielle's earliest beginnings and the pit brow girl that gave her life. Annie Hollingsworth was a beauty and before him stood a part of her legacy. He had found Annie's ways and her rich auburn hair to be as intoxicating as his favorite Scotch whiskey. Their dalliance in his carriage came back to him, then he mentally shook off the vision, needing to leave the barnacles of his misdeed buried in the distance.

"I hope I have not brought undo attention to a topic that perhaps is best laid to rest. I will have to live until my dying day with the truth of my past. I know you have forgiven me and for that I am most grateful. You know your mother and I never intended you any harm. Just to think that Arianna was kept from us all," Ian closed his eyes for a moment. Arielle was not certain whether he was holding back tears or saying a silent prayer over his indiscretions.

"Had it not been for Olivia Smithfield's knowledge and conscience your sister would most likely have remained unknown to us." Ian shook his head as he began to languish in the impact of his tainted past. "Oh, enough of this, the story has had a good result and I am relieved."

Arielle decided it best not to resurrect her feelings about her father and the shame he had inflicted on her mother. She pondered, *On both of my mum's to be precise. No good will come of dwelling on it and, as Emma has told me, 'you must not revisit your wounds, for then they will never heal.'*

"Father, I shall certainly consider accompanying you. This will however be determined by the timing of such a journey for we cannot predict what the future may hold. I fondly recall Grandmum often saying, 'We make plans and God laughs.'"

Chapter Nine

One month had passed since Alexandra ventured to meet with Sully following the devastating news Fiona shared that William had asked for Arielle's hand. She had not felt quite herself since that day. Her time had been spent hiding from the truth of the assault she had endured, a truth she realized once she returned home. Somehow she was placed in a carriage. The driver repeatedly asked her for the address of her residence, which she was finally able to mumble well enough for him to discern the location of her home.

Upon her arrival home that day, she slowly walked up the staircase to her bedroom. She sat down on her bed and looked about her room as she attempted to untangle her web of confusion. She had a headache and her mind felt like a fuzzy ball of yarn. Her body ached and the private region between her legs was wet and felt bruised. *What on earth has happened to me?* Slowly, snippets of where she had been and what had transpired began to float across her memory. *Sully, it was Sully. No, not Sully. I went to see Sully, but, oh, no, he was not home. It was Cal who invited me in. He handed me a glass.*

What was in it? Oh, come together. Thoughts, come together. Claret? No, it was stronger than that. Bourbon, perhaps. That was it, he gave me a glass of bourbon. Was it one or two glasses that I consumed? Alexandra closed her eyes tight as she sought to obliterate everything in her immediate presence to clearly see the details of her visit at Sully's.

She remembered consuming a drink, Cal sitting beside her, and then leaning into him. Then her recollection became murky and her thoughts were clouded again. *What happened? Why can I not remember everything?* A heat came over her and she felt her neck. It too felt bruised and tender like the scruff of a beard had rubbed along its length. Her chest was red and her nipples ached. *What did he do? What did he do? Oh, my god!* She exclaimed out loud as a revelation came. She pulled at her gown and tried to hide herself in it, but there was not enough fabric to cover the shame and fear that raged within her. The sudden revelation that Cal had raped her, that he had seared her straight through, seemed unfathomable. *What am I to do? Oh, dear god, what am I to do?* She repeated the words over and over again for they were all she could think to say.

Tears cascaded down her cheeks. She had taken her hands, formed them into fists and pounded on her dressing table forcing several perfume decanters to bounce to the floor. *This cannot be! This absolutely cannot be! I must tell someone! But, no, what will they think of me, what will William think? I am ruined. All of my plans are ruined.* Hateful thoughts about Cal swirled in her head. *He deserves to be dead! What kind of slime is he? And to think he has had his way with me! Oh, Alexandra, how could you let this happen? How could you be so careless!*

Thinking of herself in the third person momentarily helped her separate herself from any culpability. The act was not of her doing, but she felt responsible. *This is my body and not his to do with as he wished. And, to think this was my first time! I never imagined this would be my fate! William is the only man I ever wanted. To think that Calvin Layton of all people has soiled me! No man will want me now!* She had glanced at herself in the mirror attached to her dressing table and a fresh flow of tears released themselves down her face. She hated the image she saw. A sad and broken shell sat before her.

Now, one month had passed. Alexandra had kept to herself, making excuses as to why she was unavailable to meet William for lunch. He checked on her repeatedly, but her household staff sent him away each time saying that she was 'under the weather.' She was trying to escape the depression that threatened to further spiral her downward until this morning when, during her toilette, she was reminded that her usual monthly cycle had not yet been observed. A tremble of dread shot through her. She clutched the back of a chair for support as her legs became weak and unable to sustain her. She dropped to her knees as her worst fear was realized. *Lord, help me. Oh no, it cannot be. I am pregnant.*

She wanted to cry, but no tears would come. She wanted to scream, but no sound was emitted from her throat. She wanted to do harm to someone, but she was the only one in the room. *I am a survivor and will not be undone by this. I must find a way out of this. I will have to lose the baby. I cannot, and will not, carry a child whose seed was planted against my will.*

Her body shook as she saw Cal's face and imagined giving birth to his offspring. Anger rose from within and began to bolster her countenance. *Alexandra, what are you thinking? You cannot kill a child that is half of your flesh. Think, girl, think! There is always a way! You are wiser than this!* Solutions began to dance about in her head. *I could leave this town and deliver the baby where I am not known. I can tell William that I am going on an extended holiday. He will be curious, but he will allow me to leave. Heaven knows he will be happy to be free of me as he makes his wedding plans. His wedding. What am I thinking? I cannot leave and give William free rein to marry Arielle! They must be stopped!* An old rage caught Alexandra's attention.

Her mind swirled virulently like a tornado ready to make landfall. Her thoughts became dark and bleak as the storm of defeat threatened to overtake her. *No, I will not give up. William is to be mine. This life growing inside me will surely turn his affections toward me. Think, think, think, Alexandra. What will you do? I must devise a plan!* A thought crossed her mind. *Yes, that is the answer. Now, I must find a way to make it so.*

An idea started to form and a smile, one of very few she had shown in the last month, swept across her face. *I know exactly what I will do. William cannot give up his promise to my father. He must look after me and see to my welfare. What better way to protect my good name than to marry me and protect me from idle gossip and shame! The child will be his and no one will be the wiser. Surely Cal will never utter a word and put himself in the position of being hung, if not by a jury, then by me!*

Chapter Ten

"As they say in your neck of the woods, where are you headed old chap? Looks like, from the number of trunks you've lined up at the doorway, that you've packed all of your worldly possessions." Cal smirked as he cast a questioning look at Sully.

"We had this discussion some days ago. I told you that I would no longer be residing here and that it would be best for you to secure an honest livelihood to pay for a roof over your head, for you will no longer have me to underwrite your living expenses. And, I might add, there is no need for you to be looking me up. Our time together is done. I think it best that we go our separate ways and keep it that way."

"Well, I for one will be missing the lady folk that came to our door to see you," mused Cal who was not fully realizing the impact Sully's absence would have on his economic condition.

"Whatever are you talking about? There was but one occasion when 'lady folk,' as you call them, came to visit. Miss Whitaker brought Miss Hargrove to meet me. Are you daft?"

"I might be accused of many things, but 'daft' isn't one of them."

"Then to what are you referring?"

"Oh, I must be confused. You're right. It was just that one time that *both* of those ladies lent their beauty to our abode."

Sully shook his head. He was more certain than ever that closing the chapter on any association with Calvin Layton was warranted. He had sensed that Cal made Miss Hargrove uncomfortable from the moment she met him and he knew that Alexandra was not an admirer. *If I never see him again I will have suffered no loss*, thought Sully.

⁓

The clip-clop of the horses' hooves accompanied by the rotation of the carriage's wheels in the pea gravel lining the lengthy lane leading to the front portal of Chestnut Heights created a syncopated rhythm and a welcome sound that Sully fondly remembered from his first visit to Emma Willard's estate. *Home*, he thought to himself, *my new home*. He wondered if he dared to smile, for he felt there was so much ahead of him, so much to uncover from his mother's mysterious entry in her diary.

Alexandra has not led me astray, Sully silently reflected. *Being in this home will put me in greater contact with Miss Hargrove. I will meet her sister and will develop two allies to arrange the meeting I desire with their father, or our father as the case may be.*

As the driver drew the horses to a halt, Sully gathered his hat and a small satchel from the seat and took his exit from the coach as the driver and footman delivered his trunks onto the front porch. The afternoon was drawing to a close and the gas lanterns that flanked the main portal to the Willard estate were aglow, their flames merrily promenading in a slow, mesmerizing waltz. He wondered who would greet him on the other side. Perhaps Thomas would be there as he had been to introduce him to his living quarters. Or, would it be the odd little man, Simon Peabody, who seemed quite innocuous and, in fact, a refreshing pleasure compared to the writer whose eyes appeared to sear him through.

Sully pulled the bold doorknocker and let it loose to strike against the finely crafted mahogany door. The sound of approaching footsteps let him know that his arrival was being acknowledged.

Slowly, the full weight of the door was pulled open and the image of an angel presented itself to him. He stood firmly still as the angel began to speak.

"Please come in. Mrs. Willard said a boarder would be arriving shortly. I heard your knock as I walked through the foyer and, seeing no sign of Thomas, I thought it best to see to the door."

Words were slow in exiting from Sully's mouth. The vision before him was intoxicating. Auburn hair against smooth, white flesh, and eyes with flecks that glistened as though they had been sprinkled with fairy dust cast a familiarity to another he knew. This nymph before him was a beautiful maiden with a keen resemblance to Arielle Hargrove, her features distinguished from the other only by the difference in the color of her locks. He pictured the two of them side-by-side and forced himself into the scene imagined by his mind's eye. His wavy brown hair could make him a by-product of the loins of Sir Ian Hargrove. *If this is indeed Arielle Hargrove's sister, then this beauty before me could be my half-sister. Was this what my mum wanted me to know? Could the answer be as simple as this?* Sully's mind spun. He knew it was too early to make assumptions, but his mother, by the very nature of her writings, had opened a window that prompted him to question his lineage.

"Oh, I do apologize. Have I startled you now?"

Sully heard the nymph's words and although he felt disconcerted, his satchel dropped on his foot causing him to gather his senses.

"No, no, I am quite right. I suppose I expected to see Thomas and I was just thrown off a bit to find someone else behind the door."

"All is well then, it would seem."

"Yes, quite."

"Well, if my memory serves me well, you would be a Mr. Bernard Sullivan. I believe that is the name I heard from Mrs. Willard."

"That is quite right. And, if you do not find me too bold in asking, who are you?"

"I must say, I am typically accustomed to a more formal introduction executed by another source, but it appears we are left to our own devices. I am Arianna Smithfield and, from the sound of your voice, it seems that we are both very familiar with a shared geography across the pond."

Sully smiled with a great sense of relief. His arrival at Chestnut Heights could not have been better choreographed. Arianna Smithfield was exactly whom he hoped to meet and get to know better. She and her sister could help lead him to the truth of his beginnings. He knew they had done the same for themselves. There had been a wealth of gossip in Nantymoel about the investigations of Morgan Pennybacker and her assistant Agnes Fielding. Along with their avian sidekick, Peepers, they had secured sufficient factual information to prove the heritage of the twin sisters who had been separated at birth.

"Well, come in won't you? It is quite rude of me to keep you standing in the foyer. Mrs. Willard should be along shortly. And, I see you have some belongings that need attention. As soon as I locate Thomas, he will see to them posthaste. In the meanwhile, why don't I signal Cook to bring around some tea, or would you prefer something stronger? There is an ample supply of libations from which to choose on the buffet in the dining room."

"Tea will suit me well. I will reserve something stronger for the dinner hour if others are imbibing as well."

The two settled themselves on a large tapestry covered divan as Cook placed the tray with a teapot, cups and cookies before them.

"So, tell me Mr. Sullivan, what brings you to America?"

"I can say that I do not delight much in talking about myself. I would much prefer to hear about you. I met your sister a month or so ago when Miss Alexandra Whitaker made our introduction. I know a bit of your history thanks to Miss Whitaker's enlightenment."

"Now, there is a proper source indeed. I am reluctant to cast aspersions her way but my experiences with her have been, shall I say, less than pleasant. I am sorry. She is your friend and it is unthinking of me to say anything about her that would upset you."

"I understand. We met in New York when we were both traveling to Washington. She actually was very helpful when I first arrived. I know her personality can be strong on occasion, but she has been devoted to helping me get settled and even suggested that I seek lodging here at Chestnut Heights."

"Then for that I am grateful. I know what you mean about the importance of getting settled in a town that is so foreign. I had never ventured to America until this past year. My mum fell ill and sent me on a mission to deliver a message she could not take with her to her grave."

"That would have been the knowledge she had about your birth and the sister and the father that you never knew?"

"Precisely. Miss Whitaker has shared quite a bit with you I see for, to my knowledge, you and my sister have not been in one another's company long enough to have learned so much about each other's lives."

"Quite right. I hope I am not embarrassing you with what I know. About your father, I mentioned to your sister that I would like to meet with him. I feel there is much I can glean from him."

"About?"

Sully was taken aback. He thought Arianna would assume that he wanted to discuss her father's many business successes. *I cannot assume that she has any idea about my lumber business. Her sister may not have said a word. Or, perhaps I am being paranoid. She could have absolutely no idea that my main reason for being here is that I question whether we share a similar heritage.*

Before he could answer, bold footsteps rounded the corner as Alistair Whitfield Drake bounded into the room.

"I say old chap, here we meet again! We met the other day, so, Sully is it? That *is* the name you prefer over Bernard? Guess you did not take a liking to being called 'Bernie.' I have no objection to it, but then you are the one who has to live with your given name. I once knew a chap from Wales who went by the same moniker. Older than you by a score or more of years I should say. He managed a farm, a timber farm as I recall. His 'Sully' came from his first name. Yes, Sullivan was his first name and Ballford was his last. No, I have not got that quite right. The last name was Bamford if I recall correctly. He was a married man with a wife named Penelope, if I have got that right. Word came to me that they both had passed on, given up the ghost as they say. Happens to the best of us. Well, enough about them. No need to raise the dead."

Alistair Drake's comments had a way of bristling the hairs on Sully's neck and his latest banter was no exception. Sully knew he would do best by keeping his encounters with him to a minimum, which would be no small task with his room's proximity to Drake's. Alistair noted Sully's odd expression and passed it off as a personality defect that would hopefully disappear as the two became more acquainted with one another.

"So, I see you have met this fine maiden," Alistair continued his commentary quite happy to hear his own voice. "She's a twin you know! Double the pleasure I say! She was almost an orphan with her mother's passing until she learned the truth about her father. My what a great find you people are! It was Twain who said, 'Truth is stranger than fiction' and he could not have been more accurate!"

"Mr. Drake, I must say that discussing my family in such a way is not comforting for me. We have been through quite a year, not quite a full year actually, and I am still healing from all that was revealed to us. I would ask that you limit your comments on this topic and respect my privacy."

As Arianna finished her statement, her voice caught and tears welled in her eyes. Her reaction threw her off guard. She had not expected Alistair Drake's remarks to affect her so and decided that perhaps it was his cavalier treatment of her story that she found unnecessary and callous. He was essentially a stranger to her and she did not want to share her personal life with him. Sully pulled a handkerchief from his pocket and offered it to Arianna, which she gladly accepted. She gently blotted at the corners of her eyes then held the linen cloth in her hands and rubbed one of its corner's with her thumb and forefinger as she sought comfort in its softness. The handkerchief was embellished around all of its edges with white thread. Her thumb felt an embroidered initial. She gently moved her fingers over the woven inscription as though she were reading braille. The threads formed the letter 'B.' She looked down to confirm her discovery and saw that the letter was undeniably a 'B.' Curiosity got the best of her. She wondered why Bernard Sullivan would carry a handkerchief that held the initial of his first name. Sully watched as he saw the expression on her face change from sadness to one of inquiry. Arianna became fully aware of his gaze and prepared herself to respond.

"You are so kind to offer this to me. I am curious though. Typically the initial from one's surname would be embroidered on such a piece however, in this case, the initial of your first name has been stitched."

Sully was not quick to respond. Alistair noticed his delay and gladly enlisted his own voice to respond to Arianna's inquiry.

"Miss Smithfield, you are quite the observant one, are you not? Mr. Sullivan may not want to divulge the whereabouts from whence his handkerchief originated. A mystery can develop from the most innocuous of places, as I well know. What say you, Mr. Sullivan? Am I right?"

"You are correct about mysteries. Since they are your field it must be difficult not to see something suspect in many things you encounter however, I can say that there is nary a story behind this piece of cloth. It came to me by surprise quite frankly, and I paid little attention to the initial that enhances it. I suppose there were other things on my mind at the time. I am glad it was of use in your time of need, Miss Smithfield."

Arianna smiled, her tears a far distant memory as she studied Sully's face and found something to her liking, not only his good looks, but his calm demeanor as well. She was glad to have him under the same roof with the benefit of time to learn more about him.

"I would hand this back to you but I think it is best, and it would be most proper of me, to have it freshly laundered before it returns to your possession. That is, if that is most agreeable to you. And, Mr. Drake, it is a pity about your friends having passed for I was going to suggest that I look them up for you during my time in Wales."

"Wales? Do you have a trip on the horizon?" Sully inquired.

"Indeed I do. I leave on the morrow. Something has been tugging at me to go and visit my birth mother's gravesite."

"Will you be away for an extended time?"

Arianna was enjoying Sully's inquisitiveness about her travel, yet she wondered what was prompting him to take such an interest in her affairs. *Perhaps he is becoming too familiar for we have only just met.*

"Thank you for your interest, Mr. Sullivan. Actually, mine will be a very brief journey for this is more of a whim, or some might say a frivolous use of my time and resources, but I have the impulse to go and so I shall."

Sully was drawn to Arianna's eyes and her manner. She had obviously been reared with the skills necessary for a young woman to easily maneuver in the most sophisticated social circles. *But, what am I thinking? I must stop this attraction at once. Good lord! She may well be my half-sister. I must put any thoughts of a romantic relationship behind me for incest is not on my agenda, nor shall it ever be.* Fortunately, his worrisome thoughts were abated as Emma entered the room.

"How wonderful to find you all here in one space for me to announce that dinner will soon be served. And, Sully, the trunks you brought with you have been placed in your room. You all have time, if you wish, to freshen up for our evening meal and then meet me in the dining room in thirty minutes. Simon will join us as well. Cook has made one of my favorite roasts and has chosen from a larder of fresh vegetables to accompany our entrée," Emma smiled hoping to whet the appetites of her boarders. "This will be a lovely occasion to get to know one another a bit better."

"The menu sounds delicious, and I for one am famished. Nothing like a hearty meal to satisfy one's cravings," said Alistair as he gave a quick rub to his belly.

"I might add that if you tend to have a sweet tooth, Cook has made a decadent pound cake with fresh sliced strawberries in a simple sugar syrup and dollops of sweetened whipped cream to go alongside. It is the perfect finish for our meal," Emma said as she noted the pleased expressions on her audience's faces.

As the assembly disbanded, Sully stayed back a moment. He chose not to ascend the stairs with Alistair Drake. *It is enough that I will have to endure a meal with him. With any luck, Mr. Drake's stay in America will be limited and I will not have to hear him spouting off about his latest imagined mysteries. As I pursue my own life's unknowns, the very last intrusion I need is to be under the scrutiny of his magnifying glass.*

Chapter Eleven

The Hargrove's home in Washington was much smaller in stature and girth than his place of lodging at Emma Willard's, but Sully was not surprised. He knew their home in Wales was a large estate known by the locals as the 'Big House,' and he assumed their stay in America was a temporary one so they had no need for larger quarters. *Certainly, Sir Ian Hargrove will need to return to his colliery to oversee the continued success of his business holdings,* thought Sully. *What I am not certain of is how I am going to broach the subject of his relationship with my mum. I cannot just blurt out, 'are you my father?' But here I am. Why am I standing here, about to enter his threshold, and I have not gotten a better plan in my head?* His thoughts continued to swim about his mind as the door opened. A young woman with strawberry blonde hair and a face scattered with freckles invited him in.

"Welcome to the Hargrove's. May I ask who ye are and who will ye be seein' this fine day? Oh, and me name is Fiona. I'm known to be very helpful, so if there's anythin' ye be needin' ye can jest ask me."

"That is surely comforting to know. In response to your questions, I am Bernard Sullivan and I am here to see Sir Ian Hargrove."

Sully looked beyond Fiona and was pleased to see Arielle approaching the foyer. She brushed past Fiona to greet him.

"I hear Fiona has completed her job of inquiry. Welcome to our home, Mr. Sullivan. My father is looking forward to meeting you. I shared with him some details as I learned them from you when Miss Whitaker introduced us. He always enjoys a good conversation involving business. Today was a good day for the two of you to meet as he had a break in his meetings with the Trade Council at the Capitol. Come this way and I will lead you to his study. Thank you Fiona, you can be on your way for now."

Arielle opened one of the two large doors forming the entrance to her father's study. Fiona had properly performed her morning task of drawing back the panels of the room's cranberry-hued brocade draperies to allow the day's sunlight to show through three tall windows. Ian was sitting at his desk as Arielle escorted their guest into the room. Sully was impressed with the rich dark woods on the walls and the hardwood floors that were partially covered with a plush area carpet.

"Father, as you have expected, I would like to introduce you to Mr. Bernard Sullivan."

Ian stood and walked around his desk to face Sully. There was a familiarity about him that he could not quite place. He quickly shook off any idea that he might have known him beyond his connection to Wales and a possible resemblance to someone he knew there.

"It is a pleasure to make your acquaintance, Mr. Sullivan. I understand you have an interest in discussing business with me. I am surprised that we have not been aware of one another in the past since my business, as I am sure you are fully aware, has the need for timber. My timbermen are among the best, shoring up the walls, wedging in the timber, keeping the incidence of collapse to a remarkable minimum. We will have to discuss the stull timber you process and have you offer a bid to my overman, Paul Nesbitt."

The idea of doing business with Hargrove Colliery was an enticing one. Sully knew it to be one of the largest collieries in the region and a significant consumer of timber. He had called on one of Hargrove's agents in the past, shortly before his parents became ill. Their illnesses and subsequent deaths set him off course. He had been remiss in his efforts to revisit a business relationship with the colliery. *To be in the owner's company and to have him suggest working with my lumber company is just the entrée I need. However, in light of what I suspect about him, and if my suspicions are indeed fact, he will either embrace me with open arms as his son or reject me altogether and feel disgraced that I have come into his life.*

"I appreciate your interest in my company and I would be very happy to entertain a relationship with you, that is, a relationship with your colliery."

Ian laughed. He saw an uneasiness in the young man, which he attributed to his age but he did not dismiss the fact, as his ego was wont to believe and his nature was wont to assume, that many were intimidated by his wealth and dominating presence in a room. Ian picked up his humidor, selected a cigar for himself and offered Sully his pick of the box. After snipping the tip of each one with a cutter, Ian struck a match and both took a hefty draw through their cigar's barrels. The smell of cigar smoke soon followed, wafting its way into the parlor where Arielle was sitting working on a needle-point pillow cover. She took note of the aroma thinking that Sully's visit must be going well for her father to invite him to join him in a smoke.

"I assure you that a relationship with my colliery *is* a relationship with me. I have always found that success in business directly correlates with one's passion for the products and industry that they represent. I would not be where I am today without that passion, a strong reserve to compete with others in my field, and making every effort to assure my product is continually meeting a need."

Sully nodded. He was not sure what he expected to happen when they met, but he thought there might be more small talk, getting to know one another before the topic of business was discussed. He could see that Sir Ian Hargrove was a man of conviction who wasted no time addressing the matters at hand. *So, he says he is a man of passion. How curious that he uses that word in relation to his business world while it has prevailed in his private life. The question for me is did that passion result in my birth?* Sully shook his head hoping the action went unnoticed by Ian.

"Do you disagree?"

"No, sir. I apologize. My mind drifted for a moment and I suppose I appeared to disagree. I was merely clearing my thoughts to return to our discussion."

"I can advise you, Mr. Sullivan, to maintain your focus and stay the course. That will serve you well in all areas of your life. Please understand that I do not mean to lecture. I have shared my business acumen with many, whether they have sought my counsel or not and, I might add, most have enjoyed very successful results. In fact, my appointment to the Trade Council is a direct result of my success and the desire by others to learn what they can from me to grow their own companies."

Sully was trying to differentiate between the arrogant side of this man and the paternal side. *Do I really want to know if he is my father? He certainly has a high opinion of himself. I am not certain that I will find warmth and caring under his tough exterior. Perhaps I have been too intent on finding the truth or trying at the very least to gain a better understanding of my mum's entry in her diary. Perhaps I should abandon my plan altogether for the discovery may be too confusing or painful to know. But, what have I to lose?* He decided he was determined to see through his original reason for meeting with Ian.

"Have I lost you again, man?"

"You know, I have been so looking forward to meeting you that I am afraid I have not properly organized the many thoughts and questions I wish to pursue with you. You are very kind to meet with me and I feel very fortunate to have met your daughters. I had forgotten to ask them if they have any other siblings. Are they your sole heirs?"

"Now, that is an interesting question and a rather personal one I might add."

"Pardon me, for the question was not meant to be probing."

"I should say. You are like a fisherman throwing his line out to troll for the catch of the day. Is talking about business your bait to meet with me and draw me in hook, line and sinker for other purposes?"

"No. I seem to be going about this all wrong. I can tell you that business is of paramount importance to me and I look forward to further discussions with you if you will allow me to visit again. I suppose I was hoping we would get to know one another on a more familiar level particularly with our common ground in Wales," Sully said as he studied Ian's demeanor and asked if he was open to discussing pleasantries with him. He decided it was safe to engage in some light conversation. The thought came to him that he could reference a name recently mentioned by Alistair Drake. "In fact, where I am living at Mrs. Willard's estate, there is another boarder who is from England. He's a very interesting gentleman who is a writer of mysteries. Alistair Whitfield Drake is his name. Perhaps you have read some of his books. When he heard my nickname, he commented that he once knew a Sully but it was because of his first name. I wonder if you ever knew the family whose last name was Bamford? Sometimes it is amazing what a small world it can be and how related we can be as human beings."

Sully carefully studied Ian's face to capture his reaction to the mention of being related. Ian remained as poker-faced as he had been. Sully wondered if he was that adept at masking his reactions. *I am failing at this terribly. Unless I share my mum's name, he will never know what I am trying to divulge. I need to know if he knew her. How will I ever find this out? This may be beyond my capabilities. I fear I have taken on more than I know how to finesse.*

"Bamford. Why would I know that name?"

"As I said, sometimes it is a small world."

"Who are these people? Now you have hastened my curiosity."

"Mr. Drake mentioned their names, Sullivan and Penelope Bamford, and said that Mr. Bamford tended a timber farm in Wales. I guess I was just wondering if you knew of them?"

"I cannot say that anything about them is familiar to me but you seem to hold great interest in them. Why is that?"

"Oh, I think particularly when one is away from his homeland, that the mention of a fellow compatriot makes one feel not too far from the land that is known so well."

Sully was feeling like he had made a big mistake trying to take on the patriarch of the Hargrove family. He felt awkward and a bit ashamed to want to accuse a man he had never met of impregnating his mother solely based on a passage an ailing woman wrote in her diary. *I need to think this through with much more detail and calculation.* The two took the last draws from their cigars and placed them in a large amber glass ashtray.

"You know, sir, I feel that I have consumed a good portion of your time and do not want to wear out my welcome. Would it be agreeable for me to prepare some papers for you to review that will explain my company and provide some pricing information as well? Your suggestions and comments will be most welcomed I assure you. I imagine that Miss Hargrove has told you that I have the utmost respect for your work and value any expertise that you wish to share with me."

"That sounds like a suitable plan, Mr. Sullivan. I look forward to your return visit and to exploring our mutual interests in the business world. I shall try to think of some surnames that might be known to both of us so we shall have more, what did you call them? Oh yes, *pleasantries* to discuss."

With a nod to one another, Sully departed the study and said his goodbyes to Arielle as thoughts came together in his mind. *She and her sister are so beautiful. I would be their older sibling if my suspicions are correct, yet I do not see a marked resemblance to myself. That unto itself is not unusual. Many families have offspring that look very little like their parents or their brothers and sisters. No, this will not deter me. My quest must continue. I am determined to see this through and will enlist the aid of a professional. Morgan Pennybacker seems to come highly rated by many in this town. A meeting with Miss Pennybacker will be my top priority.*

Chapter Twelve

As he had on several nights since his arrival at Chestnut Heights, Sully sat at the dining room table quietly absorbing Alistair and Emma's lively dinner conversation. Their robust exchange about the merits of sleuthing, and its sometimes not so predictable outcomes, centered this evening on Morgan Pennybacker and her penchant for solving mysteries. The focus on Morgan did not go unheard by Sully who took note of the location of her stitchery shop. As he listened to them, his mind was drawn to a discussion he had been privy to at the Hargrove's when he stopped by their manse to deliver some literature about his lumber company for Arielle's father. As he approached the study, guided there by Fiona, one door was ajar and he overheard Arielle's mother make mention of a sibling. He could hear the sound of Arielle's father pacing the floor and from the tone of his response to his wife, he appeared to be annoyed. Fiona held out her arm to halt Sully from proceeding. Both waited out of sight just beyond the doorway. Sully began to feel uneasy, as though he were eavesdropping. He looked to Fiona to suggest they retreat to another space and observed that she appeared to suffer no such pangs of guilt.

"Quite frankly, Elsbeth, I still do not understand how you and your brother fell out of one another's good graces. It seemed to come on so suddenly. Was this of your doing or his?"

"I am surprised you mention him today. What triggered this? It seems so out of the blue to dredge up an estrangement that is decades old. It is what it is."

"There has been a lot of talk in recent days about siblings so yours came to mind."

"Talk about siblings?"

"Yes. Even that man, Mr. Sullivan, who visited the other day, asked if Arielle and Arianna had other siblings. I found it quite odd, but it made me think of your brother. I know it was very important for the girls to find each other and it would seem that you and your brother would want to make amends before death knocks at your doors. The situation between the two of you begs the question, what was the cause? Was he jealous that you had far greater wealth than he? Could it be a grudge or bitterness about something that he held against you?"

"Why siblings become estranged can take on a wide variety of scenarios, far too many for me to analyze. I guess there are times when one dredges up the past as you are doing now, whether it be for one's good or not. Some things must raise their ugly heads like a snake rising out of a basket at the sound of a snake charmer's pungi. Sometimes the past cannot be fully buried and, speaking of that, I wonder if Carson is dead or alive? The last I heard, he was roaming the streets of Shoreditch and being identified by his street name 'Ziggy.' I must say I am not proud that that is what has become of him. We were close as children, but it seems the times and his temperament shifted us to distant shores."

"Well, you know I have stated on more than one occasion that his mental state could be called into question. For example, I should say, look at his ridiculous moniker 'Ziggy.' Now, is that not a fine name to saddle oneself with? It certainly does not raise the standards for the family. It would seem my dear that you are far better off without him in your life, though I am still puzzled as to the cause for your alienation."

Elsbeth knew she was not being forthright with Ian. She knew full well why she could not be in her brother's company and, though she regretted the need to keep her distance from him, she was confident that she would never have to reveal the cause.

Sully committed to memory Elsbeth's brother's name and his nickname. Arielle's mother had not kept in contact with him and it seemed her husband was curious but took little exception to her decision. Sully wondered if Arielle knew she had an uncle who had been banished from her realm and Fiona, with eyes wide, was wondering the same thing.

⟨⟩

Sully's initial inclination was to keep his distance from Alistair Drake. His inquiring mind made him uneasy and he was concerned that he might make inroads that would usurp his mission. In short order, Sully began to reevaluate his thinking about the writer. *My father used to counsel me that it is important to keep potential enemies close at hand in order to monitor their moves. I suppose 'enemy' is too strong a word for Mr. Drake, but I am not certain that he would have my best interests in mind. Then again, if I make him feel privy to my quest, he could very well be an asset with his mind for mysteries and their resolution. I could swear him to secrecy if he is agreeable.*

Alistair was elated when Sully invited him to his first meeting with Morgan Pennybacker. He had put on his favorite burgundy hued, velvet smoking jacket for the occasion. Sully observed that the pile of the jacket's cloth was rubbed flat and thin at the elbows. A sheen had begun to develop on both sleeves from what Sully guessed to be numerous encounters with a desk's surface as the author sat and worked on his latest missive. Sully had offered very little detail to Alistair about their visit to Miss Pennybacker's suggesting that more would soon be revealed. The mere mystery of Sully's intentions whet Alistair's appetite to learn more. His first impression of Morgan when he met her at Chestnut Heights was one of professionalism, and the fact that she was a fan of his work certainly contributed to his favorable opinion of her.

The two decided to walk a portion of their trip and take in the variety of homes and businesses along their way before they boarded a trolley to their final destination, Pennybacker Stitchery. Sully had decided to don his bowler. He appeared as quite the city gent in the dome-shaped crown that suited his demeanor and his dark suit. As they passed by the storefront of Genovese Gentleman Tailor, a man stumbled from the alleyway into Alistair's path taking him by surprise. Sully recognized him immediately and was alarmed to see the condition he was in. Alistair put his hands up to push the man away before he leaned on him any further and knocked him to the ground.

"I say you must be mindful of your surroundings. Get a grip man!" Alistair began to brush the contact with the man from the soft pile of his velvet jacket.

"Well, lookie who we have here? If it isn't me old roomie! I see you've found a new friend."

"You know this man?" Alistair queried as he observed that Sully did not tip his bowler in greeting.

Sully was reluctant to speak. He had hoped to have put their association in the past and have it remain there.

"So, who is this fine gentleman? What a fancy jacket. I might like one just like it for myself."

"You need to be on your way, Cal. You have no business with us."

"Now, now. There's no need to be rude. I have a right to be on this street as much as you do even if my new home is among the lovely folk who reside in Purdy's Court," said Cal as he turned to address Alistair. "Hello sir, I am Calvin Layton and who might I be able to say I am having the pleasure of meeting?"

"Seriously, Cal you need to move along. Good day to you," Sully said with great determination to get away and move along to his destination with Alistair. As they left Cal swaying and steadying himself on the side of the tailor's building, Alistair turned back to have a second look.

He was intrigued. It seemed that at every turn there was another character to meet and another mystery to be solved. *It was certainly a lucky day for me when I happened upon Emma Willard's home to board myself. It would be delicious fun to build a tale around this man, another miscreant in my midst!*

"So, Sully my man, tell me about this Calvin Layton."

"There is nothing to tell. He and I had rooms in a house in the area. He was living in the house before I came to America. We had never met before until I answered an advertisement for a room to rent and there he was. We were cordial with one another but he was never to be my friend. An odd sort he is and he often left me feeling uncomfortable. It is advisable for both of us not to align ourselves with him. He is one of those individuals who are best left forgotten. I, for one, hope to never see him again."

"If you say so. I will let you be my guide on this, however, if he frequents this city, then the odds of crossing his path again are fairly high."

"As I said, I hope to never see him again. And, a pity about Purdy's Court. I have not been in the city long but I know that is not a desirable place to live. It is quite a shame that he prefers to sustain himself on the mercy of others rather than find gainful employment, although I am not surprised. Here, we have arrived."

Morgan's storefront was warm and welcoming. Golden numerals in the transom above the doorway read 247 F Street. A hunter green sign suspended from the storefront by a wrought iron bracket was adorned with a meandering wisteria vine motif. Below the store's name read: 'fine needlework, finishings & findings.' As Sully opened the door and he signaled Alistair to step inside, they were announced by the tinkling of a bell. Sully craned his neck around a counter stacked high with bolts of fabric and saw a young woman engrossed in filing through a pile of papers that appeared to be receipts. He cleared his throat to garner her attention.

"Oh, my goodness. Excuse me, and welcome to Pennybacker's Stitchery! How may I help you?" Agnes' words came forward with extra gusto since she knew she was remiss in not noticing her customers immediately upon their arrival. Peepers quickly turned on his perch from watching Agnes and placed his eyes directly on Sully's face.

"Whoa boy, whoa boy. Peepers say 'hello,' Peepers say 'hello.'"

"I must apologize for my little bird friend here. I have been working on his vocabulary and asking him to say 'hello' but he is very stubborn and insists on repeating exactly what I have said to him. I am sorry, how may I help you?"

"We are here to see Miss Pennybacker."

"And whom may I tell her is calling?"

"She should be expecting me. My name is Bernard Sullivan and Mrs. Emma Willard has referred me to her. I have also brought along Mr. Alistair Drake with whom Miss Pennybacker is acquainted."

"Oh, I see. Very well. Yes, we are quite fond of Mrs. Willard, a fine lady she is. Follow me this way and I will take you to Morgan's, I mean, Miss Pennybacker's office."

Alistair was dismayed that Agnes showed little recognition when his name was introduced since she too had met him at Emma Willard's. *I suppose I am not enough British royalty for these Americans!* Alistair shook off his bruised ego and followed Agnes' lead.

Both men were drawn to the warm wood furnishings in Morgan's office. The space was Eastlake in influence, adequate and well-organized, free of bric-a-brac. Like the woman herself, everything was in good order, neat, and precisely tailored. Etchings of horses in fine detail, some in full gait and some pulling carriages, were framed and hung in groupings about the room's walls and lent a rural warmth to the space. Barrister bookcases of oak in a honey-yellow stain lined the walls. Their leaded, stained glass panels appeared influenced by the Arts & Crafts movement.

Morgan stood to greet them. The jingle of coins could be heard as she fondled them in one pocket of her navy blue frock coat. The clinking of coins had become so much a part of her persona that she gave her actions little mind. It was a trademark that was calming and natural to her.

"A pleasure to see you again, Miss Pennybacker, this time on your home turf," said Alistair as he surveyed the room. "I cannot help but notice the artwork surrounding us. The equine render-ings are very well done. I like the sepia tones as well and, if I am not mistaken, the horses are predominately Morgans, is that correct?"

"Yes, you know your breeds. My late father raised horses on our family farm in Leesburg, Virginia. I have always been fond of them. They have such good confirmation and are well-suited for both driving and riding."

"Did you commission a local artist to create them for you?"

"In point of fact, they were created by me. I am not one to re-main idle, so having a sketchpad and drawing tools close at hand provides me the freedom to draw whenever I have a free moment. It is quite easy to stop when needed and pick the piece back up when more time allows."

"It seems your art is in parallel to your detective work for you have honed your observation and recording skills, both key to prop-er investigations. I would also surmise that nuance does not go un-noticed by you."

"If by nuance you mean interpreting the subtle responses or re-actions of people, I like to pride myself on that ability, which I feel is based on intuition."

"Quite right you are. Something that cannot be taught, a gut feeling that leads you to the truth. So, were you named for the breed that so enthralled your father?"

Morgan was used to the question being asked. It was a natural assumption and one that was quite correct.

"I am quite frequently asked that very question when someone becomes aware of my love for the breed. As much as I would like to think that my parents named me for the famed J.P. Morgan, I must admit that that is not the case."

Alistair felt he was with a kindred spirit and he smiled as he en-joyed their repartee. Sully, ready to get to the point of the meeting, was trying to think of a gentle way to guide the conversation his direction when Morgan spoke to him.

"Mr. Sullivan, I assume. Please gentlemen, have a seat and we can address your concerns," said Morgan as she focused her attention solely on Sully. "Tell me a bit about yourself. What brings you here today?"

"Thank you for seeing me, Miss Pennybacker. First, I would like the assurance that what is spoken before you will not be repeated to anyone else," Sully said and turned to Alistair. "And, Mr. Drake, I ask the same of you. I must be assured that this information will remain confidential if I am to proceed."

"I assure you that you will have my full cooperation and discretion in the matters we discuss. How say you, Mr. Drake?" Morgan queried.

"Unless you are admitting to having committed a murder or an act of treason, you may rest assured that I will not utter a sound to anyone. Now, there is the matter of my writing, and there may be an interesting plot twist here that I could use in the future. Of course, I would change the names to protect the innocent!" Alistair's voice went up a notch as he became filled with curiosity and anticipation.

"Then I will proceed," said Sully as he reached into the large pocket in his waistcoat and removed what appeared to be a journal. Morgan and Alistair watched as his hands fumbled to open the book and he searched to find the page he readied to share.

"This is my mum's diary. I found it among her belongings after she passed away and was unaware of its existence until that time. This page stood out for it was marked with a pressed flower, a pansy," explained Sully as he worked to maintain his composure.

"Yes, the pansy, the flower of love and remembrance. Did the flower hold any other meaning for you? Did your mother grow pansies in her garden or perhaps you know who gave the flower to her? How did it come into her possession?" Morgan inquired, trying to learn more while she developed a rapport with Sully.

"No, I am not aware of the flower's origin. I just found it curious that she seemed to have marked this page, to draw attention to it, as though her diary would someday be viewed by eyes other than her own."

"So, it would seem from your reaction that whatever is written on that page piqued your interest or drew something into question. Is that correct?"

"Yes, absolutely."

"May I see what is written or would you prefer to read the page aloud?"

Sully was not sure that he was comfortable handing over his mother's very personal possession to someone he had just met, yet he was not certain he could read the passage aloud without emotion overtaking him. He began to question his decision to engage a detective in his personal life when he himself had little evidence to prove his assumptions. *And, why did I decide to drag Alistair along? Well, there is no turning back now unless I bolt from the room, give this entire idea up, and return to Wales. What good will that do me? I will be no closer to discovering the meaning of my mum's words. I must stand my ground and move forward.*

"Mr. Sullivan, are you all right? Did you hear my question?"

"Yes, forgive me for my hesitation, Miss Pennybacker. It is just that there is a part of me that feels as though I am breaking a confidence. I know I must put that behind me if I am to pursue my original goal. Here, you may read the page."

"Aloud?"

"Yes, aloud."

"Very well. Bear with me as I become at ease with the style of handwriting." Morgan held the diary with great care, not wanting to crack its binding or damage a page. She scanned over the page Sully had chosen and then began to read:

My son must know. He must. Soon, I will not be on this earth to honor the opinion of another who swayed me from that which I felt rightfully was his to know. His father is dead now, or is he? My mind is muddled. Forgive me. He must know how much I love him and have loved him since the first day he came into my life. But, he must know more. He must seek the truth here in Wales. He must know about family. The truth is with the head of the Big House. Go, find him, find himself. Tell him to do this.

Morgan silently read through the missive one more time. In the plea in the last sentence Sully's mother was unequivocal about her strong desire for him to take action. Her words were direct and commanding. She harbored a secret that would have a direct impact on her son and Morgan was intrigued.

"I find it of interest that you have come to America and sought my services when your mother, in point of fact, has given you the clue about Wales and what she calls the 'Big House.' Tell me more about this. What is the 'Big House' and why not remain in Wales?"

"The Big House refers to the large residence of the owner of one of the nearby coal mines in my homeland, Nantymoel, Wales to be precise."

"Do you know of which owner she speaks?"

"My belief is that it is the father of someone with whom you are familiar. You worked on a case for her this past year. Her name is Miss Arielle Hargrove."

"Are you certain your mother was referring to Sir Ian Hargrove? There could be no one else? I know the man's dubious reputation beyond his business successes. I will say no more but I am sure rumors have abounded in Nantymoel for it is such a tightly woven village. I would hate to think we are making assumptions based on his history that have no bearing on your case."

"I understand. I too have tried to think this through and not abide by the aspersions that have been cast his way and in Miss Hargrove's instance proven, but what my mum wrote clearly points a finger his direction."

"This begs the question, why did you not pursue this with him in Wales?"

"When I discovered the diary, I hesitated to do anything. My thoughts were paralyzed and by the time I decided to make a call to the Big House, I learned that he and his family were living in America for a period of time. I knew I could look him up if I came here and that I would be able to use the ploy of developing a possible business relationship with him to meet with him."

"You think he is your father do you not?"

"I do. I can think of no other explanation and, without asking him point blank, which I suppose he would deny, I need your expertise to dig further into the meaning of this passage, to understand what transpired that was so important to my mum that I know."

"Was there never a time when you felt she wanted to tell you something but she held back? Was she lucid before she died?"

"No, that is just it. After my father died, she was never the same. Her mind was not always acute, she was wont to ramble on, and she died several months later. There is a part of me that wishes I had never discovered her diary. It has left me very unsettled and I feel quite awkward calling into question Mum's lack of chastity."

"Considering her mind, do you think her written words can be trusted or are they the random thoughts of someone who had seen her better days?"

"My instincts tell me that when she wrote this she was in the midst of a flashback to reality, that she was trying very hard to get her words right."

Alistair sat as though watching a tennis match. His head went left and right as he looked at Morgan then Sully during their verbal exchange. He was surprised by the revelation of the diary and the cryptic message contained within. He imagined himself as one of his characters caught up in such a tale and he too felt the need to know more. Typically bold by nature, he was not accustomed to being the shrinking violet in a room. He had remained silent, not wanting to interject his opinion unless asked, but it was becoming more difficult for him not to offer some unsolicited advice.

"May I say a word?" Alistair asked with some trepidation lest he be refused.

Morgan looked to Sully for approval. He nodded. She lifted her right hand from her desk, turned it palm side up and directed it to Alistair as an offering for him to speak.

"I am referencing the part of the passage where your mother says your father is dead. Obviously, Sir Ian Hargrove is alive and well, at least to my knowledge."

"Mr. Drake, I too examined that sentence over and over searching for clarity but you see, my mum also questioned her thinking by writing that her mind was muddled. She was correct that her husband had died, but perhaps my biological father had not."

"In all of this, you have not referred to your parents by name. Would it not behoove you to give that information to Miss Pennybacker. We know your surname to be Sullivan but what are their first names?"

"Pardon me for interrupting Mr. Drake, but at this time, their names are of little value to me unless the need should arise for me to visit the courthouse and review records that may show a birth certificate for Mr. Sullivan, assuming his mother gave 'Sullivan' as his surname. At this time I am most inclined to focus my efforts on other avenues, if there is more that you can share with me, Mr. Sullivan. If you do not mind my probing, when were you born? What is your date of birth?"

"I was born in 1868 and I have always celebrated my arrival on August 2nd. To the best of my understanding that information is accurate."

"When were your parents married?"

"They were married in 1866. They both grew up in Ogmore Vale in the village of Nantymoel so they knew each other's families very well." Discussing his personal life was not an easy task for Sully. The death of his parents still felt like an unhealed wound and the supposed mystery of his heritage was like pouring tincture over his raw emotions.

"I am wondering what other information I might glean from you? In point of fact, in my line of work I find that it is paramount to ask questions even if some are repetitious. There is typically infinitely more to be gained. Even the smallest details, or a conversation overheard can generate a previously undiscovered path that should be pursued."

Morgan's comments gave Sully a moment to reflect. He could think of nothing about his life in Wales that would be pertinent to his quest and since meeting the Hargrove sisters he had essentially only exchanged pleasantries with them. Then a thought occurred to him.

"There is something that probably has no bearing on my quest, but it may be of interest for you to know since you have worked so closely with the Hargroves."

"Let us be clear, my work was commissioned by Miss Arielle Hargrove. I had very little presence with her parents until the conclusion of her case."

"Perhaps I should not say a word about this for I am feeling somewhat like a gossip. What I have to say is probably public knowledge though I am not certain."

"You certainly have my attention. From henceforth do not 'beat about the bush' as they say on your side of the pond, get to the point," said Morgan as she grew tired of waiting for Sully to say what he had to say.

"Again, this may have no bearing here, but on a visit to the Hargrove's, I was privy to a conversation between Sir Ian and his wife. It seems he was asking about her brother and questioning why they were estranged. Lady Hargrove was dismissing their relationship as history that needed no dredging up. She also questioned whether her brother was alive or dead. I wonder, did Miss Hargrove ever mention having an uncle on her mother's side?"

"Not to my best recollection. There was really no cause for siblings to be mentioned though, now that you bring this matter to my attention, Lady Hargrove's brother might have been helpful in my learning about her daughter's adoption. He might have been a useful source. I too wonder why they have severed ties. Maybe he was not a fan of Sir Ian. I must say, you have stirred my curiosity. Was her brother's name mentioned?"

"I overheard Lady Hargrove mention his name as Carson."

"And was his last name ever stated?"

"No, just a nickname."

"And...what was that?"

"Ziggy."

"Ziggy? I wonder what prompted that moniker?"

"From the sound of the exchange between them, Sir Ian was wondering the same thing. He dismissed the name as being beneath his family's standards."

"You know, I should think I would like to look this Ziggy up. I shall discreetly try to learn his last name and his whereabouts."

"If he is indeed alive, I can help you with his possible whereabouts. Shoreditch was apparently the last location Lady Hargrove knew him to frequent."

"Shoreditch? Oh my. Not an area that I visit when I am on one of my buying trips to England. Agnes, that is Miss Fielding, and I do have a trip planned in several weeks so I suppose we could make a detour and visit the East End of London and search him out. One never knows who might be the key ingredient in the mix."

"You are opposed to questioning Sir Ian directly?"

"Note that I am not opposed. I prefer not to go immediately to the source, *if* he even is the source. We do not want to alert him, which might cause certain facts to be hidden from us. Your mention of this 'Ziggy' is of interest because he may be very willing to shed some light on his sister's life with her husband. It is worth a try to see if Miss Fielding and I can find him, talk with him, and see where our encounter leads."

Vivid memories of his mother, her loving ways, her attention to his needs, her interest in his life, her encouragement, lent a peaceful, calming air as he justified his pursuit to solve the riddle she had put in play.

"I will bow to your greater knowledge in this area, Miss Pennybacker. I marked another page in my mum's diary. There are quotations on several pages and one attributed to Lord Byron stood out. I was curious about the entry that goes like this, 'The beginning of atonement is the sense of its necessity.' These words seem to correlate to the passage we have been discussing. It is that necessity to atone felt by my mum that has driven me to secure your services. I hope that when all is said and done, I will gain a better understanding and my mum's wishes will be realized."

"In point of fact, Mr. Sullivan, we can make no assurances but will certainly do our best to find the answers to the questions you pose. Give us a bit of time. What's the expression? Oh yes, good things come to those who wait. Well, I do believe with that caveat that you may find you were better off and more settled having been kept in the dark. There are always adjustments that must be addressed when change enters our domain. I merely want you to be prepared for that eventuality."

⌣⟶

A stop at Pennybacker's Stitchery was as refreshing as a favorite repast for Elsbeth. She enjoyed the pleasure that the completion of a new needlework project brought her. The shop's air was filled with the smell of fresh fabrics, laces and trims. Shelves were filled with a variety of yarns and embroidery flosses in a rainbow of shades and hues. She paused at a needlepoint canvas stamped with a bouquet of large chrysanthemums. *This is just what I need to add to the conservatory,* she mused. She thought about the room's colors and the lush greens that filled the gardens beyond its large windows. As she began making her selections, she became aware of approaching footsteps.

"Lady Hargrove, what a pleasure to have you visit my shop today," said Morgan as she refreshed a nearby shelf with a new inventory of yarn and felt relieved that Mr. Sullivan and Mr. Drake were no longer on the premises to make her encounter. "I see it is time for another project to showcase your handiwork. When I was in your home some months ago I took note of the lovely pieces placed about your parlor. I attributed them to your fine taste."

"How lovely of you to notice. I however cannot take full credit for each piece since Arielle is quite adept at working a needle and has completed several pillows and even seat coverings in that room and others throughout our home."

"Is there something I can help you find?"

Elsbeth gave a little laugh as she thought about Miss Pennybacker's question and how appropriate it was considering her other vocation that led to the discovery of Anna Hollingsworth, her friend Maggie Galligan, and the truth of Arielle's birth. Her face flushed slightly as she thought of all that Miss Pennybacker knew about her family.

"Thank you, I think this piece will serve me well for the purposes I have in mind."

An idea came to Morgan and she decided to put it into play. *How fortuitous that Lady Hargrove has come into the shop today. In point of fact, this may be just the opportunity I need to acquire a piece of information.*

"Very well, however I simply cannot let you leave without showing you something that has become all the rage in Europe and is finding its way into framed pieces and onto pillows and lambrequins, especially for a mantelpiece. Initials are being used everywhere and in a wide assortment of scripts, Old English being of course the most popular. Here, let me show you."

Morgan reached for several packages and then paused.

"Oh, I am thinking that I failed to mention that the first initial of surnames are predominately used and they are not always one's married name. Many women are choosing to stitch their maiden name as a keepsake for themselves or to give it as a gift to a family member. Here I will show you. Your surname, what initial was that?"

"My maiden name began with a 'C,'" said Elsbeth.

"A 'C,' let me see if I can locate that letter," said Morgan as she took her time fiddling about making a bit of disarray in her inventory. "Oh, here it is, a 'C.' Was that for Clarke, Chapman, or Chase?"

Elsbeth was wondering of what interest her maiden name might be to Morgan Pennybacker. Rather than let her imagination run away with her she decided there could be no harm in divulging the last name she held until she married Ian.

"Cromwell is the last name that frequented my monogram until I became a bride."

"Ah, Cromwell. Would you be interested in one of these projects today?"

"I think the needlepoint bouquet will be enough for me today. On second thought, yes, I will take a 'C.' Not for Cromwell though, but for Clay. It will make a beautiful wedding gift for my daughter and her intended."

"Yes, I heard that your daughter and Mr. Clay had become engaged. I wish them much happiness."

"Thank you. I will give them your message but I am sure you will be able to tell them that yourself at their wedding for I am certain you will be among those on the guest list."

"It will be my pleasure to attend. Here, let me take these items to the counter for you. Miss Fielding will complete the sale of your purchases. Good day for now," Morgan said as she stepped into the hallway and returned to her office to add the last word to a notation in a file on her desk about a man who went by the nickname Ziggy.

Chapter Thirteen

The morning had been going beautifully well for Simon. He had toured the gardens and clipped several large bunches of peonies to place in a vase on the large, round table in the foyer. Just as he was completing the display, a knock sounded at the door. Looking about for Thomas to respond but seeing no sight of him, Simon proceeded to the portal to see whom it held on the other side. As he swung wide the door, he found himself face-to-face with Alexandra. *Oh, my,* he said to himself. *Just when my day was on the upswing, I have to have her in my midst.* His thoughts were very transparent to Alexandra who took full note of the expression overtaking his face.

"Well, my, my, my weird little man. If there were but two of you, what a fine pair of gargoyles you would make for the entrance posts!"

Simon was stunned by yet another insult from the one with golden locks and a viper's tongue. He heard footsteps behind him and turned to see Arianna approaching the threshold.

"Is there no ceasing the venom you spew?" Arianna said to Alexandra as she turned to Simon. "I'm sorry that you have had to hear more toxic words from this woman." She turned back to face

Alexandra. "Surely there is some devil's den you can return to post-haste and spare us another moment of your dour spirit."

"What are you doing in my face? I thought we were rid of you. You took off to visit your Welsh roots, did you not? And, I must say that I am quite taken aback by *your* words. Here I am, calling on William's aunt and being tweated, umm treated, as though I have no business on the premises. I am certain Emma Willard would find your flunction, I mean function, as a welcoming party to be severely lacking. My word, where are your social glaces, umm graces?" proffered Alexandra.

Arianna thought she heard a slur or two in Alexandra's words as her body began to sway. She seemed to be concentrating on her balance and steadied herself by holding on to the large demilune chest nearby. Arianna stepped a few paces closer to their visitor and noted the smell of wine emanating in the air about her. *Hmm, it appears this snotty twit has been imbibing, and in the early hours of the day no less. I wonder what has her knickers in a twist?*

"Alexandra, you are correct. I was away but now I have returned and, I must say, it appears *our* social graces are not the ones to be questioned if my nose does not deceive me."

"What on dirth, I mean, what on earth do you mean?" asked Alexandra, quite put off by Arianna's insinuation.

"I mean, and of course without casting unfounded aspersions your way, that the smell of claret is quite evident and I can assure you that Simon and I have not partaken of any spirits this morning."

"Move along, out of my way. What I have had to shrink, that is drink, is not of your concern. I am here to meet William and you are keeping me from him." Alexandra's tone became more emphatic as she steadied herself to proceed forward.

"Mr. Peabody and I have been in the garden a good portion of the morning. I, for one, can say that I have not set eyes on Mr. Clay this day. How about you, Simon?"

"No, Miss Arianna, no, no. I can be certain that I have not seen Mr. Clay today, not today, no, not today."

"This babble is making me feel quite ill. Please put a stop to it at once before I lose my morning meal."

"Miss Whitaker, you are looking quite pale. Let me help you into the parlor. I will summon Mrs. Willard immediately. Perhaps she has had word from Mr. Clay on the timing of his arrival." Arianna wanted little to do with Alexandra on any given day and, the thought of being her nursemaid should she decide to heave forth the contents of her stomach, held even less appeal. She shuffled Alexandra along as quickly as she could with Simon in her shadow and settled her in one of the parlor's plump chairs.

"Simon, would you remain with Miss Whitaker while I locate Mrs. Willard? I shan't be a minute."

"Oh, what more must I endure! Now I have this imp of a man watching over me. There is no telling what mischief he is preparing to cast my way!"

Arianna ignored Alexandra's latest outburst. She had observed Emma paying little heed to Alexandra's unkind words on other occasions and decided that was the best practice to follow to escape additional rantings. As she returned to the foyer, Thomas was coming along the hallway in response to another knock at the door. Arianna signaled him with a grimace that there was a visitor in the parlor and then she proceeded toward the rear of the manse in search of Emma. Thomas took a quick peek and appreciated Arianna's warning when he saw who was seated with Simon Peabody nearby.

"Why, Mr. Clay, what a welcome sight you are, yez indeed," Thomas exclaimed as he ushered William forward.

"Well, thank you, Thomas. It is always a pleasure to see you. I am here to meet with Miss Whitaker. Has she arrived?"

"Yez sir, yez sir, she has. Gwain the parlor and you'll find her there."

As William approached, Simon gave him a small salute and took his leave. He was happy to have the changing of the guard and to be relieved from monitoring Alexandra's behavior.

"Oh, my god, William, you have finally come. I thought you had forgotten. This is extreme-aly important to me, extreme-aly."

"I am glad that you have finally decided to leave your home and join the ranks of the living however, I am curious as to why you wanted to meet at my aunt's home rather than over lunch or dinner at another establishment. Are you feeling better? I have repeatedly visited your home and been told that you were not well. I have been concerned and I even sent Doc Lovering to call on you and he assured me that there was no cause for alarm. You are looking a bit pale and your speech is somewhat garbled. You are not having a stroke are you? Should I call for the doctor?"

"I am having a stroke all right, a stroke of bad luck. But, I know you will right everything for me. I wanted to meet at your aunt's because I wanted her to be at my disposal and she seems to be a guiding farce for you, that is force, and a voice of season, umm reason. We will want her blessing and I know you would want her to be one of the first to know."

"The first to know? Why are you talking in riddles?"

"Because this is not an easy conversation for me to have with you. I am aware of your affection for Miss Hargrove but that must crease, cease now."

"Alexandra, are you inebriated? What on earth is the matter with you? As I have stated, I tried to visit with you many times this last month only to be turned away. I have news to share with you and I wanted to be sure that you heard it from me. My 'affection,' as you call it, for Miss Hargrove has grown and we have made a further commitment to our relationship. I hope you will share in our joy as I tell you that we are engaged to be married."

Alexandra's face lost all remaining color. Thanks to Fiona's talent at tittle-tattle, she knew full well that William and Arielle were to be married, but hearing it from his lips sent her mood into a downward spiral. *How am I going to be able to change his heart? What am I to do if he will not honor my request to make an honest woman out of me? This situation has become supremely complicated. I must be emphatic and have him understand that there is no alternative. He must make everything right for me, for us.*

"William, let's move to the settee so we can sit together. My neck is drawing tired of looking up at you."

"As you wish. You are looking very pale. I expected my news to be difficult for you to bear, but you had to know that this was where my relationship with Miss Hargrove was leading."

William assisted Alexandra in her move to the settee and seated himself next to her. She took his hands in hers and looked directly into his eyes with earnest. She was determined to have him. *The tiny seed growing in my womb will make all the difference. I must use this unfortunate incident to my advantage. This is the answer to my having William as my own. I will make him see that this is the only way.*

"William, oh William," Alexandra's voice was pleading as she gained a tighter grip on his hands. "You are the father of my child."

William released his hands from hers as he reared back in surprise at her words. He shook his head and stared at her wondering if she had gone completely mad.

"What on earth are you saying? Have you lost your mind? This is the most outlandish thing you have ever said to me. What has been brewing in that brain of yours? Perhaps it is the effects of the drink you have consumed today for you are clearly not yourself. Really this must cease."

"No, it is true, William. I am pregnant and the child is yours. I shall see it no other way and neither shall you. You must accept the position you have put me in."

"The position *I* have put you in? You are out of your mind! How can you be with child? What have you done? Who has done this to you? Are you fabricating this scheme to render my engagement void? What is the matter with you?" Alexandra's words were wreaking havoc with William's usual calm demeanor. His anger was escalating as he moved away from her.

"I know you will not have me go through the embarrassment of having a child out of wedlock. Heaven knows the wagging tongues of Washington's elite will be hissing me at every turn, and you would not want to soil your good name. *And,* I am certain you would not have me ending the life of this seed growing within me. Marrying me is the only answer."

William was stunned. *Oh, my god! She has stooped to a new low. Her behavior has grown more peculiar than her usual bizarre standards. I feel I am living a nightmare and need to slap myself to awaken from it!*

"Alexandra, I am sure that I know what you are up to. You are trying to form a wedge between Miss Hargrove and myself. Claiming a pregnancy, and one of my doing at that, is beyond anything I would ever expect from you. You have definitely trumped yourself on this go-round. Now, get a grip on yourself and come to the realization that you and I will always remain friends but our affiliation will never go any further."

"But, William, I am telling you the truth. Our baby needs us. You must come to my aid to save our reputations."

William felt ready to explode. Alexandra's persistence was pressing his patience to its limits.

"Let's talk with your aunt. She will help you see that this is the only answer to this dilemma."

"No, Alexandra. We will not burden my Aunt Emma with your railings. First, I want confirmation from Doc Lovering that you are indeed with child. He will hold his findings confidential. Once I hear the results of his examination, you and I will have a much-needed talk about your circumstances and how they came to be. Then, and only then will we work out a plan for your future. Until that time, I want you to remain silent and never, ever speak with anyone else about this matter, especially not Miss Hargrove."

Alexandra looked away. Rejection was manifesting itself again and becoming an all too familiar adversary. Its recurrence was unsettling and more than she could bear. She had made up her mind that William was the father of the little life growing within her and she would not be deterred from her mission to have him as her husband. He was her baby's father. That is what she believed and that was all she needed to make it true. *Arielle Hargrove has another thing coming if she thinks William Clay is going to be her husband. No, he was always meant to be mine and so he shall be.*

The thought of him with Arielle made her skin crawl. *Well, I must exercise patience for he will see the weak sap has little to offer. He cannot possibly have any measure of a good time in the absence of my presence. How could he? How could anyone? No, he will come around to his senses in due time.* Alexandra raised her right eyebrow as the corners of her mouth turned up in a feline smile. She nearly purred as she comforted herself with thoughts of turning William's heart in her favor. It was a task she relished, and a task from which she would not retreat.

"Miss Arianna, you brighten my day, yes, you brighten my day. I am so glad to have you back under our roof. How I would like to take a bucket of water from the garden and douse Miss Whitaker with it. Oh, yes indeed, yes indeed, I would. You know I would never actually do such a thing, but just the thought of her caught off-guard and suddenly becoming a sopping mess would bring me great pleasure, yes great pleasure indeed. Oh, my, my, my, I should not be talking like this."

"Give your words not a second thought, Simon. She does have a compelling effect on one's psyche. I too have wished her harm – not in a cruel sense – just enough to try to set her straight. But, enough of her – tell me more about the gardens this morning. I am ready to paint some new scenes and always appreciate your guidance."

"Ah, there you are. Cook told me that you were asking for me. I thought I would find you both enjoying the great outdoors!"

"Oh, yes Emma! How lovely to see you. All is well, or as well as it can be with Miss Whitaker in the midst. She was wondering when your nephew would arrive. She said she was meeting him here so I went in search of you, however Simon informed me that William had arrived so we decided it was wise to keep a safe distance and tour the garden. I was just asking Simon to give me a lesson on some of the plantings to inspire my next works. He once told me that I always look as happy as a Jack rabbit in its natural habitat when I am outdoors."

Emma laughed. "If you don't mind my tagging along, I will accompany you. Simon's description of the flora and fauna always adds a bright spot to my day. And, I see you have augmented the flower beds with some new perennials."

"Yes, indeed I have and I can tell you that the fringetrees are becoming fully loaded with white blossoms. Their crowns are lush and round," boasted Simon, delighted to be able to share his expertise.

"Do tell me the botanical name again, Simon. I love the way you pronounce it."

"Why, Miss Arianna, you make me blush, but I thank you for helping me keep my mind sharp. Chionanthus virginicus or 'snow flower' is its name. The flowers will be full of wonderful texture for you to paint. They are like the beard of an old man – shaggy and soft in both looks and texture."

Arianna giggled as she watched the sincerity and pride on Simon's face. It gave her great pleasure to be in the company of one who appreciated beauty, the environment, and the arts as much as she did. She was fully prepared with her easel, canvas, paints and brushes to find a spot to perch herself and seize an image of what she viewed in her mind's eye.

"There he goes! There he goes! I say, yes, there he goes! Magnificent!" Simon exclaimed as he pointed to a beautiful bird that flew from one of the fringetrees onto the edge of a verdant arborvitae branch.

"Oh, my word, Simon! He has returned! I have not seen him for some months. He typically frequents the area in April. Perhaps he has his calendar mixed up and that delayed his arrival."

"Miss Arianna, with your affinity for roses, this is the bird you should capture on canvas! The chubby male, rose-breasted grosbeak is from the family of cardinals. Its scientific name is Pheucticus ludovicianus. Ah, yes, yes, yes. Named for the vivid red chevron marking his chest from his black throat down to his breast. And, did you see when he spread his wings? Underneath was the soft show of a pinkish-red hue."

"And, Arianna, he is one of my very favorite songbirds. His warble is livelier than the American Robin. His song is like a lovely thread of sweet whistles ringing through the garden's forest through July." Emma smiled as she mused about her bird watching and then her expression changed.

"Are you quite all right, Emma? It looks as though something is suddenly troubling you," Arianna inquired as she noted the disappearance of her smile.

"Oh, yes dear, I'm fine. I was thinking of Alexandra being here and meeting with William. It just appears odd that she would make arrangements to meet him here when he had no visit with me planned. I think I will go inside and see if they are still about. Maybe I can glean some rationale for the meeting. Do excuse me. I look forward with great pleasure to seeing your latest work Arianna, and it is so wonderful to have you back with us."

A s Emma entered the hallway she heard sounds emanating from the foyer and recognized Alexandra's voice, which was elevated. As she came around the back of the staircase, she saw William who appeared very agitated and she heard him shushing Alexandra.

"You *must* keep your voice down. There is no place for your hysterics here. If I receive confirmation from Doctor Lovering that your claim holds validity, you and I will discuss the next steps. We will devise a plan that will best suit your welfare. I want to hear nothing more from you until we hear the doctor's report." William's words had barely ended as Emma approached. He was so deep in conversation with Alexandra that he was caught off-guard to have his aunt within earshot.

"My goodness, Aunt Emma, how wonderful to see you," William said as he managed a quick smile to segue from the tension that had overtaken his body. He hoped his aunt had not heard any portion of his dialogue with Alexandra. She was sure to question the reason for their visit and he hoped he would be able to cull a plausible response.

"My, my, you two. I hope I am not interrupting what appears to be a serious discussion. Arianna and Simon told me you were here and you know how I never want to miss an opportunity to see you, William. And, of course, you as well Alexandra."

Alexandra attempted a nod of acknowledgment although she was not pleased with Emma's intrusion or the near omission of her name as Emma gladly welcomed her nephew. She felt ready to explode, ready to share her secret with the world, but fear of reprisals that would not serve her purposes held her back from any impulse to speak out.

"How lovely to see you as well," the tinge of sarcasm in Alexandra's voice did not go unnoticed by the gathering. "Yes, William and I have been working out some important details of our future." William shared a warning look with Alexandra hoping she would say no more about their discussion.

"Your future? I hope I am not being too intrusive but, do you mean how he will handle the affairs of your trust once he and Miss Hargrove are married?"

"I should say we were discussing affairs, so-to-speak, and other important issues that must be addressed." Alexandra turned to face William as she spoke her next words. "William has a great affection for me that has laid dormant for some time. He is finally coming to his senses and he sees the importance of rectifying his previous judgments. There will be little room for any others in his life so I would say there will be adjustments needed and those adjustments may begin with Miss Hargrove."

Emma was feeling confused and William was trying to find a way to rein in Alexandra's delusions. He knew no matter what he said she would take umbrage to it. He readied himself for her rage.

"Alexandra, let us go and leave my aunt in peace. This conversation is best ended for today. I would hate to see the differences between us sever our friendship beyond repair."

Emma could see Alexandra's unrest and displeasure. In a show of concern and comfort, she walked to her and took her hands in hers. Emma selected her words carefully in hopes of not inciting Alexandra's wrath.

"Alexandra, my mother, who was a very wise woman, used to ponder the actions of some of her peers who seemed to repeat the same mistakes time and again. One of her most recited sayings was, 'There are none so blind as those who cannot see the error of their ways.' I would ask you to think about this and try as hard as you can to see the beauty your life holds with William as your very devoted friend, yet nothing more."

Alexandra snapped her hands away from Emma and began backing away toward the front portal. Fury built inside her as she turned her back to Emma and William, opened the front door and stepped into the vestibule shouting a few words for all to hear.

"You have treated me hatefully! There is more to come, of that you can be certain!"

She stormed onto the front loggia and raced across the broad porch area to her carriage. Simon and Arianna stood as still as statues as they felt the rush of her departure stir the nearby shrubbery. They had heard her angry exclamation and wondered what had roused her into such a mad frenzy. As the door closed to her carriage, the driver jerked the horses to a start, their pace picked up speed in tandem with the mad dash Alexandra exhibited when she exited Chestnut Heights. As the carriage became a distant blur, Simon and Arianna took deep breaths and exhaled, taking in the fresh air of the outdoors and letting go of the tension ever present when Alexandra was about.

"She is quite unique, is she not Simon?"

"Indeed, Miss Arianna, indeed she is."

"Do you suspect this will be the end of her visits here?"

"There are some things that I *can* predict indeed, yes indeed Miss Arianna, but Miss Whitaker is not one of them, no indeed she is not. If you ask me about growing seasons for the flora on Miss Emma's property, I can almost pinpoint that information to the day. But, Miss Whitaker, and I hope I am not being too callous to say so, is like a wild, uncultivated weed that one tries to rid of only to have it keep popping up in another location. If my memory serves me well, it was the late statesman Franklin who said, 'A man of words and not of deeds, is like a garden full of weeds.' Miss Whitaker has great use of her tongue though not for the betterment of her fellow man, no indeed, no indeed."

"Perhaps we *are* being too harsh, Simon. Since we are sharing quotations, in my latest Lady's Book there was a quote from the American writer Ella Wheeler Wilcox that went like this, 'A weed is but an unloved flower.' You have been in the company of Miss Whitaker on far more occasions than I, however, maybe she is like Miss Wilcox's observation. Maybe she needs to be surrounded by love. Maybe, in some way, she has felt abandoned and acting out is her way of garnering attention."

"You may well be right, you may well be, but I for one do not see her extending an olive branch to any of us, no indeed, no indeed."

"Maybe then it must be we who make that concerted effort. For if not us, then who will make the first step? I am just thinking that befriending her may help Arielle and William in some way. I believe I will pursue this and perhaps it would behoove me to discuss her with Mr. Sullivan." Arianna smiled at the prospect of having a topic of common interest to discuss with Sully. She had enjoyed being in his company and would not be disappointed to have a reason to spend more time in his presence.

As Alexandra's carriage neared her home she rubbed her stomach and closed her eyes. *How can this be happening to me? What have I done to deserve this? Why is everyone always so against me? I try my best to tolerate their company only to be seen as an evil witch. When Doctor Lovering confirms my condition, William will have a change of heart, he must! Everything will fall into place as I have planned. I know it will.* Once again, denial had taken a seat next to Alexandra and, for her, it had become a healthy soul mate.

Chapter Fourteen

Arianna gathered her painting implements and placed them in her transport box made of dark shellacked wood. A handle on the top edge made for ease of carry. Brushes, paints, and sheets of watercolor paper rested alongside one another awaiting her next bout of inspiration. Her face filled with joy as she contemplated sitting among the shrubs and flowers that Simon tended so carefully. The foliage and flora were particularly lush at this time of the season and she wanted to capture as much of their beauty as she could. She never felt more like herself than when she communed with nature and documented the variety of shapes, textures, and colors in the garden.

She had selected a floral gown popping with dahlias from her wardrobe. Its colorful chiffon overlay lent a light air, perfect for the warmer temperatures and humidity hovering over the city. Her auburn hair was pulled to one side and coiled into a loose chignon with a diamond-studded comb added to ornament her coiffure. As she observed herself in the mirror before leaving her bedroom, she was quite pleased with what she saw. Smiling, she thought to herself, *I certainly hope Sully is about the manse today. Although I was away for a brief period of time, he has kept a cool distance ever since he offered me his handkerchief. Perhaps he thinks me a sniveling sop and prefers to avoid a recurrence of my display.* She shook her head trying to rid herself of the negative thoughts. *Have no worries Mr. Bernard Sullivan for today there will be no tears on my part.* With her painting case in hand, she descended the staircase in great anticipation of finding Sully somewhere in the house or on the grounds.

"Why good morning, Miss Smithfield! No more trips for you for we enjoy your presence!" came Alistair's roaring welcome. "I see you are well armed with your creative devices. If you should have a care, I saw Mr. Peabody enter the garden through the French doors while I was having some tea and toast for my morning meal."

"Good morning to you as well, Mr. Drake," Arianna said as she enjoyed their formal address to one another. "Thank you for following the habits of Mr. Peabody. However, I must ask, do you know the whereabouts of Mr. Sullivan?"

"Now, is that not an interesting question indeed? You are putting me through my paces even at this early hour. Let me see, was I put in charge of watching him this morn?"

Arianna laughed. Alistair had the ability to either humor her or encourage her to leave his presence. At times, his booming voice and overtly gregarious manner made her want to flee. There were other occasions when she observed his detached behavior, the hermit-like writer side of him, when he was perfectly content to stand back and watch the scene surrounding him. He seemed to have grown found of his accommodations and housemates for he had registered no indication that he would soon be returning to his homeland.

"He has not been dodging you of late, has he?"

"I will try not to take offense at the implication of your question," Alistair mused. "Oh, I am well aware that I have a great propensity for oratory, sometimes much to the chagrin of those about me. However, I have been practicing my silence but to no avail at times."

"Perhaps you prefer the sound of your voice above all others and that lends a certain comfort to your ears. And, if that be the case, how could you possibly draw upon silence as an option when you cannot draw the reins on offering your opinion or advice?"

"Are you suggesting that I have been trying to do the impossible?"

"Not so much impossible as improbable," Arianna smiled with a big grin as she enjoyed watching the expression of amusement forming over Alistair's face.

"You should be pleased to know that thus far, I have not spoken too much today. I have only said what I needed to say."

Arianna held back a laugh. Alistair appeared so proud of himself she refrained from dampening his spirit. Their banter, much to Arianna's delight, was interrupted by the appearance of Sully. One look at Arianna stopped him in his stride. Her beauty, her hair, her gown, and the glow on the smooth flesh of her face captured him. Her emerald green eyes sparkled with the flecks he had heard Simon Peabody describe as iris freckles. She was a glorious vision he was pleased to behold. Her journey to Wales was not overlong but he had missed her all the same. Then reality came knocking at his mind and he remembered the distance he needed to maintain between them. *Good grief, Sully, get a grip on yourself.* He reprimanded himself as he remembered that she might well be his sister. *You must not have such thoughts about her. You may remain friends and nothing more.*

"Well, there you are Mr. Sullivan. Just the person Miss Smithfield here was seeking an audience with."

Arianna blushed at Alistair's words. She had not anticipated that he would announce her desire to find Sully. *Oh, why did I say anything to that man! I wish his vow for silencing his mouth had been put into play!* Alistair realized his error and quickly worked to make amends.

"What I meant to say is that Miss Smithfield was seeking some alone time in the garden to work her wizardry on paper and was inquiring about the other borders to ensure finding some uninterrupted, quiet space outdoors."

Alistair is digging quite a hole for himself! Now he is insinuating that I want to have nothing to do with Sully! What a messy mire he is creating for me!

"Is that quite right, Miss Smithfield?" Sully asked, knowing feelings were being stirred up inside of him that he had no business feeling about this woman who might be his blood relation. However, the idea that she wanted nothing to do with him felt like a challenge for him to make her want to be in his company.

"Is what quite right?"

"That you wish to find solitude in the garden, to be alone, to commune with nature without an interloper? For if that be the case, I will rearrange my plans and visit Mr. Peabody in the garden later this afternoon."

"I should hate for you to alter your plans in any way, particularly on my behalf. I appreciate Mr. Drake's watchful eye over my painting pursuits, but I shall take no displeasure in your presence with me in the garden." As the words slipped from Arianna's mouth she hoped she was not appearing too bold in her suggestion.

"As you wish. I say we exit the confines of this room and see what blooms beyond these walls." Sully grimaced within at the slip of his tongue. He did not intentionally mean to emit the double entendre or the meaning his words implied. He decided his best course of action was to dwell no further and assist Arianna with her box of paints.

Alistair bid the two a good morning as they took their leave. He was most pleased with himself, not for embarrassing Arianna, but for the effect his words had on Sully. *If he continues to show an interest in her, I know she would never throw him over,* thought Alistair as he strutted from the room and headed up the stairway toward the library to spend several hours working on his latest tome.

Chapter Fifteen

Late June 1898
Shoreditch, London, United Kingdom

Morgan, Agnes and Peeper's transatlantic travel had gone without incident. They had settled into England's pace and grown accustomed to the nuisance of wet pavement resulting from several consecutive days of rainfall. Today, thus far, had been dry and Morgan was pleased to enjoy the fair weather to locate new fabrics, yarns and findings for her store. Now the trio was on a mission for another finding unrelated to items that would soon stock the shelves at Pennybacker Stitchery.

"I must say, for one with such an aristocratic surname, he certainly fell on hard times."

"I should say, Morgan. He is nothing more than an embarrassment to his family, so there's no wonder his sister has abandoned all thoughts of him."

"If I read the document we perused at the courthouse with all intent of accuracy, he was born in London's west end, the Royal Borough of Kensington and Chelsea to be exact. How he settled in the slums of Shoreditch is beyond my comprehension. We will certainly have to take a closer examination of the circumstances surrounding his history. As I recall, the area is grossly overcrowded, which lends itself to persistent matters of sanitation, or the lack thereof."

Morgan was less than pleased to have to travel through Shoreditch. It was an area in the East End of London that held no use for her, and strayed far from the vendors she frequented to gather new merchandise for her stitchery shop. The open carriage ride was pleasant enough, but it was the anticipation of locating Elsbeth Hargrove's brother that spurred her interest forward.

"You may stop at once," Morgan commanded the driver as they came upon the town square framed with stores, tea houses, the town hall, a church, costermongers hawking their wares, and a variety of people hustling to and fro. Agnes wondered what drew Morgan's attention to signal her to so abruptly halt the driver's course. As they disembarked the conveyance, Morgan pointed to the steps leading to the church's wide front doors.

"Agnes, it has been my experience to find many a character or two loitering about the safe haven provided by the auspices of a house of the Lord. At the very least, one of the men perched at the parish might be of value in our search for Mr. Cromwell."

The entourage of two plus Peepers walked along the pavement dodging carts and pedestrians as they approached several men sitting near the church's entry. The men were a motley crew, scruffy, unshaven, and obviously not recently acquainted with a bar of soap. The sloven gathering had Morgan and Agnes wishing they had a tussie-mussie at hand to wave before their nostrils. Upon their approach, the men ceased their conversation to observe the strangers before them. Morgan, with no inclination to waste a moment of time, immediately spoke to her captive audience.

"Good morning, gentlemen." The words had barely left her lips when the trio broke out into loud guffaws.

"Oh, blimey, now that's a good one, it is!" said one of the men. His hair was long and tied into a ponytail with a piece of twine that held his dirty brown locks at the nape of his neck against a dingy shirt collar. "Gentlemen, you say? Well, I must say it's been a wee shy of a score of years since me ears 'ave 'eard the likes of that title of refinement. But, what's that they say? Once a gentleman, always a gentleman? I don't rightly know if I be believin' that, but I'll be takin' it all the same. And, you lass, to what do we owe this pleasure?"

"It is my sincere hope that you umm…men, can assist us in locating a man important to a friend of ours in America. We understand that he resides in the ward of Shoreditch. We have never met, so I will not be able to provide a description. However, if I give you his name, perhaps he has been of your acquaintance."

"Well, lass, there be no need to be givin' me 'is name because I 'ave a name of me very own. I won't be needin' two names."

The men erupted into laughter. Morgan held her ground. She had dealt with worse and felt quite the match for drunken souls and morons who wished to bully and shame her. They would not break her. She remained as determined as her father had been with the horses he raised on their Virginia farm. Jackson Pennybacker had taught her well and she would not withdraw in fear from these beasts of the streets.

"And, just what *is* your name?"

"Now, it's very kind of ye to be askin', it is. Me name is Billy Abel and I sure be hopin' to be able to help ye ladies find yer friend."

The men bent over at their waists and broke into loud laughter.

"That's why we like ol' Billy cuz he's a very able Abel!"

Morgan took a deep, exasperated breath that she regretted because the air she sucked in was anything but fresh. The men looked at the stern expression on her face and sat up as though drawing themselves to attention. Billy was the first to speak.

"Oh, blimey, it's sorry we are fer bein' so rude and inhospitable. We should be offerin' ye fine ladies somethin' to eat but seein' as 'ow we ain't got nothin' fer ourselves we'd be hard-pressed to share a plate with ye. Now, about that friend you're lookin' for, what be 'is name?"

"His name is Carson Cromwell…" Morgan began but was cut-off by another round of laughter from the men.

"Carson! Well I dare say that's a fine name. Carson! Imagine that?"

"If you would let me complete my sentence, I understand that he is more commonly known as Ziggy."

"Common, that's a good word when ye be talkin' 'bout Ziggy! It's not me place to tell but I will. Here's the bloke ye be lookin' for comin' 'round the corner now. Let me introduce ye ladies to 'im."

Billy left the box he was sitting on, stood to his full height and swept his hand out toward Ziggy like a circus maestro presenting the next act. Ziggy stopped dead in his tracks and observed the scene before him of two women standing before a gathering of his street friends. One woman held a cage in her hands with a bird sitting on a perch. The other woman was taller and very official looking in a very tailored brown frock coat, one that Ziggy thought would have been nice to own on a cold night on the streets.

"Come on along now, Ziggy. Don't ye be afraid of these nice ladies. They is wantin' to speak with ye is all. Who knows, maybe someone 'as left ye a fortune and they 'ave come to tell ye 'bout it?"

Ziggy continued to study the scene before him. He knew he had never seen the two women before and wondered what trouble they might make for him. Trust was not something found often on the streets, he knew that full well, and he was ready to protect himself if the need be. Curiosity got the best of him as he began to approach the gathering.

"To what do I owe the pleasure of your company, ladies…and you, little bird?"

"We have a matter to discuss with you but feel it best to talk in a more private arena. Let me make myself clear, we want to remain in the public domain but free from, shall we say, the ears of others." Morgan tried to choose her words carefully. She knew nothing of this man's capabilities and would not put herself or Agnes in a compromising position.

"Well, I don't know what ye might be 'avin' in mind because this church here has been me salvation, oh yes it 'as. There's always a 'ot meal for me and I ne'er feel judged by the folks within them walls.

We're all the same 'ere, we are. All God's children…jest some 'as strayed away from 'ome and needs to be looked after like tiny babes with no way to fend for themselves."

"You have a rather interesting vision of what is your due, sir. Many would say you have made your lot in life and must take responsibility for yourself rather than rely on the mercy of others. Why have you chosen to be a burden to society?" Morgan's cold retort prickled Ziggy's nerves. His demeanor took a sudden change as he raised himself up, tall and proud, even craning his neck to give additional lift to his stature. He opened his eyes wide, looked at Agnes, then stared into Morgan's face.

"Well, well, well. What we seem to 'ave 'ere is Miss Fancy Pants who thinks she's the cat's whiskers! I'll 'ave ye be knowin' that I, Mr. Carson Cromwell, am a pillar of society. There's those on the street that will speak to my good name. Why, jest ask this bloke that be passin' us by right now. He'll tell ye 'bout me, he will. Hey, Jimmy boy, these here ladies think I be nothin' more than a bum. I need ye to be settin' them straight."

"Straight? There's nothin' straight away I can say 'bout ye cuz that's why ye got the name of Ziggy, cuz ye is always all over the place, ziggin' here, zaggin' there. Oh, ladies, he's a fine man though he'll be tellin' ye that everythin's gone horribly wrong in his life since his sister married the man from the Big House there in Wales."

"Now, Jimmy, don't be airin' me dirty laundry. That's for me to know and not fer yer tellin'."

"Ye asked and I delivered, Ziggy. Ye can't 'ave it both ways. Ye n'er said it was any secret how ye felt 'bout your sister. Ye said it was a grudge that wouldn't leave yer heart any day soon. I know ye be bitter, but fer yer own health, ye need to get past it all now." Jimmy pushed his hand in the air toward his friend as though he was dismissing him and was quite finished with their conversation. As he turned to walk away, he glanced back toward his friend. "Ye know I meant no 'arm in what I said, Ziggy. It's jest I think it's time ye got over yerself and let bygones be bygones. When ye point a finger at yer sister, yer pointin' three back at yerself."

As Jimmy resumed his journey along the thoroughfare, the bell of the church rang out the noon hour. Ziggy looked up to admire the steeple and cupped his right hand to his ear to funnel in the sound of the chimes. At the end of their peal, he smiled and looked at the women before him.

"Oh yes, the bells sing their lovely melody to me ev'ry day, they do. Their words lift me spirits like no other sound, not even the tweet of the sparrow can sooth me like these bells."

If Morgan had not already thought the man peculiar, he was confirming her suspicions with every utterance. It was curious to her that he had adopted the street vernacular by losing a consonant here or there as he spoke. She feared any information from him would be less a revelation of fact than of fantasy.

"So, the bells speak to you do they?" Morgan could not help herself from inquiring.

"Aye, they do."

"And what per se do they say?"

"Oh, weren't you privy to the songs of yer mum as a wee babe? Why me mum sang *Oranges and Lemons* 'til I gots old enough to fear me head bein' chopped off. Not a pleasant thought for a young one. Them nursery rhymes has a way of puttin' the fear in yer bonnet. But, nev'r the less, the line, 'when I grow rich say the bells of Shoreditch,' always has a nice ring to it. Something to bring hope, I tell ye, ev'ry time the clapper hits the bell!"

Morgan and Agnes were more curious than ever to know what had prompted Carson "Ziggy" Cromwell to have fallen into the lower echelon of society. *So,* thought Morgan, *his sister IS the one he has targeted to aim his blame for his condition. How I direct my questions will be critical to uncovering what I need to know.* She pondered for a moment, knowing her window of opportunity would shortly close, particularly if the church bell sounded announcing the noon hour and Ziggy's next hot meal.

"Mr. Cromwell, may I say that I am sorry for the poor start we have gotten off to. I am afraid that in my zeal to know more, I have erred and not shown the compassion you seem to so deserve," said Morgan as she began to manipulate the coins in her frockcoat.

"Now, I be likin' the sound o' that and the sound comin' from yer pocket there. I see ye've come to yer senses where I be concerned."

Morgan ignored his reference to the coins in her pocket. If the man needed a handout she would consider such a transaction after their discourse.

"Let us begin again. Do you wish to be addressed as Mr. Cromwell, or with the familiarity associated with the moniker, Ziggy?"

"Ahh, ye're such a fine lass to be askin' me. Yes, to the manner born ye are, just like meself. I say ye stick with Ziggy as I ken see we're destined to be great friends, yes great friends indeed."

Morgan commanded every ounce of restraint to keep her eyes from rolling and her facial muscles from twitching. She dared not give away her extreme lack of sincerity behind the words she prepared to speak if she wished to gain any knowledge about Carson's sister and why, as Jimmy stated, Carson held a grudge or bitterness toward her. Morgan mused, *Could it be that he was aware of her husband's infidelities and she dismissed him from her life because of his accusations?*

"Oh, it's a budgie ye 'ave with ye. What a sweet little man he be." Carson Cromwell raised his hand to poke a finger in the cage as Peepers took several steps back on his perch to avoid the uninvited greeting."

"I say, sir, you would be best advised to leave him be. He typically does not make himself conducive to approaches from those unknown to him," Agnes kept from snarling as she momentarily held her breath rather than take in another ounce of the foul air surrounding the man. She gently moved Peepers and his cage to her side.

"Aye, very well, then. Guess a good look will be 'avin' to suffice me little man if ye won't be 'avin' any of me friendship." Carson winced his eyes and smiled a lopsided grin looking like a pouch of tobacco sat waded in his cheek.

"Sir, or Ziggy as you would have it, my associate here and I have sought you out to learn more of your sister, Elsbeth. It appears, if your friend Jimmy is any barometer regarding the circumstances leading to your present choice of lifestyle, that you are less than pleased with her. We are pursuing a case to which your knowledge is key. It is paramount that you reveal all that is known to you and, perhaps you will be all the better for the telling of it."

Ziggy threw back his head and let out a howl. He would not be duped by these women or commanded to talk about the past. *Women! If these two want to know more of my sister, they can damn well ask 'er to 'er face for I won't be talkin' with 'er, of that I can be damn sure!* He squinted his eyes together, stuck his neck forward and stared directly into their faces.

"Some thin's stick like a burr. Why on God's green earth would the likes o' me want to be dredgin' up some ugly history with the likes 'o you two…or three, if you be wantin' me to count the bird?"

"Please understand that we wish you no ill effects from our conversation. You are the best authority we have to direct us through your sister's younger years."

"There are those who might say I be an authority and those who might say I be not," Ziggy crossed his arms as he delivered his message, clearly putting more physical distance between himself and Morgan and Agnes.

Morgan felt more than drained. Her questioning of Elsbeth's brother left questions unanswered, yet a curious comment by Jimmy gave her another avenue to pursue. She needed more time with Ziggy away from his street companions. He was beginning to feel more comfortable with her and his past. An idea crossed her mind, and though it was not ideal considering his state of attire or cleanliness, she would invite him to dine with her.

"You know, Ziggy, I am most grateful for your assistance. Agnes and I would like to invite you to join us for some sustenance. Upon arrival in Shoreditch, I observed a pub that might suit us all well. The Old Blue Last it is called."

"Oh, shiver me timbers as an old pirate might say. The Old Blue Last is a bit beneath me ye know. It's full of those working-class folks, not the upper crust such as meself. And there just might be the old ghost of Sir William floatin' around."

"Sir William?"

"Aye…The Bard and other theatre types chugging down an ale or two. They loved the place back in the day!"

"We have no hesitation to sharing a pint with some ghosts, especially of such fame. Will you accompany us?"

"Well, ladies, what ye've left me is no choice. I'll be 'appy to have some of that fine Truman's beer with ye."

The trio with Peepers in tow made their way along the sidewalk to The Old Blue Last just several blocks away from Ziggy's headquarters. The minute they stepped inside the pub, heads turned to view the latest arrivals. Ziggy held his head high as he paraded himself among the patrons who were enjoying pints of ale along with lively conversation.

"Hey Gov'nor!" shouted one of the men as he spied Ziggy. "To what do we owe this occasion? You haven't made your way into these parts for quite some time I'd say!"

"That's right, Squire!" called out another patron.

"Well aren't ye men bein' so kind to honor me with such laudatory titles!" Ziggy said as he beamed to be given so much attention.

"Squire?" queried one of the men. "I guess you can be callin' him that if you think his estate is the streets of Shoreditch!"

The attention of half of the pub's patrons had been drawn to the ongoing discourse and they began to explode into boisterous guffaws as Ziggy prepared to bring them down a few notches.

"Well men, say what ye will but I don't see any one of you bein' escorted by such a fine team of women. Maybe ye are the ones who need to be rethinkin' the way yer livin' these days. Now take yer focus off me and go about yer own business." Ziggy walked to a far table in the back of the room and signaled Morgan and Agnes to follow him.

"I must apologize, ladies for the behavior of me townsfolk. It seems they draw great joy from tryin' to embarrass me, but they 'ave to know that I'm proud not to 'ave the fretful life that they 'ave with worryin' about payin' bills and such. Me life's much less complicated than theirs and fer that I am most grateful."

As the threesome dined on a hearty fare of roasted meats, boiled potatoes, and a fresh vegetable medley, Morgan decided to once again broach the subject of Ziggy's sister.

"Ziggy, please forgive me for appearing to be prying into your private life but, in point of fact, I simply must request your cooperation to help me understand the reason for your sister to withdraw her affection for you. I am well aware that rifts can develop in any relationship and siblings are not exempt from such issues. Please bear with me as I inquire about something your friend Jimmy said about the distance that developed between you and your sister after she married Sir Ian Hargrove. What was it about him that caused your estrangement?"

Ziggy nearly choked as he swallowed a large portion of the roasted beef. He chased it down with a hefty draw of ale from his dimpled pint glass mug. *What harm could there be in tellin' these ladies what they want to know? After all these years, what harm can be done? Elsbeth isn't speakin' with me anyway and surely the truth has surfaced by now. And, I've kind of takin' a likin' to these two.* Ziggy looked at Morgan, then to Agnes, and finally at Peepers. He studied the bird's face, his eyes and his beak.

Peepers nodded his head and said, "Pretty boy, pretty boy, that's the truth, that's the truth."

Ziggy was taken back. He recalled better times back in the day when he was quite a handsome fellow and was often called 'pretty boy' by the lads in London's west end. *My, how times can change,* he mused.

Peepers seemed to wink at Ziggy as he dipped his head into the small trough of food in his cage. He dipped his beak in and out, in and out, as he sorted through the bird feed and nibbled on seeds then turned his attention to the dandelion leaves tied in a bunch and suspended from one of the cage's wires. *Oh, if my life could be as simple as this bird's!* Ziggy exclaimed to himself.

A barmaid paused at their table with a fresh pint of ale on a pewter tray. "Let me give ye this full glass squire. It's better than that empty one." Ziggy appreciated her kind attention and handed over his empty mug as he prepared himself to resume the path to revelation he had decided to trod.

"Ye know, ladies. I jest be thinkin' that your bird 'ere may be givin' me a message. I'm thinkin' that it's time I be lettin' the past go and free meself from the errors of me sister's ways that got me where ye find me today."

Morgan took a cleansing breath. She was relieved to have Ziggy finally agree to share information about his sister, which she assumed would lead to the revelation that Sir Ian Hargrove had indeed sired a son with another woman and that son was Bernard Sullivan.

"If you do not mind, I will ask you to please proceed."

"This may not be anythin' new to ye ladies but I'll be sharin' it jest the same. Oh, my, this is goin' back more than a score of years ago. It all 'appened 'bout the time I was married to me lovely bride, Bobbie. Roberta was her given name but Bobbie was what her family called her and it stuck with her. Miss Bobbie Wiggins to be exact. She was a beautiful girl. We fell in love right away and decided to get married in a small ceremony mind you, but very festive thanks in part to the generosity of me sister and her husband. They insisted we hold our weddin' at the Big House. Bobbie was so excited, I ken jest see the smile glowin' on her face. Such a beauty! And it weren't far after that that me sister wouldn't have anythin' to do with us. She turned on us like a wild horse unable to be tamed. I couldn't get 'er to tell me why. She jest asked that we never return to the Big House, that we keep our distance. She avoided my Bobbie at the weddin'. That was the first they'd seen of each other. I seen Elsbeth take Bobbie aside jest before we got ready to leave and they had a long talk. I thought they was becomin' good friends, like sisters, and it made me so proud. Then, Elsbeth disappeared upstairs without sayin' goodbye and Bobbie insisted that we leave. I had no idea, I had no idea." Ziggy paused and shook his head. Remembering that last day in his sister's house was a painful reminder of the demise of their relationship and the final time they were together.

Morgan was hesitant to say a word. She feared that prompting him to continue his explanation would halt the flow of the story he was finding difficult to relay. His expression had become sullen and he no longer had a lilt in his voice. She decided she would give him a gentle nudge to go on.

"Ziggy, I see this is wearing on you so perhaps you should proceed with the telling of your story so you do not have to dwell on it much longer. We are very thankful that you are willing to help us understand."

"Very well. Ye are very right indeed. This news jest came out of the blue. It was so unexpected and I must tell ye Elsbeth kept it well hidden. I feel like a fool to this day fer not seein' with me own eyes what was goin' on."

Ziggy's stops and starts were draining Morgan but she was determined not to let fatigue overcome her. They were so close to finding something out and she was not going to let the information slip away from her. Just as she was ready to make another inquiry, Ziggy began to speak.

"Jest to think that me own sister could do somethin' like that and keep it hidden from me, from us all. Thank God our parents never knew. They would never have been able to hold their heads up on the streets. If it weren't for me Bobbie, I would never have known. No never."

Morgan braced herself for the secret that Ziggy was having so much difficulty expressing. As she readied herself to speak to him, Agnes reached out her hand and placed it on Ziggy's hand. He was surprised by her touch and looked into her eyes as a gentle smile formed on her face.

"You can tell us. It will be fine. It is something you have been needing to get off your mind and we are here to help you free yourself of what you know," Agnes said as she gave a little pat to Ziggy's hand. "Tell us, what did your Bobbie tell you?"

Ziggy was surprised by Agnes' tender touch yet he felt comforted and ready to release from his lips the story that only he, his wife, and Elsbeth knew. It was time. The opportunity to release the truth had found its way to him. He looked at the faces before him and spoke. "Me wife, me Bobbie, were the mid-wife who delivered me sister's child."

Chapter Sixteen

July 1898
Washington, District of Columbia

The transatlantic travel to return home had given Morgan time to formulate the information culled from Carson "Ziggy" Cromwell. She and Agnes had remained at the pub with him until nearly the dinner hour. The trio sat tucked away in a corner booth removed just far enough away from the other patrons for Morgan to privately glean more detailed responses from him. Patrons came and went among the glow of freshly lit candles nestled in lanterns mounted about the walls and the posts of the darkly walled pub while Morgan continued her cordial interrogation of Elsbeth's brother.

She was stunned with Ziggy's claim that his sister had given birth to a child. Morgan had assumed Elsbeth was barren, which led to the adoption of her daughter Arielle. But Elsbeth had kept the adoption veiled in deceit so all about her would assume Arielle was of her own womb. Morgan was not wont to award any merit to Sir Ian's propensity for philandering, but the thought that perhaps the Hargroves did not have sexual relations, which led him to find warmth and satisfaction bedded down with others, had once crossed her mind after she learned of Arielle's adoption. Secrecy had decidedly become a trademark of the Hargrove household for it appeared many ghosts remained lurking there. Morgan was making every effort to absorb the fact that the lady of the household was as keen at deception as her husband.

She had asked Ziggy about his wife, where she was and if she could meet with her. Morgan knew he spoke of her in the past tense, but she was not sure if she was still living and had left him, or if the two had divorced over some matter. He explained that she had taken ill and died only six years after their marriage. Tears came to his eyes as he reminisced about his wife and how difficult it was to never see his sister again. He said that his wife, Bobbie, told him that Elsbeth swore her to secrecy the night of their wedding. She said they could never be seen together, that something might be said, even accidentally, that would draw suspicion her way. Elsbeth said she did not want to be remembered about what had transpired and that seeing Bobbie would be like sticking a barb in her heart. She was adamant that her brother must never know they had ever been in one another's company. Elsbeth insisted that her brother never come to visit again. She felt her harsh move was the only way to keep him from wondering why she refused to have his wife in her presence. It was not until Bobbie's final days that Ziggy came to understand the reason for his sister's extreme behavior.

He shared with Morgan and Agnes that several days before Bobbie passed, she called him close to her side, looked into his eyes and told him the story he felt could not be true. But, her words were clear and concise and he could see that it was important for her to release them. She said she wanted a clear conscience to accompany her as she left this earth. Morgan asked if she had mentioned where the infant was placed, in an orphanage or a private home. Ziggy shook his head as though he was unaware but it was more a motion of disbelief, disbelief that his Bobbie, like his sister, would keep such a secret from him. He looked up with tears beginning to stream down his cheeks.

"I ken say thank God she 'ad the good sense to go back for the baby. She rested 'im on the stone steps of the church as Elsbeth instructed 'er to do but she thought the better of it. She knew a family wantin' a child and took 'im to them. She said they were overjoyed and fine with keepin' silent about it all. It's sad I am for I ken tell you, once I learned of this I went to visit the boy from time to time. Oh, I'm not sayin' he ever saw me, but I 'ad to 'ave a glimpse of 'im. He was a handsome lad my nephew. Seemed happy runnin' in the yard and chasin' after his dog. I couldn't rightly believe that me sister would never want to see 'im knowin' she's the one who gave 'im life. And, to think all those years me was never an uncle to the lad. Oh, how me would have loved to 'ave known 'im." Ziggy shook his head and wiped his tears with the sleeve of his shirt.

Morgan took her time before pointedly asking what she had wanted to know -- the name of the family who adopted the baby abandoned so many years ago. If he had been to the home to watch the boy from afar, then he knew what she desired to know. Ziggy was slow to answer. He looked up at Morgan, then to Agnes as Peepers kept his attention fully focused on Ziggy's face. A faint smile came to Ziggy as he found humor in the bird appearing to have an interest in their conversation. He looked directly into Peepers eyes and said the words Morgan had been waiting to hear.

⌣⟶

Sully felt unmoored. Morgan, through her research, had done as he asked, however he had not prepared himself for his reaction to her findings. When she returned from England, she called on him at Chestnut Heights. She asked Emma if they could have some privacy in the smaller drawing room located just across the foyer from the parlor. It was a more intimate space that Emma used on occasion for her needlework and reading pleasure, or when the grand space of her parlor seemed too large and open a venue for private discourse.

Morgan informed Sully that she was most surprised with what she heard when Ziggy spoke the surname of the family who had adopted Elsbeth's offspring. But, Sully refrained from reacting to the family's name. He was trying to absorb the fact that Lady Elsbeth Hargrove was the woman who gave him life and ordered that he be left at a church. *What if I had not been found? What if I had starved to death or succumbed to the elements before being saved?* Sully hung his head in disbelief. The pain of rejection was almost more than he could bear.

"Mr. Sullivan, I can see that this information is taking a toll. It is certainly not what you expected to hear. You have been all along thinking that Sir Ian Hargrove is your father. You have thought that is what your mother meant in her diary entry about the answer being at the Big House. I am not sure how you wish to proceed with this information for, in point of fact, Lady Hargrove has made every effort to keep the truth from revealing itself," Morgan said, knowing there was more that needed to be said and a truth she suspected Sully needed to share. She was more certain than ever that Lady Hargrove was not the only one who had been hiding a secret.

Sully's skin had become ashen. He needed some fresh air. He needed to escape from the room, to clear his thoughts and decide how he would proceed. Morgan, Agnes, and Peepers watched as he stood to exit the room giving the trio a signal with his hand and a raised index finger that he needed a moment and would return. As he hastily entered the foyer, Arianna and Alistair walked past the drawing room and paused as they saw the familiar faces. Morgan signaled them in.

"Is Sully quite all right?" Arianna inquired, noting that he made no pause or effort to greet her or Alistair.

"We were just sharing news of our trip. He should be returning shortly, but let me ask you if I may, has there been anything that you have noticed that is unusual or that has drawn your attention about Mr. Sullivan? Anything at all?"

"Now, that is a curious question I must say," Arianna noted as she furrowed her brow and cut her eyes toward Alistair."

"Whoa, boy. Whoa boy," chirped Peepers sensing Morgan's path of inquiry.

"Well, it is quite nice to hear from you Peepers old fellow!" Alistair exclaimed as he felt the rise of tension in the air.

"I am asking for anything really. It could be the smallest thing that caught your attention at the time and then passed from your thoughts?" Morgan continued her pursuit of the missing piece that she needed to confirm her suspicions as she began to juggle the coins resting in the confines of her coat pocket.

"Hmm," said Arianna.

"Yes, what is it?" Morgan queried.

"I am just remembering a time, actually when Mr. Sullivan first moved here. Mr. Drake began speaking of my family, of Arielle and of our father, and his comments triggered my emotions and I began to cry. I was taken by Mr. Sullivan's gesture. He was kind enough to offer a handkerchief to me."

"And you found that unusual?"

"What I found unusual Miss Pennybacker, was that the handkerchief was embroidered with the letter 'B.' My experience has been that the initial from one's surname is typically what is present on linens."

Arianna's comment triggered a memory for Alistair about the same occasion when he mentioned the name of a Sully he once knew. Alistair wondered why Sully reacted so oddly when he mentioned his deceased friend and his wife.

"Miss Smithfield is charting an interesting path that now makes me wonder why Sully showed no interest in my friend with the same moniker. I mean, he did not have to go all jolly about the similarity, but he was quite silent about it, which I found odd and very unfriendly for the chap to be so uncommunicative. The handkerchief appears to be a clue we must not dismiss."

Morgan had already put the finishing pieces on the puzzle before her. Arianna and Alistair's observations gave confirmation to what she suspected. Bernard Sullivan was not going by his given name. Agnes watched Morgan's demeanor and sensed what she was about to say but held back because it was not for her to reveal what she suspected to the two standing before her. She waited until Sully reentered, thanked Alistair and Arianna, and asked that they leave them so they might talk in private.

"I hope you are feeling better, Mr. Sullivan. I know this is a great deal to hear at one time but I must add that I am afraid I have failed you with the information about the family that Mr. Cromwell declared adopted his sister's baby for it is curious that the name is not a match for yours. This is particularly troublesome because he insisted that there is no mistake about where the infant was finally placed. And poor Mr. Cromwell thinks the child he viewed from a distance was his nephew when that could not be the case because he insisted that the family was that of Sullivan and Penelope Bamford and you have presented yourself as Bernard Sullivan. Tell me, how can that be?"

Morgan, Agnes, and Peepers watched Sully's reaction. He felt the need to exit the room again but he held his ground. He took in several cleansing breaths but he looked very much like a thief who had been caught unawares. He could no longer continue under the same pretense. It was time to end the cycle of deceit and admit the truth. He looked to his accusers and announced what Morgan knew she would hear.

"I regret to inform you that I have misrepresented myself and for that I apologize. I felt that the only way I could learn the truth was by telling a lie. My name, as I am sure you know by now, is not Bernard Sullivan. I am Sully, named for my father, Sullivan Bamford."

"And your mother, Penelope Bamford is the one who has given you this gift of the truth with her diary entry so the lies may cease and find their eternal rest."

"Yes, Penelope Bamford, my mum, the one who loved, comforted, and raised me," said Sully as he choked back tears. He was overcome with the news of his heritage and the lies his life had been built upon by the people he had entrusted to be forthright with him. Gloom was descending over him and he wanted to draw it back, to lift himself up and move forward with his life. He was the same person but different somehow and he silently wondered, *Now that I know the truth, what am I to do?*

⌒

A rianna and Alistair had not stepped far from the drawing room. Curiosity had gotten the better of them both and they felt compelled to be close at hand if Sully needed their support. Morgan's presence at Chestnut Heights and her closed door meeting with Sully signaled them to circle their wagons to protect someone who had become a friend to them both. Ever since Alistair and Sully had met with Morgan to request her investigative assistance, Alistair had been anxious to have Sully keep him informed about Miss Pennybacker's crusade for clarity about his mother's diary entry. Today was the first time information was being shared and Alistair was most curious about the outcome of Miss Pennybacker's trip abroad.

Arianna had grown very fond of Sully. There was something warm and caring in his manner, a softer side that she admired along with his good looks and success as a businessman. Morgan's inquiries about him brought to mind the gravestones Arianna had observed when she visited her birth mother's gravesite in Wales a short while ago. The words neatly chiseled on her mother's headstone made Arianna feel chilled and cold like the marble itself, yet she read them aloud as though her recitation would give her warmth and solace. "Her toils are past, her work is done; She fought the fight, the victory won." She mused, *For the rest of eternity, here lay the remains of Anna Hollingsworth, the woman who gave my sister and me life and lost hers nearly in the same breath.*

Arianna wanted to defy death. Her creative mind often kept her from facing the certainty of realities. That there would be an end to which we must all succumb frequently spun her into denial, for it was far more pleasant for her to think of the living, breathing facets of life than the last gasps that would take each of us from this earth.

She remembered looking about Blaenogwr cemetery. All was peaceful and quiet. Here was a gathering of souls whose voices were now silent. Some were neighbors in death by choice where groupings of family clans were made obvious by the surnames boldly displayed on elaborate markers. Others bore positions of happenstance, their bodies placed like chess pieces into an unclaimed plot, like little pawns now removed from the game of life.

Names began to call out to her, breaking the interminable silence. Davies, Jones, Floyd, Vaughan, Bamford, Williams, and Llewellyn. The names carved into stone seemed to prick at Arianna's flesh. The urge to flee skipped across her skin as she noted the twin iron gate where she had made her entry. One portion of the gate moved gently back and forth, hastened in movement by an abrupt breeze. It was as though the gate signaled her to move, however she was uncertain whether it ushered her back or cautioned her forward.

The uppermost grave marker at the very crest of the cemetery's exit read "Yates." *How appropriate*, thought Arianna. Her mother, Olivia Smithfield, had often mentioned the surname because of its translation, "dweller by the gate." She reflected on the number of years Maggie Galligan had been a "gate keeper" of sorts for Annie Hollingsworth's oak box. Or, a "safekeeper" as Annie had instructed her. She thought of the promises and perhaps secrets held within all the coffers now buried deep underground, never to be revealed. *What a pity so much brilliance and so many stories will never be realized,* she thought as she gently walked over the sacred ground.

I cannot focus on what has been taken away, for I would be in the unenviable position of enduring a brutal sadness. What life would that be? Arielle and I both have been given so much, so many blessings. The facts of our births, our adoptions and separation for all of those years cannot be erased, but can be placed in their proper perspective. Soon she will be wed. She, William, and his dear Aunt Emma are my family now and, of course, I must not dismiss Sir Ian and Lady Hargrove. My, my, to this day, I am repeatedly stunned by the facts of my heritage.

Arianna turned from her mother's gravestone and thought of the woman who raised her as her own. Olivia had been buried in

England alongside her brother Edmund. *Perhaps I will visit Mum's grave on the one-year anniversary of her death in September. Or, it might be best to wait until Arielle has been wed.* She turned to rest a smooth river rock on Annie's headstone, a ritual of remembrance she had observed when a Jewish friend's father passed away. She was touched by the show of respect, and the symbolism the rock represented that the man's life endured through his legacy and the memory of him.

After placing the rock, she looked up and her attention was drawn to a nearby headstone. 'Bamford.' *Why is that name recognizable? I have never known a family by this name.* She studied the names and dates carved into the gray and white marble.

Sullivan Nigel Bamford, Sr.
beloved husband & father
January 8, 1830 - June 9, 1896
Penelope Mae Bamford
beloved wife & mother
February 28, 1832 - December 15, 1896
beloved parents of
Sullivan Nigel Bamford, Jr.
August 2, 1868 - ....

How unusual to have included the name of one who is apparently not deceased for there is no end date, or perhaps the child died on the same day it was born? No, there is space awaiting the date of death. I still find this most unusual for what if he were married and chose to be buried with his spouse? Arianna shook her head and wondered why she was dwelling on something to which she might never find an answer. *Why am I even drawn to this headstone?*

As Arianna began to walk away, the name Bamford struck a chord in her memory. *Yes, it was the writer Alistair Drake who mentioned to Sully that he once knew someone who was called 'Sully' but it was in reference to his first name and not his last. What a coincidence this is that I have come upon the burial site of Mr. Drake's friend. I shall have to make a note to mention this to him when I return to America.*

She looked about the vale. The verdant grasses and patches of wild flowers made her think of the gardens her mother cultivated outside their brownstone in England. It was her mother who gave her an appreciation for growing and nurturing plants and instructed her to notice the smallest details in the parts of flowers, shrubs, and the wildlife that visited their yard and the parks nearby. She gave her mother great credit for the artist she had become and she was grateful for the guidance and encouragement her mother lent so she could pursue her love of art. *I do miss everyone in America, but there is something begging at me to someday return to my roots and build a life here where my history grounds me.*

Her thoughts were brought back to the present as she looked at Alistair and shared her experience at Blaenogwr cemetery with him.

"I only share this with you because you mentioned your friend Sully Bamford and so, here I was visiting my birth mum's grave and that family's name is adjacent to my mum's. It is quite a small world. I guess all of this concern about our Sully, though it is his last name that is Sullivan, has got me remembering that gravestone."

Alistair was surprised to learn that her birth mother's resting place was in such close proximity to his friend's. He was growing impatient waiting for the doors to the drawing room to open. He began to pace about. *What in the devil is going on in there?* No sooner had the thoughts swirled in his head than the drawing room doors opened and Sully signaled Alistair and Arianna to enter.

Morgan, Agnes, and Peepers were seated. Sully stood and pointed to two empty seats, which Alistair and Arianna gladly accepted. They had both grown tired of dwelling in the foyer and welcomed a spot to rest.

"Step up son, step up son." Peepers began to chirp the refrain he had often heard carriage drivers use to signal their team of horses to move forward.

Peepers' levity brought a faint smile to Sully's face. He needed the distraction the bird provided as he gathered his thoughts trying to determine how he would proceed. He felt someone of importance was missing from the group, someone he wanted to be present. He held up his hand in a request for everyone to wait one moment as he stepped into the hallway and spotted Thomas.

"I say, Thomas. Would you please summon Mrs. Willard to come and join us?"

Within a few moments Emma entered the doorway and looked about the room. She was surprised to see Morgan, Agnes and Peepers. She knew that they had been abroad but was unaware of their return. She could feel the tension in the room and wondered why Sully had asked Thomas to call her in. *What on earth could be happening now?* Emma pondered as she smiled to greet everyone and chose a seat in a large, tufted-back chair. Arianna and Alistair pointed to the silver salver well-appointed with crystal glasses and decanters of Scotch and claret. With a nod from Sully, Alistair poured a glass of Scotch for himself and Sully and a glass of claret for Arianna. Emma declined a beverage wanting first to hear the reason for the gathering of the ensemble. Sully looked to Morgan as though needing an opening remark and she intuitively responded.

"Mrs. Willard, Miss Smithfield, Mr. Drake, some information has come to our attention, which we have shared with Mr., umm, with Sully here. He wishes to be candid with you about what we have learned because he trusts your friendships. I hope you will hear him out and lend whatever support you can as he adjusts to his newfound knowledge."

"Pretty boy, pretty boy," chirped Peepers.

"Thank you, Miss Pennybacker...and Peepers," Sully spoke slowly, cracking a faint smile Peepers' way. He hesitated periodically as he drew another sip of the amber libation that was helping to bolster his nerves. He detailed Morgan's findings in brief, from beginning to end, and credited her for the thoroughness of her investigation. He was not yet ready to disclose what he knew about Elsbeth Hargrove. He wanted to approach her himself and see if she would be forthright or continue to perpetuate her lie. He announced that he had been abandoned and adopted by a family named Bamford. Arianna's eyes opened wide in surprise. *Bamford! My goodness! Is this an insane coincidence? Bamford?*

"That's the truth, that's the truth," came Peepers' retort.

Agnes gave a stern look in Peepers' direction. He began to pace about the floor of his cage looking for errant pieces of his feed to make the appearance that he was unaffected by the reprimand.

"Bamford? How can that be when your name is Bernard Sullivan?" Arianna was feeling confused and hoped that Sully could bring clarification.

"In my efforts to solve the mystery surrounding the words in a passage in my mum's diary, I decided that I had to suffer the use of an alias for at least the time being. I was accustomed to being called 'Sully' so it was a rather easy moniker to assume. My given name is Sullivan Nigel Bamford, Jr."

Arianna felt rattled to the core. *This man to whom I have grown so fond has led me to believe he was of a different name. How I am to believe anything about him? Is he a total fraud? Does he have a successful timber business? Is anyone telling the truth anymore?* She felt compelled to speak.

"Excuse me for interrupting your speech, but I am wondering if I am the only one feeling completely duped here? We have known you as Bernard Sullivan, a successful businessman from Wales and suddenly you are Sullivan Bamford, Jr. Forgive me for adding to your, shall we say upset, but we need to know who this stranger is in our midst!"

"And, I for one must say what great good fortune has come upon me to be among a host of miscreants! Forgive me if I appear insensitive but you people are the fodder every writer hopes to stumble upon. You all have truly outdone yourselves!"

"Alistair please remember yourself. This is not the time for such statements or focus on self," Emma reprimanded. Morgan considered Alistair's outburst rude under the circumstances. He may have been one of her favorite authors but he had just lowered himself a few notches in her esteem. Sully ignored Alistair's comments and refrained from responding to his retort.

"Everything else about me is as I have presented it to be. I have one more very important step to take regarding the results of Miss Pennybacker's discoveries and I intend to make a visit tomorrow that will hopefully verify all that I need to know. I am very sorry to have caused you, Miss Smithfield, and the rest of you any disservice for I meant none. I have been on a mission to seek the truth and as it turns out, I was not on the correct course, or assumption, until I hired Miss Pennybacker. I hope you will please bear with me and continue to consider me your trusted friend despite the only difference being my name. I might add, Miss Smithfield, that I would like for you to accompany me tomorrow when I pay a visit to the Hargrove's home."

Arianna was not certain how to respond. She was curious about Sully's need to visit her sister's residence but wondered if he merely needed to discuss business with Sir Ian. If that was the case, then she had no need to go with him other than the fact that she enjoyed his company, or she had until she learned that he was not whom he said he was. Hopefully, Arielle would be there and they could visit while he completed his mission. The only way to satisfy her curiosity was to accept his offer and tag along.

"Very well. You have piqued my curiosity Mr. Bamford and it will give me a very welcomed chance to visit with my sister. However, I should have thought that someone who was becoming my friend would have been forthright from the beginning yet, your secrecy appears to continue for you are not revealing the purpose of your visit to the Hargrove's residence."

"That information is best saved until the morrow," came Sully's succinct reply. His apprehension was mounting concerning the reaction from the lady of the manse when he confronted her with Miss Pennbacker's findings. But, he had not come this far not to pursue and bring to closure the twisted details of his arrival on earth. It was time for Lady Hargrove to unburden herself and he was determined to tell her so.

Arianna's expression held a glimmer of displeasure. She was not pleased to be put off but she acquiesced not wanting to contribute to Sully's distress. She knew full well what it was like to have lived a lie and the emotional waves one rode arriving at acceptance and forgiveness. *No, I shall not place my feelings over his. I value his friendship and will gladly support him in any way I can.*

As the cast of characters disbanded and found their way to their rooms for the night, the curtains closed on the scene before them. Peepers' exclamations of "That's the truth, that's the truth" and the soft jingle of coins in Morgan's coat pocket could be heard throughout the foyer as she and Agnes took their exit with their feathered companion.

"So there we have it," said Morgan stretching her neck and raising her chin in the air. "That information and Mr. Bamford's confirmation provides verification enough for me about the story told to me by Mr. Carson Cromwell. He said he was telling the truth and so be it, he was."

Chapter Seventeen

"Why, Mr. Sullivan, what brings you to our door this day and with my lovely daughter! What a pleasant surprise! I must call for Arielle for I know she will not want to miss your visit." Ian emitted a cheerful greeting that was not met by Sully's expression. Arianna's face revealed a reticent smile as she stepped into the foyer. She was happy to see her father, but the curiosity she held about the nature of Sully's visit was heavy on her mind.

"Father, what has happened with the household staff that you are here greeting us at the threshold?"

"Yes, it certainly appears that they have taken their leave. However, Fiona is about doing some task in her usual lackluster manner and the others are preparing our victuals for the day. So, I was left to my own devices. Come in, come in."

Sully was losing his verve. He felt as though the energy needed to confront Lady Hargrove was quickly escaping him. Having Arianna at his side was his one saving grace. She knew part of his truth and had not yet abandoned him. He hoped she would remain steadfast about their friendship. He had asked her to keep her silence about the knowledge she had gained about him from Miss Pennybacker's presentation at Chestnut Heights until he had the opportunity to speak with Lady Hargrove. He was relieved to hear that Arielle was home for he wanted her to hear his story directly from him and not place the responsibility of the telling on Arianna. How to go about this whole thing perplexed him. He had devoted great thought to the most humane way to approach Lady Hargrove and had determined that he would first meet with her and then insist that she gather her husband, Arielle, and Arianna to make them privy to all that had transpired. The time had come for her to face the decisions she had made that had had such a dramatic impact on the lives of others, particularly himself.

"So, again, tell me what brings you here today?"

"Actually, I asked Arianna to join me for reasons that will soon be known, but I first would like to speak with Lady Hargrove. Is she at home?"

"She is. May I inquire as to the topic of your discussion?"

"For the moment, it is important that I speak only with her. I am sure you will quite understand after we speak."

"Please forgive me if I sound a bit snobbish, but I should say that as cryptic as you are being, it shall quite be up to Lady Hargrove as to whether or not she wishes to engage in conversation with you. I shall go and get her."

"Very well, I understand and thank you for your understanding."

Elsbeth had not been expecting guests nor did she have plans to leave the manse all day. Her work with her lady's group and their activities at her church had been postponed. Ian had announced that he was not planning to go to his office, which made little difference in her day since he typically sequestered himself in his study only appearing in order to take his afternoon and evening meals with her in their opulent dining room. Her attire was very simple. She wore a dark navy blue linen dress with a full skirt whose hem barely brushed the dense Bristol carpet. Its sleeves were long and cinched at her wrists with a short ruffle that mimicked the ruffled edge of its neckline. She walked first to Arianna and leaned forward giving her a brief hug. Then she turned to Sully and gave a nod of her head.

"Mr. Sullivan, my husband tells me that you wish to speak with me and me alone. I must say that my curiosity precedes me so you will find me quite agreeable to sharing an audience with you. Sir Ian, if you do not mind, we will proceed to your study. Shall we, Mr. Sullivan?"

Arianna could hardly keep her face from showing a reaction every time Elsbeth referred to Sully as Mr. Sullivan. She knew he was about to tell her that he was using an alias, but why he thought that would be important or of any interest to her was a mystery. She knew he seemed troubled. Other than requesting that she not say anything to anyone until he cleared her to do so, their carriage ride from Emma's to the Hargrove's was wrapped in silence.

As Sully and Elsbeth entered Ian's study and pulled the doors shut, Ian and Arianna stepped into the parlor joining Arielle who had also been summoned by her father to receive their visitors. The three were having difficulty making small talk. Time seemed to be standing still as their minds remained focused on what was transpiring behind the closed doors.

Sully suggested that Elsbeth sit while he stood. He had decided that his opening remarks would focus on his life in Nantymoel, his business, and then his family name. He wondered if Elsbeth would appreciate his candor when he approached the most difficult portion of the story he needed to tell. There were words he hoped to hear from her, her testimony, and her account of the facts. He was reminded of Morgan's words of warning that there may well be denial on Elsbeth's part and gaps in the truth. Morgan wanted to protect him from setting his hopes too high and he remembered she had warned, "Many times one remembers something as they want to." He held high expectations that he could convince Lady Hargrove to finally put the truth out in the open where together they could help soothe each other's pain from the truth and begin the healing process. *If healing is possible, if I can accept her actions, if I can let this go,* thought Sully.

He told Elsbeth about his mother's diary and his assumption that Sir Ian was his father. Elsbeth's eyes grew wide waiting to hear that yet again her husband's escapades were delivering another child he had sired. Quickly, Sully informed her that that was not the case. He told her about hiring Morgan Pennybacker and her pursuit and questioning of Elsbeth's brother. Elsbeth's heart was racing. Suddenly everything she had so thoroughly dismissed from her mind came roaring back, including the reason for her estrangement from her brother and his wife Bobbie. She defended her reason saying she was not fond of the woman he married. Sully challenged her response letting her know that he knew there was more to the story. And, when he announced to her that Bobbie had made a deathbed confession to her brother, there was nothing Elsbeth could do. She was trapped in what Ian always referred to as 'inevitability.' For her, there was no escaping the truth of her past and, now, before her was the son she never knew.

Sully was spent. Reiterating all of the information Morgan had gathered left him completely drained of energy and warmth for the woman before him. Here was his birth mother, yet she was a total stranger to him. Elsbeth was unsure about what would be expected of her now. *Oh, my god!* she silently exclaimed. *What am I to do? Should I embrace him? No, he will want nothing to do with me. I must accept that. I betrayed him and he must hate me. So here is this handsome man, Sully, my son, raised by the Bamfords. And, Sully tells me that my brother knew where he was and went to watch him from afar.* Elsbeth shook her head and felt her chest tighten. Her face was cloaked in guilt and regret. Everything was crushing in on her and she had no way out.

Sully was having his own battle with emotions. *What do I say to her now? There is nothing between us but time.*

An aura of frigid air circled the two as they stood frozen in time staring at each other yet seeing nothing in particular. Both had become numb and it would take more than this inaugural meeting of mother and son to find any ties that would bind them to one another. Elsbeth was grateful that she was not standing for she knew her legs would have certainly failed her. *What am I to do now? Lord help me, what am I to do?* She thought about seeking absolute forgiveness from a power much stronger and greater than herself but wondered who was she to ask? Why should she be absolved? Sully was equally torn. He knew only one reason for elation and that was the fact that he and Arianna were not related by blood. He could thankfully pursue his interest in her without any moral confines.

Slowly, Elsbeth rose from her chair. She looked straight into Sully's eyes and he looked into hers as they locked on the resemblance, the familiarity between mother and son that had been unknown to them for a score and ten years. There would be no hugs, no embrace, as each tried to gain some semblance of normalcy from their newfound knowledge. Elsbeth exited the study as she had entered it with curiosity. Not the curiosity about what would be revealed to her but the curiosity of what would transpire for the rest of her days. She knew Sully would join the others in the parlor and impart the details that threatened to turn her life into shreds. *What will Ian say? How can I face him? Surely something good must come from this. That is my prayer, yes, that is my prayer,* Elsbeth begged as she ascended the staircase that seemed to have doubled in size, the weight of her feet hanging heavy on each tread she trod.

Sully joined Ian, Arianna, and Arielle in the parlor. He very thoughtfully told Arielle and her father about his reason for coming to America, his mother's diary and his, albeit inaccurate, suspicions about his parentage and Sir Ian. It was all he could do to contain Ian's outburst when he felt summarily accused of having fathered Sully. Next, came the hardest part for Sully to relay. He felt like an informant, a traitor that should be hung for treason to speak aloud about his birth mother in such a fashion. He told about Elsbeth's brother, which brought a look of great surprise to Arielle. When she looked at her father for verification he nodded his head. *Another ghost that has been living amongst us. An uncle, an uncle that I have never been privy to know! Oh, when will the lies and the hidden truths cease?* Sully's news was making her feel sick to her stomach. He paused to let his audience collect their thoughts and as he did, something very unexpected occurred. Ian went to Arielle and Arianna and took their hands. The girls were caught off-guard by his action, his sudden show of affection. It was uncharacteristic, yet welcomed. He held onto them as he struggled to speak.

"To say that I am surprised by this information is a supreme understatement. I want you both to know that I was never aware of Sully or any connection to my wife. She, and she alone, will need to come to some explanation and understanding of what she has done and how we will all move forward from this moment on. This cannot be dismissed nor is it a simple situation." Ian was shaking as he delivered his well-chosen words. He was embarrassed yet he knew he needed to go to Elsbeth to hear from her the truth as she wished to tell it. He only hoped that she would not perpetuate the denial that had held her captive these many years.

"I hope you will all understand that I must go to my wife now," Ian said in a low, reverent tone as he released his daughters' hands and exited the parlor.

Arielle was the first to speak. She sensed that Sully wanted to be with Arianna without an immediate audience. The house was well staffed and she and her parents were readily about to be called upon if Arianna's need for assistance arose. Arielle had no fear, for what she was beginning to know of Sully was that he was a man of purpose and conviction determined to seek and find the truth. She respected those traits, traits she admired in her William and traits that would see them all through what appeared to be some tough times ahead.

"Since your given name has been exposed, I must refrain from calling you Mr. Sullivan so, I will proceed with Mr. Bamford if that suits you."

"Miss Hargrove, you know that you may call me Sully. Nothing about the moniker for my first name has changed."

"Very well then, Sully. I will bid you and my sister adieu for now. Please remain if Arianna so wishes. I am sure that you both have much you wish to discuss."

Arianna turned to Sully as Arielle left the room. All was quiet. It was just the two of them suspended in what seemed like interminable time and space. Arianna felt ready to reel. First, Sully had lied about his name and now, he had held back what he knew about the origin of his beginnings. *He had even suspected that my father was his father!* She closed her eyes at the thought and when she opened them Sully had stepped several paces closer to her. She could almost feel his body heat as her face became warm. She put her hands on her cheeks to verify the sensations she felt hoping to quell their display. Sully moved forward several more steps and took her hands in his. A rush of adrenaline raced through her torso at his touch. A smile came over his face as he watched her hold her breath and brace herself for his next move. *Breathe, Arianna, breathe,* she coached herself wondering if he intended to touch her lips with his and then he spoke.

"The silver lining for me, dear Arianna, is that you are not my half-sister. I so feared that we were of the same father and could not advance our friendship to something more."

"Are you saying that you quite fancy me, Mr. Bamford?"

"That I am, Miss Smithfield."

Chills of delight rushed through Arianna's torso. She was elated and almost needed to hold onto her legs lest her feet decide to dance for joy. Now she knew why Arielle had mentioned to her that there was a familiarity about Sully when she first met him at Alexandra's insistence on her visit to his residence. He resembled Elsbeth, particularly about his eyes, and his coloring was hers. The information was nearly more than she could fathom, but accept it she would as Sully leaned forward and their lips touched, softly and sweetly, and every ounce of worry and tension melted right away.

Sully and Arianna had long since left and Arielle had returned to her room, but Ian summoned Elsbeth to his study. When he saw her face he was instantly concerned about her countenance. Her face had become ashen as though the grief of all she had lost had come bearing its full weight on her body and soul. And, though the son she had given away so many years before had been brought back to her, she felt she had lost him again. *How will he or could he ever forgive me for my actions. How could I have been so uncaring and thoughtless?*

I am nothing, absolutely nothing. My life has no meaning anymore. And, my brother! Why could he have not let sleeping dogs lie? He has ruined my life!

Images whirled in Elsbeth's head. She thought she had left her secret buried in her womb yet it was now, deep in her core, that the wrenching pain of guilt grabbed at her insides. She felt sick, nauseous, and put her arm across the middle of her abdomen. She swallowed hard to keep the rising threat of regurgitation from revealing itself. She no longer felt like herself, the self she had risen to, the self she wore like a mask that kept her hidden from the shame she bore one score and ten years before. Now, her mask had been removed and her disgrace was fully exposed. Her demeanor had taken on a somber air for she felt she would never regain the respect of her family. Her feeling of melancholy was broken by Ian's voice that brought her back to their conversation.

"Elsbeth, you have no doubt unburdened yourself by this disclosure, however, just imagine the burden you have placed upon not only my being, but that of our daughter and her sibling. Your revelation, in a sense, sanctions my indiscretions or must certainly make them easier to accept. It is readily clear that underlying, or should I say hidden, circumstances, upon their rising have lent a parallel to our mutual behaviors, a balance so to speak, making our pasts exceedingly more palatable to one another than they might have been without the knowledge we both now share." Ian's words were exacting but his posture lacked his usual fervor.

He was no longer parading as the pompous peacock. His ceremonious feathers, though copious as ever, were lackluster in appearance. Though he felt an odd fraternity with Elsbeth, he was subdued by the truth of her actions, of her history that was presenting itself to him today. He knew he had no right to think ill of her, or to judge her, for he had been the purveyor of far worse betrayals. In recent years, he had turned the tide of his past and abandoned the precarious courses he had been wont to set to suit his fancies. He was a changed man and would nary think of casting aspersions on his beloved Elsbeth. However, whether it be his ego or the compassion of his soul, he sensed a wrestling within.

"I simply cannot bring myself to believe this, any of this. First, and foremost, I cannot believe that you have lied to me all these years! Why on earth would you do such a thing? What were you thinking? To lie, Elsbeth, is unforgiveable!" Ian was nearly manic in his declarations as he began to pace about the space before him. His face was red with fury.

"Sir Ian, you must calm yourself and, I might add, refrain from casting stones my way, for you sir, have a past more tainted than mine. I take umbrage at your accusation that I have lied to you without cause. I felt that it was in your best interest for me to hold silent, merely keeping from you actions that took place well before we met. And, I might add, actions I have buried in the deep recesses of my mind. Trust me, for if I could but wind back the clock, I would."

"Trust you? No, no, no. I cannot believe my own wife has fooled me in this way, for god's sake! Why, it is unheard of!"

"It would seem that you are more distraught by not knowing than you are by the revelation that I bore a child out of wedlock," Elsbeth said, as the velocity of her voice seemed to elevate an octave.

Ian shook his head trying to shake out the feelings pressing against his skull. His mind was a jumble of anger and disbelief. He felt as though the stages of the grieving process had been set upon him and he could not preempt their onslaught.

"Sir Ian, I urge you to look at me. The person you see before you has not changed. I have stood by you all these years and fully expect that you will in turn do the same for me. Together we are our greatest strength. We still need one another," Elsbeth's voice cracked as the emotions of the moment enveloped her and another wave of nausea tried to present itself.

Ian could hear the fragility in her voice but was wont to satisfy his desire to comfort himself from the sting of her disclosure.

"I know I dare not seek your absolution for the actions of my past. Perhaps your reaction is the comeuppance I deserve. However, it seems we are of the same ilk, cut from the same cloth, and perhaps that likeness has served us well in the past and will continue to our advantage for the future."

"I must ask. Who is his father?"

"That I cannot tell you."

"Oh, dear god woman! Were there so many suitors you cannot know who sired your offspring?"

"You have me so flustered! I have meant to say that I prefer not to say. A name will make no difference now."

"What of the boy? What if he seeks the answers to his past?"

"He simply cannot know what I do not know myself. There was an outing – a late evening picnic with a large group of us -- some known to me and others visiting from distant shires. We were having a gay time and much drink was consumed – far more than I have since imbibed and…"

"Oh, my god, Elsbeth! Are you saying you were taken against your will? You were raped?"

"Please remain calm. This is a difficult conversation. I cannot and will not throw accusations about for I feel I am as much to blame for the encounter as he. One thing led to another and here I am today sharing with you a shameful time in my history. One of my great fears was that on our wedding night you would be apprised of the knowledge that I was not a virgin. But, saints preserve us, the drink made you amorous but numb to the fact that it was not my first time. I must admit it was with some relief that I made it through that first night being bedded by you."

Ian felt a new sense of agitation as he listened to her words and realized that he had been unaware of the tainted package he received on his wedding night. *To think she kept this from me,* Ian shook his head in disbelief.

"This is beyond my reasonable comprehension! I want to know the name of this man, this boy, who soiled you!"

"You may want but you will not get. I never saw him again and I kept my being with child hidden from all who knew me. He is fully unaware that our assignation resulted in an offspring. I have no way of finding him nor do I wish to seek such information. The past shall remain the past for the benefit of all."

"But, he is a louse to have had his way with you."

"Is this the pot calling the kettle black again? How many girls have you had your way with? For all I know, Arielle and Arianna are not the only children you have sired!"

Ian decided to hold silent. Until the year past, he had no idea that his loins had produced the two beautiful young women he now knew were his flesh, his daughters. He hoped there were no others for such knowledge would only magnify the complications to his life.

"Sir Ian, giving up the baby born to me without the fence of matrimony was the most difficult, heart-wrenching act I have ever endured. Until these most recent revelations, I knew not whether the baby had survived into adulthood. I never knew where the baby was taken after I instructed the midwife to leave him on the steps of our church. How was I ever to imagine that my brother would meet and marry the very woman that delivered my infant? This is all Carson's fault! He has ruined me! All these years I have blocked from my mind the images and questions of that day rather than be haunted by wondering about the child's welfare. It was the only way I felt I could survive. Then, you and I met, and four years later we were married. This was to be the happiest time of my life. To begin anew with the actions of my past erased – a clean slate. How was I to know that my son would find me?"

"It is quite remarkable that inevitability has come knocking at our door yet again, Elsbeth. Like water seeks its level, it is inevitable that the truth will rise to surface itself. So, here we are. What to do, what to do? Here I was, dignified by the title of knighthood, yet it is quite extraordinary that I feel anything but dignified now. And for you to blame your brother for this mess is ludicrous. He is not responsible, you are! And, to think you banished him from your life over this! It's quite appalling!"

"Perhaps you should think how I feel, how I have felt all these years, married to you and not being able to conceive. It has been incredibly difficult for me to remain barren having the knowledge that I was impregnated years ago only to let the infant leave my life. Rather than be perpetually haunted, I had to push these thoughts out of my mind as best I could. I guess this is the punishment I deserve for the error of my ways."

"We will rally and we will move past this as we have so many other things in our lives," Ian assured but warned, "This will take time and will not come to us overnight."

"This may be more than I am able to bear for seeing the expression on Sully's face, his sadness, his anger, his questioning the choice I made, has made me feel quite ill. My body is feeling weak. This reunion is beyond anything I ever imagined. Meeting my son face-to-face, a grown man before me, is a shocking surprise. I am not quite sure I will survive the disgrace I have placed on myself and my family." Elsbeth could stand no longer and fell into a leather wing chair next to her husband's desk.

Ian was alarmed. He wondered if Elsbeth was being overly dramatic until he surveyed the expression on her face. Her jaw was taut and her face quite pale. She appeared weak and limp and began to close her eyes.

"El, what is it? You truly are distraught. Let me get you upstairs where you can rest comfortably. Tomorrow will shed a brighter light on all of this and we will make our plans to move forward. We have Arielle's wedding to look forward to and you know the months will pass quickly for they always do."

Ian called on Fiona's assistance to escort Elsbeth to her room and get her settled. As he pulled her bedroom door shut, he looked down, closed his eyes, and softly murmured a prayer for her health and comfort, then he returned to his study. He had business to attend to and had devoted all he could to her needs this day. *This too shall pass for it is inevitable,* he muttered to himself and shook his head in absolute denial.

Chapter Eighteen

The spate of unruly episodes at the colliery had given Ian cause to remain in persistent communication with Paul Nesbitt, the colliery's overman. Their correspondence by post had kept Ian apprised of the possibility of a walkout by the pit workers. As much as he could ill-afford the colliery to be shut down, even for a period of days, he had encouraged Nesbitt, as his manager, to keep the leaders of the strike movement advised that the hardships for the men in the pit and their families would far outweigh any deleterious effect on the coal mine's management. Most of the men lived payday to payday, and the mine owned many of their homes. To rise up against ownership was a risk that needed to be weighed with utmost thought and care, for far more than hot tempers were at stake. For the men, mining was not only their way of life, it was their means of survival, their way of supporting their families, and for that they held great pride.

The South Wales Coalfield, known to the locals as Maes glo De Cymru, was a vast region of South Wales valleys rich in coal deposits. Hargrove Colliery was a leader among them. The past year's aggregate output formed some of the largest tonnage recorded in the history of the mine. Ever since The Miners' Federation of Great Britain organized itself in 1888 in Newport, Wales, the regional and local miners' unions had gained more force with the Federation's power behind them. Gareth Lewis and Thomas Davies led the local Ogmore Miners' Association comprised of the workers at Hargrove Colliery. Ian knew the two men to be hard workers in the pits and clear thinkers who had a strong influence on their fellow workers. He also knew that they were not exempt from stirring the pot and creating some hot headed reactions from their cohorts.

Although the everyday workings of the colliery were foremost on his mind, he had been additionally burdened with worry over Elsbeth's health. Since taking full responsibility for her past actions that resulted in a son she never grew to know, her condition continued to worsen. She kept to herself, isolated in deep reflection as though she could never cleanse her soul and spirit from her past decisions. *The threat of a strike could not be coming at a more inopportune time,* thought Ian. *With Elsbeth ill, my allegiance is divided. How can I stay in Washington and ignore this most critical time for my business?* He paced the floor of his study, deep in thought, searching for a solution to the position the latest news from Nesbitt put upon him. He was never one to stray from danger or a challenge, though he had certainly strayed in other ways, yet he reasoned, *how could I leave Elsbeth? She has always stood by me and I must give her the same consideration. What am I to do?*

He walked to his desk where his eyes caught on a carte de visite of Arielle. He looked into her beautiful, very capable face and had a thought. *Perhaps I can convince her to go, to take my place, to be my emissary. It may be difficult for her to leave her mother at this time as well, but I will make her understand the extreme need for representation in Nantymoel. Certainly she will take comfort in knowing that I wish to remain by her mother's side. She will see that my heart is in the proper place and, if all goes favorably in Wales, she will return in due haste. Perhaps Elsbeth's health will have improved and all will be well.*

Ian stepped from his study into the foyer where Fiona was passing by. "Fiona, What are you doing?"

"Oh, nothing, sir."

"It's quite well to note you have not availed yourself of change. Now, make yourself useful and find Miss Arielle for me. Tell her I want an audience with her in my study."

"But, sir, I was just about to plump the cushions in the parlor."

"Well, the cushions will have to wait. Do as I ask and find my daughter for me."

"Yes, sir. As you wish, sir." Fiona dipped in a modified curtsy and made her way up the staircase as Ian rolled his eyes and shook his head.

Arielle was startled by the knock that came to her door. Her mother's decline had kept her on alert, never knowing if the next knock would be the bearer of bad news. Doctor Lovering had said her mother might rally from her malaise, but Arielle had seen little improvement.

"Come in."

Fiona opened the door just enough to peek her head into the room. She looked around as though she anticipated someone else to be in the room, then disappointment formed on her face when she saw only her lady, Arielle. There would be no juicy story to tell to the other household staff and for that she was dismayed.

"Come in, Fiona. Why are you looking around like a frightened mouse leery of a feline? What is it?"

"Oh, miss, it's jest that yer father is asking that ye come to 'is study. Let's see, 'e says 'e needs to 'ave an audience with ye."

"An audience?" *Probably more like a command performance,* Arielle thought to herself. "Very well, Fiona. Please assure him that I will join him in a few minutes. Then you go about your other duties that keep you far afield of the study doors."

"Why, miss, what might ye be suggestin'?"

"I would be suggesting that you mind your own business. No eavesdropping in other words. There is no need for you to concern yourself with my conversation with my father. If the need arises for me to apprise you of any details, you can trust that they will be revealed to you. I do not mean to insult you, Fiona. I am merely trying to prevent you from getting yourself into affairs that are not your concern and to which you were not invited."

Fiona sulked from the bedroom. Her day was not going to her liking. She was getting quite bored with her humdrum everyday life and was hoping for something exciting to change her focus. More often than not she thought of returning to Ireland to see what her homeland might offer, but she was in need of the monies she earned working as a housemaid in America even though most of her income was sent home to her relatives who were eager to claim the money as rightfully theirs. So she continued to muddle about at the Hargrove's and dismissed the thoughts of returning to the lichen acres of the Emerald Isle any time soon.

Arielle entered her father's study where she found him sitting in his desk chair with a letter in his hands. Her first thought was that another enlightening correspondence had been received. In the past year, she had adjusted to enough shocking news. *Thank God for William. If not for that dear man rescuing me in the rain and identifying me after the carriage accident, I might never have recovered from my injuries. And now, the news about Sully and an uncle I never knew existed! What more can this family bear?* She shook her head as she reflected on her last word.

"Oh, Arielle, there you are. Good. Please come and sit down. There is something of supreme importance that I must discuss with you. Please sit and hear me out before you give me an answer."

"But…"

"No, just sit. I will explain everything."

"I will sit as you request, however, first I must know the topic you wish to discuss. Please tell me this is not another crisis for this family to face."

"Of that I cannot assure you."

"Father, please, you are scaring me. What is this about?"

"Rest assured it is about the lifeblood of this family, my raison d'être, besides your mother, of course. To be exact, it is about the colliery. Nesbitt and I have been in constant correspondence during my time here on Capitol Hill with the Trade Council. As I mentioned to you before, along with the idea that you would accompany me on my next trip to the colliery, trouble has been brewing for several months and there is the threat of a strike. Your mother's condition is of great concern to me, as I know it is to you. However, I feel that I must remain here. I am only comfortable with this decision because I know of your capabilities. You understand the coal industry and you know how I conduct my business. I must say, I have taught you very well and I value your opinion. There is no one I trust more and I need you to be my agent, to represent the company's side as we are confronted with this opposition. We must at all costs avoid a bitter and prolonged fight. "

"You would send me, a woman, into the mire to fend off a batch of hostile men? As much as I appreciate your confidence in me, I am not sure that I am well able to take them on. Equally, I would not want to disappoint you or have any harm come to the company or myself for that matter."

"I know my trust in you is well placed and I will instruct you well before you leave for Wales to arm you with all the verbal ammunition you will need to squelch an uprising. There are certain concessions, within reason, that I am willing to make. And, as for your safety, Nesbitt will be with you as well as my solicitor, Benjamin George. The two men you will need to watch are the leaders of the Ogmore Miners' Association. The president is Gareth Lewis and his sidekick is Thomas Davies. The locals know him as Tommy. They are well-liked and respected. If you can reason with them, they will bring the others along with them. Understand that a strong show of solidarity may be the welcome mat that greets you. I know you want to be here with your mother, but I feel very strongly that I must remain at her side. She will understand your absence and, if all goes well, you will not be overlong in your visit to Nantymoel."

"Father if you insist I go, then I must make a firm request that Fiona accompany me. It would be best for me to have a companion for my journey, and she is most aware of the operations at our home in Nantymoel. She will be most capable of finessing her way about the manse with the balance of the household staff."

"You give the girl entirely too much credit. She is quite daft on her best of days. Her presence here, or lack thereof, will hardly be noticed. Certainly she may accompany you. Her absence will provide me with a holiday of sorts." Ian's last words exited his mouth in an exasperated puff. Though he treated Fiona fairly where wages were concerned, he held little tolerance for the girl's behavior and her mediocre completion of her chores. She would be one less set of hands to assist with Elsbeth's care, but he was equal to the task of rallying enough help from the remaining staff to suit his needs as a caregiver.

"There is one more matter that I wish to discuss and that is of your mother's brother, Carson. I want to send word to him about her declining health and request that he travel to America to see her. My hope is that her health will improve. I am certain that her estrangement from his has taken a toll over the years. Now that the truth is out about Sully, it would seem there is little reason for them to maintain their distance. I understand that he has fallen on hard times so I will send the funds needed to cover all of his travel and lodging expenses."

"Will you ask Mum how she feels about this? Perhaps she does not wish to see him."

"Your mother is in no position to doubt my judgment on this. It is for the best, particularly if her health should take a turn for the worse. However, I will suggest that he reside elsewhere only in the event that she have any difficulty with his proximity."

"Very well then. I shall look forward to meeting him. It will be but another step on the path of enlightenment that has mapped the course for this family of late. An idea just came to me. Shall I ask Emma Willard if she can provide lodging for him? With Sully there, they could become better acquainted for he is truly his uncle. I recall that Miss Pennybacker said that Mum's brother visited Sully's home on occasion just to catch a glimpse of him."

"I think that is a splendid idea. Yes, make the necessary arrangements with Mrs. Willard and I will contact Carson through Miss Pennybacker."

Alexandra had become less inclined to accept any assistance from her household staff with her daily valet. Her corset could no longer hold back the truth and she could not bear to view the questioning looks that were certain to cross their faces as they helped her step into her garments that were becoming too snug for comfort. Cecilia came knocking at her door, opened it and peered in only to be promptly dismissed by Alexandra with a sharp wave of her hand. The girl had been with her for five years and had weathered a myriad of her mistress' moods. Still, she was determined to perform her tasks by helping her prepare for her day.

"Miss Alexandra, if you will allow me. I put one of your favorite gowns in your wardrobe. It's been freshly laundered and would be lovely on you today. I'm sure it will be a perfect fit for it has a loose bodice and is not as cinched at the waist as is the style of many of your gowns."

Just as I thought! Cecilia has observed my weight gain. I must make a feasible excuse to throw her off course before she shares any suspicions with the rest of the help.

"Why, Cecilia. Thank you for the delicate way you have approached the fact that my affinity for sweets is taking a toll on my waistline. I guess one cannot always have what they want, though that is not a doctrine that I prefer to endorse or live by. I will pay more attention to my diet and suggest you help me by telling Cook to limit the desserts at our dinner meal. Now that we have that understood, show me the gown about which you are speaking."

Cecilia walked to the wardrobe, opened its double doors and removed a gown made of royal blue silk. The gown's bodice was ruched and had an overlay of ivory lace, perfect for concealing a change in one's figure particularly around the mid-section. Alexandra reasoned that the leg o'mutton sleeves with their puffy upper arms that narrowed at the wrist would be an excellent distraction to keep eyes away from her abdomen.

"I see why I keep you in my employ, Cecilia. You are absolutely right that this gown is just what I need to wear today. I have a special visit in mind, someone I must call on, and looking my best will be a necessary asset."

Pleased that she had won the favor of her employer, Cecilia helped Alexandra into her gown, then brushed and styled her hair into a loose chignon that touched the nape of her neck. She selected a gold necklace for her to wear with a large teardrop-shaped blue sapphire and a pair of matching earrings. Alexandra admired herself in the mirror attached to her dressing table and smiled with the satisfaction seen on the face of a cat that anticipates its prey. *This will do quite well. I am ready for my outing.*

T he silence of the night provided an unwelcome venue for the raging thoughts that bombarded Arielle. The realities in the forefront of her mind were daunting enough, but her subconscious mind was waging an unrelenting war with her psyche. She would have much preferred a calm closure to the day's events, but that was not to be. *My life seems to be in constant turmoil. When will it ever end? My strong desire is to escape, to pretend none of these things are happening, to find a quiet space and envelope myself in it.*

She could think of no better way to find balance in her life before she tackled the affairs of the colliery than to make a trip to Chestnut Heights and visit with Emma. Her sage ways always lent a pacifying effect. Fiona had selected a fuchsia gown for her outing. The deep pink shade was a dramatic contrast to her raven locks and cast a warm, rosy glow to her cheeks. Pearl drop earrings complemented the strand of eight-millimeter pearls she wore at her neck. She admired herself in the large cheval mirror in her bedchamber quite surprised to see that, from appearances, her night's sleep had not taken the toll on her visage that it had taken on her emotions.

The drive up the long lane to Chestnut Heights was always met with pleasure. The grounds were pristine thanks to Simon's talents and his watchful eye, and the front portal and vestibule within held fond memories of her very first visit to the manse when William rescued her from the elements and she was first introduced to Emma. She had so much to share she hardly knew where to begin. *Alexandra and William. I will begin there for I want Emma to look out for him, to protect him from her in my absence. The news of my mum and Sully can comprise my next order of business. How do I even tell her such disgraceful news? How can she not think less of me to learn that I have two parents of the same ilk? My family tree continues to grow in inconceivable ways.* Arielle shook her head in disbelief. She looked to the heavens with a brief, silent prayer. *Dear Lord, Please let there be no more to which I must adjust. My trip to Wales will be harrowing enough. It is time for peace and tranquility. Keep William safe from harm. Amen.*

Thomas led Arielle into the parlor where she awaited Emma's arrival. Her wait was brief for within moments Emma made a graceful entrance and with her usual broad smile she warmly greeted her guest by taking her hands in hers. She gave them a gentle squeeze before she released them and sat on the plush divan placed against the wall opposite the fireplace.

"It is such a delight to see you! William told me that you have a trip planned abroad and I have been so in hopes that you would afford me the opportunity to see you before you sailed away!"

Arielle tried to muster a cheerful face but the weight of her mother's revelations like a powerful gravitational pull threatened to rob her of the ability to feign joy. She quickly fought the forces tugging at her emotions, determined to first speak of Alexandra before she mentioned Sully. *For all I know, Sully has already spoken to Emma, though she does not appear to be aware of such alarming information.*

"Yes, about my trip to Wales. There is something I wish to ask."

"Anything for you, my dear."

"It is about William and Alexandra."

"My goodness, I am surprised to hear you use their names in the same sentence as though they are a pair. You needn't worry about that relationship. You know William only has eyes for you and you are engaged for goodness sake!"

"I know, I know. It is just that she can so tax his nerves. I want to protect him from her as much as possible. Her schemes seem to be never-ending. I am sure she is conjuring up something as we speak."

"You know, my dear, Alexandra is not that much different than ourselves."

Arielle felt quite taken aback. Was Emma, her mentor, her confidante whom she so regaled, suggesting they were of the same ilk as her nemesis? Was there a bitter side to Emma she had not observed? *Perhaps this was not the best idea for me to visit today. To think that Emma is finding sympathy for Alexandra, has she gone mad?*

"Emma, I am confused by your statement. Alexandra tries to inflict ill will at nearly every turn. I have never seen such traits in you, and I am quite certain I have no such desires."

Emma looked carefully at Arielle's inquiring face before she spoke her next words. "Let me see how I can say this without any offense intended. I mean simply that, if we were to strip ourselves down to our bare souls, we would find a commonality. Alexandra may act out, in quite devilish ways I might add, but the poor dear so wants to be loved, albeit on her own terms. I fear her father did her quite a disservice catering to her every whim. Hers is a learned behavior that she has not been able to escape."

"I guess that my hope is, that in my absence, albeit this is a temporary arrangement, that you will watch over William so he is not overly burdened by her demands. I have been privy to several of their acrimonious conversations and, quite frankly, one such hearing is enough. I am certain that my blood pressure rises every time she begins one of her tirades and I for one have had more than my fair share of surprises in recent days. I care so deeply for William that I wish him spared of having to deal with her as much as possible."

"You may rest assured that I will keep a watchful eye over him, though you and I both know he is very capable of managing his affairs. Let's put talk of Alexandra to the side for now. I am sensing that there is more on your mind. What surprises have come your way?"

"I hesitate to tell you only in that you may think quite the less of me. It is really shocking news and it relates to someone currently residing in your home."

"I may be aware of more than you know and hope you will understand why I failed to say anything from the moment you arrived. I felt the information was for you to share with me. You know I am not one for gossip."

"Has Sully told you? You know about my mum, our mum?"

"Actually, Miss Pennybacker came calling soon after her return from the United Kingdom. She met with Sully and then he asked that Arianna, Alistair and I join him in the drawing room. Arianna was shaken to see him so upset. Alistair poured him a glass of Scotch. After several long sips, he and Miss Pennybacker told us what had been gleaned on their journey and that your mother had confirmed the information to be true. I am so sorry that you have had to endure yet another blow to your family's history."

"Emma, you know how puzzling my life has been this past year and now, here I am again. I find myself in the throws of another quagmire created at the hands of my parents. Why is this happening? I find myself asking, why, why, why? Give me a reason for this latest turn of events."

"I fear you will find no comfort in the whys. Some things in life seem without reason and hearing someone's explanation or excuse is not always cause for consolation. I have heard it said, a lie well told is better than the truth. From what I understand, your mother took it upon herself to put a wedge between the truth and her reality of that truth. What she was able to conceal formed a cocoon she was comfortable to live in for a time, but it was inevitable that that would serve as little defense once the facts emerged. Secrets always return home unless they are taken to the grave."

"So are you saying that I am to excuse her actions? To dismiss them as she did, as though she did not make an egregious error in judgment?"

"Quite the contrary. My dear, Arielle, I am merely suggesting that it is time to face what has come to light, to acknowledge your mother's actions and to move forward for your own health and sanity. The facts as we now know them will not be altered. What we must alter is our thinking about them."

"Oh, Emma. I do apologize. I am not in my best-composed state. My mum's revelations have taken a toll on her health. She is not well and I want to feel empathy for her but I am finding it difficult to understand and forgive her, and I appear to be challenging your good judgment, my good friend. Please excuse me for my poor manners. You are so important to me and I would never want to jeopardize our friendship."

"Fear not. You are equally as important to me and, of course, to William. That is a reality about which we can all rest assured! I pray for your mother and for your comfort. And you know, a silver lining for your sister and Sully is that he is not related to the two of you by blood. I have watched their interest in one another grow, yet he was denying his attraction to your sister because he thought you were of the same father. You need only watch the happiness in your sister's eyes to see the good that has come from the truth."

"You are always so comforting to me and you remain my voice of reason. It may seem ridiculous and petty considering my mum's actions however, you know there is another matter that has my nerves on edge. Traveling such a distance on my father's behalf at this time, during this difficult period with my mum's health has me less than confident. There is a part of me that relishes the thought of meeting with the pit workers and another that questions my raison d'être. What is my reason? What do I truly think I can accomplish? I question my ability to stand before the masses and make any difference in the outcome of the colliery's affairs."

"You have stepped into the arena of the opposite sex and cannot hope for more than animosity at the onset. One might advise that perhaps you should decline your father's suggestion that you go in his stead. Please do not misunderstand me. I know full well you are supremely capable with quite the mind for business. I am merely reluctant to have you place yourself in such a potentially hostile environment. What has William advised you to do?"

"He, I assure you, is not without concern. However, he knows I will have Paul the Overman at my side, and father has retained his solicitor to oversee the proceedings. William knows I prefer not be held back and has every confidence in my knowledge and ability to maintain a strong presence with the colliers."

"Then, my dear, you shall go with my blessing knowing you will be evermore in my prayers for your success and safety. God will give you the strength and grace you need. You are braver than you think and stronger than you know. This is not a foreign area or subject to you. You know it well and have been raised with confidence. You know, as much as my darling Horace adored Shakespeare, I was equally enamored with the poetry of Lord Byron. I am reminded of his lovely piece, *She Walks In Beauty*. This particular poem is so fitting and seems written especially for you." Emma smiled as she looked toward the ceiling and began a recitation:

> *She walks in beauty, like the night*
> *Of cloudless climes and starry skies;*
> *And all that's best of dark and bright*
> *Meet in her aspect and her eyes;*
> *Thus mellowed to that tender light*
> *Which heaven to gaudy day denies.*
>
> *One shade the more, one ray the less,*
> *Had half impaired the nameless grace*
> *Which waves in every raven tree,*
> *Or softly lightens o'er her face;*
> *Where thoughts serenely sweet express,*
> *How pure, how dear their dwelling-place.*
>
> *And on that cheek, and o'er that brow,*
> *So soft, so calm, yet eloquent,*
> *The smiles that win, the tints that glow,*
> *But tell of days in goodness spent,*
> *A mind at peace with all below,*
> *A heart whose love is innocent!*

Arielle smiled. Emma knew her so well. She knew how to tap into her sense of calm and deflate any angst threatening to rise up in her.

"That was beautiful, Emma! And...so dramatically presented! Your inflection and diction shows a hidden talent. Were you perhaps associated with the stage and have been keeping that fact from me?"

"Perhaps in another life, certainly not in this one! Horace was the one inclined to aspire to being front and center on the stage. He adored the theatre and was always wont to attend the latest showings at the New National. I know I told Alexandra about the time the wonderful actress Ellen Terry graced our home one evening after her performance in MacBeth. I will not bore you with that story, and I am sorry to bring up Alexandra, but it was quite something to have Miss Terry banter lines back and forth with Horace. They were a very entertaining pair for our guests."

"Oh, Emma. What a wonderful memory that is indeed. I look forward to many happy moments to come. It would seem that I deserve some joy and calm to befall me. There is a part of me that worries that William will tire of my family's ghosts although, thus far, through all I have shared with him, he has not yet retreated."

"I understand your concerns however, through it all he has remained steadfast. The only thing you must do now is pack your worries. Just remember to keep your balance for there will always be more to come in life, the happy and the sad. We do not know what is in our next chapter, which is probably for the best. There can only be so much planning and preparation for what tomorrow brings."

Chapter Nineteen

T he gas lanterns had not yet been shut off at the Hargrove residence when Alexandra approached the front door. It was early in the day, but evening's edges had long taken off their guard and the sun had revealed itself, so there was no need for additional illumination. *Humph. They must be so accustomed to burning mass quantities of fuel at their discretion that they have little concern for waste. I suppose that is what happens when abundance prevails. The coal mining industry must be very prolific for Sir Ian Hargrove. Well, we will see how the wealthy family copes with my revelation!*

Her knock was answered by Fiona who looked at their visitor and took several steps back to protect herself in the event that Alexandra came charging through the door. Fiona knew she had not earned Alexandra's favor when she shared what she knew at the Palais Royal department store about Mr. Clay and Miss Hargrove. She needed to be on guard to incur Alexandra's wrath if that was the reason for her visit. *What on earth is she doin' here this day? I can be sure Miss Arielle did not mention that she would be comin' by for a visit. I best be calm so she leaves me be.* Fiona stood very still. Words seemed trapped in her mouth for nary a greeting exited from her lips.

"So, the cat has finally gotten your tongue. How nice to see. Why are you not doing your job? Invite me in, will you?"

Fiona moved back a few more steps to allow space for Alexandra and the skirt of her gown to swoop into the foyer.

"Are you not curious about my visit? Are you not wondering whom I have come to see?"

Fiona nodded, affirming her interest but afraid to utter a sound.

"Very well, then. It seems I will just have to blurt it out. I have come to see you. Let me first ask, are any of the Hargroves about this morning?"

Fiona shook her head.

"My this is a fun game you are playing. Perhaps we should try charades and see who comes out the winner. So, this will do quite well not to have any Hargrove under foot because I want to share some news with you and, since it seems you are unable to speak, this information will go no further than the two of us."

Fiona was spellbound. She could not imagine why Alexandra Whitaker would confide in her. *Is this a trick she be playin'? What could be the purpose of her visit? I'm feelin' quite confused and a bit worried at that.* She forced herself to find her voice, face her fear and speak.

"Excuse me. Ye be wantin' to tell me somethin' that no one else ken know?"

"Can you believe it, yes, I am entrusting you with a secret and I hope it will not go beyond these walls."

"I jest can't imagine what would be so important fer me bein' privy to without the others knowin'."

"Well you will see soon enough. I know you care about Miss Hargrove's welfare and I thought it would be wise for you to encourage her to end her engagement to Mr. Clay."

"End her engagement? Mercy be, why in the world would she be wantin' to do that?"

"There, you have finally asked me what you need to know and the answer my dear is that I am pregnant with Mr. Clay's child. He certainly cannot marry her when I am carrying his baby."

Fiona fell back stunned and numb. Fortunately the coatrack in the foyer kept her from collapsing to the floor. She felt the heat rising on her cheeks as though every freckle had converged to form a burnished flame across her face. She knew Alexandra's reputation was to be vile on occasion but she had no idea that her morals had been cast so low.

"This ken not be so! Ye are spreadin' this evil and I will not be believin' it! And here, with Miss Arielle gettin' ready to leave on a journey!"

"How can you be so sure? How can you doubt me? Ask Mr. Clay, he knows the truth and he is keeping it hidden from your dear Miss Arielle. And what is this about a journey? Where is she off to?"

"Not that it be any of yer business but she is goin' to visit the Big House and help her father with his work." Fiona's head was beginning to feel like her brain had been taken over by balls of fuzz. *That would be explain' the sallow look her skin has takin' on but, how can this be true? Miss Arielle would be so upset to hear this news. Miss Whitaker is right though, for there is no way I ken be tellin' her about this claim this blonde witch is makin' jest to be cruel and try to have her own way. I need to see her out of here before Miss Arielle returns.*

"Stunned are you? I knew you would be. It is definitely a lot to learn. Shocking I know, but I felt it was my duty to inform you so you could do your very best for Miss Hargrove and have her put an end to this idea of marriage to Mr. Clay. She will be upset initially, but she will recover and be much the better for it in the long run."

"Jest how do ye think I might go about tellin' her to end her engagement without tellin' her what you've jest told me?"

"Oh, you are a smart enough girl to figure that out. I will leave you now and wish you a good day. Oh, and much success with the job you have ahead of you."

Alexandra swished her skirt around as she headed to the door to leave. The grin on her face went from side-to-side. She was exceedingly proud of herself. She had told Fiona that she did not want the information to go beyond the walls of the Hargrove manse for she knew the girl's propensity for gossip. Alexandra felt assured that Fiona would be hell-bent to share what she had learned within those very walls.

"Fiona, why are you fidgeting about so much? You are as nervous as a canary being spied by a hungry cat," Arielle queried, annoyed with the girl's manner.

"It's jest that I have to beg ye to do somethin' that I know ye won't be wantin' to do, but ye have to."

"Must the world be full of riddles? You have piqued my curiosity. Spit it out! Say what you have to say!"

"Ye jest ken't marry Mr. Clay. Ye jest ken't!"

Arielle had never felt the frustration with the girl that her father always seemed to feel, but today she was testing her tolerance. Fiona surprised herself at her difficulty in immediately blurting out what she knew. She felt very dedicated and wanted in no way to harm Arielle or disprove her loyalty. *But if I dun't tell her, then I'm not bein' a help to her. Fiona, ye have no choice gel, ye've got to let the truth come to light. Ye'd be doin' her a disservice, ye would.*

"This isn't an easy thin' fer me to be sayin' but I ken't think of any better way then to tell ye. Ye know Miss Whitaker?"

"Of course, I know Miss Whitaker. Why would I want to speak of her this afternoon?"

"Well, Miss Whitaker paid a visit and had some very interestin' things to say. She asked me to keep quiet about our little conversation, but the silence is more then I ken bear."

"I swear, Fiona. You are making me crazy with the circles you are forming with your words. My mind is going around and around trying to imagine the nature of this conversation you are attempting to have with me. And, the fact that Miss Whitaker asked you to remain silent is utterly ridiculous for she knows you have rarely been considered, and please do not take this in an unkind way, a paragon of virtue when it comes to confidentiality. What is this about?"

"Well, ye asked and I'm goin' to give it to ye. Miss Whitaker has a condition."

"A condition? What condition?"

"Well, I dun't know if it be polite of me to use the word for her condition."

Arielle rolled her eyes and let out a sign of exasperation. If the girl did not speak up soon, she was going to lose her composure.

"Let me be the judge of that, Fiona. Now tell me what it is you need to say."

"If ye say so, Miss Arielle. It's jest that Miss Whitaker says she is in the family way as me mum always said."

"The family way? She is going to have a baby? Good lord! How did this happen? Oh, excuse, me, I do not know why I am asking you for that information for how would you know?"

"This is the hardest part for me to say, Miss Arielle. Miss Whitaker told me that the baby is Mr. Clay's."

Arielle wanted to laugh out loud. The very idea that Alexandra was pregnant with William's child was so outrageous that Arielle was not sure whether she wanted to scold Fiona for spreading such a rumor or dismiss her from her room until she collected herself.

"Fiona, I have never heard anything so incredulous! This is absolutely preposterous! And, to think you have listened to the words of a woman who is keenly jealous of me. Why, she would search for any excuse to undermine my future with Mr. Clay."

"I ken only say what I heard with me very own ears and I wasn't doin' any eavesdropping this time. It was told directly to me."

"Well, you have a very fertile imagination, however it is not very prudent of you to believe what Miss Whitaker has claimed."

"I ken understand yer thinkin' on that, Miss Arielle, but I ken also tell ye that she was lookin' a bit thick about the middle. Maybe it's jest that she's been dinin' on too much rich food. I'm sure that be it. I know she's always likin' to stir things up, so this is probably one of those occasions when she's tryin' to get the best of us."

"Fiona, I hear every word you are saying and the words make no sense whatsoever. What a sorry state of affairs this is that Miss Whitaker thinks she can fabricate such an enormous lie and have us believe it! I for one am going to dismiss this topic from my thoughts immediately and I suggest you do the same."

"It's sorry I am, Miss Arielle, to be sayin' any of this to ye. I jest care so much about ye and didn't want ye to learn about this some other way."

"As far as I am concerned, there is nothing to learn about. This is a fairytale created by Miss Whitaker and we will close the book on it as we would any other tale."

"Right ye are, miss, right ye are."

"I do not understand why Miss Whitaker does not find her behavior beneath her. She was raised by far higher standards. Her father would be appalled by her antics."

"That she may have been milady, but as me mother always told me, ye can put silk on a goat and it is still a goat."

Arielle appreciated Fiona's levity but she was ready to seethe. *Alexandra has done it again! She is determined to find a way to have William to herself, so what does she do? She devises an unconscionable scheme with every intention of ruining our relationship. But, this scheme trumps anything I have ever known her to be capable of attempting! To think she has such a low opinion of herself that she would risk her reputation and prove herself to be of such unbridled morals! But, oh my god! What if this is true? No, I will not doubt Will. I will do what I told Fiona I would do. I will purge this from my mind and think of it no more. But, how can I leave America with a question in the recesses of my mind? I must sleep on this and see what wisdom tomorrow brings.*

⌒

A knock at the front portal broke the cadence of Ian's conversation with Arielle. He had called her into his study this morning to refresh and finalize the information about her trip to Wales before he departed for meetings at the Capitol. Arielle's mind was less than focused on her father's words. Her night's sleep was restless with dark images of figures standing before her with disturbing news. She was unable to decipher their messages as they glided in and out of the scenes in her mind's eye. Upon awakening, she remained unsettled and a dull headache kept her from being at her best in her father's presence. He had taken note of her demeanor but decided to dismiss it from his attention rather than take time away from the matters at hand.

Fiona's footsteps could be heard making haste to the manse's entrance. As she pulled back on the door's brass hardware, she gulped and swallowed hard at the sight of the flaxen-haired visitor who had become more of an intruder than a guest to the Hargrove home.

"Oh, my. What a greeting I am receiving from the hired help. You would think I had cast a spell on you and, now that I think of it that would be a pleasant turn of events. Now, step aside and let me enter or have you lost all sense of grace?"

"Miss Whitaker, ye need ta be waitin' here 'til I announce yer presence."

"Please, do not be ridiculous. I am no stranger to this residence and will not be held back." Alexandra swished her gown to give her feet full clearance to quickly move toward Ian's study. She paused at the doorway where the partially closed doors made her privy to the conversation that had resumed. She recognized Arielle's voice at once and that of her father. Something about an impending journey was being discussed. Fiona stood behind Alexandra in an attempt to clear her from the space, but Alexandra swatted at her like an unwelcome fly. Fiona was not to be easily dismissed. She held her ground, quite pleased to be able to eavesdrop under the ruse of keeping an unwanted guest at bay.

"Tell me you will not be distracted by the separation this trip obviously imposes on your relationship with Mr. Clay," Ian said as he looked at his daughter and studied her face looking for any sign of regret concerning her decision. "I am fully aware of your importance to one another and, with your impending marriage, I want to feel completely assured of your abilities as my emissary at the colliery."

"You may pack your worries, Father. William is my sun and my air. Without him I feel I cannot breathe. However, with that said, he will be forever present with me in my heart and mind. With that knowledge I shall be able to be apart from him for this period of time."

Alexandra's eyes rolled as she shook her head trying to shake away the dialogue that fell upon her ears. She began a snide mumble repeating over and over, "My sun and my air, my sun and my air, my sun and my air," all the while making a sour face as though her palette had suffered a distasteful morsel. She lifted her right foot and stomped it to the floor with an equally resounding "Argh!" that would have impressed many a plundering pirate.

Ian and Arielle were both startled by the outburst and turned to locate its source just as Alexandra pushed through the doors of the study firmly planting her feet before them. Fiona, in hot pursuit of the home's visitor, fell forward and against Alexandra as she scrambled to impede her.

"Good grief, you have nearly taken me to the ground! Get your wits about you!" Alexandra shouted at Fiona as she shimmied her body much like a duck ruffling its feathers. Upon regaining her composure, she looked at the two before her who appeared quite stunned to have had their conversation interrupted in such fashion.

"Why, Miss Whitaker, I see you have yet to recover your deportment of grace and courtesy. And, Fiona, you never cease to amaze me with your inability to keep visitors at their proper distance," Ian spoke very directly with nary a crack of humor present on his face.

"Alexandra, I, like my father, am not well pleased to find you barging into our home with wild abandon. Pray tell what brings you here? More rumors to sprinkle about?"

Alexandra held her thoughts for a moment before finding her voice to speak.

"I am most disappointed for it seems this freckle-faced nymph has not spoken with you about my visit the other morning. It would appear that I have arrived just in time."

"In time? In time for what pray tell?" said Ian in his most authoritative tone.

"Oh, sir, forgive me. I was speaking to your daughter."

"You have burst into my study and therefore are expected to reveal the status of your visit to all before you. You, young woman, are the uninvited and, I must say, without losing all sense of propriety on this side of the pond, this is not the first occasion in which this home has found you so."

Arielle decided she needed to intercede before the bull-headedness of her father locked horns with Alexandra's stubborn resolve to have her way at all costs. *If Alexandra is determined to continue her charade, the last thing I need is for Father to hear her declaration about William.* The reality of the information Fiona had shared with her came back bringing the ache in her head to the foreground once again.

"Alexandra, what do you have to say to me?"

"Well, are you not the curious one? I am so pleased to know that you have any interest in what I have come to say. However, it is a delicate matter that is best discussed among women. I fear your father, and your Bridget here, are best left to their own devices while you and I have little chat."

Arielle was relieved that Alexandra had enough decency to keep silent about her claims in her father's presence. Ian looked to Arielle. She gave him a nod. With her signal, he excused himself from the study as he guided Fiona by her elbow out of the space and closed the doors. The two departed to separate spaces in the manse. Ian had determined that his curiosity would be sated after the testy Miss Whitaker exited his home. However, Fiona was hell-bent on hearing more without restraint. She waited just around the corner, inside the parlor's alcove to ensure her employer would not see her shimmy up to the study doors. With Sir Ian out of sight, she made her way to the study and peered through the wee space of light emitted between the twin doors. She saw that both of the women were standing. *Oh, I have missed it, I have. Why Miss Arielle has her hand to her mouth and Miss Whitaker has her hand on her belly.* Then she heard Alexandra speak.

"I tell you, this is the sorry truth! Well, I say 'sorry,' but that is truly not what I mean to imply. I am grateful to have this out in the open between the two of us so you understand what a mistake it is for you to trust a man who has obviously forsaken you for another. His intensions are not true to you, and I thought it best for me to share this knowledge even though it may leave me with a tainted name. I have warned you for months that William loves me. Perhaps, if you had shown him more affection, *if* you know what I mean, he would not have to go elsewhere for his manly pleasures. I have given him that release and I might add that he is quite good…"

"You must stop this minute! I had hoped we had begun anew with a new chapter in our relationship that would have civility prevail. But, oh no, you choose to ruin any chance of a reconciliation between us. It will be impossible to salvage any vestige of friendship. I will not hear another word from your lying mouth! This is the most preposterous and outlandish thing you have ever done! Why you would subject yourself to such claims is beyond my comprehension! How could you ever imagine that I would doubt William's love for me and his propriety? Your accusation, admission, whatever you choose to call this incredible tale, is without basis and is one of the lowest, most despicable acts you have ever perpetuated! And, to think you have shared this with my lady's maid. You should be horsewhipped!"

"Ah, so she told you, has she? The world seems to be full of snitches. I asked her not to let this news go beyond the walls in which we were speaking," Alexandra laughed.

"Why on earth would you imagine that my lady's maid would be obligated to secrecy on your behalf?"

"On second thought, she held true to my request and told you here, *within* these walls. I did not think you would take this news very mildly, for it is so hard to hear that your intended has had a very intimate relationship with another."

"Stop! I tell you I will not hear another word from your mouth! You must leave my home at once before I ring the bell and have the full weight of our household staff upon you!"

Arielle was seething. She felt like swooning. Her legs felt so numb she was not sure they would carry her across the carpet to the doors. She needed to open the doors to gather fresh air into her lungs and remove Alexandra from her presence. She had tried so diligently to accept her and include her in her life, to accept her for William's sake. But, this was beyond all reason. Alexandra was a toxin that needed to be snuffed from their lives. *Oh, my god, thought Arielle…what if her claim is true? What am I saying? What am I thinking? Oh, my god, this woman has made me doubt the love of my life. What is happening to me? Why does this vixen have such control over me? Why do I allow her such power?* Arielle shook her head to clear the webs threading through her brain as she nearly shoved Alexandra forward to the front portal to rid herself of her sight.

"Careful now! In my condition, you want to treat me with respect," Alexandra said with a wry grin as she sashayed out the front door.

Arielle closed the door with a vengeance. She liked to think she had become numb to Alexandra's outbursts, but the truth was evident in the sting her words left against her skin. Her mind whirled. *What should I do next? How can I possibly broach the topic with William? I cannot place myself in such an improper position to speak with him about such a delicate topic. What if Alexandra is telling the truth? Oh, my god! What am I to do?*

Answers were coming loud and clear to Fiona whose eavesdropping ears were back in the parlor's alcove. She had barely escaped the opening of the study doors as she scampered back into her hiding place. *I ken tell ye, I ken be speakin' to Mr. Clay 'bout the visit from his blonde friend, yes indeed I ken! Oh, Jesus, Mary and Joseph…what if it all be true what the woman said? What then will it be for Miss Arielle? Oh my, her heart will be broken fer sure!*

Chapter Twenty

Arielle's night's sleep was erratic and filled with dark and foreboding nightmarish visions until her dreams were punctured by the sound of Fiona's voice urging her to awake. She gave herself several much-needed minutes to face the morning, then slipped from her night covers and went to sit at her dressing table. As she looked in the mirror she blamed Alexandra for every puffy bag she saw beneath her eyes. She pinched her cheeks and worked to make her complexion suitable to face William. She had sent word to him to meet at her home before noon, that there was something important for them to discuss. Upon receiving her request, William assumed it was something related to their wedding or her upcoming trip to Wales. He had no idea what was to greet him when he arrived at her home.

Arielle had refrained from sharing with her father the nature of Alexandra's visit, although he was quite curious and nearly demanded to be told what had transpired under his roof. Arielle was able to abate his concerns for the time being feigning a headache with the assurances that she would inform him as soon as she was feeling better.

"Fiona, please bring my lavender gown to me. I am in the mood for something subdued, nothing bright and flashy."

"It's goin' to be a pretty day, Miss Arielle. Won't ye be wantin' somethin' with more color, somethin' more festive like one of yer floral prints?"

"No, the lavender gown will be sufficient. I will not be going out today. There is much to do to pack for my journey, which we will work toward later today. Mr. Clay is coming to visit so I will not have time to focus on my travel wardrobe until he departs." Arielle gave her instructions with sadness in her voice. *Departs. As I depart for Wales, he may be departing from my life. How can I even think of a trip abroad when my whole world is crashing into little pieces like a broken crystal vase rendered into disparate shards?*

So, Mr. Clay is coming today, thought Fiona. *I have to hope the master and the misses are not home so I ken be the one to be greetin' Mr. Clay the minute he arrives. I best be keepin' Miss Arielle upstairs 'til I've got the chance to say a word or two to him.*

"Fiona, you appear distracted. Please remain focused on my toilette so I am not delayed when Mr. Clay arrives."

Arielle was in no mood to discuss with Fiona the topic of Alexandra's visits. She knew Fiona's curiosity would not be sated with her silence but further discourse was inappropriate, especially since she needed to hear what William had to say about the matter. It was all she could do to attempt to erase Alexandra from her mind and, so far, her efforts were failing her. *She is a fierce foe! Here I am, planning to leave the country, to leave Will, with a building mountain of uncertainty. I must get this settled if I am to maintain my sanity and be in the right frame of mind to handle the issues surrounding the colliery. Emma once said to me that God does not give us more than we can bear. Events of late are certainly testing that statement and my strength!*

"Yes, sorry I am. I was jest thinkin' that it would be nice fer ye to be makin' a grand entrance and sort of float down the stairway in yer gown. When Mr. Clay comes, I'll be gettin' the door and then I'll come up and announce his arrival to ye. That will make fer a very fittin' entrance."

Arielle pondered Fiona's suggestion. She certainly did not want to look anxious when he arrived by being front and center in the foyer. Perhaps Fiona's idea was best. He could wait below while she slowly entered the foyer and it would give her a chance to gauge his mood.

"You know, Fiona, I think you have a brilliant idea. Yes, I will await from my chambers your announcement of Mr. Clay's arrival."

Fiona's fingers fumbled with the last tendrils of Arielle's hair as she anticipated the details of her plan and a nervous smile crossed her face. She laid out Arielle's amethyst briolette earrings and briolette necklace with a ruby drop. The set, willed to her by her grandmum, had become a favorite since her mother informed her that the ruby drop denoted her birth month. Arielle excused Fiona, deciding to complete the accessorizing of her outfit by herself.

When the doorknocker sounded Fiona was caught off-guard and jumped. She had been standing at-the-ready with so much anticipation it seemed like an eternity had gone by before the arrival of their guest occurred. She gathered her senses and raced to the front portal before another knock could come that might be heard by Arielle. William stood on the other side looking as dashing as ever. Fiona always felt like melting in his presence and today was no exception. *Oh, to have his arms around me and feel his breath on my neck! What a fine specimen of a man he is! He is so delicious!*

"Well, Fiona you are looking quite fine this day. What has you in such lively spirits? You pulled open the door with such gusto I thought the suction alone might draw me in." William chuckled as he watched a rosy blush roll across Fiona's face.

"My, my, Mr. Clay. Ye always have a way of makin' me forget what I was supposed to be doin'. Please come in. Miss Arielle will be comin' down in a minute but before she does, would ye be kind enough to step into me lord 'n master's study for a quick word?"

"This seems very important to you. Is everything all right? There is nothing wrong with Miss Hargrove is there? Is that why she has not come downstairs?"

"Oh, no sir. She'll be along in jest a bit." Fiona was beginning to rethink her plan. *What am I thinkin'? What if I say what I'm meanin' to say and he turns on his heels and leaves? Oh, what to do? I could be doin' a disservice to 'em both and puttin' me nose where it don't belong.* Fiona was concerned but she decided to forge ahead.

The two stepped into Ian's study and Fiona cautiously closed the doors so she would not be heard by anyone else about the manse. William studied her actions growing more and more curious about her behavior. He questioned being alone in the room with her but decided to allay those concerns and hear her out. Fiona stepped away from the doors, clasped her hands together and began fidgeting with her fingers. She became aware of her movement and shoved her hands into the pockets of her apron.

"Mr. Clay, I don't know quite how to say this, but there's somethin' I think ye should be knowin' and I'm jest goin' to blurt it out and I hope you don't think unkindly of me but I ken think of no other way and I jest think so much of ye and of Miss Arielle that I can't have you not knowin' what I be knowin."

"That is quite a string of words, Fiona. Now, slow down why don't you and get to the point of what you need to 'be sayin' as you say."

"Ye know Miss Whitaker, well, I mean, I know ye know her. Well, she came to see Miss Arielle and she said some things that were the same things she had been tellin' me and had been swearin' me to secrecy and I be tellin' ye now because my heart will break if this be true and ye and Miss Arielle will be callin' off yer weddin'."

William was taken aback and hesitated to make any further inquiry but he wanted to be certain about the topic Alexandra had shared.

"When you say she swore you to secrecy, what were you to keep silent?"

Fiona removed her right hand from her apron's pocket and put the nail of her index finger between her teeth. She needed a moment to think about how she would speak something that was unspeakable in mixed company. Pausing with her finger in her mouth gave her the time she needed to draw up the expression her mother used whenever one of the girls in their village became thicker in the middle.

"Well, I hope it be all right for me to say what me mum always said. Miss Whitaker's up the flue, you know, in the family way. There I've said it and I hope ye don't think no less o' me."

Embarrassment would have prevailed for William if shock and dismay had not gone to the forefront of his mind. He felt the blood rage in his veins. He had no idea that Alexandra had been to see Arielle or that she had shared her story with Fiona as well. He was trying so desperately to have Alexandra see reason and to aid her in her condition, but she was obviously doing everything within her power to foil his attempts to make the best of her complicated situation. *How could she do this? Has she no pride or concern for her reputation? She is willing to ruin our friendship and threaten my relationship with Arielle. Just when I think she can find no more dastardly deeds to add to her repertoire she stoops to this!* William took a moment to regain his composure and to settle the thoughts flying around in his brain. He pondered how to respond to Fiona and how to face Arielle, if indeed she would appear downstairs to see him as planned.

He had spent some time exploring options with Alexandra after Doc Lovering confirmed that she was indeed with child. He had tried to persuade her to name the man whose seed she carried, but she was steadfast in her determination to have him remain nameless. She would hear nothing of his idea of taking an extended journey and returning with her offspring where she could claim any number of explanations, among them that she had taken on a deceased relative's child as her ward, or that she had been married and her husband had died. Nothing that William suggested seemed to placate Alexandra. His suggestions only lead to her threats to end the pregnancy. He could still hear her rantings in his ears.

"I am telling you that I will hear nothing of the sort from you! I shall end this pregnancy at all costs! Those knitting needles I purchased from Pennybaker's Stitchery may serve me well in this regard, or perhaps I should visit the apothecary and purchase ingredients to accompany some tansy oil or try a lye douche! I have been reading about these things and I will follow through! If you will not save my good name by marrying me it appears I have no other recourse but to cause the miscarriage of this thing growing within me!"

William had pleaded with her. "Please, Alexandra I beg you to reconsider such desperate actions. You may damage yourself for life or cause your untimely death by consuming such toxic concoctions! I implore you to look at this situation rationally."

William took a deep breath and closed then reopened his eyes to clear the tension building within as he relived their conversation. Alexandra may have been speaking boldly, but he knew she valued her life and would not intentionally bring harm to herself. So far, her threats were idle and he hoped they remained that way.

Fiona was becoming undone by William's silence and concerned that she should never have spoken aloud to him or given any merit to Alexandra's tale. But, she cared for him and would not see him blindsided by the flaxen-haired bully. She was compelled to warn him and she had, the rest was up to him. He cleared his throat and began to speak.

"Fiona, I will discuss this private matter with Miss Hargrove. I am sorry that you have been privy to Miss Whitaker's assertions and I am duly sorry for any worry such knowledge has caused you. Please know that I will see to the well-being of all concerned to the best of my ability. Now, if you will kindly let Miss Hargrove know that I am here and that I wish to see her."

Fiona performed a mild curtsy and quickly exited the room to retrieve Arielle. As much as she enjoyed William's presence on most occasions, she was thankful to find her distance from him now. Although she felt justified in telling him what she had been told, she was very nervous about the outcome of her actions. She knew her place was to stay far removed from the personal lives of the ones she served, but her ability to restrain herself from wanting to know more, and the rush of excitement she always got from the knowing, kept her at less than arm's length from many closed doors and private conversations. *He didn't deny what Miss Whitaker said. He knew! What if he and Miss Whitaker…oh my!* Fiona rushed the thoughts from her head as she raced up the stairway, tapped once on the door to Arielle's room and entered abruptly.

"Good grief, Fiona! What on earth is the matter with you? Your tongue is nearly hanging out like a wild and thirsty canine! Get your wits about you. I take it that Mr. Clay has arrived and stirred such beastly behavior in you. Am I correct? Is he here? You need to gain more composure in his presence."

Out of breath, Fiona panted, "Yes…he…is." She inhaled a full breath of much needed air. "Downstairs…in…the…master's…study."

"Why there and not the parlor? Is my father home? I thought he had left for the Capitol. Why did you escort Mr. Clay to the study?"

Fiona thought for a moment before she spoke. "Oh, it's jest that I was doin' some work in the parlor and had things moved about and thought it best to take him into a room more fit for company is all."

Arielle shook her head. Fiona's explanations were somehow open to suspicion. She could understand her father's impatience with Fiona although she was not supportive of his unkind remarks to her. Fiona watched as Arielle stood to leave her room. She felt like blocking the doorway to prevent her from exiting but she knew her actions would be drawn into question and delaying her visit with Mr. Clay would ultimately serve no purpose. *Me mum always said 'the truth may be bitter, but it's better to get a taste of it than swallow a pack of lies.' I wonder why me mum is comin' to me mind so much this day? It's all this talk of mums and babies I guess and Ireland seems so far away. Maybe I'm jest missin' home is all.* Fiona resisted her impulse to descend the staircase and lend an uninvited ear. Instead, she busied herself by tidying Arielle's chamber and prayed that the sound of wedding bells would remain in her mistress's future.

⁓

Arielle found William standing in the foyer as she made her entrance. She stepped cautiously on each stair tread with her gown raised just enough above her shoes to allow for safe clearance without exposing her ankles. It was just as she had hoped. Here he was, as dashing as ever, watching her decent and the elegant sashay of her gown along each step. She was the epitome of style and grace, her head held high and her eyes set on him. She wanted him to see her grand entrance and relish the vision of her. If Alexandra's claims were fact, then she would raise herself above the shame and blight her intended had placed on their relationship and grow from strength to strength. She would not be brought down by the whims of folly of others. She had determined herself to usher in resilience.

William offered her his hand as she approached the last step, which she graciously accepted. He was surprised not to see the usual light in her eyes and the ready smile that always greeted him.

"You look lovely, Arielle. I am glad you sent for me to come. I suppose it would be proper for me to ask what prompted the invitation?" William knew his words seemed aloof but he saw no reason to waste time and dodge the inevitable. *In light of Fiona's surprising revelation and the look on Arielle's face I am afraid our visit today is going to be quite unpleasant. However, what if that was not the reason she asked for me to come? I would be wise not to broach the subject unless she does.*

"It is good that you have come. There is a matter of some importance that we need to discuss. Let's step into my father's study, shall we?"

"The study?"

"I would have suggested the parlor for it is a far more pleasant place to visit, however I have been informed by Fiona that she has created a state of disarray in that room and, actually, she had informed me that you were waiting in the study. I was surprised to see you in the foyer."

"I would not miss a moment of your beauty," William smiled and dipped into a modified bow trying to bring a smile to her face to no avail.

In force of habit, Arielle left the doors to the study partially ajar, as she was wont to do in the presence of a member of the opposite sex. She fully trusted William, or had in the past, but she wanted to avoid any tittle-tattle from the household staff if they observed them alone behind fully closed doors and, with Alexandra's admission, she questioned the level of trust that existed between herself and William.

"So, it has come to my attention that we have much to discuss. There is a rumor circling that has caused me great anguish."

William stepped toward Arielle and tried to take her clasped hands in his. She withdrew her hands and placed them down alongside her gown. He was taken aback by her sudden rejection of his intimacy. *How will we ever get through this conversation if she does not allow me to comfort her?*

"I am trying desperately to understand your mood. I would expect you to be reveling in the prospect of our nuptials."

"Prospect. What an excellent choice of words to use, a nebulous word, vague with no assurance that something is actually going to occur. It would seem the *prospects* of our marrying have been reduced to none."

"Arielle, what has distressed you so?"

"Will, I know there is someone else, or someone else that must be considered, and that has now come between us."

"Someone else? Pardon me for saying this, but are you mad? There is and never will be anyone else for me but you. There are things I am not so sanguine about, but our bond is not one of them."

"I have heard the news and I just cannot fathom that you have chosen Alexandra to end any hope of our future together."

Arielle was afraid she would lose William. Her words became a whisper as she made every effort to bring her voice back from the edges of worry that threatened to silence her.

"What has Alexandra to do with our future? How can she possibly factor into the life we have planned with one another?"

"The fact that she claims to be carrying your child! I do not want to believe any of this, but how can I not? Even though I acknowledge that this is coming from Alexandra who is one never to be trusted, she has been very emphatic in her claims and she showed no remorse in telling me about her condition. Does your aunt know of this? Emma must be shocked and most disappointed in your behavior!"

William was quite taken aback that Alexandra was spreading her venom and defaming his character with such gusto that Arielle was wont to believe her ranting. He was determined not to allow Alexandra to form a wedge between them. He needed to put a stop to her fairy tale at once and bring Arielle back from the brink of ending their future together. He stepped closer to Arielle only to have her step several paces back. Her action again caught him by surprise for she seemed afraid or repelled by his proximity.

"Arielle, please. Let me explain."

"Keep your distance. How will you ever explain Alexandra being with child? And, I repeat, your child so she claims!"

"I have done as much as I am able to thwart Alexandra's ambitions. She is hell bent on dividing us. And as far as my aunt goes, to my knowledge she has not heard a word of this. I will of course make her privy to Alexandra's claims but you must know that I am in no way responsible for the fix she has gotten herself in. You know this in your heart of hearts. Her actions and words to you are her vile attempt to control our lives. We must ignore her and move forward with our plans. I have presented her with several options for her choosing and I assure you that none of them include me becoming her husband."

Arielle began to sob. Her body shook as the reality of losing William engulfed her. Alexandra was a powerful force and thinking that either of them could put a stop to her agenda seemed far too formidable a foe. Cautiously, William stepped forward wanting to comfort his future bride but respecting the privacy of her space at the same time. He needed to assure her that worries where Alexandra was concerned were unfounded.

"Arielle, I can say little more than emphasize the words, 'I love you and only you.' We have a bright future together and it does not include Alexandra or the situation she has gotten herself in. I am not tethered to her by her father's bequest or the child she is carrying."

"But she names no other than you. I am so confused and I regret having such a delicate discussion with you. I feel so improper. How could she do such a thing to you, to us, to herself? This is the most desperate and vile move on her part! I could not fathom devising such a plan. She is without scruples and to think I was trying my best to befriend her and give her the benefit of the doubt after her shenanigans last year! This is what I get in return! Heartache and slander!"

"There is nothing in this world improper about you, Arielle. I am relieved that we can be this candid with one another. If it is of any comfort, she has also not revealed to me the name of the man who has gotten her in a family way. I asked her to speak openly with Doc Lovering about this hoping she would confide in him but she has continued to hold her tongue on this matter. I am willing to help her, but certainly not by becoming her spouse. You must believe me that I would like to see justice for her if she was perhaps taken against her will, but you must also believe that I had nothing to do with this. Please, Arielle, say you believe me. You never need to fear that you cannot trust me."

William was offended by the affront on his character but he would let those feelings lay low where Arielle was concerned. He knew she had been dealt a harsh blow and he was determined to do all he could to shelter her and see her through this latest storm manufactured by Alexandra.

"Oh my goodness, Will. I cannot believe that I have stood here doubting you. I am so ashamed and hope you will forgive me. Alexandra's news has thrown me into an emotional tailspin that I can only spiral out of by being with you. I had to hear your voice, I had to have confirmation that we are meant to be together and cannot be driven apart by her outlandish assertions. You always lead me to safety and yes, I trust you with all my being. I can only imagine how trapped and responsible she has made you feel. I am forever sorry for questioning your morals and your good name. You are the most steadfast and sincere man I have ever known and for that I am most grateful. I love you and never want to lose you," Arielle words flowed as more tears washed along her cheeks.

Simultaneously, they moved toward one another. William proffered a handkerchief, which Arielle took to dab at the tears on her face then she reached her arms out to him. He circled his arms around her waist and held her in his warm embrace. They released their hold on one another and looked into each other's eyes, his ocean blues meeting the sparkles in her emerald green orbs as he leaned forward matching his lips to hers in a slow, moist kiss. He pulled her closer to him, their kiss lingered as his tongue slipped between her lips searching for hers, which she gladly offered. Their passion ignited with the anticipation of what was to come as husband and wife as they stood together and said everything they needed to say without uttering a word.

Chapter Twenty-One

Wwilliam escorted Arielle into the train station, for he assured himself he would never let her risk injury and suffer the fate that befell her at the same station just one year prior. He would be forever thankful that Doctor Lovering called for his legal assistance on a patient labeled 'Jane Doe' who became misidentified as Olivia Smithfield. Had it not been for that twist of fate, it may have taken many more months for Arielle to recover and be returned to her proper home.

He gently took her arm as Fiona trailed behind finding herself easily distracted by the hustle and bustle at the station. William guided Arielle across the walkway and up the steps toward the ticket window. His grace was in perfect companionship with hers. Her gown swooshed and then fell back into place as she gained sure footing on the landing.

"We have made it to our destination without incident, and for that I must thank you, sir," Arielle said as she released her arm from William's.

"*Sir*, you say. Have we digressed to such formalities Miss Hargrove?"

"Oh, Will. You know I am simply making fun and trying to be light of spirit for this is a difficult day for me. If I could have it any other way I would see Father off on this trip and not find myself entangled in the workings of the colliery. But, with Mum so ill, one of us must be there to represent our interests and save Nesbitt from the hoards of unrest with the workers. If I can stave off a revolt and resulting strike, it will serve us all well."

"I know, my dear. I too am feeling the pangs of your departure but I understand the importance of this trip to you and your family. I will keep abreast of your mother's health and send posts to keep you informed. I trust we will receive the same from you after you have had time to assess the situation in Nantymoel. Without sounding old-fashioned or like a stodgy old bird, my concern is for your welfare. The pits are controlled by men and I am not so sure they will take to having a woman at the helm."

"Those are very salient thoughts and I share your concerns, but I have small choice in this matter. I must admit, there is a part of me that is anxious to put what little I know about the business of coal to work. Nesbitt has assured my father that every precaution for my safety will be put in place. Please refrain from worry."

"I expect Nesbitt, as you call him, to exercise an abundance of caution on your behalf."

"You can rest assured my father has instilled every ounce of fear in him for my safe return."

William took Arielle's hands in his and then lifted them to his lips. He placed a soft kiss on the top of each one. Her eyes began to fill with tears, for saying goodbye was never an easy task, and she too was not at ease about what lay ahead. She gave his hands a squeeze as they released their hold on one another.

"Be sure you come back to me, Arielle."

"I will come back to you. And, Will, please take comfort in the fact that as long as I remain in your heart, I am never too far away."

"I will be feeling you close to me, my love."

As she turned to approach the passage to the train platform, William could not take his eyes from her. She was his one, his only, and if she never returned to him, he knew he would never love again.

Nantymoel, Wales
In South Cymru

Arielle's heart was heavy as she stepped from the carriage onto the soil at the crest of the colliery. Her ocean voyage from New York's port was uneventful for which she was thankful. She knew she had enough unknown ahead of her with the colliery's workers that might foster some rough seas in her near future. The trip across the Brecon Beacons through the Rhondda had been pleasant enough as she viewed the valleys that were lush with green in sharp contrast to the land with which she was so familiar surrounding her father's coal mine. Her mind wandered to what she had left behind, her dear William, Alexandra's claims, and her failing mother. She could not shake off her last vision of her as she kissed her goodbye. She felt perhaps it was folly for her to leave her in her sick bed. Her condition could worsen at any moment, not leaving sufficient time for her to return to the states to be at her side. True, her father was there, but she was unsure that his bedside manner would be the tonic her mother needed to ease her transition from this world to the next. *Oh, please Lord do not let it come to that.* She shook her head in an attempt to erase the image she held of her mother, fragile and worn, not the vital woman who had raised and loved her for a score and three years.

Paul Nesbitt had sent her father's carriage to meet her in Ogmore Vale for the final leg of her journey to Nantymoel. The fancy turnout, recognizable with its highly lacquered finish and distinctive crest on the passenger door, offered a comfortable mode of transport. Her father had designed the crest with a trio of bright yellow canaries sharing one neck in the hopes that the trinity would encourage God to watch over the colliery and keep it safe. One of his favorite Latin expressions: Carpe Diem was arched at the top of the crest's shield. *Seize the Day, yes,* thought Arielle.

She appreciated the confidence her father held in her ability to work through the problems facing the management of the mine. Nesbitt had done all he could to placate the ire of the men and the union they had formed to protect their safety and their wages. She was being thrust into a mire unfamiliar to most women but one she had prepared herself for by listening to her father's tales of meetings with the Trade Council at the Capitol building and overhearing conversations the male cartel held during their retreats for brandy and cigars in her father's study. *No, I will not try to extricate myself from the difficulties that may certainly ensue. I will face them head on. Seize the Day,* she repeated to herself.

Despite the shadow bearing down on the colliery, Nesbitt appeared only slightly the worse for wear. Arielle, as did her father, held him in high regard. She knew that in her father's absence, the colliery's continued success rested on her family's trust in him. There was no preventing the current state of affairs at the mine. Labor unions were prevalent and negotiations were inevitable, but she felt confident that with a cool head and a thoughtful response compromises could be met without militancy overtaking her family's livelihood.

"Miss Arielle, it is good to see you, and good that you have come. Your father informed me of your mother's poor health. I extend my sincerest hope that she will not succumb to her ailments and will be fine and fit upon your return to the states."

"Thank you Nesbitt. My mum's condition is dire indeed and it is with great heaviness of heart that I have come here. That said, since it was impossible for my father to be present, the unrest at the colliery must be addressed before it is beyond control. Additionally Nesbitt, and this is in no way a reflection of or a change in our family's affection for you but I feel it would be proper for you to address me as Miss Hargrove throughout the proceedings with the workers. It will be quite enough of a challenge to be before them as a woman without their eyes upon me as the little child of their employer."

"Miss Arielle, umm, excuse me, Miss Hargrove, I quite fully understand and will refrain from the use of your first name whenever in their midst. Perhaps I will refer to you as Miss Hargrove throughout your stay here."

"Very well. So, tell me, Nesbitt, how does it go now? What are the latest claims and demands being made?"

"It is brutally complicated. I have documents to share with you drawn by our solicitors and the representatives that will help to shed light upon the pit workers and what they see as their plight."

"Essentially, in summary, what would you say are the most prominent of their concerns?"

"I'd be saying their main concerns are their wages and their working conditions. Some of the men have grumbled about wanting a shorter workday too. Most of them have many mouths to feed and are just scraping by. Then there's the worry that is ever present, particularly with the womenfolk, that their men will suffer a fatal accident at the hands of their cavernous workplace. There's talk of a union, quite strong talk I might add."

"So, you have a meeting set for tomorrow I understand. Where are we to be? On the grounds of the colliery?"

"We thought it best to meet in a neutral place and hopefully one that will shed some of God's light on the proceedings. We're meeting in St. David's Church. One of the men said he asked the principal at St. Andrew's Music Academy in Cardiff if he'd play the Hallelujah chorus on the organ if the meeting went in favor of the workers. That ought to keep its seventeen pipes vibrating loudly!"

"I should say. I believe his name is George Bull. He is quite well respected in Ogmore Vale and has been an inspiration to the young people, encouraging them to take an interest in not only the folk music they have grown up with, but also the various eras of the classical composers. I just might request the pleasure of his fingers on the keyboard if we all leave the meeting without a blemish to our names or bodies," Arielle mused, trying to relieve herself of the more serious thoughts burdening her mind.

The church hall was a sea of men, filled beyond capacity with the pit workers jammed one next to the other. Arielle questioned her place there as a fleeting thought of retreat passed through her mind. She had a mission and felt well able to accomplish it even though an ever-present touch of fear tapped her now and again. She shook her head. Numbers and hostile faces would not deter her. She would make her father proud and more importantly make herself proud. Complying with the demands of the workers would only be acceptable if the colliery could maintain a healthy profit margin. She was determined to find a way to accept the formation of a union and ensure that it would benefit all parties involved so neither the business of the colliery, nor the livelihood of the workers would suffer. If they were akin to allowing all sides of the issues to be heard, she hoped good senses would prevail for all.

As she positioned herself on the altar before them she felt courage fill her veins. She nodded to Benjamin George, her father's solicitor, who not only offered the legal support she might need, but also served as a much needed ally. *How fitting that this be my stage for this meeting. No, I will not be the sacrificial lamb they anticipate me to be. I will be strong.* As she looked the men in the eyes, one must have detected a hint of fear.

"We are not barbarians, miss!"

Arielle lifted her shoulders and addressed the gathering. "And, I have not claimed you to be. With all due respect, gentlemen, I ask you to hold your tongues until what I have to say has had the proper hearing." Arielle drew in a shallow breath to gain sustenance. Had she taken a heartier breath it might have had the men thinking there was a weakness evident in her demeanor that could easily be taken advantage of and she was not about to let them think they were getting the best of her.

Nesbitt, or Paul the Overman as the men called him, spoke up. "First, men, let me introduce Miss Hargrove to you. As you have been informed, she is the daughter of our colliery's owner and is here as his representative in light of his wife's poor health. Also present is Mr. Benjamin George who represents Sir Ian Hargrove as his legal counsel. He will prepare any necessary documents should the need arise. So, I will now turn over these proceedings to Miss Hargrove."

"So missy, what have you up that sleeve of your Bonnie dress? You come to us in such fancy clothes and from the Big House and all…what could you know of our lives, our needs, the way we scrape together every morsel of bread we have to put before our wives and children!" The worker shouted and raised an angry fist as Nesbitt looked on, ready to protect Arielle if the need should arise.

She paused and thought about her couture that Fiona so carefully helped her assemble that morn. *Perhaps I would have been wise to appear as a barrister and wear a frock-tail coat and horsehair wig. Had we met in a court of law rather than a church hall, perhaps the men would show a modicum of respect lest they be jailed.* The conduct of the men made them appear void of the fear of reprisal. Their very livelihoods hung in the balance and yet they were ready, willing, and able to risk it all to have themselves heard.

"Sir, I am here to work for the good of all concerned with harm to none," Arielle responded having much preferred to reprimand him for his poor manners and lack of grace. "There are those of you who take exception to my gender, but I assure you, I did not come here to take tea and dine on crumpets and minced pie."

"Oh, malu awyr! You just be here to mince air! It's nothin' but empty talk you be spreadin' about!" The worker looked at the men around him as he tried to stir their ire and he searched their eyes to be sure they were of the same mind. "Arglwydd mawr!" he shouted to the gathering, "Great Lord, we do work hard enough for the pittance that comes our way!"

"That's right, it is!" came the lament from a worker who appeared to be two score old. "The monies we get do not pay the piper! We can no longer simply hope for more, we must take this into our own hands if tomorrow be any different than today!"

"Right you are, Gareth! Me fambly and me 'ave been down and out long enough! It's time for change and I be sure we're goin' to get it if it takes me dyin' breath to make it so!"

A rousing cheer of camaraderie filled the hall as Arielle tried again to gain control over the tension in the room that had the walls nearly pulsing with their anger. She had heard the name Gareth mentioned by her father as the most likely to lead the pit workers in their cause. She set her eyes on him and wondered what her best tactic would be to win his favor. With him as an ally her work to quell the men's concerns would be completed with greater dispatch.

"Aye!" shouted a stout man who rubbed the coarse gray whiskers on his face. "And who do ye be thinkin' ye are miss, tellin' us how this meetin' will be proceedin'? Why, ye be nothin' more than a bastard child of his lordship. Bastard child, bastard child!" A hush came over the gathering.

"Shame on you, Archie Redmond, to cast such aspersions on this fine lady. You'll be lucky to work another day in her employ." Nesbitt would have none of their rabble-rousing ways. "It's a bully you're bein' and you've got to stop it now!" Nesbitt stepped forward with every intent to intimidate the worker and keep a healthy space between Arielle and the worker.

"Oh, she not be my employer. It's 'er old man who is. I not be afraid."

Arielle was stunned at the man's slur against her, yet she knew Nantymoel was a village as close as bark on a tree. It should have been no surprise to her that word had traveled fast through every cottage. One step in the Double Duchess and the sharing of a few pints of ale would have the rumor going round and round. *Yes,* she thought, *it was inevitable. I should have anticipated some mudsling-ing coming my way. The townsfolk were curious last year when Morgan Pennybacker and Agnes Fielding appeared with Peepers and began making inquiries about my father and my birth. It was only a matter of time before questions were asked around and answers were given.*

She felt a tinge of embarrassment to be a witness to the rail-ings of the workers but, like it or not, she was tethered to the col-liery and would not be released of her obligation there. Despite the ramblings of some of the men that challenged her good name and intentions, she would not be deterred from her mission to subdue the unrest at the colliery by finding a reasonable solution for all.

The solicitor had heard enough of the gruff worker. He knew it would take little more for others to join his chant. He had experienced negotiations with workers at another colliery where epithets led to throwing punches and a nasty brawl.

"You, sir, are quite mistaken. Miss Hargrove has every authority here as representative of Sir Ian Hargrove."

"I should say, Archie. Ye best be listen' to the solicitor here," came the words from a woman's mouth. "It's a bully you're bein' and my best advice is that ye not be bite'n the hand at feeds ye or butters yer bread. "

Arielle looked in the direction of the words that were spoken, as did the rest of the gathering. The female voice was a familiar one. She searched the back edges of the room and there she was. Arielle's mind swirled with the thoughts of the last time they had been in each other's company. Visions of a small cottage on Wyndham Street whirled about with images of this voice telling her about a woman she had never known. There she was, in a far corner, defending her now just as she had defended her birth mother, Annie Hollingsworth, so many years before. There she was, Annie's dear friend, Maggie Galligan.

Chapter Twenty-Two

William had decided that the only way to suppress Alexandra's thoughts of putting an end to her pregnancy and intercede on her threat to tell his aunt about her condition on her own terms was to take her for a leisurely ride in Rock Creek Park and share a picnic lunch where they could calmly, he hoped, discuss the reality of her circumstances. He would then surprise her with a visit to Emma's where he would insist that Alexandra tell her the whole truth and hopefully reveal the name of the man who soiled her. He was determined to see him brought to justice without drawing undue attention to Alexandra and the Whitaker good name.

The air was free of humidity, which was a rare occurrence during a Washington summer where the atmosphere was thick and radiated like a wall of heat. There were many others in the park enjoying the cooling shade provided by the canopies of the large specimens including American elms, river birches, and maples that were among the many varieties of deciduous trees throughout the grounds. William's conveyance pulled up to the edge of a walkway. As the horses came to a full halt he exited his carriage and turned to assist Alexandra whose face beamed to be seen in public on a date with the one she considered her intended. She continued to make herself believe that William's affections would come her way. *It is just a matter of time before he finds that he no longer needs Arielle in his life,* she mused. *How wonderful that she is far, far away. I hope she remains abroad…or suffers some mishap that would erase her from my life for good!* Her last thought even made her shudder at its harshness although it was not the first time she had ever wished someone dead and it would probably not be her last.

"You look as though you are feeling quite well today, Alexandra. Not to be trite, for I have heard it said of other women in your circumstances, there seems to be a special glow about you."

Alexandra's smile grew even larger. She looked about for any heads turned her direction so she could begin her proud promenade and nod her head accordingly in acknowledgment of their attention.

"Why, thank you, William. You know you may take the full credit for my appearance, baby and all, since being with you always brightens my day. I was actually amazed that you called on me to go out like this. To what do I owe this gesture on your part?"

"I thought the beauty of nature might be the perfect backdrop for us to clear the air about a few things."

"Oh, please do not tell me that we are going to dwell on this little bundle growing inside me when we both know this situation is easily settled by you deciding to do the right thing and marry me. Why, it is silly and actually quite mean of you to think any other way."

"We simply cannot keep harping on the same topic every time we are together. Let's have our midday meal in peace and enjoy this beautiful day."

"You know William, denial is not a solution to this problem that is not going away any time soon or ever for that matter! If all goes well with the delivery, we will have this child for ever and always!"

William's nerves were becoming threadbare. He had had it with her narrow vision that always found its focus on him as her baby's father and her spouse. *I certainly hope that Aunt Emma can talk some sense into her. This has gone way too far and seems to find no end in her mind.*

They found themselves diverted to other topics, even worrisome issues such as the Washington Evening Star's reports about the latest developments in the Spanish-American War. Tensions had been on high ever since the sinking of the Navy battleship the USS Maine in Havana Harbor in February. President McKinley had been opposed to going to war but public demand fueled by inflammatory stories in the press forced his hand. Their minds were diverted to lighter topics as several cyclists wheeled by, three on an American Star bicycle, two on a penny-farthing, and one on a safety bicycle.

"Look at him go on that wheel, William!"

"It has become very popular as an alternative to the penny-far-thing. I guess I need to give it a try sometime for it appears far easier and safer to move about than those high wheelers. I almost cracked my head open going over the handlebars on one occasion. I was about to hit a large rock and broke too hard. I was thrown right over the large front wheel. Now, that was a lesson learned that I hope never to repeat again! I for one am glad for the new technology and the wheels that are approximately the same size. With the chain drive there is a more natural ease of movement."

"I have always been afraid that the skirt of my gown would get caught up in the spokes and I would be twirled down to the ground. I assure you this is nothing I shall try in the near future, that is, unless you break my heart and refuse to make me your wife. An accident of that sort might be the answer I have been seeking to put an end to my current situation."

"There you go again with your threats, Alexandra. Please stop yourself before you call in such misfortune by cursing yourself. Let's enjoy the fine repast before us and then I have one other stop for us to make that shall remain a surprise."

With William's poker face Alexandra wondered what he had up his sleeve. She knew he was inclined to reveal only what he chose to so she decided to remain compliant and nibble on the variety of offerings in their basket of food. Roasted chicken, chilled aspara-gus spears, wedges of cheeses with crusty bread, and a platter of strawberries and grapes provided an ample buffet for their dining pleasure. A small basket of cookies and thin slices of glazed sour cream pound cake added the sweet finish to their meal.

"You know William, I could dine like this with you again and again if you would have me do so. In fact, on more than one occa-sion in the past, and it has become the far distant past I might add, you have promised me an outing to Tolchester Beach. It would be such fun to board one of the Chesapeake Bay steamships and spend a day enjoying the many delights the area has to offer. We could have a picnic in the shade there, take in the amusement park, and enjoy the musicians performing at the pavilion. What say you about that?"

"I say that is a trip that would require some time and planning. Let's save that for a future discussion."

William was pleased that his plan to lighten Alexandra's mood was working. Now it was time for their journey to Chestnut Heights. *If all goes well, she will say the name of her suitor. I will finally have the answer I desire but, what am I thinking? What do I do once I have that information?* William knew such knowledge would add an additional burden to the actions he would need to take to resolve the state Alexandra was in. *What should I do? What will I do?* He wondered how far he would go to bring justice for her.

⟨⟩

Within minutes William and Alexandra arrived at Emma's and were greeted by Thomas. He noted that William's aunt was walking about the manse with one of their boarders, Mr. Drake, and he suggested that they might like to wait in the parlor while he located her.

"Miz Willard will be mighty pleased to seez you Mr. Clay, yez in-deed she will," Thomas said as he left the room barely, but respect-fully, giving a nod to Alexandra. He had ignored her before. She dismissed his snub as the hired help not appreciating who she was. *If he truly understood my stature, he would know how important I am and treat me accordingly! I suppose even for someone like the prominent Emma Willard it is hard to find good help!*

"Well, if you ask me…" Alexandra's words were cut short.

"No one has but, I for one am certain that will not curtail your intentions," smirked William knowing Alexandra would not hold silent her thoughts.

"Now, William. Just when I thought you had turned a page on your rudeness toward me you strike again. It's a pity you treat me so."

"If you could assure me that what you have to say is in no way a slight to another, then by all means do proceed."

"My comments are merely observations that, I might add, are right to the point. While others may dilly-dally around and not state what they are truly thinking, I do not suffer from that affliction," Alexandra said with a curt smile as she smoothed the skirt of her gown.

"Some would say your ability to perpetually flap your tongue laden with criticisms toward others is indeed an affliction from which you should try to rid yourself. Taming the tongue is a virtue you should try to achieve."

"Well, isn't this a fine observation on your part! Honestly, you should allow me to complete my sentences before you begin passing judgment!"

"Very well, proceed away."

"I was simply going to say that Arielle's mother has little voice when it comes to explaining her actions for she, as it turns out, is no different than her husband. As my nana often said, 'It's like the pot calling the kettle black.' Why, the two of them are of the same ilk and should be ashamed of their lack of moral conviction."

William had been taken aback when he learned that Alistair Whitfield Drake had taken it upon himself to speak to Alexandra about Arielle's mother's longtime secret and the truth about Sully's birth. The information brought great delight to Alexandra who found the news to be another layer of tarnish on Arielle's family's name. Her main regret was that Sully, whom she thought was her friend, kept from her the truth of his name and his true purpose for coming to America. Her other, more upsetting regret was that her plan to have him form a relationship with Arielle did not come to pass. She was willing to give him the benefit of the doubt and decided that a second chance on their friendship was in order. She still managed to find every opportunity she could to rub what she termed "the sordid details" into many of her conversations. Today was no exception.

"Alexandra, you must exercise caution when you cast aspersions on others. Assumptions are easy to come by but are not based on fact. You would have to walk in their shoes, so to speak, to know what transpired in their lives and why certain decisions were made."

"So you would excuse their lack of morals and accept the standards they have ruled to be acceptable?"

"Look at the state you find yourself in. Would you want to be so judged?"

"Are you blaming me for my condition? Have you succumbed to the daggers others wish to throw at me?"

"Absolutely not! You were a victim, or so you have implied, of a very unsavory character and I would be the last to victimize you further by casting blame your direction."

"I am thankful to note that, but I hold my ground when it comes to the Hargroves, and that would include Sir Ian's daughters who have probably inherited his wily ways."

"Watch yourself now. Whether the senior Hargroves exhibited a lack of moral turpitude or not, is not for me to decide. I would say they have lived productive lives and their actions will remain on their consciences for the remainder of their time on this earth. We all have events that impact our lives in varying ways, not one of us is exempt from that. Surely you miss your father's presence, as do I. You know he would want you to be happy. I would implore you to find the good in people. It would do you a world of good."

"He *would* want me to be happy and that is where you come in. You know how much I want to be with you William. Why can you not see this is not some passing fancy? I will never know true happiness without you and this child will need a father like you. And, perhaps the phrase, 'familiarity breeds' that my grandmother used to recite applies to our situation." Alexandra gently put a hand to her belly and looked down as she gave it a rub.

"Alexandra, seeing your maternal instincts beginning to surface is heartwarming however, we have had this same conversation on many occasions and the result is always the same. You must release yourself from this dream, this vision, this whatever name you wish to put with it. My heart is with Arielle and that will never change."

A sense of seething rolled through Alexandra's veins. It seemed no matter what ploy she presented to William his response was perpetually the same. She prepared herself for one more retort when Emma and Alistair entered the room.

"I say the entire world seems to be undergoing a revolution of sorts! All of these gadgets are entering our lives at record speed and we are to accept them or be left in the dust! What will be next?"

Alistair's booming voice shook Alexandra to attention. His strong personality was a match for her own and she was quite enjoying his repartee of late. The two had developed a bond, somewhat like a secret society.

"Why, Miss Whitaker, I presume!" Alistair laughed as he borrowed a phrase from the fictional detective he so loved to emulate.

"Yes, good afternoon, Alexandra and my dear William. Alistair and I were just examining the walls in Chestnut Heights to see what impact the coming of electricity will have throughout the house. We are all so accustomed to the candlelight and oil and gas lamps that I cannot imagine what it will be like to have instant illumination! I know I have refrained from making this conversion, but we must find our places in this changing world or be held in the past."

"I think it is a very wise move on your part, Aunt Emma. I look forward to the many conveniences sure to come from the advances in manufacturing."

"This is so true, William. In fact, I was speaking with my friend King Gillette at a dinner party last week and he revealed to me that in just a few short years his plan is to improve shaving for men by developing disposable razor blades. He said they would be thin with a very moderate price point. Now, will that not be a welcome addition to personal grooming."

"Sounds like I should make an investment in the steel trade. If his invention becomes popular with the general public there will be an increased demand for the commodity."

"Spoken like a true businessman old chap! Perhaps I should follow your lead and share in the wealth!" Alistair was always game for a new venture to pad his coffers when the revenue from his writing projects was having a lean showing.

"Alexandra and I were having a similar conversation on an outing today about all the change happening in not only this country but in the world."

"Quite right you are!" Alistair exclaimed. "Your fine aunt and I were sharing the latest news in the Star and reading more about, literally, the bloody war. That charge up San Juan Hill, though I believe the Cubans call it San Juan Heights, on the first of this month landed quite a nice victory for your boys. It would seem that the commander of that group, what do they call themselves, yes, the Rough Riders, will always claim some notoriety in the history books for his and their efforts. That commander has added another feather in the cap of his family's name. Yes, I am certain the Roosevelt's are proud of their son Theodore's leadership."

"Fortunately for industry, as we were discussing the economy before, it will not be plagued once again by economic woes such as those brought upon us by Garfield's predecessor. It appears the economy is having a taste of resurgence from the depression we have been suffering," William noted as he gave a nod to President McKinley's promise for stable money based on the gold standard.

"I remember reading about the dispute over your man Hayes' election. It was so controversial that the news made its way across the pond. Many felt he should not have been elected because he had not gotten the popular vote as that other man, you know, as Tilden had. Those disputed electoral votes gave your president the nickname, 'Rutherfraud!' We in the U.K. found that quite refresh-ing, particularly with all of the political cartoons that ensued!"

"I can tell you that my clients in the railroad industry hope to never see a financial panic like the one endured in '93. Several of them went under and lost a fortune in the process."

"I hope that had no ill effect on your financial tills, Mr. Clay!"

William simply smiled and declined responding to Alistair's rather personal inquiry. He wondered if it was going to be possible to get Alistair to take his leave so he and Alexandra could sit with his aunt and relay the difficult circumstances that plagued Alexandra's future and William's peace of mind.

"You men are about to bore me to tears with all of this talk about the state of the economy and other matters that are best left to your men's cigars and bourbon tête à têtes! To think by your vote that you can make any difference or have any control over the ac-tions of your leaders is profoundly ridiculous! They arrive in office and do whatever they please to suit the monied gentry who pad their coffers!" Alexandra's comments gave William the entrée he needed to make a request of Alistair.

"Mr. Drake, without appearing rude, I wonder if you would mind if my aunt and I had a moment with Miss Whitaker? Our visit should not be overlong."

Alistair was drawn to attention as he wondered what was so im-portant that William required a secret, confidential meeting with his aunt, the mistress of the house and Alexandra.

"Why, certainly, Mr. Clay. How could I deny your request when I am but a boarder and you are family? I shall be only steps away if the need should arise for you to call on me for any number of pur-poses. For now, I shall bid you adieu."

William was relieved to have Alistair leave of his own volition without creating a scene as he was so often wont to do. Alexandra looked puzzled as she questioned William's need to be void of Alistair's company and Emma had an expression of curiosity as she contemplated the direction her nephew's actions were proceeding. William took a deep breath before he began to speak.

"Aunt Emma, it is with a heavy heart that Alexandra and I come to you today to share some news that may be off-putting or uncomfortable to hear but, at the same time, must be heard and dealt with."

"My dear William, you are frightening me with your delay. Please tell me of what you are speaking?"

"Alexandra, it might be best for you to share your news with my aunt. I feel you should speak on your own behalf."

Emma could feel the tension in the room and was beginning to feel a touch undone by it. She was determined to hear William and Alexandra out, but the suspense was building and she had had quite enough of it.

"One of you needs to speak right now. There can be no more delay. What on earth is going on?"

Alexandra felt the same tension Emma was experiencing and knew exactly what William expected her to do. He expected her to relay the story of her pregnancy and the details of it that led to the condition she now found herself in. She could see no way out.

"Well, here goes, and I hope you do not think enormously less of me, or him, when you hear what William so wants me to say," Alexandra said as she waited, feeling like choking on every word. "I am in a family way and William, being the gentleman that he is, would like to make an honest woman out of me by marrying me. However, as you know, he is engaged to Miss Hargrove, which certainly complicates the issue. Truly he needs to let her go and assume the responsibilities he has toward me. There should be no question from any among us that his duty is to marry me."

Emma looked away from Alexandra and focused her attention on William who shook his head. Alexandra would classify his movements as denial, but Emma sensed there was much more to the story. She adored her nephew and knew he was a man of honor. If he was in any way responsible for the state of Alexandra's condition, he would accept that and they would not be having this conversation. Emma took a few moments to process the words she had just heard. *How did this happen? How was Alexandra put in this position to be in impending motherhood? And, now my dear William has to once again come to her aid. Has she finally found the one link that will weaken William's resolve and ruin his relationship with his true love?* Emma was determined to get to the bottom of Alexandra's claims.

"William, I would ask that you give Alexandra and myself a few moments together, if you do not mind. Some things are best left to the women folk to discuss." Emma felt in her heart of hearts that William had absolutely nothing to do with Alexandra's condition and she was unwavering in her pursuit of the truth.

William stepped through the foyer and out through the front vestibule onto the grand front porch. Its depth from the manse's façade shielded the interior from the sun and made for a welcome retreat from the summer's heat. Some time in the open air would be a healthy change and give him the needed space to pace about and gather his thoughts. He was not aware that Alistair had remained in the foyer tucked behind the lush portières swaged across the parlor's opening. Emma stood and moved to a seat next to Alexandra on the ample brocade covered settee.

"You know, my dear that the best policy is to unburden yourself with the truth. There can be nothing gained by anything less than an honest portrayal of oneself. I will help you in any way necessary. And, of course, you know William is at your disposal but you must allow us to know how this came to be. Who is responsible for your condition?"

Alexandra found pleasure in the fact that William's aunt was not holding her responsible for the state she was in, but she was not going to let loose the name of the man who violated her. She wanted nothing to do with him ever.

"Mrs. Willard, I do appreciate that you have not appeared to judge me in this matter."

"How can any of us judge you when we are not one of us without sin? The sins may vary in severity, but whether it be even the smallest lie or misplaced gossip the fact remains that a lie is a lie and gossip is gossip and neither provides a benefit to others. Without trust, there can be no relationship. We must always strive for trust."

"I guess I should say that it is admirable that you do not suspect that William could possibly be the father of this child and, as I have told your nephew, I am not comfortable sharing the name of the man who has caused me to be in this condition. My stand shall not deviate from that position. As you can imagine, this is nothing that I am proud of and I hope that this innocent child will not be thought of as a bastard since William refuses to clear my good name by marrying me. That would be the simplest and kindest of tasks."

"We have discussed time and again that William's heart is with Miss Hargrove. You would not want to add a loveless marriage to the vitae of your life. You must very seriously and thoroughly come to terms with what has transpired and make arrangements accordingly."

Tears began to well in Alexandra's eyes. She felt alone and isolated. No one was seeing her situation as she did. *Everyone hates me,* she thought to herself as the tears began to build and cascade down her cheeks. Emma leaned forward to comfort her only to be brushed aside by Alexandra as her tears increased and her sobs turned into a crying tirade. Emma saw that there was no consoling her and announced that she would locate William and suggest he take her home. Alexandra fell over on the cushions of the settee and buried her face in a needlepoint accent pillow. As her sobs became more pronounced, Alistair decided to slip from his hiding place and offer any assistance he could. He entered the room very quietly with due caution, so quietly that Alexandra was unaware of his presence. She began to speak as she pounded the pillow and the arm of the settee.

"How could this happen? How could he do this to me? My world has been turned upside down! Pregnant! How can I be pregnant and by such a scoundrel as Calvin Layton! I will not parse words! Calvin Layton will regret the day he laid a hand on me! I will see to it that he pays!"

Alexandra pounded the pillow several more times before she sensed that she was not alone. She feared that Emma or William had entered the room and, thanks to her carelessness, they would know her secret. Slowly, she lifted herself up. As she wiped her eyes the vision that came into view was Alistair Whitfield Drake.

"You should have made me aware of your presence," Alexandra blubbered as she attempted to collect herself. "I was speaking to myself."

"Let me suggest that when you are speaking solely to yourself that you speak more softly so others are not privy to your conversation. From the sound of things you are in quite a fix, I must say. Without being so bold considering your condition, I know from my own up-bringing, though lower class that it was, such topics are not spoken in polite company and especially not with the opposite sex. So, my suggestion is that you rally all the allies that you can including my-self. I take it that Mrs. Willard and Mr. Clay are aware of your circum-stances and that is why they essentially ushered me from the room."

"Please Mr. Drake, I beg of you not to breathe a word about the name you heard me call out. It is disturbing enough to me that you are now aware of the delicate condition I find myself in, but I do not want anyone else to know who assaulted me."

"Assaulted? This cad, Calvin Layton, assaulted you?"

"Yes, I was assaulted! There was nothing consensual about this, I assure you."

"This is a name I have heard before from Sully. In fact, I have met him."

"Oh my god! You met him. The very thought of him sickens me!"

"His is one of those faces that linger in one's memory. We stum-bled upon him, or I should say, he stumbled upon us on F Street. Sully mentioned in passing that he was relieved to be living at Mrs. Willard's to remove himself from the man that boarded with him at his other residence. Something shady about him he implied. I should say that is an understatement! He informed Sully that he was living in a place called, let me see, I believe it was called Purdy's Court. He needs to be horsewhipped or worse! I say we pool our resources and bring him to justice!"

"Purdy's Court, oh my, but why am I not surprised? Please do keep your voice down. Mrs. Willard will undoubtedly be returning very soon with Mr. Clay and they must not hear this man's name. I will not name him or involve the authorities because my name and reputation will never be the same. This must remain between us."

"As you wish. His name shall remain our secret although it may work its way into a storyline of mine someday for I find you a fascinating study in fierce femininity!"

On Alistair's closing words he and Alexandra turned to see that William had entered the room. He was pleased to see that she had regained some of her calm but he was curious about Alistair's comments.

"Well, what have we here? Alexandra, has Mr. Drake been a comfort to you? Aunt Emma was alarmed at your behavior. She said you were distraught but it appears that that storm has passed. What is this I hear about a name that shall remain your secret?"

"Now, now, William. First of all it is impolite to eavesdrop and secondly, Alistair inadvertently overheard us discussing my situation. You know he has such an inquiring mind as a former journalist turned mystery writer. He asked, and it was a rather bold move on his part I might add, about the man responsible for my situation and, as you have just stated, I told him that his name would remain my secret."

"Quite frankly, it sounded like the man's name is to remain a secret between the two of you. Is that true? Does Mr. Drake know that which I do not?"

"William, please let's not have any overreacting where this is concerned. I think it best to table this conversation for nothing is to be served by dwelling on it. I feel very strongly that fate will have a way of resolving any concerns we have about this said man."

As their discussion continued to revolve in circles, William decided it was time for him to take his leave and return Alexandra to her residence. He had an uneasy feeling. Alexandra's sudden calm was unusual as was Alistair's subdued demeanor. The two appeared to share a common knowledge and to have formed a pact that he hoped would not lead to the surfacing of any more mysteries beyond those finding their way onto the pages of one of Alistair's novels.

Chapter Twenty-Three

Nantymoel, Wales
In South Cymru

"Defiant she be just like the gel who carried her in her womb, me sweet Annie fach. You butties best be rememberin' Annie Hollingsworth and show the respect she's due, God rest her soul. And show her youngin' respect too ye old fools! Oh, Annie worked the mines as good as any of ye. She were one of us and so were her wee babe, Miss Hargrove. Look at her. Just look at her. She's givin' all of ye a time ta be heard. She won't forsake her heritage. Heaven knows if Annie fach had lived, Miss Hargrove would be sittin' in one of these here chairs and not leadin' this meetin'. Now, hush your mouths and let her be heard." Maggie's speech had reddened her face and puffed her body up almost double in size like a proud toad ready to do battle with its venom.

"Maggie Galligan, ye best be sittin' down and not stirrin' a pot ye've got no business in," shouted one of the older colliers.

"Hush now, Edwyn! No one has squelched ye or any of the others from speakin' what ye will so me thinks it's high time I be puttin' an end to yer rantin'. Why dun't you give Miss Hargrove a chance to have her say. I bet ye will be learnin' somethin' whether ye planned on it or not!" Maggie was furious and ready to raise her fist and shake it at the angry gathering.

"We *will* have our voices heard!" shouted another to which several others joined in to chant.

"Did not those among us attend chapel? What evil be skulking about in yer souls? Cast it off now, I say to ye, and force yerselves to listen to what she has to say. Ye may be better off for it! Now wouldn't that be a pretty surprise fer ye and yer famblies?" As the gathering pondered Maggie's questions, a rumble of discontent traveled like rippling water that came to rest as Thomas Davies stood and gained the attention of the workers. He was a voice the men knew to be on their side as one of the leaders, along with Gareth Lewis, of the local miners' association and most were willing to quiet themselves and give him his due respect.

"Men, this meeting is an important one fer one an' all. Our concerns 'ave been noted by the mun at the top and that's a good sign I be sure." Thomas Davies' words ushered a calm that spread over some of the crowd but not all. There was still a pulse of agitation that filled the room.

"Aye, I would find meself agreein' with Tommy here. Sir Ian Hargrove 'as sent his ambassador to us, his daughter, because 'is wife is very ill. Let's let her 'ave her say." Gareth Lewis looked about the room as he finished speaking to see if there were nods of agreement.

"Miss Hargrove, may I introduce two of the men who are leaders in the vale. Tommy Davies, who spoke first, and then Gareth Lewis," Nesbitt pointed to the men as he made their introduction to Arielle. "They are very active in negotiations for the workers and lead our local Ogmore Miners' Association."

Arielle knew their names from her conversation with her father before she embarked on her journey to Wales. She was glad to be able to identify them and she fully intended to meet with them as she worked toward establishing a common ground that would work to the advantages of the colliery and its workers.

A new chant arose among the gathering. "Tommy, Gareth! Tommy, Gareth! Tommy, Gareth!"

She awaited the din of the chant to die down before she spoke. "I have not suggested that you be not heard nor shall I. Gentlemen, there is no need for an uprising. Let us see that cool heads prevail and let us see what good comes from that. I am pleased to make the acquaintance of Mr. Davies and Mr. Lewis. I understand that they share your views and will be proper spokesmen for your cause."

"Our cause ye say! Well, ye can't be forgettin' Abercarn. It's blazed in me memory though it was a score ago! Oh, such a sad, sad time in the Rhondda Valley! At last count it was two hundred and sixty-eight mun and boys killed in that mine. I had fambly lost and they told me how sad it be for them to 'ear that steam whistle blow. They ran as fast as they could run to the pithead only to learn that their loved ones was trapped, never to be seen again. We 'ave the same threat at Hargrove. Them lamps we be usin' are our death sentence as much as the firedamp!"

Arielle knew well of what he spoke. Her father was forever checking the safety precautions at the colliery. He knew that the presence of coal dust was enough of a concern for the workers but sometimes the high-sulfur coal seams contaminated with pyrites could cause firedamp explosions when the pit worker's tools struck. Hargrove Colliery had been switching over to the new electric lamps that were more reliable and unlikely to ignite firedamp. The resulting lethal afterdamp sent carbon monoxide, methane and other gasses throughout the tunnels leaving death and destruction in its wake. Canaries had been worth their salt in checking the mine for gasses and alerting the miners to the invisible dangers lurking below. Arielle remembered enjoying the mass flight of the birds out of the tunnels. She delighted in knowing that all was well and no gasses were present if the birds once again saw the light of day.

"As many of you know, we removed the Davy lamps many years ago and are now replacing the Geordie lamps, removing them from the mine. The new lamps along with the ventilation procedures we are instituting should make for safer working conditions and peace of mind for all. The mined-out areas are being made airtight to bar oxygen and make the areas impervious to gases." Arielle's summary was a testament to her preparation for this trip to ensure she was up-to-date with the colliery's procedures. She thought of her discussions with her father as she continued.

"In addition to the provisions related to wages and working conditions, Hargrove Colliery will construct a Miners' Hall specifically suited as a gathering site for both union meetings and socials. On its grounds we will erect a monument, as a memorial to remember all of those who have suffered and also to respectfully honor the many lives that were taken from our valley at the hands of the coal mine."

"At the hands of the master of the mine ye mean -- his lord almighty, Sir Ian Hargrove! Oh, the greed! His breeches just get richer and richer while the rest of us struggle by on a mere twenty-two shillings and 7 pence!"

"Right you are Edwyn!" shouted Trystan Jernigan. A hewer, he knew how important his position was in the mines. Without his hard work and that of the other men in his section their earnings would greatly suffer, for their wages were in direct correlation to their output. "We men haven't seen a rise in our wages for the likes of two years past and at that we were only increased by one and a quarter percent! We're nothing but paupers!"

"Hear now this, O foolish people, and without understanding, which have eyes, and see not, which have ears, and hear not." Maggie Galligan's words resounded throughout the walls of the church as she garnered the attention of the workers who came under her spell. It was as though the vicar had delivered a message from on high to calm the tensions of everyone gathered in the place of worship. "Maybe the words of Jeremiah will find a place in yer hearts today. It's best ye be listenin' and really hear, and open yer eyes and really see. Ye want to be doin' the best not only fer yerselves, but also fer yer famblies. Gareth, Tommy, I say you and Miss Hargrove take the words her solicitor's written down and 'ave a meetin' to iron this all out. Ye know what the mun and their butties want, so go about gettin' it done."

"Thank you, Mrs. Galligan. Your words are appreciated. As I have stated, the matter of wages and their increase will be a top priority during my meetings with Mr. Lewis and Mr. Davies. They will serve as your representatives and bring to the table all of your concerns." Arielle spoke with great aplomb considering the toll the pulse of the gathering was taking on her nerves. She would not be bullied by the men. She was determined to hold her ground not only for her father's sake as his representative, but also for her own satisfaction. She felt secure in her abilities to conduct a successful meeting and resolve the issues bearing down on the colliery. She knew the men saw her father as a callous man who ruled the mine to his best advantage, but she further knew that deep inside, her father had a heart that cared about the workers, their families, and the well-being of the entire village of Nantymoel. He had an invest-ment in their welfare, for without them his business would fail and the village would disappear into a rolling mire of coal dust.

Arielle was also fully aware that the advent of advances in manu-facturing and increased industry were making coal a fuel of choice and putting the energy resource in high demand. In conversations with William, he would occasionally note the large-scale use of coal in the railroad industry to fuel locomotives and the fact that many of his clients had made great fortunes from the machine tools they developed to operate the factories that were becoming more and more prolific as the century drew to a close. She was determined to maintain Hargrove Colliery's prominence at the top of the industry.

"You have now heard that Miss Hargrove will meet with Tommy and Gareth. You have also heard her commitment to you and the desire of her family to respond to your requests and see that certain improvements are put in place. So, now I ask that everyone go qui-etly to the security of your homes. I will see you at work in the morn-ing and as soon as I hear the results of Miss Hargrove's meeting I will call everyone together for an announcement." Paul Nesbitt was relieved to see the workers acquiesce and start toward the door, although he heard several mumble with serious doubt that nego-tiations would go in their favor. As the men began to disperse, the pipes of the church's organ bellowed and the men began singing the lyrics of **Calon Lân** *that translated into English as* **A Pure Heart**:

Beyond the Rose

Nid Wy'n Gofyn Bywyd Moethus
Aur Y Byd Na'i Berlau Mân
Gofyn Wyf Am Galon Hapus
Calon Onest Calon Lân
Calon Lân Yn Llawn Daioni
Tecach Yw Na'r Lili Dlos
Dim Ond Calon Lân All Ganu
Canu'r Dydd A Chanu'r Nos
Pe Dymunwn Olud Bydol
Hedyn Buan Ganddo Sydd
Golud Calon Lân Rinweddol
Yn Dwyn Bythol Elw Fydd
Hwyr A Bore Fy Nymuniad
Gwyd l'r Nef Ar Adain Cân
Ar l Dduw Er Mwyn Fy Ngheidwad
Roddi l Mi Galon Lân

I Don't Ask For A Luxurious Life
The World's Gold Or Its Fine Pearls
I Ask For A Happy Heart
An Honest Heart A Pure Heart
A Pure Heart Full Of Goodness
Is Fairer Than The Pretty Lily
None But A Pure Heart Can Sing
Sing In The Day And Sing In The Night
If I Wished For Worldly Wealth
It Would Swiftly Go To Seed
The Riches Of A Virtuous Pure Heart
Will Bear Eternal Profit
Evening And Morning My Wish
Rising To Heaven On The Wing Of Song
For God For The Sake Of My Saviour
To Give Me A Pure Heart

The harmonies of their voices cast a cautious pall into the night's shadows. Theirs was a song of hope as the sound became increasingly faint and spread over the village like the salient prayer of one beseeching salvation from a higher source. *I may be considered the gentler sex, but I was not so properly educated to merely sit back and do nothing. Where there is a will, there is a way, and I plan to find a way, with fairness to all, to settle the grip the men think they have on the lifeblood of this colliery,* Arielle thought to herself. She may have been raised in the Big House, but deep in her heart she felt the pangs of her countrymen. For them, mining was an inevitable cycle of generation after generation and there was no way out. They had been reared to faithfully follow what they had been taught and knew, and, God love them, they knew the mines.

Chapter Twenty-Four

Nantymoel, Wales
In South Cymru

Arielle's night's sleep was interrupted periodically as she shifted about making adjustments to the covers and the mattress in her bedroom. Fiona had freshened all of the linens but she was surprised to find that her room at the Big House felt like a stranger. She was longing to be back in America and close to William. She snuggled with her pillow and imagined William's scent on the pillowcase. She closed her eyes as she drew in the image of him, his blue eyes, his dark, wavy brown hair, the cleft in his chin, the subtle pulse of the muscle in his cheek when something aggravated him, and the way her mouth burned with fire when he kissed her. Tingling sensations surged through her veins. *If all goes well with the miners' association tomorrow, I can be on my way before the week's close,* she mused as the dreamy warmth of her bed and sweet thoughts of William sent her into slumber.

The next morning, a prescient dream awakened Arielle and readied her with confidence for the day's agenda. *All will be well,* she assured herself as Fiona fussed about preparing her toilette and seeing to her gown and accessories. In her dream, there was amicable conversation, and a vision of handshakes, nodding, and smiles. *This meeting will go well for it must. I want to make Father proud, but I also want to take pride in myself that I was able to enter the domain of men and accomplish the goal I set forth.* She smiled as she viewed herself in the mirror and smoothed down the fabric on her dress made of silk moiré in a soft raspberry shade. Its watermarks created by the varying tension in the weave of the warp and weft of the fabric gave a shimmer that bounced light about the surface of the cloth. *This is a happy dress. It will serve my mood well today.*

"Well, Miss Arielle, today's a big day fer ye and I want ye to know that I fer one wish ye well."

"Thank you, Fiona. It will be to both of our advantages for my meeting to be successful for then we can venture back across the Atlantic. I miss my life there and I am very concerned about my mum. The last post I received from my father was very vague. He probably did not want to worry me. I hope we find that she has vastly improved when we return."

"I ken tell ye Miss, that will surely be me hope fer Lady Hargrove too."

N esbitt met Arielle at the Big House. With assistance from the footman, they boarded her father's carriage and instructed the driver to take them to St. David's Church. Benjamin George, her father's solicitor had suggested that they return to their original meeting place for their talks with several members of the miners' association. It was a convenient and neutral location and, by the very nature of its being a house of the Lord, it would hopefully not encourage any scene of violence.

Arielle wanted to settle the existing troubles at the mine as efficiently as possible. The men bowed to her as they refreshed their introductions. After all were seated, she looked to Mr. George to begin the discussion.

"Essentially, you have heard the complaints of the men. Wage is a primary concern in addition to their working conditions," Benjamin George said as he studied Arielle's face for a response.

"We were all pleased that there were no threats directed at the men. We were glad that you didn't stir up their ire and fears by threatening to close down the mine, fire them, or take away their homes," added Gareth Lewis.

"Right ye are, Gareth," said Thomas Davies. "The conditions at the mine are better than they was but they ken be even better for the men. The miners want better pay, better houses, and better livin' so they ken give their chil'ren better educations then they 'ave got. The main thing Miss Hargrove is that we want things to keep improvin' for all the years ahead. This coal business is our life."

"First I want to thank you, Mr. Lewis and Mr. Davies for the commitment you have to the colliery, its workers, and the influence you have on them. I can see that the men feel that you represent their eyes and ears. Although the men expressed themselves in a forcible manner at the meeting last evening, their militancy was subdued, they remained restrained and I credit you for that. I want to discuss the areas of concern and determine an agreement we can reach with the best intentions."

"Thank you, Miss Hargrove. I believe I may speak for all of us gathered here that we appreciate your earnestness," said Benjamin George.

"It is important to my father, myself, and Paul the Overman that the men have every facility of convenience and comfort that can reasonably be provided and applied. I assure you we will persevere with untiring efforts to revisit issues raised by the workers as time progresses. We understand the feeling of isolation that can occur when living in a village and there is a closeness that develops among the villagers and a need for equality. For now, the issues of wages and safety are two concerns that deserve our immediate focus."

Gareth and Tommy looked at each other and nodded in agreement. They felt the concerns of the workers were well known to them from previous association meetings and that their opinions were fairly presented the night before. Arielle noted their agreement and spoke briefly and to the point.

"Our goal is to disarm antagonism and worry. We want to work with fairness to all and keep communication open. We feel this is the only way to maintain proper relations and avoid disaster for owners and workers alike. Solidarity is a mainstay for a first-class business and first-class work."

Both Gareth and Tommy were pleasantly surprised by Arielle's knowledge of the colliery business and they equally admired her ability to negotiate with them. After several hours of intense discussion and a protracted back and forth of the issues in an effort to seek their common ground, all of the parties involved were able to find a mutually satisfactory resolution. The men came to see Arielle as a strong, yet fair-minded, woman who was well-prepared to stand her ground in a man's world. They also knew deep in their hearts that they and the other men, although they talked tough, wanted to avoid a strike lest they be left for weeks or months without wages to support their families. Arielle was relieved that both sides maintained a civil manner and that a strike was averted.

"We have your good word on this? About the raise in wages, that is?" asked Gareth.

"You have not only her good word but I have drawn up papers here that will be signed by all parties to bind us to these terms," said Benjamin George as he ushered forth the papers for signing.

Signing ensued and a mutual good feeling seemed to reign as the men shook hands and bowed to Arielle. She had effectively erased any doubt that her father would not support her actions. They had signed a contract, an agreement to raise wages, to form committees to monitor any future safety concerns, and to establish an Injury Relief Fund to aid families should their main wage earner fall victim to an injury that kept him from the workplace. Her work was done for now. She breathed a huge sigh of relief knowing she could safely report to her father that the colliery would continue to operate with a healthy profit margin.

Nesbitt suggested that they stop into the Double Duchess and enjoy a light repast and some ale. Arielle accepted the offer. She was quite elated to be done with negotiations and happy to move on to lighter subjects although her mother's health weighed heavy on her mind. Thoughts of William were the saving grace helping her to maintain her calm.

In the far corner of the pub sat a lively group of men with their full tankards hoisted in the air. They were singing a robust rendition of a song very familiar to Arielle. She had heard it sung on many occasions by the pit workers as they made their way home united both in voice and by the grime on their faces from an honest day's work. Over the rough-hewn wood table, an occasional splash of ale took flight as they swayed to and fro in song. Their voices formed a harmonious blend as smooth as freshly churned butter. Some took the lead, baritone, and tenor vocals, while others sang base in their native Welsh, then began a second round in English.

> I am a little collier and gweithio underground
> The raff will never torri when I go up and down
> It's bara when I'm hungry
> And cwrw when I'm dry
> It's gwely when I'm tired
> And nefoedd when I die
>
> I am a little collier and working underground
> The rope will never break when I go up and down
> It's bread when I'm hungry
> And beer when I'm dry
> It's bed when I'm tired
> And heaven when I die.

Big smiles and the clanking of tankards added to the general feeling of bonhomie shared by the men who were not only the lifeblood of Nantymoel, but also the heartbeat of Hargrove Colliery.

Arielle watched the men from afar, neither wanting to engage in conversation with them nor put a damper on their celebration. *Good news certainly travels quickly in this village,* she mused. They sang the song through a second time then raised their glasses in a salute as they chanted: "What do we value we might be asked and the answer is always true. We value our famblies, our lives, our jobs, our friends, that's as clear as the sky is blue."

She and Nesbitt finished their victuals of roasted beef and potato mash. Nesbitt took the last swig from his mug of ale. Arielle had opted for a glass of claret, which she finished and declined a refill when Dolly the barmaid swept by their table with a towel in hand to wipe up an errant spill on the table beside them. Arielle took in the scene. Here were common folk enjoying one another's company, hardworking folk trying to make ends meet, and all of them were taking a moment and some of their hard earned money to pause and celebrate what they had. Arielle was glad to be a part of the reason for their celebration and although she was quite ready to return to America, she worried about what would greet her there in the days ahead.

Chapter Twenty-Five

Washington, District of Columbia

A listair was descending the stairway when he heard bold voices coming from the parlor. He recognized the tone of Alexandra's voice laced with the sour notes she was wont to cast about. Then the refined accent of his homeland surfaced. He knew the voice to be that of Arielle Hargrove who was trying to subdue Alexandra with little effect. Next he heard the repetitive language of Simon Peabody coming to the aid of Miss Hargrove. Simon was becoming so excited that his words became a series of stutters. *Ah, Miss Hargrove has returned from her trip abroad,* thought Alistair. *No wonder Miss Whitaker's ire has been raised. She has adopted her usual form. This should be great fun to witness!* Alistair picked up his step and raced down the staircase.

Emma's voice could be heard as she spoke up to intervene on behalf of Arielle and Simon, but Alexandra was not to be silenced. Alexandra attempted to gain support from Simon for her condition by blaming Emma's nephew. Simon was taken aback and so was Emma. She could not believe that Alexandra was making her personal life an open book. *It is so sad to me that the girl simply shows no shame. Here she is airing her dirty laundry for all to see.* Until this moment, Simon had not been aware that Alexandra was with child. *She has stooped to the lowest, yes the lowest, yes, yes, yes, the lowest of lows. Low, low, low, not much lower can she go!* Simon fumed. He had listened to all he could of Alexandra's latest claims. He was tired of her bullying and could not hold back his tongue.

"My, my, yes my indeed. You could use an elixir of some proportions to improve your personality, yes indeed. It cannot be easy, no, it cannot be easy being you, and please forgive me for saying so, indeed, forgive me, for it is difficult enough being around you." Simon flinched as Alexandra moved toward him. He feared she was ready to strike out with her hands as well as her words.

"So, it seems you have deemed yourself my personal alchemist. How fine and charming of you, little man. While you are mixing up potions, why don't you work on one that will grow you to a proper height? I am quite surprised you have not slipped into a mole hole as you conducted your work in the garden, or perhaps you have and even the moles have cast you out."

"Say what you will if it pleases you to do so, yes indeed, if it pleases you. I have had to put up with worse than you in my lifetime, yes indeed, that is true. You are the one who must fear being shunned for your condition out of wedlock, yes indeed, that is true. My mother for one would hiss you."

Simon was feeling uncomfortable with his verbal exchange with Alexandra. Rudeness was not his favorite companion yet he found her behavior appalling. She held her ground and was not about to mellow. It was unlike him to become confrontational, but she had pushed him to his limit by making accusations that upset Arielle. He adored her and would not see her harmed physically or emotionally. Emma felt like a referee at a boxing match and was ready to send the fighters to their respective corners. Arielle closed her eyes and took a deep breath. She had been back from Wales for a very short time and had looked forward to her visit with Emma yet here she was back in the throws with Alexandra as though she had never left. *Some things never change and Alexandra is one of them!* Her thoughts railed around and around inside her head.

"I forget, Alexandra. What is your purpose for being here? Ah, yes, I guess you thought that perhaps you would find William here. Well, I hate to disappoint you but he was called away by a client so you have wasted your time and ours."

"Well said, Miss Arielle, well said, yes indeed, well said," muttered Simon.

"You are both ignorant if you think that I would 'waste my time' as you say and stop here on the mere chance that William would be here. I have many more important things to do than make such unscheduled visits. Actually, and not that this is the business of any one of you, I came here expressly to see Mr. Drake. Is that not the truth, Mr. Drake? Have we not discussed the truth in the past?"

Alistair stood at attention wondering where Alexandra was going with her comments. She was being so loose-lipped, he wondered if next she would be calling out the name of Calvin Layton. *Has the girl gone mad? I thought that 'truth' was ours and ours alone to do with as we discussed. Surely she is not going to tell the world that which we have agreed to hold secret...is she?*

"Oh, right you are Miss Whitaker. How clumsy of me to have forgotten."

"Truth? Truth? What truth could you possibly, yes, possibly have at your disposable? Why the word, yes, the very word must be totally foreign to you!" Simon's body rose up then settled back down.

"My word, you look like a hot air balloon, all puffed up and ready to take flight. If you do not exercise caution, you may end up like Pilâtre de Rozier's poor passengers who came crashing down to their deaths! Let me see, do you resemble the sheep, the duck, or the rooster?" Alexandra was particularly pleased with herself to draw upon knowledge she had recently read in her monthly issue of Godey's Lady's Book.

Emma was finding her status as referee a particular challenge. There seemed no relenting on Alexandra's part. Her pregnancy was not softening her with maternal instincts. She was more determined than ever to cast disdain among those in her midst, particularly toward Simon.

"Alexandra, Mr. Peabody does not mean to be unkind but I must say that I cannot bear the direction your conversation is going and must ask that we all remain civil with one another at the very least. As you know well enough, I expect everyone within the walls of Chestnut Heights to be treated with respect. I cannot emphasize that enough. Additionally, we have a new boarder arriving at any moment and I would not want him to happen upon this ill-natured scene." Emma was ready to ask Alexandra to leave if her behavior did not take a turn for the better. She hesitated a moment to watch Alexandra's reaction to her words as Alistair spoke up.

"Pardon me all, but I cannot resist joining in the fray. If you would like Mrs. Willard, I will set her on a proper course. Perhaps I could take you aside Miss Whitaker and interview you to set the story line for my new novel. I think I shall title it, *The Capitol Shrew*, yes that will serve me quite well. I shall set the story in this nation's capital at the Capitol building and have the antics of congressmen and senators create a mystery about the shrew's questionable past. It should make for a lovely quagmire of clandestine affairs and politics, not that that is anything new to the world of politics in my country or yours!"

Alexandra was ready to stomp her foot like a bull ready to charge a scarlet-cape-wielding matador. Her patience had worn thin with the sword fight of words in which she was forced to participate and she was not certain whether Alistair was making fun of her or trying to divert attention away from her condition. Whatever his purpose, she was losing the parlay and knew the only way to regain her win was to exit the premises and devise a new strategy. She had hoped, as Arielle thought, that William would be at his aunt's. *No wonder I did not find him at home. Off with a client when I need him. Oh, this makes me so angry! He is becoming more and more thoughtless when it comes to my needs!*

"You know, you all bore me to tears! The whole lot of you! And Mr. Drake, you disappoint me for I thought we had soothed over some of our differences and formed an alliance of sorts, yet here you are teasing me as deliberately as the others. I have absorbed all of the insults I can for one day! I shall take my leave!"

Much to her chagrin, no one begged Alexandra to remain. Their unified silence fanned the flames of her discontent and added greatly to her bruised ego. Just as she approached the front door a loud knock sounded from the other side. She stepped away and backed into a corner in the foyer not wanting to be mistaken for the hired help. Soon Thomas was rounding the corner and greeted the visitor welcoming him inside. Emma stepped into the foyer and quickly regained the smile that had left her face while she dealt with Alexandra.

"Welcome to Chestnut Heights. I take it that you are Carson Cromwell."

"You are quite correct, madam."

"Do you prefer to be called Mr. Cromwell?"

"I will assume that I am among friends and should say that you may forego my formal name and call me Ziggy. That will be quite all right by me."

"Very well, Ziggy. I am Emma Willard."

"It is a pleasure to meet you although, as I look about at the worried expressions on the faces before me, I must wonder, I haven't picked a proper time to come have I?"

"Your timing is fine, Ziggy. Your arrival is being met with great anticipation. Let me introduce your niece, Miss Arielle Hargrove. I understand that Miss Pennybacker filled you in by post about the circumstances of her birth and adoption by your sister and her husband, Sir Ian Hargrove. Everyone present here is aware of this information that we only learned last year thanks to the efforts of Miss Pennybacker and her assistant, Agnes Fielding whom you met when they visited you in Shoreditch, I believe. That is the correct location is it not, Arielle?"

"Yes, Emma. You have remembered everything very well. Should we announce Mr. Cromwell's arrival to Sully?" Arielle queried as she turned to face her uncle. "I know he is anxious to meet you, sir."

"Sir? My word. I am in hopes that you will feel comfortable, I mean I would be most gratified to have you call me Uncle."

Arielle thought for a moment. She had not ever met this man, but he had a warmth about him, a street smarts that made her feel at once at ease."

"Yes, I think I would quite like that, Uncle. Would you prefer Uncle Carson or Uncle Ziggy?"

"Might I say that we should keep things simple and all stick with the name I have come to associate with myself so, Uncle Ziggy it is."

"Uncle Ziggy! Uncle Ziggy!" Alexandra and Alistair formed a chorus as they shouted his name in unison. Alexandra shouted with alarm for she had no idea that an uncle existed in Arielle's realm and Alistair shouted because he had first heard Ziggy's name when he and Sully met with Morgan Pennybacker. Now, here he was in the flesh.

Emma and the others stared at the two of them. The assembly was forming an unwitting cast of characters and the fact that Alexandra was still in their midst was generating additional angst. Simon, rather than lift his wire-rimmed eyeglasses up onto the bridge of his nose, let them rest a slipped distance down, which forced him to squint as he looked up at the gathering, his nose raised in the air. He resembled a groundhog sniffing the atmosphere about him and the image brought a subdued smile to Arielle's face.

"And, might I make an observation? You people are mad I tell you and I adore it!" Alistair boldly exclaimed. "So, the infamous Ziggy has been found! Brilliant! Well done, old chap! I bet you led Miss Pennybacker on quite an adventure, especially if she had to endure some of the sights in Shoreditch! And to think we have you here and then we have your sister's revelations and Miss…"

"That is quite enough Alistair," Emma cut his words to the quick. She was afraid his next words would be to relate Alexandra's news, which she felt would be most inappropriate. Alistair realized he was becoming carried away with excitement as he relived all that had transpired of late.

"I should say, it's rotten luck you're having but there are so many potential stories here, it will take me months to sort them out!" Alistair beamed at the prospects.

Emma feared that his statement meant he would remain indefinitely in America, which she hoped would not be the case. She had never evicted anyone from her home but there was a first time for everything. She signaled for Thomas and instructed him to locate Sully and bring him into the grand parlor. Within a few minutes, Sully entered the room with Arianna. She had one arm through his and in his other hand he carried her box of painting supplies. Although one never knew who would be on the premises at Chestnut Heights, she and Sully were surprised to see Alexandra and Arielle in the same room since they knew that they were at odds with one another once again. Then their eyes went to the stranger in the room. Sully felt immediately that this must be Elsbeth's brother. He saw the resemblance they held with one another and knew he was among family.

Ziggy realized he was staring at his nephew and worked to capture the words caught in his throat. He wanted to voice the thoughts he had not been able to share for all these many years. Now, here he was. No longer the little boy he had watched at play. Here was a handsome man he hoped to know better and he hoped to retrieve the time lost between them. *God bless you, dear Bobbie, for telling me the truth that brings me to this day. And God bless Miss Pennybacker for finding me and seeking the answers. It is a day to revel in the joy of what has been found.*

All were quiet as they watched the long-awaited reunion. Gracefully, Arielle strode beside Sully, the swish of the crinolines under her gown made a hypnotic sashay. She paused and looked to Arianna with a smile.

"My dear sister, it is my pleasure to introduce you to Sully's and my uncle, Mr. Cromwell. He has made a long journey to be with us. He has come not only to be at my mum's side but also importantly, he has come to finally meet Mr. Sullivan, I mean, Mr. Bamford. You can all see that it is taking me some time to get used to his new identity. Nonetheless, Uncle Ziggy, this is my beautiful sister, Arianna and with her is your nephew, Sully."

Arianna nodded her head as she released her hand from Sully's arm to free him to greet his uncle. The two men stood statue still for a few moments until Ziggy broke the silence.

"This is a day that I have treasured the thought of for so many years. I understand that Miss Pennybacker relayed to you that upon learning of your birth and adoption when my dear wife was on her deathbed, I would on occasion visit your father's timber farm. Oh, not so that anyone knew. I kept my distance. I just had to have a look at the young man that was of my sister's flesh. I was trying so hard to understand what she could possibly have been thinking when she gave you up. I can tell you that she had to have been very scared and she must have thought that you would have a better life if she let you go. Elsbeth is not a cruel person. I am sure she felt it was the best thing she knew to do at the time. In hindsight, she would probably make a different choice. I hope you can forgive her for her decision but that, of course, is solely up to you."

Sully was neither about to declare his feelings about his birth mother before her brother, a man he was coming face-to-face with for the first time, nor with the audience surrounding him. It would take some time to feel a bond with him and to think of him as family. And, he was working very hard to find any level of acceptance or forgiveness for his mother for her actions. His emotions were still very raw. He wanted to touch Ziggy, to shake his hand, to welcome him into his life, but something held him back.

Arianna studied Sully's face and could see the conflict in his eyes. The room was held in awkward silence until she took Sully's hand and the two stepped forward toward Ziggy. She smiled at Ziggy and lifted Sully's hand forward in a gesture of goodwill. With caution, Ziggy took Sully's hand. Their handshake lasted only a few seconds but it was a first step toward healing, toward getting to know each other, toward coming to terms with the labyrinth of lies and hidden secrets that wreaked havoc with their family, with their lives, with how they would greet tomorrow.

Chapter Twenty-Six

August 1898
Washington, District of Columbia

Emma and her household staff had busied themselves all morning sorting through the variety of items donated by her wealthy friends for delivery to the less fortunate residents of Purdy's Court. Emma, along with her colleagues at the Woman's Home Missionary Society, had taken on as their mission the impoverished area that lay in the shadows of the Capitol. They were determined to aid the indigent souls, many Italian immigrants, who lived day-to-day surviving predominately on the handouts of others. Her friends were instructed to leave household goods with flatware, kitchen knives, bowls, clothing, and non-perishable provisions at the Lucy Webb Hayes Training School for Deaconesses and Missionaries at 1150 North Capitol Street Northwest. The Methodist Episcopal Church ran the training school and Emma had sent Thomas to retrieve the provisions with her driver. Emma had met on many occasions with former President Hayes' wife, Lucy, who was the namesake and first president of the eight-year-old training school. Emma assisted in its operation and lent a hand with funding for the newly built Sibley

Memorial Hospital whose construction in 1895 was very generously underwritten by William J. Sibley.

Her friends did not disappoint her. They had provided multiple boxes laden with clothing for men, women, and children, sacks of shelf-stable food, and blankets, brooms, and toiletries among many other miscellaneous items. Emma knew it would all be welcomed and she instructed her staff to load the boxes into her carriage for transport to First Street. She would have Thomas accompany her driver again today to aid in the distribution of the goods. Emma shook her head as she recalled her last trip to Purdy's Court with Alexandra. *What a trip that was! Why she ever thought to linger in the streets without a chaperone after her vile comments about the place is beyond me. She of all people knew the history there and the "germs and vermin within" as she referred to the residents. My, my, I suppose she learned her lesson and fortunately came to no permanent harm from the man who tried to assault her.*

After examining each box to ensure its contents contained an equal array of provisions, she placed a letter from the Society on the very top. The letter informed the recipients of the source of the donations and contained well wishes that included a bible verse from John 6:35, "Then Jesus declared, I am the bread of life. Whoever comes to me will never go hungry, and whoever believes in me will never be thirsty." As she closed each box lid, she rested her hand on top and shut her eyes as though giving a blessing and sending it off to do the most good by providing for the needs of others. She felt great satisfaction with her volunteer work. It humbled her to help others and see firsthand the improvement she was making in someone else's life. She remembered her mother's recitation of Luke 12:48, "For unto whomsoever much is given, of him shall be much required." She had been blessed with much and placed great expectations on herself to give back to society.

"What's this we have here?" Alistair asked loudly, breaking the silence of the moment. "Are you parting with your belongings? Don't tell me you have fallen on hard times and I will have to find another roof to cover my head! Is that so?" Alistair gave a hearty laugh, then thought about the impropriety of his statement.

Emma was not well pleased. The author was beginning to wear on her nerves and she wondered when he would be taking leave of not only her home but also the Washington area. He had been entertaining for a time but his presence had worn thin like the elbows of the velvet jacket he donned at the dinner hour. Sully and Arianna too were tiring of him. It seemed his only ally of late was Alexandra who Emma noticed had taken a liking to him on her most recent visits to rattle the walls of Chestnut Heights with her abrasive personality and ongoing threats about William's responsibilities toward her.

"Good morning to you, Alistair. My work in the community should come as no surprise to you for you have been aware of my whereabouts on many mornings as I meet with my committee of ladies working diligently to assist families in need. Thomas is going to join my driver to transport these provisions today."

"What they need is to get off their duffs and find decent work so they can feed the mouths of their family without waiting for handouts. As I know well enough, and in my esteemed opinion, you ladies do these people a disservice by providing for them. Their cycle of poverty just keeps perpetuating itself thanks to your helping hands."

"Perhaps you need to learn more about the nature of our work. It goes far beyond the provisions you see before you. We counsel the families, particularly the heads of the households, to help them thrive on their own volitions and to wean them from requiring assistance beyond their doors. You must have similar programs in the United Kingdom." Emma was becoming exasperated and weary having to justify her work, her cause.

"Well, I dare say, I was not meaning to be rude. I just felt the need to voice my opinion."

"I know you did not mean to be unkind, however, perhaps you should keep your opinion to yourself in this house for I have found that unsolicited advice is rarely welcomed against the ear of the recipient."

"Touché. A point well made. I would think your work contributes to your good standing in the community and keeps your name in the news, which cannot be a bad thing. In my line of work publicity is always a good thing whether good or bad. It keeps my name in the public view." Alistair lifted his torso like a proud peacock ready to strut about.

"You know Alistair, there are times when one has to go for the cause, not to get publicity, or recognition, or your name in the morning news. For me, even with all of my associations over the years with politicians, this is not political. I feel strongly that it is important to just think how you can help others and feel you are blessed that you can do this. It is an enormous way to count your blessings."

A thoughtful look overcame Alistair's face. He pondered for a moment Emma's words and her obvious dedication to her cause. She had been equally kind to him by welcoming him into her home and insisting that he be spoken about in a respectful way. He must respect her and her sincerity. A thought came to him.

"I see I have acted irresponsibly by speaking out in this fashion and I would like to make amends. I would like to join Thomas on his trip to deliver the items you have collected. Perhaps the trip will allow me to rethink my opinions and see firsthand the squalor, I mean living conditions, of those you have chosen to assist. Perhaps it will be a way for me to right a wrong. Who knows? I might find a fresh storyline in the midst of these unfortunate folks!"

Emma wanted to tone down Alistair's boisterous response and the only way she could think to do so was to accept his offer and agree for him to travel with Thomas. *Right a wrong? What on earth did he mean by that?* she pondered. *He must mean righting his misconceptions about charity work. If a visit to Purdy's Court will avail him that then so be it.*

"Very well. I appreciate your help and I know Thomas will too. Do follow his instruction for Thomas is very accustomed to driving through the area and back alleyways. You want to be aware of pick-pockets and the like."

"Pickpockets are no strangers to me. We have them all over London, especially near Tower Bridge. I am rather looking forward to being among the likes of costermongers and miscreants. Great characters they all are!"

Emma looked away for a moment as she pursed her lips and rolled her eyes to the side so Alistair would be unaware of her reaction to his words. As her staff removed the boxes from her parlor, she watched Alistair somberly follow along carrying one last box like a pallbearer issued with the task of seeing the dead off on their final journey. The man, like the genre of his writing, was still a mystery to her despite the many weeks he had been a boarder in her home. She felt she had only skimmed the surface of his personality and she was apprehensive about his true reason for wanting to tag along with Thomas. Perhaps time would tell.

His was a gruesome sight to behold. His body was askew in a macabre pose, slumped in a sitting position with his back against the alley's wall, its brown bricks stained with large spurts of blood. His arms were limp at his sides with clots of blood clinging to his chin and dripping down upon his chest from the ghastly slice across his neck that nearly decapitated him. His eyes were bulging wide as though, in the last moments of his life, he had caught the full image of the person who caused the final breath of air to be sucked from him. The greatest quantity of blood appeared to have originated from him, but some may have come from his assailant, for it appeared from surface wounds on his hands that he attempted to struggle, to fight off the one intent on bringing his life to an end. His legs were splayed left and right indicating a loss of ability to stand and protect himself. Here he was, lying defenseless like the women he preyed upon, whom he captured in a weakened position, and with whom he had his unruly way. Now, his time had come to suffer the consequences of his actions.

He was alone except for the company of several rats curiously wriggling their noses at his corpse. And, a parade of beetles had begun to make diverse tracks up his legs and across his torso giving his chest a sense of movement that made it appear that he was breathing. Such was not the case. For Calvin Layton, his life ceased the way he lived it. He had no care or respect for others and seemed to be void of a conscience. A violent end in a dreary alley, left like a lump of discarded garbage, seemed a fitting sentence for the crimes he had inflicted on others. There would be no one to mourn him, no tears to be shed, and no one to celebrate his life. He would be buried as the pauper he had become. After Sully, who underwrote their rent and provisions, had moved from the brownstone they shared, Cal relegated himself to the lower classes and came to linger among the other vermin of Purdy's Court.

"I say, Thomas," Alistair shouted as he came running out of breath toward the carriage, "Do you have a moment? There is something I need for you to see."

Thomas signaled the driver to hold back the horses as he stepped from the carriage. As he approached Alistair, he observed what appeared to be blood on his hands and wondered if he had injured himself delivering some of the boxes. Not wanting to overstep his authority, he began to speak with an ounce of caution.

"Yez, Mr. Drake. What ken I do for you sir?"

"Over there, in the alley. It's a rather wicked sight but I didn't know what to do. I am not of this land and so I'm not quite sure how you chaps handle these sort of messes."

Thomas was confused by Alistair's comments. *Messes?* Thomas wondered if he had spilled a box of provisions and was unable to pick the items up by himself. The smear of red on his hands added to the confusion.

"Come along, man. You need to have a look!"

Alistair was becoming agitated. His face was turning red as though his blood pressure was sky high and his arms were beginning to shake. Thomas decided the only way to calm him was to go in the direction he was pointing. Alistair took the lead as Thomas followed, walking along the street then turning into a nearby alleyway. As the two stepped around a large storage container Thomas saw the "mess" to which Alistair referred. His eyes popped nearly as large as the victim's as he took in the scene before him. He was at a loss for words and wanted to exit the area as quickly as he could before he was accused of having anything to do with what appeared to be a violent attack that resulted in murder. He had been in Purdy's Court last year when Alexandra was attacked and he wanted no part of the lynch mob that was certain to form around him.

"I dun't know nothin' 'bout this, Mr. Drake. We's gots to get out o' here and I mean now." Thomas could hear footsteps getting closer and the sound of voices. A window shade lifted, then the window slid up and a head looked out over the sill.

"What are you men doing down there? What has happened? Oh, my god!"

Thomas could think of nothing but to flee. He ran from the alley and back up the street to the carriage. Alistair saw several men and women walking toward him. As they got closer and closer, he too fled, following in Thomas' wake. They both jumped into the carriage before the entourage exited the alley and entered the street. The coast was clear for their getaway as Thomas motioned the driver to have the horses step along quickly. Thomas caught his breath and turned to Alistair.

"Mr. Drake, please excuse me for askin' this but how did you get that blood on yer hands?" Thomas asked cautiously not wanting to overstep his position, but he could not let go of the gory vision playing in his mind's eye.

"Are you accusing me of something, Thomas?"

"Oh, no sir, I's not. I's just curious is all." Thomas' limbs began to shake. He was glad to be sitting in the carriage for he feared his legs would fail him if he tried to stand. Though he knew Alistair Drake to be somewhat eccentric in his ways and speech, and he had heard talk that his novels involved mysteries, he did not think murderer comprised his ilk. Perhaps he was mistaken.

"Well, sometimes it is best to mind one's own business. I assume you have no objections to that? But, if you must know, when I discovered the man in the alleyway, I went over to him to see if I could offer him any aid and then I saw that was a moot point. I suppose that is how the blood ventured to my hands."

"All right, all right then," said Thomas who was less than satisfied with Alistair's explanation. For now, he was relieved to be away from Purdy's Court and the dead man in the alley, but he wholeheartedly wished that, if the need arose, someone else could vouch for him besides Alistair Whitfield Drake.

Alistair sat back to catch his breath. He too felt relieved to be seated in the carriage and on his way back to Chestnut Heights. He wondered why he felt no remorse for the dead man. But, how could he feel remorse? He knew the man and he knew what he had done. Calvin Layton had gotten what he deserved and there was no more to be said.

As the crowd grew around the victim's body, a doorway several yards away opened presenting a female with a head of coiffed blonde hair. She watched as the men and women turned to one another in animated conversation, some in fear, as they questioned the scene before them. Several uniformed officers arrived and began making inquiries hoping to find witnesses to the attack. She heard them ask if anyone knew the victim's name. She knew, but she would neither shout out his name nor come forward with any details. Seeing him lying there lifeless brought her comfort. He had gotten the comeuppance he richly deserved. She was grateful, and as a smile began to form on her lips, she realized that the gathering had distracted her from the crimson fluid that had run onto her hand. As she prepared to put on her dark gray gloves, the sight of blood startled her. *How could I be so careless? How could this have happened? Now what am I to do? I must wipe my hand free or be accused of some wrongdoing.* Alexandra lifted her gown to its underside and wiped her hand clean. Satisfied with her impromptu and rudimentary toiletry she covered her hands with her gloves and discreetly walked in the opposite direction of Calvin Layton's body. *This is a day to rejoice,* she thought as she accelerated her step to her waiting carriage and reflected on the man who molested her. *He was an evil man and his fate has been sealed with evil.* Uncharacteristically she shuddered. She was glad Cal had met his end but she worried about the part she had played in his demise.

***

Retaliation was becoming a theme with Alexandra and remained paramount on her mind. Her anger for Arielle had only been subdued by her anger for Calvin Layton. And, then there was William. She could never be fully angry with him, but she knew she had plenty of anger to go around and she would not spare William her wrath. There was a wedding on the horizon and now she was free to focus all of her energies in that direction. *Oh yes, there will soon be church bells ringing but I swear they will not be in celebration of Arielle's wedding vows. Oh no, for I have my own vow to honor and that is to be certain that William is saved solely for me and no other.*

Alistair sat in the parlor at Chestnut Heights. He had been sitting for quite some time but he still felt short of breath. The visit to Purdy's Court had drained him of the fervor he needed to approach Alexandra. He felt compelled to talk with her as quickly as time would allow. He was determined to question her about her day in Purdy's Court. As he fled the scene, he saw someone who resembled her slip from the alleyway into a door not far from Cal's body. *Could she be a cold-blooded killer? How could she have the strength to administer such a severe slice to that Layton chap's neck? Adrenaline is a mighty force,* Alistair thought. *Weaker souls have found amazing strength in times of need. And, meanwhile, I believe Thomas thinks I am the one who perpetrated the attack on Layton.* Alistair trembled as he imagined Alexandra's actions. Although he sensed that Thomas suspected he had some involvement in the attack on Cal, as far as Alistair knew, Thomas was holding his tongue and not sharing his suspicions with any others.

Soon after they began delivering the boxes of provisions to the doorways that lined the poverty stricken enclave, Alistair saw a man that resembled Cal staggering as he slipped out of the window of a first-story residence. *Perhaps the chap had already been roughed up a bit. Maybe he was caught unawares by the man of the house as he had his way with the lady of the house? I would say it served him right, but that was a horribly nasty way to go even for scum like him.* Alistair was trying to make sense out of what he had seen and still could not bring himself to fully believe that Alexandra had wielded the knife that killed Cal.

Alexandra sat alone in her bedchamber unable to wash away the mental remnants of Purdy's Court. She was surprised at her reaction to the scene that still played vividly in her mind. *So disgusting, so disgusting, but it had to be. Who could have predicted such an outcome?* From her spot, tucked away behind a partially opened doorway, Alexandra periodically had looked about the alleyway. She saw Alistair walk past Cal who stumbled in the alleyway and she noticed that Alistair looked back at Cal in recognition. She hoped Alistair would not take matters into his own hands and wield the sword of justice he had proclaimed should be dealt when she blurted out Cal's name at Emma's and informed him of her plight. Alistair had been ready to do battle with Cal and for that she was as content as a purring feline. She appreciated someone who appreciated her and, for now, Alistair was her best defense against any of her foe.

⌣‿⌐

Thomas was never happier to see William at the portal of Chestnut Heights. He needed his counsel and could think of no one more appropriate with whom to share his concerns.

"Mr. Clay sir, I's wonderin' if I could talk with you 'bout somethin' that's been troublin' me. It won't take but a minute of your time, sir."

"Of course, Thomas. What is it?" William had not seen Thomas so distraught since last year and the episode with Alexandra in Purdy's Court when Thomas was nearly accused of attacking her.

"Well, Mr. Clay sir, it's like this. You knows the other day when Miz Willard had all those things from the mission to go to those poor folk on First Street? Well, I was with Mr. Drake and I hopes I's not speakin' out o' turn or nothin' but that man they found dead in that alley, well sir, Mr. Drake had blood on his hands and I'm rightly scared that he might jest be the one that killed that man. I mean, we jest ken't have him at Miz Willard's ifin' he's a murderer!"

"Here Thomas, have a seat. I read about the man they found there in the Evening Star. The article in the newspaper said that the authorities do not have a suspect at present. I can see that this is disturbing you. Tell me what you know. Did Mr. Drake give you an explanation about the blood you observed on his hands?"

"Yez sir, he shore did and I's wanted to believe him, yez sir, I's surely did but it jest dun't make no sense to me. Mr. Drake acted like he done knew the man. Do you think he did knows him?"

William pondered the information Thomas was presenting. He needed more information to pursue Thomas' concerns and thoughtfully determined that a conversation with Mr. Drake with no delay was in order. His aunt's welfare and that of her boarders could not be compromised.

"Thomas I appreciate your candor, your honesty that is, as always. Tell me, is Mr. Drake about?"

"Yez sir. I sees him steppin' in the big parlor jest a little bit ago. I thinks he's still in there but I beg you, not to says anythin' to him 'bout what I tolds you."

"You can rest assured that I will not mention our conversation to him. And again, thank you for coming to me with this concern."

William paused to collect his thoughts before he made steps to approach Alistair in the parlor. As he thought of the tactics he would invoke to learn the truth about the day in Purdy's Court, William paraphrased a quote of George Washington's he recalled from his days in law school, 'Offensive operations, often times, are the surest, if not the only means of defense.' He prepared himself as though he were ready to do battle in the courtroom. He took a deep breath, cleared his throat and made his opening statement.

"Ah, Mr. Drake. Just whom I was hoping to see."

"I say young fellow, to what do I owe this honor? Or, should I refer to you as Your Honor?"

"Quite unnecessary, I assure you. You flatter me, Mr. Drake. Although there may be some judgments handed down today, I, personally, do not hold the status of judge in the courtroom."

"Judgments? My, my, you are taking on a serious tone. Would you like to explain yourself?"

"Well, I am well aware that you appreciate a great mystery and create many of your own. I was reading an article in the Evening Star about the murder of a man in Purdy's Court. Curiously, the murder occurred the same day you and Thomas were delivering items for my aunt's charity. I wonder if either of the two of you were aware of any commotion or any other details that would be pertinent to this case? I understand it is yet to be solved."

"You sir, are not accusing me of a crime are you?"

"Oh, my goodness no. But why are you so quick to ask?"

Alistair held back his retort as Thomas entered the room to announce a guest. Before he could get the words out of his mouth, Alexandra swept into the room, albeit at a somewhat slower pace than usual given her condition. She smiled as she took in the vision of her handsome William Clay.

"William, it is true you *are* here! Why, when Thomas told me you were here I thought what wonderful luck this day has brought me! "

"Good afternoon, Alexandra. What brings you?"

"Well, what a pathetic welcome that is. Not, 'How wonderful to see you, Alexandra' or 'My, you look wonderful, Alexandra.' What is the matter with you that you have lost all sense of grace and gentlemanly charm?"

"Forgive me, Alexandra, but Mr. Drake and I were having a discussion before you entered so abruptly. Let's begin again. Alexandra, you look lovely. Now, what brings you to Chestnut Heights?"

Alexandra's temper began to settle. She had received a compliment from William even though she had to pry it from him, but she was less than sure that she wanted to broach the subject in William's presence that she had come to discuss with Alistair.

"How have you been getting on?" Alistair inquired, thinking it was important to acknowledge her condition without saying the socially inappropriate word 'pregnancy.'

"Thank you for asking, Mr. Drake. I am feeling quite well. So, if I may be so bold as to ask, what is it that has you two so entwined in conversation? May a lady enter your realm?"

"My dear Miss Whitaker, Mr. Clay was inquiring about my trip to Purdy's Court with Thomas and that rather rabid story in the news about that poor chap that met his death the very same day. Quite a murky mess, if I do say."

Alexandra was taken aback. She had come to discuss that very topic with Alistair and had no idea the story would stir an interest in William. *Why has he focused on that story? What could any of this mean to him to garner his sudden interest?*

"Why the distressed look, Alexandra? You look as though you have seen a ghost." William studied her expression and waited for her response.

"I feel that I am being cross-examined, William. Really, this is not a courtroom. You can only imagine how distressing that news story was for me. Why just one year ago I could have been left in an alley with my throat slit if not for Thomas coming to my aid. And to think, Sully roomed with that low-life..." Alexandra's words trailed off as she realized her blunder. As far as she knew, William was unaware of anyone's connection to Calvin Layton and she preferred to keep it that way. *This pregnancy must be taxing my brain. I cannot believe I was so foolish to let this slip. Now what to say?*

"What is that you say, Alexandra?" William queried and prepared to probe further.

"Oh, I mean, how odd of me to say such a silly thing. Sometimes I wonder where my mind goes. I meant to say I wonder if Sully has heard the story of that low-life? Perhaps we should summon him."

"Alexandra, you are acting quite unusual. I see no need to bother Sully. Now, if you do not mind, I will continue my discussion with Mr. Drake. Sir, let me rephrase my question. When you and Thomas were at Purdy's Court, did you witness anything in relation to the murder of the man found? Did you witness the deceased?"

Alistair held his silence for a few moments as he worked to craft his response. He could not in good conscience reveal Alexandra's secret, yet he knew if William made any inquiries of Thomas that he would undoubtedly mention the blood he saw. And, Alistair knew it was Alexandra he saw in the alley. *Oh, why could I not have spoken with her before Mr. Clay became involved? I need time to sort all of this out.*

"Mr. Drake, is this question confusing for you? Why the delay in responding?"

"No, no, Mr. Clay. What do you mean by witness exactly?"

"That seems an odd question from a writer of mysteries. Do you truly need the word defined for you or, as they say in your country, are you just having a go with me?"

Alistair began slowly to speak as Emma entered the room. A sign of relief came over him as he looked to Alexandra for moral support and an opening to escape William's line of questioning. He knew he needed a way out and the sooner the better.

"Pardon me for intruding, but what is this I hear about a murder in Purdy's Court? Seems a very glum discussion to be having on such a glorious day. You should be out in the garden. Arianna and Sully are there with Simon taking in the beauty of the perennials that have not fully lost their blooms. Oh, Alexandra, I did not see you there dear. I hope you are feeling well. Now, back to the murder. I have not yet read the news story. What was the man's name? Are you discussing this because he is someone known to us?"

"Actually, Aunt Emma, I realized that the day the donations that you and your woman's guild collected were delivered to Purdy's

Court is one and the same with the day the man was found dead. I was merely curious to learn whether Mr. Drake or Thomas might have witnessed something that may have seemed innocuous at the time but could have bearing on the case."

"Well, that is interesting. Tell me, what was the man's name?"

In unison, as though they were making a knee jerk reaction to Emma's inquiry William, Alistair and Alexandra responded, "Calvin Layton." Alistair and Alexandra cut their eyes at one another shocked that either of them were prompted to answer. Emma stared at the trio finding it curious that they all spoke at once. *What in the devil is the matter with me?* Alexandra asked herself as she looked to Alistair who appeared to have the same question forming on his lips. *I mustn't be involved in any part of this discussion,* she reprimanded herself as she waited to see who would speak next.

"May I have a moment with Miss Whitaker?" Alistair asked and signaled Alexandra to walk with him into the foyer. William and Emma looked at each other then cut their eyes toward the two in transit from the room.

"Before I answer Mr. Clay's inquiries, I must ask you a question. That day, in Purdy's Court, I saw you. Why were you there?" Alistair asked Alexandra in a very hushed tone.

"Excuse me? Are you suggesting that I had something to do with Cal's death? I came here today to talk with you and ask the very same question? I saw you in the alley when Cal walked past you and you turned to look at him. You must have recognized him from the time you and Sully saw him on F Street. You are the one who told me that he should be brought to justice for what he did to me! You are the one!"

"You know I was there strictly to deliver the donations for Mrs. Willard. I had no other purpose or agenda but I must ask if you did? I clearly recall your words that you would see to it that he pay for his actions against you."

"I did have an agenda, but it went awry. I really do not know why I am even talking with you about this. This is ridiculous. Just when I thought we were friends you accuse me of murder!"

"Keep your voice down or we will have the wrath of the household upon us." Alistair's words had barely left his mouth when William and Emma entered the foyer. Emma gave a stern look to them both. William had shared Thomas' concerns without naming him. He had kept his promise to Thomas although he knew his aunt was savvy enough to put the pieces together to know the source of his information. She would hold that confidence but she would not have the plague of worry overtake her household. She had asked her nephew why the name of the murdered man was familiar to her and then remembered that Sully, one day in a passing comment, had briefly mentioned the name of his former housemate. Now, Alexandra and Alistair were acting oddly in tandem and she was determined to unlock the reason for their mysterious behavior.

"What on earth is going on? With all of this whispering you appear to be hiding something. Both of you need to come back into the parlor at once and reveal what you know." Emma uncharacteristically commanded Alexandra and Alistair to follow her orders and the two took heed and walked toward the parlor like prisoners about to meet their final fate.

Chapter Twenty-Seven

Emma and Alexandra took their seats on opposing settees while William and Alistair stood on either side of the fireplace like sentries posted to keep watch over the realm. Emma stared first at Alexandra. Her head was tilted down and her eyes were closed as though she were in prayer, which Emma seriously doubted, and then she turned her attention to Alistair.

"This is quite enough. There appears to be much more to this topic and I will not stand for any more nonsense. Do I need to call the authorities or can we discuss this civilly?" Emma queried as she awaited a response.

Alexandra was indeed not praying. She felt trapped and closed her eyes in an attempt to manage the multitude of thoughts racing about in her head. *Oh, that Calvin Layton has ruined my life! I can feel no remorse for he has gotten exactly what he deserved!*

"Well, Mr. Drake, if you want a roof over your head tonight, I think it is time for us to share all that we know," Alexandra said as she took a deep breath and continued. "But how could I possibly be expected to feel badly about the loss of someone so despicable?"

"You say the word despicable with such authority. What brings you to this degree of hatred for this man?" Emma inquired, wondering how Alistair and Alexandra had come to know the deceased.

"Perhaps you should go first Mr. Drake since you have been so intent on broaching the subject. I would be quite content to let the topic drop to the wayside as it should without involving others."

Alistair was taken aback. If he were to tell his side of the story it would implicate Alexandra. *Why does she want me to speak first? She must wholeheartedly believe that I am the one who led the evil chap to his death. What more is she hiding?*

"Are you certain Miss Whitaker, that you want me to reveal all that I know? You seriously want all the wretched details to be spread about?"

"I would suggest that you proceed before Mr. Clay and Mrs. Willard tire of your delay."

"Very well, as you wish, although I do not think it is my place to tell." Alistair was tiring of Alexandra's repellent personality. *However, if she wants me to explain our focus on this man, then I shall proceed.*

"Please let me begin by saying that things are rarely what they seem. It is with some difficulty in speaking these words aloud that I hesitate to go on for I am concerned that I am breaking a confidence..."

Alexandra could take no more. As far as she was concerned her life was in ruin and she no longer had control of her fate. Her heart raced and her breathing became labored as she looked at Emma and then to William and spoke the words she thought she would never confess.

"If you must know, Calvin Layton is the awful, awful man that caused me to be in the condition that I am in today and I am forever grateful that he is dead and would have it no other way! He raped me! He was the scum of the earth!" Alexandra began to sob.

Stunned silence overtook the room. Emma was the first to move as she walked over to Alexandra, sat next to her and held her in a comforting embrace. William stepped behind the settee and placed his hand on Alexandra's shoulder in a show of support. Alistair stood with his eyes popped and his jaw dropped. He thought Alexandra was prepared to explain how she ended Cal's life, not name the nefarious man as her baby's father. *Perhaps next she will tell the rest of her escapades in Purdy's Court. I for one am curious to know.*

Emma waited for Alexandra to regain her composure. William was trying to process all that he had just heard. He thought Alexandra would never release the name of the man who caused her to be in a family way. An element of guilt washed through him along with anger that someone of his gender would force himself upon her. *How I wish I could have protected her from this assault.* He knew he could not reasonably guard her day-by-day but he felt a strong sense of obligation, a commitment to her father to keep her safe. *Alexandra is her own worst enemy,* William reflected, not wanting to cast blame her way, but knowing her relentless pursuit of him found her making hasty decisions and taking inappropriate actions. *Did she intentionally place herself in harm's way? I hate to admit that I am in agreement with her that thankfully the scoundrel is dead. He saved us from bringing him before the court to face charges and risk soiling Alexandra's name. For that, I am grateful.* He was trying to find a silver lining in Alexandra's revelation. She was with child and that fact would go unchanged. William shook his head. *A man like Calvin Layton most certainly had compromised himself on many occasions and made many enemies in his time. There is no wonder he met the fate to which he was destined.*

Alexandra repositioned herself on the settee, drew in a deep breath and looked to Alistair. She wanted him to continue his explanation for the fateful day in Purdy's Court.

"Mr. Drake, please proceed with your details of Cal Layton's death. We would all like to hear what you were doing in that alleyway." As Alexandra spoke she saw the look of surprise overtake Alistair's face.

"Since you are urging me to do so, I will. As Mrs. Willard is aware, I volunteered to accompany Thomas to deliver donations to the residents of Purdy's Court. Once there, as I was readying myself to leave one of the residences by way of an alleyway, I passed by a chap that looked familiar to me. Upon a second look, I identified him as Calvin Layton whom I had met some time back when

I accompanied Sully, Mr. Bamford, to Miss Pennybacker's shop. At any rate, when I completed my deliveries and was prepared to return to the carriage, I saw Mr. Layton's limp, bloodied body and walked to assist him, but the chap was too far-gone. I am sorry to say that I had some of his blood on my hands and I am afraid I scared Thomas. I had him come see the chap's body to see if we could help but Thomas knew there was no hope and he felt it was urgent for us to return to the carriage and return home to Chestnut Heights. Now, Miss Whitaker, perhaps you can explain the reason for your presence in the alleyway? I saw you in a nearby doorway as I turned to leave the alley."

Emma and William quickly turned their heads to Alexandra. They were both shocked by Alistair's claim that she was anywhere near the murder scene. Alexandra was once again appalled by his suggestion that she was in any way responsible for Cal's demise although she felt she was.

"Well, well, Mr. Drake, is this not a fine way to turn the tables and cast doubt about the nature of my visit to the lower classes of this city? Do you seriously think you were the only one conducting good deeds that day? And, are we to believe what you have to say about the blood on your hands? Why the very knife you delivered to that Mrs. Brown is the very knife that took Mr. Layton's life!"

"Miss Whitaker, who is Mrs. Brown? And, I thought we had grown to become friends, yet you are casting aspersions my way and calling into doubt my verbal documentation of events," said Alistair as he raised himself up into a formal posture.

"It is time the two of you stopped your sparring. Alexandra, you must tell us why you were there that day and what you saw," William ordered as he stepped closer to her to reinforce his determination to have her finish her tale.

"It all began very innocently. When I learned that Mr. Layton was frequenting Purdy's Court, I decided that I was going to confront him about what he had done to me. I suspected that no one would know me there so it would be a discreet place to have it out with him. As I walked down the alley, I saw Mr. Layton enter a residence and I waited for him to come back out. The residence was familiar to me for it is the same one that I visited last year with you, Mrs. Willard. I believe it was the home of Mrs. Brown. You know, the one with all of the mouths to feed living in perpetual squalor. Well, several minutes later, I saw a man that I recognized whom I had hoped to never see again. You remember the man who attacked me last year, the one with the limp? Well, he was one and the same! The same snarly grin, with some teeth missing and the ones remaining tarnished the color of strong tea. I could see the coarse stubble on his face and oh, those hands with the stubby fingers!" Alexandra grimaced as she recalled his appearance. "So, to ensure my safety, I quickly found an alcove to hide in where I could watch where he went and I saw that he entered the same home. The next thing I knew, Mr. Layton and the man were struggling with one another. The man was wielding a large knife and threatening Mr. Layton with it. Then Mr. Layton began to run and the man began chasing him yelling horrible words, calling Mr. Layton all sorts of names and I heard him say, 'You'll pay for this! No one has sex with my wife and gets away with it!' Then he kept yelling, 'I'll kill you, you bastard!' And the next thing I knew, the man, I guess I should call him Mr. Brown since he said the woman was his wife, caught Cal by the arm, swung him around and put the knife to his throat. I could not bring myself to watch the rest. Everything became very quiet. I peeped around the corner of the alcove and could see that Mr. Brown was gone but Mr. Layton was there, sitting propped up against the brick wall perfectly still. I waited in the alcove a few minutes longer and heard footsteps coming into the alley so I held my place. I poked my head out once again as two men hurriedly left the alley and one turned back but it did not occur to me that you saw me. I have been concerned about my role in Mr. Layton's death but not disturbed that he is dead."

"Alexandra what role do you feel you had in his death?" William queried and Emma nodded her head wanting to hear Alexandra's response.

"Why, if I had taken that man to court last year for his assault on me, he would not have been around to attack Mr. Layton. Obviously, without my testimony, the authorities had very little on which to build their case so in that respect, I feel responsible for that man running the streets."

"I can tell you Alexandra that this incident must not remain a secret. I will go with you to the authorities and you may give them a statement about what you saw so they can bring Mr. Brown to justice for his actions. He is a threat to society and must be dealt with. This you cannot let slide. You are a witness to a murder and you, in all good conscience, must come forward."

"Why, oh why must I always be the one coming to the aid of another? When will it end? Now you want me, yet once again, to subject myself to the litter of the lower class when I am most assuredly the victim! What is wrong with you people? William can you not assist me on this? And to think I was concerned about the blood on my hands!"

"Blood? What blood? Are you using this as a euphemism for a greater act you have performed?" William was aghast.

"My goodness no! It is simply that when I turned to leave the alcove, my hand brushed against an exposed nail in the doorframe and broke the skin on my finger. I began to bleed and worried that I would be accused of some wrongdoing so I used the underside of my gown to wipe away the blood so I could freely retreat for my home."

William was surprised that he was inclined to believe Alexandra's depiction of the events in Purdy's Court. He felt empathy for her although, for Arielle's sake, he needed and wanted to distance himself from Alexandra, from her antics, from her high drama. He would speak to the authorities and find a resolution to the case of the murder of Calvin Layton without compromising Alexandra in the process. He would have her and Alistair provide sworn affidavits that would be admissible in court. Hopefully, neither of them would ever have to appear before a judge and jury. He closed his eyes for a moment to reacquaint himself with calm. Peaceful visions began to overtake him as he looked forward to a life away from Alexandra's constant demands and her relentless pursuit of him. Him, the prize she wanted that he knew she would never obtain.

Chapter Twenty-Eight

S tress had gotten the best of Elsbeth and had no doubt led to her decline. Ian's tone, whenever in her presence, and his avoidance of her on many occasions in the weeks past, had fed her spirit with toxins that were eating away at all the good she had left. She had become reclusive, wanting no one to trespass on her solitude, and she preferred the confines of her room above any public display. But, of late, conversing with herself no longer aided in lifting her morale. Her heart felt full of empty hollows. She found the quiet of her space to be akin to the hushed chambers of a tomb where nothing existed but barren walls devoid of life.

For Arielle, visits to her mother's room offered little solace. She was still trying to make sense of the secret her mother had held mute all these years. Her father's assignations had been enough to bear. They at least carried with them the gift of a twin sister. But now, with her mother's revelation, she had a brother of sorts and an uncle she had only recently met. Though of no blood relation, she and Sullivan Bamford shared the only woman she had known as 'Mother' for a score and two years until Morgan Pennybacker's investigation shed a different light on what she had believed to be true. For Sully, his search had led to the same woman to call 'Mother,' if he chose to do so. Arielle closed her eyes and took a deep breath. *This too shall pass,* she said silently aloud as a whisper awakened her quiet.

"Arielle," Elsbeth's voice came methodically slow and soft. "I am so pleased you have come to my room."

"I am sorry. I did not mean to interrupt your slumber. Doc Lovering said it was best for you to rest. I thought I would sit by your side just to keep you company should you need any assistance."

Elsbeth knew by her daughter's tone that she would be present on her own terms. Arielle's voice was aloof, not issuing the warm, loving sounds to which Elsbeth had been accustomed.

Arielle searched her mother's face. It was the worn and weary face of someone she felt she hardly knew. *How could I come to live with two people who have such illustrative pasts? What was God thinking when He placed me in their hands?* Arielle shuddered as another thought crossed her mind. *What other secrets lay hidden that will raise their ugly heads for me to bear? I pray there will be no more surprises on the horizon.*

"No, dear. I am glad you have come," Elsbeth drew shallow breaths as she made every effort to have her words flow. "I know I have already apologized to you but, I fear you are not willing to accept my deep, most sincerest apology for causing further angst to come your way. I had put this in the past and buried it in the far recesses of my mind."

"Mum, the 'this' you mention cannot be put off so lightly. 'This' involves a human being, a person who has feelings, hopes, dreams and desires that have been held captive by a hunt to find you. Keeping 'this' hidden has not served you, him, or any of us well. There are adjustments and acceptances that must be made, but they will not be made over a period of days or weeks. 'This' will take time and inordinate amounts of prayer and patience. And to think I have had an uncle whom you have kept secret from me. If not for Sully's desire to learn more, I might never have learned of Uncle Ziggy."

Arielle was reminded of a time when she sat and chatted with Emma. Emma's sage observations always blanketed her with warmth and optimism. She thought about their discussion regarding the power of prayer and Emma's words, "There's always something in every day that is worthy of prayer, my dear." *Her words are no truer than at this crossroad in my life,* thought Arielle as her eyes held their gaze on the frail vision before her. Although she had not yet crossed the threshold of forgiveness, she hoped her mother would rally. She hoped there would be happier times on the horizon for them all when they would be able to shape some element of acceptance about all that had come before.

She knew her uncle's visit to her mother several days earlier was met with mixed enthusiasm. There was a hurt between them, a blemish that would need to quickly heal if either of them was to let forgiveness prevail before going to their graves. Her mother had seemed to rally after Ziggy's visit, but any elation about her improved condition was short-lived as her health began to plummet. His visit today found their time spent in quiet company. Elsbeth drifted in and out of sleep as her brother kept watch over her and wished he could call back the years they had lost. When Arielle returned to sit with her mother, Ziggy left his sister's room with a heavy heart sensing she was not long for this world.

"Arielle, as I have repeatedly stated," Elsbeth quietly said as she began to cough, "The decision I made a score and ten years ago was made with my best judgment at the time. On reflection, there were perhaps other, more suitable roads for me to have taken. But, the past is the past and I shall not dwell on what might have or should have been."

"Mum, with all due respect, your denial, or ability to forget the past, does not require me to forgive or accept your decisions. I hate to appear so harsh, particularly when you are not well, but I feel compelled to state my feelings."

Elsbeth knew in her heart of hearts there was little of consequence she could say that would divert her daughter's distain with her past. She had been determined to sweep up the rubble that had become part of her life and lay out all the demons to bear the truths, the realities that must be faced before she passed from the earth. She was proud of Arielle, the woman she had become, and her ability to face the challenges at the colliery and come to a successful resolution for the workers with little impact on the financial wings of the business.

A knock came to the door and it opened without the caller waiting for a response from within. Ian stepped into the room. "Oh, ladies, I hope I am not interrupting."

"Oh, no, Father. In fact, I am afraid I am monopolizing Mum's time and making her weary. She will find it refreshing to have you join her and I will take my leave."

Suddenly, Elsbeth became very agitated. She began to moan and shift her body about in the bed sheets.

"El, what is it?" Ian questioned, sensing her condition must have taken a dramatic change for the worse.

Elsbeth's writhing continued. She tossed her body from side to side, disheveling the bed sheets in a frantic display. Ian moved closer to still her wild thrashing, fearful that a seizure had overtaken her ability to control her movements. He laid his hands against her shoulders and gently, but firmly, applied pressure willing her body to stop its erratic motion.

"Elsbeth, my dear. You must improve for, as you said to me only a short time ago, we still need one another and we have so much to which we can look forward," Ian's eyes visibly welled with tears as he took his wife's hand and lifted it to his cheek. Her hand felt very cold against his warm skin. "Oh, El. I have not been very understanding. I have behaved like a bumbling fool these past weeks. Please forgive me for my behavior toward you. Arielle, Doc Lovering is in the next chamber. Please go to him and tell him he is needed at once."

Arielle moved swiftly, the sashay of her crinoline against the skirt of her gown was the only sound audible as her mother fell into a hopeless abyss. The emotions swirling about her were becoming more difficult to decipher. At certain moments, anger overpowered any sense of love she held for her mother, yet her heart was wont to let compassion lead the tumult raging within. She tapped on the doorframe of the nearby bedchamber and entered to find Doctor Lovering conversing with Sully. She had not been aware of Sully's presence in their home and wondered what good could be rendered from his consultation with the doctor. She put those thoughts aside to focus on the most pressing matter at hand. Her father's urgent request to immediately bring the doctor forward superseded any explanations she could muster.

"Excuse me, Doc Lovering. My Father asks that you come to my mother's room posthaste. Her condition has considerably worsened. And, I must ask if you have seen her brother? Is my uncle still about?"

Doctor Lovering stood quickly, paying no heed to Arielle's question. He bid Sully adieu with a hand signal that suggested their conversation would have to hold. He entered Elsbeth's bedchamber and at immediate glance knew her health was dire indeed. He placed his fingers on her forehead as he reached and grasped her hand. Her forehead, warm from a residual fever, was in stark contrast to the icy chill of her hand. Her body had become a barometer for a terminal diagnosis. Just as the doctor reached toward her face to lift her eyelids, Elsbeth shouted out as her eyes shot wide open.

"Bring Sully here!" She tried to lift her body from the bed sheets only to fall back in weakness upon the ivory white linens. Her right hand went up into the air like a scepter to usher him forth. Doc Lovering took her hand, trying to bring it back down upon her mattress, but she fought him off as though a greater force called to her. Arielle had found her uncle sitting reflectively in her father's study and suggested he accompany her upstairs to her mother's room where they joined Doc Lovering and her father.

All in the room were at once stunned and turned to explore the expressions on one another's faces. Ian looked at the doctor and nodded his head. The doctor exited the bedchamber to retrieve Sully and effectuate his patient's wishes. He knew her time was measured and he would gladly answer her peal. It was not his place to judge her decisions or her history. His oath required him to stick fiercely to the regimens for healing, without ill doing, for the good of his patients, no matter what their lot or actions in life.

Sully was sitting on a settee in the upper hallway, slumped forward with his head in his hands. He heard the approach of footsteps and slowly raised his eyes to welcome the doctor's advance.

"Son, it is time. She has called for you and requests an audience with you. You of course, may do as you choose. I would suggest to you, for your own sake mind you, that you honor her call and go to her. She has but moments remaining on this earth. This will be your final opportunity to be in her living presence whether you exchange a word with her or not."

Sully's first thought was to shake his head to affirm he would not go to her. Thoughts swirled...*This woman I was never given the choice to know as my mother, this woman who allowed someone to leave me, a foundling, forsaken on the barren stone steps of a church.* He shuddered to imagine an innocent infant left so casually and carelessly with no way to fend for itself. *Who would have such a hard heart? Who would allow such a thing? Why did she not want me? Who could forgive themselves for such an act? No, she can go to her grave knowing she hurt me beyond repair.* Anger was having its way with him. He was continuing to struggle in the wake of the painful aftermath of the truth.

"Son, what will it be? Time is of the essence," Doc Lovering's words were direct but laced with a tincture of gentle compassion to allow Elsbeth's son time to see his thoughts through.

At first, no movement came from Sully. He remained seated as he allowed all of the thoughts in his head to meld into a cohesive bundle. He mentally weighed all of the newfound knowledge about his birth. It was so fresh it stung like a new wound aggravated by grains of salt. *This woman is dying. This woman who is my mother. This woman who left me like a common mutt, a stray with no place to call home. Oh, why do I feel this pull, this need to see her off before she gives up the ghost?* His thoughts continued to rage for what seemed like minutes until he lifted his body from the settee and faced the doctor.

"Thank you, sir. I will join you in her room. I cannot say for sure why, but there is a part of my flesh that will not deny my origins."

"I understand, son. Blood forges a bond and you are answering that call. It is for the best – you will come to see that." The two walked quietly into the space now filled with Elsbeth's final world. Her family surrounding her bed looked to Sully and made a space for him to join their circle. He looked at the weak shell of a woman before him. She was a stranger, the mother he had only recently met, yet she possessed a familiarity that he had hoped to come to know.

Sullen faces, trying to resurrect parting smiles for Elsbeth, did their best to hold back tears. The imminence of death was in the air. Ian stroked her hand, then moved his fingers to her cheek. It too had gone cold. It was as though her blood no longer cycled through her body to nourish her extremities. He was losing her, and nothing in his power would change the course now set.

"Is Sully here?" Elsbeth's weak voice quizzed the air patiently awaiting a response.

Sully at first did not respond. He looked to Doc Lovering who signaled him to speak.

"I am."

There was a long void before Elsbeth spoke again. The formation of her thoughts into words was taxing every ounce of her strength, but the words, she would, she must say. Her voice, barely audible was no more than a faint whisper as she struggled to deliver her last words.

"Sully, oh, Sully. What have I done, what have I done? Forgive me son for I knew no better at the time." Elsbeth's breathing became shallower. "And Carson, I so regret closing you off all these years." She had summoned the ability to make her declarations and would take that satisfaction with her into eternity. A flood of memories whirled through her brain…distant, fuzzy flashes of a full life, of a childhood, of a young woman, of a wife, of a mother, of a sister. It was her life slipping away like the slow drip from a faucet with the droplets spiraling down the drain.

"My dear El, I know we have had our differences, but among them there has always been love. Through all these years, I know your love is more than I have ever deserved. Know that I love you and always will. You are my strength, my light, and you will continue to shine with me all my days. Oh, my dear El, please do not go, I will miss you so."

She had lost all capacity to speak. Her body was too weak. Ian continued to stroke her cheek as a single tear fell from her eye and she was gone.

⁓

Gentle sobs came from Arielle as she looked to Sully and took his hand giving it a tender squeeze. Her conciliatory gesture was met with sad eyes that bespoke volumes about the turmoil he had undergone since he became aware of the truth of his beginnings. His expression pulled at her heartstrings and she at once made it her vow to help see him through it. She knew firsthand the shock one could experience when the veracity of the details of birth were revealed. Morgan Pennybacker had done her professional best to ease the weight of the newfound knowledge about his relationship to her mother, but even her very adept skills could not cushion the affect of such astounding news. Her focus turned to her uncle who moved forward and stroked his sister's face. He took his fingers to his lips, kissed them and placed the kiss on Elsbeth's cheek.

Arielle looked to her father. He was pale and his face was drawn. She had not witnessed such a dire constitution surrounding his visage since he had been called upon to explain his association with her birth mother, Anna Hollingsworth. Once again, he appeared broken and alone. She released Sully's hand and went to her father's side.

"Father, she always knew how much you loved her and she loved you in return, unconditionally. Please let me know what I can do to ease your pain. I know arrangements will need to be made and I can assist you with those. We will make it a beautiful ceremony to celebrate Mum's life. She would want it that way."

Ian began to sob and his body shook. Arielle had never seen such emotion from him, and it caught her quite off guard. His typically stoic and reserved demeanor had been ripped open by his wife's death. *My dear Elsbeth has gone to her ancestors.* He looked at Arielle and shook his head in denial. He could not believe their years together had come to an end.

"Later," Ian replied as he touched Arielle's shoulder and reluctantly left Elsbeth's body. Slowly, he exited the room and carried with him the inescapable burden of a heavy heart.

I t was a beautiful day, almost too beautiful for a funeral, although Arielle much preferred a clear day to the thought of standing under a parasol during a heavy rain. She needed no additional element of gloom to hang over the proceedings for her mother's burial. She slipped her arm through William's as they walked past the gravestones lining their path. Each monument stood before them like a respectful honor guard for the dead.

"I missed you so very much while I was at the colliery. My travels only made me fonder of home," said Arielle as she gazed up at William.

"That is heartwarming to hear my dear, but I thought you would always think of Wales as your home."

"Wales will always hold a very special place in my heart. It is my place of birth and a place I intend to never forget. I will go back to visit, but my home is where you are and that is here in America."

"That warms the cockles of my heart," William said as he smiled a playful smile. "You are foremost in my thoughts when we are not in one another's company and days without you are longer by far. I am grateful for your success at the colliery that availed your prompt return."

Arielle wanted to melt at his words. *He is such a fine, fine man. I am the luckiest woman in the world to have him by my side.* For a moment she was lost in his eyes, his presence, until the reality of place and event returned to her mind. Her father had made the decision to bury her mother in America. His work on Capitol Hill, the seat of government named so by Thomas Jefferson, was consuming more and more of his time. He reasoned that to bury his wife in Wales would keep her far from him. He was comforted to think she would be several miles away rather than a journey away across the Atlantic. Washington Parish Burial Ground, more commonly called Congressional Cemetery, would be her final resting place. The cemetery on E Street in the city's southeast section pleased Ian. Elsbeth would be in repose among some of the best civil servants and other notable souls who had contributed to the country's history and served it well. Among the graves, cenotaphs had been erected to honor war's fallen, impressive, lasting monuments to those who should not be forgotten.

A large group had gathered at Elsbeth's gravesite. Several members of the Trade Council, ladies from Elsbeth's woman's society at church, and a small cluster of friends comprised those paying their respects. Fiona stood out among the household staff as she held a place of prominence in front of the others not wanting to miss a moment. Emma and Simon were in attendance standing with Morgan and Agnes. Alexandra kept to herself in the shade beneath a large oak tree. *I wonder why she is holding herself back?* Arielle thought to herself. *Not that I am disappointed to see her keep her distance from Will, it is just most unusual for her to linger in the shadows. Perhaps she saves her best behavior for when she is commemorating the dead. Or, perhaps it is her condition that causes her to retreat from the scrutiny of others.*

The Reverend began a simple graveside service. He spoke to Elsbeth's strengths, her life of service to her family and those less fortunate. There would be no mention of secrets and lies for they held no use now. The words redemption and 'cleansing of the soul' were incorporated into the text of the Reverend's speech, his way of giving absolution to her memory and spirit and offering comfort to her family. Ian had asked that the children not be singled out. He knew explanations would be complicated and Arielle and Sully were comfortable with his decision. Arianna too agreed with her father's wishes.

Ian felt a closeness to Sully that extended beyond their mutual affinity for business and their success. He was part of Elsbeth, of her flesh and blood, and that tie was one he did not want to unbind. When Ian learned of Sully's talent for song, he asked if he would sing a hymn at the service. Sully was reluctant at first, still healing from all that he had learned about his birth, but something deep in his gut told him that he needed to acknowledge his birth mother's death and he much preferred to use his voice in song than read a eulogy that he felt would be impossible to properly compose. He selected, "O Love That Wilt Not Let Me Go," a hymn by a Scottish minister named George Matheson. As he sang the heartfelt lyrics with his tenor voice in perfect pitch, there was nary a dry eye among the gathering:

O Love that wilt not let me go,
I rest my weary soul in Thee;
I give Thee back the life I owe,
That in Thine ocean depths its flow
May richer, fuller be.

O Light that followest all my way,
I yield my flickering torch to Thee;
My heart restores its borrowed ray,
That in Thy sunshine's blaze its day
May brighter, fairer be.

O Joy that seekest me through pain,
I cannot close my heart to Thee;
I trace the rainbow through the rain,
And feel the promise is not vain
That morn shall tearless be.

O Cross that liftest up my head,
I dare not ask to fly from Thee;
I lay in dust life's glory dead,
And from the ground there blossoms red
Life that shall endless be.

Ziggy beamed at him with pride through sad eyes. *To think this is my nephew, Elsbeth's issue.* He bowed his head praying for peace and healing to overtake his life. The Reverend concluded the service with a partial reading of Revelation 7: "They are before the throne of God and serve him day and night in his temple; and he who sits on the throne will shelter them with his presence. Never again will they hunger; never again will they thirst. The sun will not beat down on them, nor any scorching heat. For the Lamb at the center of the throne will be their shepherd; 'he will lead them to springs of living water.' 'And God will wipe away every tear from their eyes.'" Then he concluded with, "Dear Lord, we commend Lady Hargrove to your care that she may be born to eternal life. Let us bow our heads and pray as I read, 'A Prayer For The Dead':

God our Father,
Your power brings us to birth,
Your providence guides our lives,
and by Your command we return to dust.

Lord, those who die still live in Your presence,
their lives change but do not end.
I pray in hope for my family,
relatives and friends,
and for all the dead known to You alone.

In company with Christ,
Who died and now lives,
may they rejoice in Your kingdom,
where all our tears are wiped away.
Unite us together again in one family,
to sing Your praise forever and ever.
Amen.

A solemn hush had overspread the gathering. They took guidance from the Reverend as he motioned for those who wished to join in the process of committing Elsbeth to her grave. A flood of emotions overcame Ian as he nestled a hearty sum of exhumed dirt in his hand. He held it reverently and fondled the compact soil while saying a silent, salient prayer. Slowly and ceremoniously, after what seemed an eternity, he released the moist mound onto Elsbeth's coffin. The granules of clay spread along its length, their solitude became broken by shovelfuls of terra cotta that began to descend into her grave. The larger clumps of dirt exuded a hard, hollow sound against the wooden funerary chamber as the cemetery's regiment of gravediggers completed the process of tucking Elsbeth's mortal remains into Mother Earth.

Ian's eyes were swollen from weeping as he turned to his daughters and gave a nod to Sully and Ziggy. He addressed them with choked back tears. "I never want the sting or the pain of losing her to leave me. I do not want ever to forget Elsbeth." He turned and began to walk away with unabated grief.

Arielle, holding close by William, put a hand on her father's shoulder. He leaned into her and the two embraced as Arianna laid a hand on her father's back. Sully, Ziggy and William looked on, once again surprised to see Ian in such a weakened state. His style was always one of stoic reserve. It was indeed a rare occasion when he publically revealed a vulnerable side. Arielle slowly pulled away from their embrace.

"Father, I am glad you were there for Mum. I am glad you were able to help her through her final journey." Arielle tried to comfort her father as she turned to her uncle and gave him a nod of gratitude. He had accepted her father's invitation to come to her mother's side and for that she was thankful.

"I was where I needed to be and where I wanted to be," Ian said as he pulled a handkerchief from his pocket and blotted his eyes.

"And, Sully, you too," said Arielle. "I know it meant the world to Mum to have you come to her when you did. We will be forever grateful to you for that."

Sully was beginning to accept the losses that he had felt on many levels. First, his parents were deep in their graves, then his identity was drawn into question by his mother's entry in her diary, and now his birth mother's passing left him twice orphaned. He felt he had lost himself, the self he had known for a score and ten years. For a time, he was not certain what was real in his life. Before him was a family of no blood relation with whom he suddenly had ties. They had welcomed him and were willing to accept him into their fold.

Arianna stepped to his side. She placed a hand on his shoulder. "I share my sister's sentiments. Though Lady Hargrove and I were only acquainted for a short period of time, I know Arielle saw her as a devoted mother. You saw in the end how she cared for you and how she regretted the decision she made so many years ago. I hope that brings some comfort. Please know that we are here for you."

Sully could not help but have a subtle smile begin to form on his face as he looked into Arianna's eyes. He was growing more and more fond of her as each day passed. Knowing they were of different parentage greatly relieved them both for she too was becoming quite enamored with him.

"You have all been so kind to me, a stranger who was not forthright with you. Thank you for accepting me."

"It may be too soon to ask and perhaps not appropriate to discuss on a day such as this, however, I am curious as to whether you will remain in America or do you find that your business in Wales comes calling you home?" Arielle asked more for Arianna's benefit than her own.

Arianna swallowed hard as she awaited Sully's response. The idea of his leaving America was more than she wanted to consider.

"I mean, Will and I hope you will remain here for our wedding. After hearing your beautiful voice, the ceremony will be an even greater occasion if you would favor the gathering with a song. I have just the hymn in mind. We can discuss the particulars later. What do you say?" Arielle cast a smile at William who nodded in wholehearted agreement.

"Nothing is so pressing that demands my return to Wales and I would hate to miss your upcoming nuptials. Thank you for inviting me and for including me in your ceremony. I will be honored to sing."

Arianna was relieved. Arielle looked at her face, saw the expression of relief and winked an eye at her. Their lives would forge on. The sun would set on today and rise on tomorrow and they could all focus their attentions on happier times ahead.

Chapter Twenty-Nine

Mid October 1898
Washington, District of Columbia

Arielle held the heavy ivory card stock in her hand and studied the words before her. It still seemed a dream that soon she and William would wed and she would become Mrs. William Clay. A shiver of joy eased through her torso and a smile brushed across her face as she read the invitation aloud.

Sir Ian Hargrove
requests the honor of your presence when his daughter
Arielle
is united in marriage with
Mr. William Clay
at St. John's Church
Washington, District of Columbia
on Wednesday, 26th October 1898
at 2:30 pm.
a celebration will immediately follow at
the estate of Mrs. Horace Willard
Chestnut Heights

Her thoughts turned to images of William holding her close, his strong arms enveloping her and making her feel safe, secure and loved. She imagined their first kiss as husband and wife, and the long-awaited moment when they would be alone and could close the doors on the outside world and fully release the building passions burning inside. *I have so waited and longed to be his, to give him pleasure. I hope I will be all that he has wanted and more.* She held the wedding invitation against her bosom and took a deep breath, soaking in the love it represented.

"You appear deep in thought, my beautiful sister, and with that smile on your face, I can probably guess exactly of whom you are thinking," Arianna teased, relishing in the happiness she knew William brought to her sister's life.

"Oh, Arianna, you are quite right. This is such a wonderful time in my life. I just wish my mum could be here to witness my joy."

"She will be well aware, of that I am sure. She will be smiling down on you from the heavens as you and William take your vows for a lifetime of happiness together."

"I am so saddened by her loss and I know Father has yet to recover. It took him an inordinate amount of time to finalize the arrangements for her funeral. He said he wanted everything to be perfect for her. I am thankful that he made the decision to bury her in America although I still feel that she is so far away. I mean, I know she will remain with me always, in my heart and mind, but she is not by my side."

"You could imagine that she is. She knew of your pending nuptials and was so thoroughly happy for you. She showed you great love through all the years that you had together and no one can ask for more than that kind of unconditional love. I believe she used to say that you were 'born of her heart.'"

"Yes, she did say that indeed. The past year was just so severe on us all. The silver lining for me is to have had you come into my life. I am so grateful for Olivia's revelations. Had she taken her secret to the grave, we most likely would never have found one another." Arielle shook her head to erase the thought from her mind.

"Now, onward to brighter topics before we find ourselves dwelling on the past and not looking toward the joys that today and tomorrow bring. I hope you do not mind, but I observed a missive signed by you lying on top of one of your paintings. It was a poem that I assume you wrote and it was quite lovely."

Arianna laughed. "So, you have found me out have you? Yes, on occasion, the visions I see to paint equally inspire me to write a few words. Sometimes the words develop into poems and other times they simply become an affirmation of a feeling that I want to hold onto."

"Well, you, my sister, have a great talent beyond the brush. Your gift with words is astounding and so vivid. It would bring me, and William, great joy I know to have you prepare a reading for our ceremony. Oh, please say you will." Arielle's eyes danced as she clasped her hands together awaiting Arianna's response.

"But, of course, you have only to ask. It shall be my great pleasure and honor to compose a piece especially for the vicar to read at your nuptials."

"The vicar? If that is your preference then of course we will so abide. But, how special it would be for you to perform the reading. Would you sister?"

"Your wish directs me forward and I am most obliged. I will see how the day progresses and perhaps begin composing something especially for the two of you today."

A rianna sat at her desk with paper, pen and ink before her. She was determined to write a missive not only suitable to the occasion but befitting her sister and her intended. Theirs was a bond that would endure the test of time, of that Arianna was most assured. She struck the point of the pen to the parchment. Initially, there came no response from her fingertips that held the stylist at the ready. She closed her eyes and began to think and think, putting great pressure on herself to say something profound, something that would be remembered, something that would hold meaning for all whose ears her words would fall upon. Nothing came.

"Oh, my. It seems I have taken on a task greater than my abilities," Arianna said to herself aloud. "I must persevere. I must instill confidence in myself. Mum always encouraged me to take on that which I thought I could not do. My paintings are proof enough of that. Every stroke of the brush as I apply paint to create my botanicals is evidence of the risk I take to put my art in the public view."

She closed her eyes again, shutting out all of the reality encompassing her. A few moments passed until it seemed at once she felt comfortable as ink from the pen's point began to ease upon the paper before her. Words flowed and flowed as though guided by a hand not her own. She read through the first series of words then the next. She repeated her reading, taking much satisfaction in the feelings the words before her imparted. She added more words, forming verses until she came to her final pen stroke and the missive was complete. A poem, a special poem, written solely for her sister and her groom-to-be was finished. She titled it, *Love's Embrace*, and it would remain in her safe keeping until she shared it with all in attendance on Arielle's wedding day.

⁓

Fall was softly descending on the city. The crisp edges of leaves were beginning to curl and nature's paint box had begun to splash vivid shades of red, yellow, orange, purple, and brown on the foliage of deciduous trees. The abundant chestnut trees lining the driveway to Emma's home formed a colorful canopy that would enrich the promenade of carriages on William and Arielle's wedding day for the reception at her home. Large iron gates at the driveway's entrance were opened wide like welcoming appendages for Arielle's conveyance to make its journey along the lengthy roadway to the circular drive. As her carriage pulled up in front of the manse, her body tingled with excitement imagining her wedding day. She knew she only needed William to make her happiness complete, but the idea of a lavish party at Chestnut Heights to celebrate the beginning of their lives together was something she would not deny William's aunt who was intent on making their wedding day a memorable one. Parties at the Willard home were always met with great anticipation. Emma and her staff saw to every detail for the comfort and enjoyment of her guests. Her parties were talked about afterwards for weeks and months and usually made the society section of the Evening Star. As Arielle began to step from her carriage assisted by the footman, Simon rounded the corner of the manse and made a quick dash to greet her.

"Why Mr. Peabody, how lovely to see you on this fine morning!" Arielle had a fondness for Simon. In addition to his vast knowledge of horticulture, he had always made her feel welcome and on several occasions he had come to her defense, particularly when Alexandra was present.

"Lovely is definitely the word for the day, lovely, yes, lovely is the word. My, my, my Miss Hargrove, I say my, my you are looking especially radiant and lovely today!" Simon blushed as he rapidly delivered his words as though the moment would evaporate for him to compliment Arielle.

"Thank you. You are so kind as always. I hope my timing is good and that Mr. Clay has preceded my arrival. We are to meet with Emma to finalize some of the details about our wedding reception," Arielle shared as she made her way onto the loggia of the stately Italianate home.

The stunning architecture of Chestnut Heights always captured Arielle's breath. Multiple arches spanned the width of the home's façade and above them on the dwelling's second story were double doors opening onto a large balcony trimmed with a bowed iron balustrade. Above the upper windows, ornamentation in an embossed fruit and swag design lent an air of sophistication and softened the edges of the brick and sandstone structure. Arielle and Simon made their way to the front portal that was flanked on either side by large urns filled with evergreens. Simon opened the door and stood back for Arielle to enter. He blushed again as he extended the courtesy to the raven-haired one whom he so admired.

William was standing in the foyer anxiously anticipating her arrival. When she stepped through the doorway he was engulfed by her grace and beauty. He had to seek personal restraint to avoid running forward to her and taking her up in his arms. *There will soon be more than ample and appropriate times for me to embrace her and hold her close and love her,* William mused. Arielle looked at the handsome man before her. She was drawn to him in ways that made her want to lose all sense of self-control. His sexual attractiveness was becoming more difficult to ignore as a hot ache grew in her loins. The sensation surprised her and she hoped her feelings were not evident to William as quivers surged through her limbs.

"Arielle you look so beautiful, wonderful in fact, but you seem to be trembling. Is everything all right?" William asked as he moved closer to her.

Her behavior gave him the perfect entrée to reach out and take her in his arms. Arielle welcomed his embrace. His proximity gave her comfort but at the same time flamed the feelings aroused in her by being in his presence. She felt a warm flush come to her cheeks and hoped it would dissipate before she withdrew herself from William. Although she feared the sensations she was experiencing would be beyond her control, she knew it was only proper, and her obligation as a woman, to assist William in controlling himself. Simon watched as the two held one another, feeling somewhat embarrassed to be privy to what he felt should be their private moment. Fortunately, he was rescued as Emma swept into the foyer.

"Ah! There are the lovebirds! Now, now, let us maintain our propriety. There will be time enough for that kind of display. I hate to sound like an old matron, but we do not want people to be wagging their tongues about the two of you. I know some of my noteworthy friends like to proclaim there is no such thing as 'bad publicity' but I take exception to that. For now we will maintain the highest standards for personal conduct."

"Aunt Emma, you *are* sounding like quite the prude and just when I thought you were coming into the modern age," William teased as he released Arielle and gave his aunt a kiss on the cheek. "My goodness, we are engaged and in two short weeks will be husband and wife."

"That is exactly my point dear. Two weeks will pass very quickly. Come, let's go into the parlor. I have laid out my file with all of the details for your special day. I want to be sure you both are pleased with my ideas. Of course, this is a group effort and your input is paramount to the final plans for your reception. Arianna has made some wonderful suggestions as well. You know she loves both of you so. Oh, your wedding is just going to be the most wonderful day! Come Simon, you may join us too if you like."

Emma sent Thomas to find Arianna so she could join them. Thomas returned rather quickly saying that Miss Smithfield sent word saying "thank you" but she was occupied with something and that they could proceed without her. *Hmm, Emma wondered,* as did the others. *I wonder what she is up to?* She smiled as she reflected that Sully had returned from a meeting on Capitol Hill with Sir Ian Hargrove. *Perhaps he has found Arianna and is sharing the highlights of his day with her.* Emma particularly liked the thought of that.

"I know it is your desire to do that which is customary so I was talking with my florist about the floral arrangements to flank either side of the altar at St. John's and we think it is a lovely tradition to twist the stems of some of the flowers to represent two lives becoming one. I hope you like that suggestion?"

Arielle and William looked at each other and smiled. They knew his aunt would tend to the smallest of details and they appreciated her desire to incorporate symbolism into their special day. They nodded in agreement as Emma continued.

"And, of course Simon will be instrumental working in tandem with the florist regarding all of the floral arrangements for the reception," Emma said as she gave a nod to Simon who filled with pride. "And, as you are leaving the church, I thought little white satin pouches of birdseed for each of your well-wishers to toss in the

air would be a nice touch. All of the guests will be able to participate in a celebratory way and our winged friends will be happy to
benefit from the festivities. Oh, and this is one of my favorite ideas!
There is a stable in Rock Creek Park with white horses that we can
hire to pull the carriage that will transport you from St. John's back
to Chestnut Heights for your reception! What do you think? Oh,
and I have much more to share as you can only imagine."

"I think you have everything under control as usual, Aunt
Emma and I adore you for it. Why it appears there is nothing for
Miss Hargrove and myself to do but be present and everything else
will fall into place thanks to your detailed planning on our behalf."
William grinned at Arielle and his blue eyes gleamed. He walked to
his aunt and gave her a kiss on the cheek. "You are always so wonderful to me. What a lucky man I am to have such special women
in my life."

Arielle hoped he was not including Alexandra in his cadre of
special women. *Why has the thought of her popped into my head? I must
not let thoughts of her cast a pall over my wedding plans.* As she brought
herself back to the subject at hand, William took her hands in
his and looked into her eyes. The iris freckles in both of her eyes
seemed to dance as the light through the parlor's windows shone
on her face. He was mesmerized as he stared intently at her feeling
even more certain that he wanted to tell her now about a thought
that had been brewing in his head.

"Arielle, I have been thinking for some time that my home,
which will soon be your home too, has never had a formal name. I
have always been so fond of Chestnut Heights and the fact that my
Uncle Horace named his home for the trees he favored and amply
planted on the grounds here. I want our home to represent something important to us so I have been working an idea around in my
head."

"You intrigue me, Will. I think that a name for your, our home is
a charming idea and I am anxious to hear what you have in mind."

"Actually, your middle name factors into my thinking. I have
been doing some research. Conveniently, your middle name means

'meadow.' Since our home is surrounded by meadows and soon we will take our vows to love and honor one another forever, I thought the perfect name for our home is 'Everleigh.' It will forever be our home and your middle name is Leigh. What do you think?"

A small puddle of tears welled in Arielle's eyes. Emma was touched with a similar emotion. She was always proud of her nephew. His success as a corporate lawyer had established his solid reputation in the city and allowed him to make a very healthy living, but it was his humanity and grace under pressure that she admired the most. Simon could hardly contain himself. He was so pleased that William revered Arielle so much that he chose to name his home for her. *Yes, this is a lovely day indeed!*

"I am truly honored and delighted. Yes! How wonderful it will be to think whenever I am away that I will be returning to Everleigh and to you. I love the sound of it." Arielle felt swept away with joy.

"And, now to the food for the reception. Cook, as you know, is a master at many things including pastries. We have discussed your wedding cake and she is prepared to create several tiered layers of cake with swags of garland circling each layer accented with small white birds perched about and, of course, roses. The cake will be covered in white fondant icing, which Cook will also use for the swags and other adornments. We are also planning a plentiful buffet of meats with fruits and vegetables to represent this season of harvest. There shall be an abundance for all and of course an orchestra for background music while we dine and lots and lots of dancing!"

"I may have to refrain from partaking of the 'abundance' or poor William will not be able to carry me over the threshold! That is a customary ritual in America, is it not?"

Everyone laughed. The atmosphere was one of happiness and excited anticipation. As their laughter began to subside, Thomas entered the room with a silver salver carrying champagne glasses and a bottle of the chilled beverage.

"Thomas, your timing is perfect. Thank you for remembering my earlier request. You may place the tray right over there. William, please be a dear and help Thomas distribute a glass to everyone." As Emma completed her sentence, voices entered the foyer and Sully and Arianna entered the parlor followed by Alistair.

"Well, it looks like we will be needing another bottle and several more glasses, Thomas. Come in everyone. Please join us in celebration. We are getting a head start on the wedding revelry! This is such fun! It has been a very long time since I have been filled with joy of this magnitude. I would say it is not since I learned that the two of you were engaged! All good things to one and all!" Emma toasted as she raised her glass in the air, brought it to her lips and took a hearty sip.

"Oh, Emma! Have you heard that Sully is going to grace us with his voice at our wedding?" Arielle took a sip of champagne then raised her glass in a salute toward him.

"And, I actually have another request of him," William said as he turned toward Sully. "Sully, it would bring me great pleasure to have you stand as my best man in witness to our union. Do I have your acceptance?"

"Thank you, yes, I will be honored to do so," Sully responded equally pleased to be in the wedding party since he knew Arianna was to be Arielle's maid of honor.

Arianna took Sully's hand and gave it a gentle squeeze. The action did not go unnoticed by anyone in the room. Emma had watched their fondness for one another grow. Sully was a frequent visitor to the gardens when Arianna was working on a painting and her work had become more prolific. There was a refreshed gaiety about her paintings and a focus on the process of applying layers of color until they had a tactile quality about them. The petals of the flowers and their leaves and stems seemed to be lifted from the canvas. Emma had declared that one was more beautiful than the next.

"I think it is wonderful that you will sing at the wedding Sully, and stand as my dear nephew's best man. Perhaps you will want to join the musicians and lend your voice to some of their compositions as we dance the night away? I for one vote 'yes' for that!" Emma was elated to have all of her plans falling so flawlessly into place. "Now, tell us Arianna, what is the latest addition to your work? It must be a challenge to find something new to paint for it seems you have documented every nook within the walls of the gardens at Chestnut Heights and I might add that is much to Simon's pleasure and mine!"

"I can tell you that she is finding the change in seasons very beneficial to the inspiration for her art work," Sully beamed.

"I would say that inspiration comes in many forms not the least of which might be your interest in her...talent," Emma said, quite tickled with the pause in her delivery. She looked at the two watching their expressions, which did not disappoint her. There was definitely something brewing between them. She looked forward to watching their relationship develop into something beyond friendship and their mutual appreciation for the arts.

Arianna looked to Arielle hoping her sister could rescue her from the direction the conversation was going. A knock came to the front portal. *Ah, saved for the time being,* Arianna thought to herself. Within a moment, Ziggy appeared in the doorway. He hesitated before fully entering the parlor, waiting to be certain he was not interrupting a private gathering.

"Mr. Cromwell, how good that you have returned while we are together for a somewhat impromptu celebration in anticipation of your niece's wedding! Please come in and join us in a glass of champagne," Emma encouraged as she filled a glass and passed it his way.

"Why thank you, I do not mind if I do. I have just come from the cemetery and after paying a visit to my sister, this is a very welcome fortification for my low spirits. Oh, excuse me, for I haven't meant to put a damper on these festivities. I can tell you that in all the time I spent on the streets in Shoreditch there was never anything to drink as fine as the libation I hold in my hands right now with you fine folks, and I thank you for that and for making me feel so welcome."

Arielle walked over to her uncle and put her hand on his shoulder. She appreciated that he would visit her mother's grave, let the past slip into its proper setting, and release any grudge he might have held against his sister. She was glad to have him in her life. His presence kept her mother's memory alive. She hoped to get to know him better and perhaps help him find his way to a better existence beyond the life of a street dweller. *Perhaps Father can help him in this regard. I shall have to discuss this with him.*

Alistair had been unduly quiet, seemingly taking in the wedding plans for which he felt he had no need to offer input. It was after all not his affair. He had only in the past few months even come to know the people gathered in the room and, although he had come to enjoy their company, he felt a distance between himself and them, especially Emma whom he sensed only tolerated his presence at times. He had already determined that he would sequester himself upstairs in his room on the big day. He would devote himself to his writing to drown out any of the frivolity on the floor below. He studied Emma's face. *She is a comely woman. Obviously she is very bright and a sophisticate of style, albeit somewhat that of a matron's garb but, my goodness, look at her age. Although, I would say we are of the same generation, which gives us some common ground from which to build. Oh, it is wicked of me to have thoughts of her this way.* He looked to Simon who too had had little to offer to the discussion but was enjoying his glass of champagne and the camaraderie of the group.

"Well, this has all been well and good but if you do not mind, I am going to dismiss myself and head for my chambers. I have a chapter that has been giving me fits and I hope to be able to work out some awkward dialogue between two characters. Let me say that I wish you both much happiness in your future together."

"Why, Mr. Drake, there will be time enough for you to offer your congratulatory salutations at our wedding. We certainly hope you will attend the ceremony at St. John's and the reception following here at my aunt's home," William said as Arielle nodded her head in confirmation.

"What a lovely thought! I had no idea! I thought your wedding would be a day for family and close friends. Are you certain you want me there? I mean, I shall be quite honored to attend and I thank you!"

"The saying the Italians use, *Chi entra come amico, parte come famiglia* or translated, *those who enter as friends, leave as family,* is an expression that my aunt has quoted on many occasions. We want you to attend our wedding and we would have it no other way. We are very pleased that you have accepted our invitation."

Emma surprised and embarrassed herself when she let out a sigh. It was subtle but audible just the same. Of course Alistair would be invited to attend the wedding. She had just not wasted any thoughts on him. It would be unkind to omit him from the proceedings when everyone else boarding in her home would be included. She took in another breath that was audible as well and drew the attention of everyone in the room.

"Oh, I apologize. Perhaps it is the drink that has fatigued me, or the excitement about the details for the wedding. Have no fear, I will rally and be in fine and fit form for October 26th," Emma assured as she mustered a half smile and stood to leave the room.

Alistair watched her make her way past the brocade portières draped on either side of the parlor's entrance. The sashay of her gown added an elegant rhythm to her promenade. He wondered if her sigh was directed at him, then he quickly released that thought. *Of course, anyone would be honored to have me on his or her guest list. What on earth am I thinking?* Alistair smiled as he imagined himself at the reception. He pictured the grand parlor as a large ballroom with guests lining the perimeter and others in a lively two-step circling about the dance floor, some high stepping in two-quarter time. He saw himself with a partner, spinning her slowly about during the last waltz of the evening. He shook his head wondering if his mind's eye was playing tricks on him for the woman whose face turned and looked him straight in the eye was none other than that of Emma Willard. *I must be losing my mind or hallucinating! Get a grip on yourself man!* Alistair bid his adieus to the others and retreated upstairs to the solace and security of his room before any more unfathomable fantasies rattled his brain.

Chapter Thirty

As Sully stepped up to the front portal of the Hargrove residence, he noted that the draperies were pulled fully across the windows, which made him wonder how long Sir Ian would observe a period of mourning and shut out the healing light of day. *Maybe I should rethink being here. Maybe it is best that I first seek out his mood and make no assumptions that he will be in favor of the question I wish to pose to him today.* Sully hated doubting his intentions. Talking with Sir Ian was a necessary step that he did not want to delay. Fiona answered his knock and walked him past the smaller parlor where he saw Arielle tending to a large needlework on a standing frame.

"Why Mr. Bamford, I wonder what brings you to our home today?" Arielle asked. A broad smile lit up her face. Her intuition told her why he was there and she was most pleased. Sully smiled in return and gave a nod of his head as he proceeded to her father's study with Fiona continuing to lead the way.

"Sir, Mr. Bamford has arrived," Fiona announced as her fingers twisted the lower edges of her apron. "Is there anythin' you'll be needin'?"

"Thank you, Fiona. No, that will be quite all. You may go about your other duties for now and please stop that fidgeting!"

The clear ring of crystal against crystal sounded as Ian removed the decanter's stopper and poured a full round of amber courage into two waiting glasses, one for Sully and one for himself. Sully had requested the meeting as a courtesy to ask for Arianna's hand in marriage. He knew she was still in the process of getting to know her father, having only learned of him one year past, but he felt it only proper to observe the formality and seek his blessing, especially in light of Elsbeth's death. Ian suspected that the young man's mission involved a proposal, and he was delighted to think that Sully considered his feelings and opted to speak to him before he took the final steps to propose. A smile crossed Ian's face, one of the few he had been able to muster since Elsbeth's passing. He was determined to get back on course and absorb himself in his work with the Trade Council, which would require him to remain in America for several more years. He had a proposal of his own he had decided to make, but first he would see how comfortable he felt after this meeting with Sully. If all went well, then he would proceed with the request he had in mind.

"Fiona leaves a more than adequate amount of room for improvement as a servant. She has skills that are barely worth mentioning but, at the very least, she keeps these decanters amply supplied for occasions such as these. Come son, have a seat," Ian said as he ushered Sully to a nearby tufted leather chair with the wave of his hand.

Son, thought Sully. *Was that not my fear when I thought he was my father? That I would have to call him father and he would call me son? Well, I guess I need to get past that now for we will be father and son, if not by blood but by marriage.*

"I thought some libation would serve us both well to bolster ourselves for our ensuing repartee," Ian joked, trying to lighten the mood and put Sully at ease. Ian knew his manner could be off-putting and he wanted to assure that Sully felt relaxed and welcomed in his presence.

Sully took an over zealous gulp of Scotch, which caused him to draw back and clear his throat as he swallowed. *Collect yourself,*

Bamford, Sully spoke silently to himself. *This is no time to suffer a choking fit!*

"Are you quite all right? Here, let me give you another pour. Even though this one is 21 year aged, the first tasting can surprise your senses. Your next taste should be quite pleasant and smooth. These single malts, matured in oak casks, are among my favorites." Ian was feeling in a festive mood, one of few he had experienced since his loss.

Sully was pleased to note that although the draperies were indeed blocking a view of the outdoors, they were not an indication that a somber mood had overtaken the residents of the home. Ian replenished Sully's tumbler with theatrical gusto, more than ready to get on with their visit. Patience had never been a great virtue of Ian's. He had grown impatient of mourning and was determined to focus on his family, on the living, and to be a proper patriarch to his daughters. *It all comes down to family. That is the most important, and I have had to learn that the hard way,* he silently reflected. Ian was thinking that he would like Sully to get to the point of his purpose for their meeting so he could get to his. Sully took a second draw of Scotch with no ill effects.

"There son, just as I told you, smooth and delightful. Warms the cockles of your heart, does it not? We should have had Mr. Clay join us, but there will be plenty of opportunities for that I am certain."

Ian's attitude and the Scotch were making it very pleasant for Sully to feel comfortable and ready to pose his question to the senior Hargrove. He cleared his throat and addressed the man who would become his father-in-law.

"Sir Ian, it is with great admiration for you that I seek your agreement on a topic very close to my heart. In fact, I assume that you know full well why I have called on you this day. It concerns Arianna and something we both desire."

"Well, I say spit it out son. What the devil do you wish to ask?" Ian's tone was sharp and the expression on his face became serious. Sully wondered what had caused him to take such a harsh tone and then Ian laughed. "I am just having a wee bit of fun with you. Go ahead and ask your question for you know I am going to say 'yes.'"

Sully was relieved. He would need to remember that Ian had a playful, if not sadistic, side to him. That knowledge might serve him well in the future.

"Right you are, I shall get right to the point. Sir Ian, I wish to marry your daughter, Arianna. We have grown to love one another and wish to take that bond to the altar. It is my hope that you will give your blessing to our union, which we will delay until Arielle and William are married. I adore Arianna. She is everything I have ever wanted or dreamed of for a friend and a lifelong companion." Sully realized that in his zeal to ask for Ian's approval, his words were flowing so rapidly that he needed to bring them to a halt. "What say you?"

"You will find no hesitation in my response of absolutely yes! I already had my fun in delaying my answer with Mr. Clay when he came to me to ask for Arielle's hand. So, you see, you benefit from his being your predecessor on this topic. I have seen how radiant Arianna is in your presence and I have heard your kind words whenever you have spoken about her to me before our meetings on Capitol Hill. To witness that joy is all that a parent can ask. I know you will serve each other well and I shall be proud to have you join our family." Ian was beaming as he gave Sully a gentle slap on the back and clinked his glass against his in an unusual display of camaraderie.

Sully was relieved. He knew a meeting with Sir Ian could be unpredictable but he could not have asked for a better outcome. He knew exactly how he wanted to propose to Arianna and he would put that plan in motion posthaste.

"So, now that we have completed that part of our agenda, I have a proposal to make to you that will, of course, have to meet with Arianna's approval as well. You are well aware from the Trade Council meetings you have attended with me that my position on the Council is to be extended. What I thought would be a temporary stay will now keep me in America for several more years. While I am happy to serve, this leaves a void at the colliery and limits the time I can take to venture across the Atlantic to keep abreast of my business," Ian cleared his throat, took a sip of Scotch and continued. "Arielle did a fine job acting as my personal representative to avert an all out strike by the pit workers. In fact, I was quite impressed with her performance and received a superlative report from my solicitor and Nesbitt, the colliery's overman. The man knows the workings of the mine from the inside and out. I could not ask for a better employee and he knows the men, their families and the village. But, with all of that said, there needs to be a man at the top, so to speak, someone on-site like an owner who has a huge stake in the success or failure of the colliery. Arielle and I have discussed this matter and she prefers to assist in any way she can from here as she builds her life with Mr. Clay. So, what I am proposing to you, Sully, is that you take that position. You act as the head of Hargrove Colliery. I know Arianna has expressed a desire to return to the place of her birth, to the surroundings that were familiar to her birth mother, Annie Hollingsworth. She said there is little for her in England since Olivia Smithfield's passing so I would think Wales would suit her quite well. And, you can live at our estate."

Sully's mind was whirling with the magnitude of Ian's proposal. It was a dream come true to be selected to serve in such a capacity at the colliery, yet he had his own business to consider. He could not and would not let it dissolve into nothingness. He had spent too many years building the timber business and it also carried with it the legacy of his father who trained him on their farm to be a master sawyer. He would have to confer with his overseer and determine how the businesses might be merged to suit the needs of his employees.

"Your estate? Ah, yes, the Big House." Sully was delaying an affirmative response to give himself more time to digest Ian's offer. *What to say? What to say?*

"Son, I know this is quite a bit to absorb in one sitting. You, of course, have your timber business to consider. But, we all have competing priorities. There is a way to make all of this work and I am sure you will find a way. Give it some thought and get back to me as soon as you can. Present the idea to Arianna and see where that leads you both. My hope of course is that it leads you home to Nantymoel."

Ian and Sully shook hands as a gesture of a conversation to be continued. Sully had made his first step in seeking a future with Arianna and Ian had made his first step in laying the foundation for a future generation to run his colliery. *Elsbeth would be pleased,* Ian thought to himself and choked back a tear.

"Where in the world are you taking me, Sully? I think I shall ask Thomas to give me a hint!" Arianna was filled with excitement hoping that the outcome of their outing would be what she anticipated.

"It was quite thoughtful of Mrs. Willard to provide Thomas as our escort but, I assure you, he will not be revealing our destination. I want it to be a surprise."

"So it seems that you have gone to great lengths to arrange our time together today. I am not certain whether I should think of you as clever or as a sneaky one not to be trusted." Arianna gave a light-hearted laugh as she teased the man she had come to love. She enjoyed watching the appearance of the dimple on his left cheek whenever a smile graced his face.

"Please do not tell me that you are going to break my heart by name-calling or I shall have to resort back to being Bernard Sullivan and see how that suits you." Sully realized as the words left his mouth that the issue of his false name was not the most appropriate thing for him to proclaim since it brought into question his trustworthiness. "I apologize. That was not the best example to bring forth."

"No apology necessary. I was merely teasing you. But, I will admit you are making me nervous with so much secrecy and intrigue. Will we soon be at our destination?"

"We are but moments away."

Arianna looked through the carriage's windows. She caught a glimpse of the gardens at the Executive Mansion as the conveyance made a turn from Pennsylvania Avenue onto 17th Street where it came to a full stop just past New York Avenue. She looked at the building and then the signage that read, "Corcoran Gallery of Art and Corcoran School of Art." *This is curious. An art gallery? Perhaps I was wrong to think Sully had other intentions. It looks like he intends to tour the latest exhibits at this gallery.* Disappointment came over Arianna. As much as she appreciated art, she had envisioned a different scenario for their outing, something romantic, somewhere less public. Sully smiled and took her hand to exit the carriage. He saw the expression on her face, but hoped his plan would soon bring gaiety back to her disposition. She let go of Sully's hand and lifted the skirt of her gown as she stepped over the curb and onto the walkway leading into the gallery. Sully offered his arm to her for their promenade, which she gladly accepted. As the doors opened, the docent who acknowledged Sully by name welcomed them into the vestibule.

"Welcome to the Corcoran, Mr. Bamford."

"Thank you. May I introduce Miss Arianna Smithfield?"

"What a great pleasure it is to meet someone of your talent, Miss Smithfield. Quite impressive."

Arianna was taken aback. She was happy to accept the docent's praise, however she wondered what he could possibly know of her work.

"Is everything ready?" Sully asked the docent, which only added to Arianna's curiosity.

"It is indeed. Here, let me lead the way."

Once again, Sully offered his arm to Arianna as they followed the docent through the building's atrium and past several exhibits until they came to a halt at the doorway to a small gallery room.

"I will leave you here. If you have the need of anything else, please do not hesitate to ask."

Sully thanked the docent then turned to Arianna and asked her to close her eyes and keep them closed as he guided her into the room. Surprises and the unexpected made her uncomfortable. She preferred to be well-planned and in control of her surroundings, but how could she not trust Sully's intentions this day? She complied with his request, not peeking even once to see where he was taking her.

"You may now open your eyes!"

Arianna was stunned. She was surrounded by her artwork. Her paintings were installed on the petite gallery's walls as well as several carefully placed easels. It was as though gardens as fresh as those depicted by Monet had created a botanical paradise for her to enter. She was at once amazed and she found herself unable to speak for a moment. Sully was ready to burst from his frock coat. To see Arianna's paintings so beautifully displayed made his heart soar and to see how taken she was with the scene before her confirmed for him that his idea to surprise her with a gallery exhibit of her works was an excellent plan indeed. Arianna began to walk about the space visually taking in each of the installations. She paused and looked at Sully.

"How? How did you manage this? How did you manage this without my knowing? This is absolutely amazing! I am so honored and thrilled to have you do something like this for me."

"I hope you will not be upset with Mrs. Willard and Mr. Peabody for they are the ones who informed me about the closet where you were storing your completed pieces. The idea came to me to visit here and see if the powers that be would entertain the idea of having a very accomplished student of Redouté's style exhibiting her work for a period of time. The gallery agreed and Mrs. Willard informed me that you rarely went to the storage closet because Mr. Peabody enjoyed taking your finished pieces and cataloging them for you. So, I felt that it was reasonably safe to remove them when you were out and transport them here to surprise you."

"I can barely speak. I have never had my work exhibited in a gallery. This is such an honor and the dream of every artist to be recognized, to receive validation for her style and technique. I simply cannot thank you enough."

"I actually can think of a way."

"A way?"

"Yes." Sully reached into his coat pocket and removed a small black velvet box. He faced Arianna, took her hand and placed the box in her palm with his hand resting over its top. She met his loving eyes with hers as he began to speak. "I can only hope that you will give me an affirmative response when I ask you something that has for weeks been paramount on my mind." Arianna raised an eyebrow as Sully continued. "You, Arianna, mean so very much to me. I delight in your beauty, in your brilliant mind, in your many talents, in your kind ways, and your gentle heart. It would bring me extraordinary pleasure if you would agree to marry me. I have asked your father for your hand and he has given us his blessing. Please say that you will become my wife."

Arianna needed only a moment to formulate her response. She felt the box move in her palm as Sully's nerves got the better of him. She placed her other hand on top of his to steady his nerves and without further delay replied.

"Yes, oh my goodness, yes!"

Together their hands went to the box. Sully lifted the hinged lid to reveal a large, brilliantly cut diamond ring set in platinum. Arianna's eyes popped at the sight of the beautiful gem. Sully removed the ring and placed it on the ring finger of her left hand. She took the fingers of her right hand, touched the stone, and gently moved the ring side to side enjoying the way the light in the room bounced about the various cuts in the diamond. She and Sully looked with enchantment into each another's eyes as she raised her chin to greet the advance of his lips on hers. Happiness filled them both as their kiss lingered, arousing a vibrant chord within them that would only be sated by their union. Sully raised his mouth from Arianna's, reliving the warm, velvet sensation of her lips. He wanted to kiss her again and again. His body was demanding him to do so, but he restrained himself. He would rather delay his desires than soil this tender moment.

"Mr. Sullivan Bamford, you have made me the happiest woman on this earth! I adore what you have done for me and I adore you! I cannot wait to tell Arielle. She will be equally happy for me, for us!"

"I think your sister suspects that we would become engaged. She saw me when I went to talk with your father."

"You mean Arielle has known all along and kept it a secret from me?" Arianna smiled. "I am just teasing for I am pleased that she would not spoil your surprise."

"I have the feeling that you anticipated the outcome of this day."

"I can say that I hoped you would ask me to marry you, but I never suspected that you would go to so much effort to arrange this showing of my work! This is beyond anything I could have imagined!"

"The pleasure of the effort was all mine. There is more that we need to discuss."

"More? Now you are making me nervous. What is it?"

"I think you will take pleasure in what I have to say however, I have not made a firm decision. Your input will determine how I respond to your father."

"Please delay no further. What has my father asked of you?"

"When I spoke with him about proposing to you, he asked if I would oversee the operations of Hargrove Colliery in his absence. He said his duties in America would extend for several more years. He was aware of your desire to live near your birthplace and he has offered us his residence, which comes fully staffed. How do you feel about this?"

"Oh Sully, my goodness, this is wonderful news! I need no more time to consider the possibility for I can think of no better way to begin our lives together. But, what of your timber business?"

"I will speak with Sir Ian and see what we can do to merge my company with the colliery in a partnership of some kind. Your father's mine uses a fair amount of timber and with considerable expansion to additional collieries in the Rhondda and other neighboring valleys we should do quite well with volume. Financially it would be a very stable and profitable venture, I can be sure."

"Then to Wales we shall go!" Arianna wrapped her arms around Sully's neck and embraced him in a lingering hug. She was buoyant and blissfully happy and never wanted to let go of him or the sensual feelings racing like a raging river through her bloodstream.

Chapter Thirty-One

October 25, 1898
Washington, District of Columbia

Alexandra was reeling. She questioned what her life would have been if William had agreed to marry her and assume the responsibility and fatherhood of her baby. Then reality appeared before her and raised its ugly head like a persistent devil standing on her shoulder, poking her to her senses with a pitchfork. William had declined her and she felt the pain of his rejection. She tried to reason why he had not accepted her offer, and then the harsh truths of his rejection came to her full force and sent her into an irrepressible downward spiral. She seemed incapable of grasping the dangerous depths of her infatuation. She had become desperate like a languishing rose deficient of precipitation and thirsting for a drop of rain. She was hell bent on quenching her thirst by meeting with William one last time before his marriage. She had taken a ride on a Herdic Phaeton Company omnibus that dropped her several blocks from his estate. The staff informed her that he had gone to visit with his aunt so she promptly re-routed herself to the steps of Chestnut Heights. She took a deep breath and knocked on the front door. Thomas too took a deep breath as the opened door revealed the flaxen-haired one who was notorious for bringing turmoil to the residence.

"Good morning to you, Miz Whitaker. Is it Miz Willard youse here to see?"

"How ridiculous of you to ask such a thing. By now you must know that it is Mr. Clay whose company I wish to be in. Where is he?"

Thomas was not surprised by Alexandra's conduct. He had seen her at her worst on several occasions and wondered if she even had a best. He felt sorry for William and the burden he endured watching over her. *That Mr. William is a saint, yez he sure is. Up there with the best of them for puttin' up with this one,* Thomas shook his head as he mused to himself.

"Step along and bring him to me at once! There is no time for you to delay!"

Thomas walked to the back of the house and soon William came walking up the hallway toward the foyer. He politely greeted Alexandra who insisted that they have a private discussion. He had little tolerance remaining for any conversations with her for they were always filled with the same content. He hoped that this was the last time that he would have to hear her out. He suggested they step into his uncle's study where they could be alone and refrain from inciting the rest of the household with her discourse. Alexandra wasted no time in beginning her tirade. Her tongue was as sharp and ready for battle as an unsheathed sword.

"But, you must know, William, you must! This is what my heart wants! What my heart needs! I cannot, and I will not deny myself. You, and only you, are all I have ever desired and hoped for. I must have you hear and know this or I shall regret it all of my remaining days. I cannot drive you from my thoughts! Please do not tarry with me and break my heart. I shall never be the same without you and, quite frankly, I do not know how I will ever go forth! I must have you, for you were always intended to be mine! You know that is what Father wanted!" Alexandra's fervent plea was taking an emotional toll but she was not to be thwarted. Her body heaved with desperation and despair. As she raised her voice to a new decibel, tears began to descend upon her reddened cheeks.

William was surprised at the callous shield overtaking his demeanor. He had experienced so many of Alexandra's outbursts, there was little room left in his repertoire of compassion, and there was no hope of reasoning with her. He had tried and failed on numerous occasions to assuage the burdens she was responsible for placing on her heart. He would not be moved by her latest efforts to sway him away from Arielle. Threatening him with a pregnancy not of his doing was worrisome enough. However, discounting his efforts to help her conceal her circumstances and confront the perpetrator left him bereft of viable alternatives.

"I dare say Alexandra, with all due respect, you must come to grips with yourself. You make me appear like a possession of yours, a thing easily manipulated and molded into whatever pleasure you cast…like a spell you have firmly set."

"Good grief, William! You make me sound like quite the witch, casting spells about, ready to make victims of any soul I deem worthy of my lair! You might as well have stricken me with an onerous plague or pierced me through with a poisonous sword, the taste from either would be no less painful or fateful than your hateful proclamation!"

"Please avoid the drama, Alexandra. I feel our conversation will have no welcome end. You know I am committed to Arielle and shall have no other. I have for years sought your best interests and looked after your welfare. I had hoped to prepare you and give you the most capable wings to thrive on your own recourses under the guardianship of your father's well-intentioned wishes and the preparations he held in place for your livelihood. You must find refuge in all that he set aside for you and go forth with the resolve that I will forever be your friend, but nothing more."

"Friend, friend, friend! Must you repeat something that has no romance attached to it? *Friend*? I am suddenly no more than that of a faithful hound, man's best friend? I will not be satisfied with such status! A good home, a warm bed, and a bowl full of canine gruel will neither honor nor soothe my spirits. You know me far better than this. Please William, please let me love you. Let me be all that my heart desires me to be for you. I beg of you! The woman you think you love is nothing but a man in woman's clothing! Off she went to Wales to conduct business meant for a man without a care that you were left behind. You should question her femininity!" Thoughts spun in her head as her movement became more frantic. *Why, oh why does he find Arielle so captivating? I simply cannot understand! I cannot see her charm, her allure!*

Her desperate pleas were making her wane. She felt she was losing every ounce of energy she needed to sustain her hold on William. She was falling into her own personal abyss of abandonment and there seemed to be no way to find her way back into William's good graces. *Why can he not see the intensity of my love for him? What must I do to have him turn from Arielle? This is my worst nightmare! There must be some way to halt this ridiculous path he has taken! What am I to do? What am I to do? Think, think, think!* The word was repeated again and again in Alexandra's mind. She felt like banging her head against a wall to gain a clearer vision or, at the very least, dull her senses so the agony of his dismissal would inflict far less pain.

"William, please, I beg of you," Alexandra urged with fresh tears mounting in her eyes. "My love is here waiting for you to take it, to feel it."

William hoped to sufficiently douse her flames of passion. He took one step closer to her and laid his hand on her shoulder. She shuddered and shifted her shoulder away, releasing it from his touch. She, as always, was at once at odds with herself, wanting his touch, but reproaching his advances. For Alexandra it was all or nothing, and she could not accept second best. She could not accept friend. She could not accept a pat on the head or a rub on the snout with a treat thrown in for good measure. She would not be placated like a hound by such simple pleasures. She wanted him, all of him, and would not stop until the wants, wishes, and desires of her heart were met. She would stop his marriage to Arielle by any means. She would make him love her and her alone. He would learn to see that she, Miss Alexandra Whitaker, was his true love and all that he needed in this world. *Tomorrow will be my day of reckoning, my day of victory, and my day to have William proclaim his love for me. Yes, tomorrow will be a very sad day for sweetie, sweet Arielle Hargrove. I will not let her win. She will not have my William. Tomorrow, her supposed wedding day will be the end for her. I will see to that.*

The others in the house had become aware of the loud voices coming from Horace's study and they began making their way to its entrance. William was traditionally fond of the room for it held so many treasured memories. It was the place where his late uncle passed along his words of wisdom and mentored him to become a successful lawyer. Today however was an exception to the warm images he conjured of visiting with his uncle and exploring the wide variety of his books that filled the floor-to-ceiling bookshelves. Alexandra had taken any pleasure from the day with her tirade. As she marched to the doorway and opened it to exit, she was surprised to see that a small crowd had gathered.

"Well what do we have here, an eavesdropping entourage? Are your lives so dull that you must linger about and put your noses in the affairs of others?"

"Alexandra was just leaving. I apologize for any discomfort we may have caused in your home, Aunt Emma," William expressed as Alexandra twisted away from the guidance of his arm.

"How quickly I am dismissed! I have much more to say on this topic!"

"I would say there is not much more you can say about the topic, thankfully. Let me walk you to the door."

"And Mr. Drake, I thought you were my friend! Have you nothing to say to commend me? Would it be a crime for you to find a word of praise to cast my direction if for nothing else but my ability to stay focused on a topic and ride it until the end?

"The bitter end, some might say," Alistair muttered, hoping his comment went unheard.

Emma heard him and, although she was pleased to hear him admonish Alexandra's behavior, she feared that his statement would spur her to spew more venom.

"My observations about so many who have crossed my path since I have been in America are based on a variety of influences," Alistair said as he continued his remarks. "From the senior Hargroves, to you, Miss Whitaker, to you, Mr. Bamford, and oh, let us not forget the stories you have shared about the Smithfield and Hollingsworth women – why I should say that the crime of which they all are collectively guilty is that of omission. There is no mystery to the fact that had they not harbored secrets your lives would have been very different indeed, as would theirs. It was inevitable for the truth to be told. There is usually no hiding it you see, and it has been my experience that some who do hold their tongues about their suspicions usually find a confidant with whom to bare their souls. My yes, there are many complexities to love gone wrong and decisions gone awry! Maybe I should direct my writing efforts to romance novels, although the way of love can be a mystery unto itself, would you not say, Mrs. Willard?"

Emma was caught off-guard by Alistair's statement and wondered why he was directing his last comment to her. She was considering how to formulate a response as she studied his face, which had taken on a very pleasant and relaxed appearance. Alexandra had had her fill of Alistair's tone and left the manse in a huff without bidding anyone a formal adieu. Her day had not gone to her liking and she needed to rally her strength to prepare herself for the challenges tomorrow would bring her way. Emma looked about at the others in the room, and then turned to address Alistair.

"I cannot imagine anyone considering me an expert when it comes to romance for I had but one love in my life. Horace and I enjoyed a charmed life as is evidenced in this magnificent home he commissioned for us. Yes, I was truly blessed to have such a stable and loving man in my life. I miss Horace every day."

"Oh, do not get me wrong. As I have said in the past, you people are mad and I adore it! I do so fancy your style! And, as far as your opinions regarding romance, one never knows what might spark a flame of interest in another. Some things that seem to have gone dormant spring to life when most unexpected, wouldn't you agree?"

Where is he going with this dialogue? If I were not mistaken, I would say he is flirting with me! Emma felt unnerved at the thought as her cheeks flushed with heat. It was a sensation she had not experienced for many years. *How can Alistair Whitfield Drake be having this effect on me?*

⁓

"W̲ere you absolutely surprised?" Emma enthusiastically asked when Sully and Arianna returned to her residence along with Arielle.

Arianna's eyes were sparkling as she gave Sully's hand a squeeze and then proudly displayed her newly acquired diamond engagement ring for all to see.

"I can hardly contain myself I am so happy! I could not wait another minute to tell my dear sister, so Sully suggested we stop by to tell her and my father. This has been the most wonderful day! And, I thank you and Mr. Peabody for the part you played in assisting Sully with the acquisition of my artwork."

William could say the same about the day now that Arielle was in his presence. He would not allow Alexandra's visit to take a further toll on his good spirits. He walked to Arielle and took her hand. She gave his hand a squeeze and leaned into him.

"Just look at all of the lovebirds in my presence! I feel especially blessed to know all of you and to have you in my life. Yes, I am truly blessed indeed!" Emma's smile broadened as she admired the couples before her.

"And just think, Aunt Emma, tomorrow all of your plans will come to fruition as Arielle and I take our vows," William said, seemingly hypnotized by Arielle's beauty.

A tingle of excitement enveloped Arielle as she looked into his eyes. She was quickly drawn into the strength of his being and could hardly wait for tomorrow to come. *Tomorrow he will be mine and I his,* she mused. Her heart was bursting with love and desire. She felt a heat come over her face and hoped no one observed the pink blush that she was certain filled her cheeks. William noticed, but said not a word as he gazed into her eyes. Her nearness made his pulse quicken. *Tomorrow cannot come soon enough,* he thought, for the wait was becoming more than he could bear. He was eager to take her home to Everleigh and to have her savor the intimacy of his touch as he explored her body and she his. "Mr. and Mrs. William Clay," he pondered aloud and added with a broad grin, "I love the sound of that."

Chapter Thirty-Two

Wednesday, October 26, 1898
Washington, District of Columbia

Arielle peeked into the sanctuary. She was glad to have a few quiet moments alone to take in the beauty of the scene before her. Nosegays of roses in luscious shades of red, yellow, and orange adorned each pew. Wispy sprigs of baby's breath gathered with variegated greens were tucked among the flowers, while tendrils of ivory, cocoa, and burnt orange satin ribbon cascaded from each bouquet. The floral displays created a lush and fragrant aisle for the soon-to-be promenade of the bride and groom and their guests. Two large white urns placed on either side of the altar were dramatic with tall arrangements of hydrangeas in antique shades of russet and burgundy, peach-colored lilies, calla lilies, aralia leaves, long-stemmed roses, some with their stems intertwined, and lengths of ivy trailing over the top edges of the urns. William had promised Arielle that their wedding would abound with roses and he was true to his word. She smiled with deep satisfaction as she noticed another detail attended to by William's aunt.

Upon Emma's instructions, satin pouches filled with birdseed to shower over the bride and groom rested in a large crystal bowl and baskets of rose petals sat in wait for the end of the ceremony for guests to gather handfuls and joyfully toss them into the couple's path. Emma said tossing the petals was a symbol her mother proclaimed was important. Her words were, "To assure a happy journey through life, the newly married should walk upon a carpet of flowers."

Emma had also shared the history of St. John's Church with Arielle. It was as dear to her as the special services the church provided for those in need, which kept Emma involved in her volunteer work at the settlement houses in nearby Purdy's Court. Arielle was startled from her concentration by the sounding of the church's Revere bell that shook the serenity of the sanctuary. Since its installation in 1822, every hour on the hour, the striking of the bell's clapper resonated against its sides. Emma had informed her that the decorative instrument of percussion was so named because Paul Revere's son, Joseph, had cast it.

Arielle's mind drifted to the day she and William met with the man who would officiate at their wedding in order to finalize their vows and discuss the hymns and readings that would complete their service. William had teased her when she reverted to her roots and referred to the man as a vicar.

"The vicar, what is his name? I know I should remember. It is just that Emma has been our liaison and this is my first time in his presence."

William smiled. He was always quite taken with the charm Arielle exuded when her Welsh roots slipped from her lips.

"What, Will? Why do you smile at me so?"

"The smile, you can rest assured, is not meant to mock or to make fun but, in the States my dear, the one you mention is known as Reverend. The rector of St. John's is Reverend Alexander MacKay-Smith."

"Oh, say what you will, but I do suspect there is a tinge of teasing in your tone," Arielle said as she smiled back and warmly took his hand in hers. Through an alcove came the sound of footsteps. Arielle released William's hand as the rector entered the sanctuary.

"Alex, here you are! Oh, forgive me. We are in your hallowed chambers so I believe your rightful title is warranted. Reverend MacKay-Smith, I am most pleased to introduce you to my intended, Miss Arielle Hargrove."

"Ah, Miss Hargrove. I have heard so many wonderful platitudes about you from Mrs. Willard. It seems you can do no wrong where she is concerned!"

"You are very kind to say so, Reverend. I feel much the same about Mr. Clay's aunt. She is kind and wise and a great ally. But, oh, I am afraid that I am embarrassing myself. Please do not misunderstand, for I am not suggesting that I am of the same caliber as Mrs. Willard."

"My lovely bride-to-be is being very humble. You will note the grace about her after only a short while in her company."

"Indeed I do, indeed I do. Well, this is a great pleasure for me to finally see the two of you together. Come, let's discuss the plans for your ceremony."

Arielle's mind drifted back to the moment at hand. It was time to slip into her bridal gown and ready herself to meet her groom.

"Sir Ian, Agnes and I want to extend our condolences to you about your wife's passing. We were present at her service but did not have the opportunity to speak with you. We are so very sorry for your loss." Morgan's face was stoic as she observed a sad expression wash over Ian's face.

"Yes, Arielle and I lost the light of our home. Lady Hargrove was a quiet but central presence in our lives and gave our home stability. She is sorely missed but will never be fully gone. In my memory she lives and, for now, we must move on because today is a day to rejoice in my daughter's and Mr. Clay's happiness. Lady Hargrove will be very much in my thoughts for I know how much she wanted to see this day. Thank you for being here and for your kind words."

Morgan and Agnes, with Peepers in tow, walked to a pew several rows down to take their seats for the ceremony as Ziggy walked into the church and caught Ian's eye.

"Carson my man, just whom I wanted to speak with before the ceremony gets underway. I have been so consumed with a variety of details both personal and work related that I have failed to meet with you about a topic that, if you say 'yes,' would bring me great pleasure and I hope it will be mutually beneficial."

"Sir Ian, you have my undivided attention. What is on your mind?"

"The colliery is on my mind, you and the colliery to be exact. You are aware, I am sure, that Sully and Arianna have become engaged. The idea of their union pleases me very much for I have come to know Sully and he has an astute business mind that will continue to serve him well. They both long to return to Wales so I have asked him to be my eyes and ears and oversee the operations of Hargrove Colliery. Along with Nesbitt who is my overman, they will make a solid team."

"And what does this have to do with me?"

"I would like to offer you a management position as well. This is an idea that Arielle brought to me. I see you as being very effective with the workers, knowing their needs and causes. I would like you to keep pace with their daily lives at the mine and become a liaison of sorts to convey what you learn to both Nesbitt and Sully. And it will be important that you keep everything documented. You will receive a very fair wage that should keep you living in comfort the rest of your days. How does this sound to you?"

"It sounds like I would be a fool to say no to such a proposition. When do I start?"

"As soon as you return home, well, to Wales that is. I take it that you have no attachments to Shoreditch?"

"You take that right. I am happy to leave that chapter of my existence and never revisit it. This is very kind and generous of you. I am not sure that I quite deserve it."

"You have endured a wrong that must be put right. Accepting my invitation to come to America and mending your relationship with your sister before her death was the beginning of putting things back on the proper course. Thank you for agreeing to my offer. I know Elsbeth is smiling from the heavens," Ian said as a tear came to his eye. "My goodness, I had best get back to my duties as the father of the bride. We have much to celebrate this day!"

Ian walked to the back of the church to the waiting area where the wedding party was gathering. He spotted Sully and as he approached him Sully came forward.

"Just whom I was hoping to see. Sir Ian, I wanted to inform you that Arianna and I have discussed at length your proposal that we live at your estate in Wales while I oversee your colliery."

"Yes, yes, and what was your decision?"

"We have collectively decided that we are very receptive to your offer and accept it without any further delay."

"Very good. Now, that is settled. I want to let you know that I have asked Carson Cromwell to be in a management position at the colliery as well. I am very confident that the two of you, in concert with Nesbitt, will be a driving force for the continued success of the mine and that you will take it into modern times with all of the advancements in industry." Ian's words picked up momentum until he remembered where he should be putting his focus. "Well, forgive me, but that's enough business for one day for we are in the business of getting a couple married. Let's find our places."

Ziggy slid into a pew next to Morgan, Agnes and Peepers. He knew he had them to thank for finding him and reuniting him with his sister. His thoughts turned briefly to Elsbeth. *How I missed her all those years. When I think of all we could have shared. Alas, so many missed opportunities.* He reflected on his arrival in America and his first visit to her home. Although she gave him a warm welcome, he saw that the youthful spark was gone from her face and the energy she had exuded when she was first married had waned. Worry and fatigue had overtaken her emotionally and physically. She sat up in her bed as he walked closer to her and took her hand. They held onto to each other for what seemed like an eternity, trying to erase the hurt, find forgiveness, and restore some of the time lost to them as brother and sister.

When they finally spoke, it was of the old times, the days growing up, their parents, and all the good that had been in their lives. There came little mention of the reason for their parting and although he forgave Elsbeth, the memory of what she did would fade but never vanish. Ziggy wanted to be able to consider the circumstances of their estrangement to be water under the bridge, in the past, a prologue that could not be altered. His concentration was broken by a question.

"So, I asked how are you, Mr. Cromwell? I was telling your brother-in-law that we are very sorry about the passing of Lady Hargrove. We hope your time spent with her provided some closure to the events of the past."

"Oh, pardon me, for Elsbeth, in fact, was uppermost on my mind. I fear I became lost in my thoughts. Yes, yes, you were quite right to find me and Sir Ian was very generous to provide the funds for my passage here." Ziggy thought about the good fortune of the job offer he had just received. His brother-in-law was a man of enlarged experience in the coal industry and his careful management had led to his unparalleled success. *Things are definitely looking up for me, I must say,* Ziggy reflected.

Morgan noted the change in Ziggy's speech. He had abandoned the street vernacular she had heard him speak in Shoreditch. When a tap on the shoulder from a guest in the pew behind them distracted Ziggy, Morgan leaned over to speak to Agnes.

"It is interesting how quickly he has fallen back on his proper English tongue. A refreshing improvement, I might add." Agnes nodded in complete agreement as her peripheral vision spied the woman who had desired Ziggy's attention.

"Look Morgan, behind you," Agnes said under her breath. "Won't Miss Hargrove be surprised to see her here?"

"Whoa boy, that's the truth, that's the truth," squawked Peepers as he spun around in his cage.

"She will indeed," Morgan said as she, Peepers and Agnes turned to face the altar.

As the organ music segued to announce the bride's entrance, William looked with great anticipation at the doorway to the sanctuary as Arielle stepped into the threshold on her father's arm. Her beauty took his breath away. Her gown, designed by one of the sisters who founded the Fox Dressmaking Company of New York, was exquisite. The fitted bodice, made of cream-white silk brocade enhanced with tiny pearls, accentuated her petite waist. The silk brocade continued onto the gown's skirt held full by several petticoats that lifted the skirt's train ever so slightly to allow for freedom of movement. Modified leg o'mutton sleeves scattered with pearls were full at her shoulders and then tapered to her wrist with one dozen covered buttons and a small flounce of imported lace at the cuff. Her veil of silk tulle, attached to a coronet of diamonds borrowed from Emma, matched the length of her gown's train. Her raven locks were swept into a loose chignon studded with pearls. Ecru satin slippers with one-inch heels peeked from under her gown revealing a hint of her silk stockings embroidered with roses. Pearl briolette earrings with diamond studs were at her ears while a simple strand of pearls adorned her neck. Cream-white kid gloves with a slit for the placement of her wedding ring finished her ensemble. She was a vision in beauty and grace.

Arianna and Emma had insisted she carry on the tradition of the Old English rhyme: "Something olde, something new, something borrowed, something blue, and a silver sixpence for her shoe." Emma's diamond coronet served as the "something borrowed;" Arielle's gown was "something new;" her mother's strand of pearls were "something olde" to link her to her past; a blue linen handkerchief with her new initial 'C' for Clay represented "something blue;" and her father offered up the sixpence to be worn in her left shoe to symbolize future prosperity. None of those things crossed her mind when she saw her future husband waiting near the altar for her to join him.

William was so stunningly handsome she could barely stand still. She wanted to run immediately into his arms and be enveloped by him, smell the warm musk of him, and forever be entranced by the tenderness of his gaze. He stood tall in his dark brown cut-away tailcoat with an ivory pocket square, a double-breasted ivory waistcoat, and an ivory shirt with winged-collar. His dark brown cashmere trousers with thin gray stripes, patent leather button boots, and pale tan kid gloves completed his exquisitely tailored ensemble. Sully was dressed in a similar fashion in a brown tuxedo jacket with matching trousers. Both men had a russet colored rose boutonnière in their lapels.

Sully looked at Arianna as the processional music played and she stared back at him with longing. She was stunningly beautiful in her bronze gown made of imported satin. It was the perfect back-drop for her emerald eyes. They sparkled as she shifted them back and forth taking in all that she could of her fiancé. Like Arielle's gown, it too had leg o'mutton sleeves with a dozen tiny covered buttons running partially up the sleeves from her wrists. Her auburn hair was swept up in wavy tendrils that fell onto her shoulders from a diamond-encrusted hair comb secured in her hair at the base of her neck. Sully was anxious for the ceremony to get underway so he could take her in his arms and dance the night away at Chestnut Heights. For Arianna, the overwhelming desire to be closer to him was becoming more than she could contain. A warm blush came over her cheeks as she returned her focus to Arielle and her father.

Ian and Arielle began their syncopated stroll along the white cloth laid down the full length of the aisle establishing a pure path to the altar. Suddenly, Ian felt a strong bump to his side as Alexandra appeared and attempted to shove him out of the way and move past him. At first he thought she was simply late for the ceremony and was determined to make her way into a pew. Then he realized that her intent was anything but pure as she pushed harder against him nearly knocking Arielle to the floor. She was dressed as a bride in a white gown with a long train and veil to match. Within a moment, Simon jumped from his seat in a pew at the back of the sanctuary and stepped on Alexandra's train halting her in her tracks. As she jerked at the train to free herself of him, he rolled down putting his full weight on her gown's train making it impossible for her to move forward. Ian quickly turned and quietly admonished her as he signaled to several men Arielle had never seen before to guard her. He had anticipated that there might be an incident and he was fully prepared with a security detail if anything unruly occurred. Two of the men helped Simon to his feet as they ushered Alexandra from the church. William and Sully were ready to charge up the aisle when they saw her dressed as though she were the one to be married, but they held themselves back when they saw Simon jump from the pew and onto Alexandra's gown and two other men take her by the arms and escort her out. Simon brushed himself off and shook his body to restore his suit to its proper form. Ian patted Arielle's hand giving her comfort as they resumed their promenade.

"I would never have guessed that the smallest among us would do the biggest job," Ian whispered to Arielle with a smile forming as he relived the sight of Simon rolling down and thwarting Alexandra's plan.

"Simon has come to my aid in the past. He is quite resourceful and it seems you were, as usual, well-prepared for an outburst of this sort. Very prescient on your part. I thought Alexandra would have given up her pursuit of William once our wedding was underway."

"The girl is relentless. What a sorry soul she is. I will deal with her later. For now, we have a man waiting before us to begin his life with you, so here we go," Ian said as he gave a little pat to Arielle's arm and they proceeded to the altar.

Along the way Arielle took her eyes from William for just a moment to look left and right to acknowledge the faces of the large gathering of family, friends, and close acquaintances who filled all of the church's pews. She recognized some of Emma's theatre family, several in flamboyant attire, her father's colleagues, associates of William's, and several judges and government leaders. Here sat Washington's finest, a veritable *Who's Who* montage of the social elite. Arielle paused momentarily in her gait as one face stood out among the others. Ian noted the change in her pace and knew whom she had spotted in the pew behind Ziggy. There she was, Maggie Galligan, with a smile as wide as Wales. Arielle had last seen her during the negotiations at the colliery and she was fully unaware that she had been invited to her wedding.

"Ah, you have seen the surprise guest William and I planned for you," Ian whispered as he gave a nod in Maggie's direction. "We thought it would be a proper way for you to have a part of your birth mother here. Mrs. Galligan was a good friend to Annie Hollingsworth and so proud that she could know her offspring. So, we sent her the fare to cover all of her travel expenses and her lodging during her stay."

"I am without words. This is so unexpected and thoughtful of you both," Arielle said as the two continued their stroll. Her father was revealing a softer side of late, a side to which she could grow quite accustomed.

⌒

Reverend MacKay-Smith greeted the congregation of witnesses to William and Arielle's wedding with an opening salutation and several readings including First Corinthians chapter 13 verses 4 through 7. Then he motioned for Sully who moved from his place beside William and stepped onto the riser of the altar to sing the Welsh love song, *Tra Bo Dau*, known in English as, *While There Are Two*. He sang first in Welsh then in English. Tears came to Ian's, Arianna's, Arielle's, and Maggie's eyes as Sully so beautifully sang the traditional words of their homeland. Although he sang alone, the clear resonance of his voice had them imagining the full support of the Treorchy Male Voice Choir. They relished in the song's lyrics, "For every day my choice I bless, My love I'll never rue, His gentle voice, his sweet caress, Is constant fair and true; Rich years are fading and constant, Beauty will wither and wane, With love so pure, will I endure, while our two hearts remain."

"We will now have a reading by the bride's sister, Miss Arianna Smithfield. I understand that she has written this original composition especially for this occasion. She has titled her poem, 'Love's

Embrace,'" the Reverend said as he motioned for Arianna to stand near him. She softly cleared her throat and began to read:

Love's Embrace

When faced with the emotion of love, its power, its potential,
one wonders and reflects, "What course will it travel?"
For, when the beating of two hearts come in harmony as one,
unified in spirit and devotion,
there exists a great bond that transcends space and time.
Love develops a transparency, like still waters reflecting the river basin
below,
and we see our true selves and our selflessness.
The mighty forests surrounding the river envelop us,
as we feel the embrace of a new branch
pointing toward a destiny that brings strength and hope
and a growing desire to keep fresh what brings us to this day.
We pause.
We celebrate this moment.
And, we give thanks as we anticipate the many blessings of love to come.

When Arianna completed her recitation and walked to stand once again beside her sister, Arielle touched her hand in a tender gesture to thank her for her beautiful words.

"And now for the vows," smiled the Reverend as he opened his prayer book and began to recite the words that William and Arielle would exchange to promise to commit themselves to one another. As they repeated his words as instructed, the awareness of the congregation faded away. It was just the two of them with a man in a clerical robe guiding their words but not their emotions. Agreeing to love, honor, and obey one another for the rest of their days in sickness and in health, for richer, for poorer, until death do they part, were commitments they willingly made and gladly accepted. They had waited long for this day to come and they were going to cherish every moment of it.

"Now the rings," said the Reverend who turned to Sully who placed two wedding bands in the Reverend's hand. "William and Arielle have given me the following words that they wish to convey to one another. I might also note that they have inscribed their rings with their initials and today's date, an additional commemoration to record the significance of this day. William, as I say the words, please repeat them after me as you place this ring on Arielle's finger."

William took the ring and as he slid it onto his bride's finger he said, "Arielle, milady, I give you my heart and my hand. Let this ring serve as a symbol of our bond of mutual respect, of friendship, and of love."

A tingle went through Arielle as the Reverend gave her William's ring and she said, "William, kind sir, I give you my heart and my hand. Let this ring serve as a symbol of our bond of mutual respect, of friendship, and of love."

The heat between them was becoming more intense. Arielle ached to have his fingers touch her, to find their way all over her body. She was brought back to her senses and the reality of the moment as the Reverend came to the conclusion of the service. He read from Matthew 19 verses 4 through 6, which made Alexandra's skin crawl. She had found her way into a side alcove of the sanctuary with one of Ian's hired men fast on her heels. He held her back from proceeding any further, but the bible verse continued to sting her ears: "Wherefore they are no more twain, but one flesh. What therefore God has joined together, let not man put asunder." Alexandra wanted to scream to the heavens but she knew the man overshadowing her would quickly squelch her efforts. She listened as the Reverend announced them as husband and wife and watched them, both beaming with joy, turn to face their celebrants. They caressed one another with a kiss on the cheek, and then made their way up the aisle carrying with them the responsibility of promises made while Alexandra melted into a hopeless heap of white on the cold tile floor.

Chapter Thirty-Three

The team of Spanish-Norman horses pulled the deluxe carriage fitted out in white leather seats to a halt in front of Chestnut Heights. The beautiful white mares, a regal mix of the Spanish Andalusian and the French Percheron breeds, offered a commanding presence and elicited a rousing cheer from the guests on the loggia awaiting the arrival of the bride and groom. William proffered his hand to assist Arielle from the conveyance as they and their entourage of guests made their way into the grand salon. Lit candles and floral displays abounded. Servers were passing food and drinks on large salvers and voices became enthusiastically engaged in conversation.

Arielle spied the wedding cake on a large, round, skirted table at one end of the salon. It was resplendent in autumnal splendor. Rounds of white cake in ascending order from large to small formed its seven tiers. Smoothly covered in a white fondant icing, the cake was piped with pearls of buttercream frosting and enhanced with plump roses in rich shades of russet, red, and yellow, beautifully appointed by leaves in several tones of green. Icing formed in swags of garland circled each layer accented with small white fondant birds. A bouquet of icing roses was nestled on the very top and added the crowning touch. Arielle had requested the cake's design as a tribute to her birth mother. The seven layers represented the number of letters in Arielle's name and the month and day she was born -- a number she felt provided her with the good fortune of finally being united with her sister, Arianna. And, the roses. They kept Annie Hollingsworth ever present in her life. Though she had long since passed, her birth mother was like the symbol of the lingering summer rose she and William witnessed one year past that had found its way through a crevice in a stone wall. *Yes,* she thought as she looked at the sweet confection, *my mother is the rose beyond, for I steadfastly believe that the rose still grows beyond the wall. She is more with me today than she has ever been.*

A tinge of guilt passed over her like a shadow cast to bring her back to the present. She was not forgetting her mother Elsbeth, for she had raised her and loved her as her own. She had set an example of dignity, grace, courage, and love under sometimes strenuous circumstances and for that Arielle would always be grateful. She had forgiven the secret her parents had long-held about her adoption and the revelation from her father about his philandering ways. She would not dwell on what could never be changed. She had a sister and now a husband to brighten her future, and she was filled with gratitude for her many blessings. And, there was Sully. He had unexpectedly come into their lives, and though they were not related by blood, she felt a kinship to him like a darling brother. She hoped his visits to America would be frequent so their relationship could continue for years to come. *And, Uncle Ziggy, what a joy he is and such a fond reminder of my mother.* Arielle's attention was brought back to the festivities before her as she heard her father clink a utensil against his glass to gain the attention of the guests.

"Excuse me everyone. If I might have your attention, I would like to propose a toast to the newlyweds." Ian stood as proud as a peacock as he turned to acknowledge all about him with his glass held high. "William, it is with much pleasure that I welcome you into our family. You and Arielle mean the world to me and I know you will make each other exceedingly happy. I had thought that I would have Arielle's mother on my arm for this momentous occasion, but

God in his good graces had another plan." Ian became choked up at his reference to Elsbeth. "But, I can unequivocally tell you all that my dear wife more than anyone would want mirth to prevail today. So, to the bride and groom I repeat the words of the French author George Sand, 'There is only one happiness in life, to love and be loved' and I salute you."

Rousing shouts of "here, here" could be heard among the gathering as guests emptied their glasses of their contents and the catering staff made their rounds to replenish beverages.

"Whoa boy, whoa boy! Relax, relax!" The loud squawk from Peepers garnered Arielle and William's attention.

Agnes gave a gentle wiggle to his cage to settle him down as she looked about to see what had ruffled his feathers. Alexandra sauntered onto the dance floor. No longer donning a wedding gown, she was more suitably dressed in a royal blue gown of velvet with an empire waist and ruching that disguised her present state.

"Shush, Peepers. That is quite enough," Agnes admonished.

"Oh, let him have his fun. It appears he is trying to ameliorate the situation and the other guests seem to be enjoying his intuitiveness. Once again it seems that he is an excellent judge of people," Morgan observed as she watched to see if anything more would come of Alexandra's presence in the room.

William and Arielle were surprised to see Alexandra at their reception. They thought her episode at the church would have rendered her feeling embarrassed and defeated. But, here she was again. William walked to her without causing undue attention and quietly gave her a word of warning.

"The stunt you pulled at the church must not be repeated here. I will have no more of your displays and, I see that Sir Ian has his men at the ready should you make the mistake of attempting to wreak any additional havoc. Enough is enough, Alexandra."

Alexandra looked at him feeling ready to spit. She held back her anger but her distress was building. She was like a wild, untamed horse growing increasingly defiant in response to the restraints being placed upon her.

As the musicians positioned their instruments to begin play, William very capably took his bride in his arms. Arielle was so taken with his warm embrace and the emotions of the day that she felt ready to swoon. For her, this day had been one of great planning and great anticipation. Alexandra's many attempts at interference might have denied them this day of resounding joy, but thankfully she had failed. Arielle looked up into her husband's eyes and fell into them. Even in the most enchanting of dreams, he was everything and more than she could ever have imagined.

Emma watched as the two began to sway to the music. Her thoughts turned to her wedding day and Horace holding her in his arms just as William was holding Arielle. *Such a long, long time ago,* she mused.

"You are deep in thought it appears? What a glorious day this has been. I must admit it is easy for me to succumb to a happy ending. Speaking of that, might I have this dance?" Alistair inquired as he held his hand out for Emma to join him.

She surprised herself when she accepted his offer without hesitation. *What an unexpected turn of events,* she thought as Alistair led her in a waltz about the dance floor. *Upon our first meeting and the many months he has lived in my home, I never suspected that I would be this close to this man. Will wonders never cease?"*

William watched his aunt and saw the joy in her step. *Yes, Uncle Horace would want to see her living her life. I know that would be his wish.*

Arielle nearly laughed when she saw Simon approach Agnes for a dance. She rested Peepers in his cage on a nearby chair and the two made their way onto the dance floor among the growing crowd of participants. Fiona stood on the sidelines tapping her feet to the music while Morgan observed the scene and jingled the coins in her pocket. Ziggy walked to Morgan and said something, which caused her to cease the manipulation of her coins and suddenly they too were among the dancers.

Ian watched Fiona wanting to be part of the festivities. He was afraid that brows would be raised if he asked her for a dance, so he signaled an associate from the Trade Council, a young, flame-haired

Irishman who readily stepped in to whisk her about. Arianna and Sully were as lost in their own world as were the newlyweds. They continued to dance from one song to the next never seeming to tire of dancing or the loving hold they had on one another.

William held Arielle closer and caressed her with his strength, both gentle and strong in the same whisper of time, then the two glided about the dance floor touched only by the eyes of the on-lookers who formed a circle of unconditional love around them. Their feet picked up speed as the tune became livelier and William held on more closely to Arielle lest he spin her across the room. As the musical composition met its crescendo and the pace began to slow, the bride and groom waltzed and waltzed in gay abandon as though they were the single souls in the space – no outside force could penetrate their bond. Arielle's spirit had never been lighter. She was in the arms of the love of her life and longed for their dance to never find its end.

William lifted Arielle in his arms, much in the same manner he had on their first meeting in the spring of 1897 when she was fleeing her home in the middle of a rainstorm. He had res-cued her and introduced her to a broader world with new faces, new friends, and new revelations. She rested her head on his shoulder as he carried her across the threshold of Everleigh. Here they were for the first time in William's home as husband and wife. *Our home,* thought Arielle. *Our Everleigh,* she sighed as she snuggled against William's neck and took in the wonderful, masculine scent of him.

"Yes, it is our home and you may do with it as you like. Buy what-ever you want and furnish it as you please."

As William spoke, Arielle lifted her head and looked into his eyes. They had waited all day for this moment, this time alone, this time to become one. He brought his lips to hers in a deep, passion-ate kiss. They explored each other's mouths as their tongues play-fully tagged one another arousing their senses. Arielle pulled back, not to escape but wanting more. She was breathing more heavily as was he and he knew it was time to make their way to their bed chambers. He carried her up the staircase stopping on the landing to kiss her again before proceeding to their room. With his booted foot, he pushed the room's double doors wide-open and made his way to the edge of the large canopied bed where he released Arielle from his arms.

"I want you in every way."

Upon those words, William released the combs from Arielle's hair and ran his fingers through her lush, raven locks as the tendrils tumbled along her soft, creamy shoulders and cascaded down her back. He looked into her eyes and she into his as their passion ignited. His hand slid down and then up the full side of her gown causing a tingling sensation to rise within her. She felt a moistness in her loins as he raised her lips to his, enveloping her in the wet hunger of his mouth. His lips moved lower where he placed gentle, tickling kisses along her neck. Arielle moaned. Calling for more, she raised her arms about his neck and ran her fingers through the full thickness of his chestnut waves. Slowly, William turned her to have full access to the back of her gown. He placed his lips on the nape of her neck as his fingers adeptly unhooked one button at a time to reveal the fine symmetry of her back. She shuttered as his actions caused the tingling sensations to revisit her loins. He turned her to face him as he carefully slid her gown from her shoulders letting it and her petticoats puddle to the floor.

He drew her to him bringing her chemise against his shirt. Arielle smiled and leaned away as she fondled his tie, loosening its knot and slipping it from the shirt's collar. She looked into his eyes as one by one she unbuttoned his shirt, then ran her hand over the hair on his chest. He took her hand in his and held it against his heart.

"I love you more than you can ever imagine, Arielle. The joy of this day shall remain with me forever."

"And for me, sir."

"Ah, I hear formalities have regained themselves, milady."

Arielle grinned as a playful smile crossed her face.

William pulled Arielle closer to him. His hand moved up and down her torso resting on her thigh. In massaging motions his hand went around and around on her thigh as his kisses moved from her lips to her neck, finally resting between her breasts. His hand left her thigh and came up under her right breast. Gently he squeezed at her soft flesh until his fingers came upon her nipple and he brought his lips down to suckle the sweet nectar of her flesh. Arielle groaned as her body writhed in motion to his advances. Her hands moved in slow, virgin steps to release the buttons on his trousers. Their heart beats advanced in response to the carnal sensations racing through their limbs and groins. William's trousers fell to the floor. As he stepped from them, he removed the final vestiges of undergarments from his bride's body. Growing with anticipation, he looked at her naked form. Intermittent flickers of light cast from the gas lit lamp on the bedside table provided an ambient glow. He was ready to be one with her and could wait no more.

He pulled her close. Arielle took in a deep breath and let it softly spill all over William's chest. She laid her head against him, then leaned back and ran her fingers through the soft mat of hair on his chest. He smiled and pulled her closer. It was all so new to her, yet so natural. Time slowed as she savored his every touch. As her body rubbed up against him, she felt a hard bulge as his maleness rose with a determination to be sated. The two began to rotate and rub one against the other. Soft groans and sighs emitted by Arielle urged William forward. Deftly, he swooped her into his arms and laid her down on their wedding bed. Down he came on top of her and reached between her legs to ready her for his entry. Ever so slowly, he made his way inside as Arielle writhed in perfect rhythm to welcome him. Their motion gained more and more intensity until William released the fullness of his manhood and Arielle cried out with an ecstasy of pleasure she had never felt before. She tugged at him wanting more, wanting to feel the exhilaration again and again. William answered her plea with kisses up and down her torso, his lips resting on her breasts as his hands made their way to her buttocks. He turned her and lifted her up as she positioned herself on her knees. He held onto her hips and pulled her against him as he found her opening and slowly entered. His pumping back and forth became more intense as she groaned and rocked wanting more and more. He came inside her just as she cried out his name. Indescribable sensations overtook the two as they moved and rocked until William eased himself from her.

They had wanted each other in every way and had found fulfillment beyond Arielle's wildest dreams. *To think, this is only the beginning,* she thought to herself. She rolled onto her back and looked up at her groom. William slid beside her, held her hand and stroked her face.

"You are everything and more than I ever dreamed I would have in my life. You have always given me great pleasure and now, the ultimate gift of your intimate self. I love you so very much. To think the fate of a rainswept eve brought us into one another's lives. We are truly blessed and I will always be grateful that our paths crossed when they did."

Arielle watched every word from William's lips. She could not imagine loving anyone more than she loved him now. He had touched her very being and made her senses come alive as never before. She took his hand that held hers and moved it to her chest. She looked into his blue eyes with love and adoration.

"Please know my dear William, you hold my hand and my heart and always will."

William's marriage to Arielle stirred a renewed rage within Alexandra that was reaching an uncontrolled climax. She was broken and not to be consoled. She had been unable to halt the shadow spreading across her heart. Her mind whirled with images of the two of them together, his arms around Arielle, arms that should have been enveloping her, and his kiss to Arielle's lips, kisses that should have been hers to receive. Tears stained her face as she rubbed her eyes to erase the visions bombarding her. To think of them coming together as husband and wife in every carnal sense of the word sent toxic shivers throughout her body. *If only Father were here. He would have seen to it that Arielle would have been no more than a passing fancy. He would have set William straight. He was destined to be mine, but she ruined it all.* Alexandra could barely get her words to come together. She was seething with jealousy and anger and felt an intense sensation to scream, to throw something, to do damage. She needed an escape to find solace, turf familiar to her, where her wild spirit could roam free. *I will return home. I will go to the stables. Father always encouraged me to ride, to clear my worries by becoming one with nature, one with my mount.*

She journeyed by coach from Chestnut Heights to the Whitaker estate but the trip was less than sufficient to calm her nerves or cool her fury. She was determined to find a means to let go of the vicious aura swirling about her. It was threatening her ability to form a new plan to end William's marriage to Arielle. *An evening ride will be my salvation! Marriage is not so sacred that it cannot be put asunder! Though I am with child, William will see the error of his ways and come to love me as his true love. He can divorce her! He will love me unconditionally, and he will come to love this child as his own flesh and blood.*

Not tarrying to change into her riding habit, Alexandra raced to the stables. Her favorite horse, Blaze, greeted her with a welcoming neigh. Opening the stall door, she guided him out to the mounting block her father had commissioned for her to make it easier to mount the stately Tennessee Walker that was fourteen hands from his hooves to his withers. In her agitated state, carelessness prevailed. She was neither in the mood to take the time to properly curry him, nor would she have him under saddle.

Blaze raised his head and, like a barometer of warning, let out a higher pitched neigh. *Now, now, boy. Not to worry. We have ridden in this fashion in the past.* Upon her words, Alexandra stepped up, gathering the skirt of her gown in her hand as she straddled the horse's girth and settled herself on his back. His gait was easy and rhythmic as he followed the lead of his mistress. The sound of distant thunder did not deter her from her course as she patted Blaze's neck and gently poked her heels into his sides to spur him forward. She was determined to feel free of the events of the day. *Come Blaze, we will ride into the Wide, Wide World! Nothing will stop us! I will show William that I am invincible and strong. I will prove to be everything he ever wanted and he will soon be done with his mate.*

'The Wide, Wide World' was the moniker her father, the late Andrew Whitaker, had given to a portion of the acreage on his estate. It was a flat, verdant area, encircled at its perimeter by forests of deciduous trees co-mingled with massive pines. It was the perfect arena for her. She had been raised with little or no boundaries and the anger burning inside her urged her forward to test the very edges of the wide-open space.

Wistfully alone, except for her mount, and guided by a faint beam of the moon's light that intermittently broke through ominous clouds, Alexandra set out on a furious ride, invoking a full gallop from Blaze as she dug her heels into his girth and gathered fistfuls of his dark amber mane. She rode in reckless abandon, tears obscuring her vision. Blaze answered her fervent plea, moving onward faster and faster, his hooves churning the soil beneath them. The night's air was heavy with impending doom. Suddenly, an earth-shaking crack of thunder resounded across the *Wide Wide World* startling Blaze and causing him to rear, nearly spilling Alexandra to the ground. A second clap of nature's fury spooked Blaze, causing him to rear again. Alexandra held tight her grip. She was one with her horse and would entrust him with her destiny. When his front legs returned to the ground, he took off more rapidly than before. It seemed there was no holding him back. The two were of one mind, hell-bent on an escape that superseded safety and security. For Blaze it was the reality of the storm that set his beastly pace in motion -- for his mistress, the reality of the events of late set her on a perilous course. Reality periodically escaped her as the fantasy she had created danced about her head. Truth no longer mattered. She imagined herself with William in a realm of their making until reality reappeared and she could not be consoled. She felt damned, unloved, betrayed, and would have no other vision enter her mind's eye.

She called out loud, "Oh Father, you truly were the only sensible human being for you understood me!" Her words, gripped by a gust of wind, became garbled, and her thoughts, as opaque as the heavens that veiled her ride, could not keep pace with Blaze's hasty and deliberate stride, yet she felt no fear. She was determined to ride the rage inside her to the end.

Under the edges of the night's sky she found shelter in her thoughts as ink-dark clouds more foreboding than their predecessors filled the endless nocturnal void. Another clap of thunder rattled the earth and sent Blaze forward with renewed gusto. Spectacular flashes of lightning vehemently lit the sky as the two, rider and horse, were one against the elements. Thunder began to rumble its wrath across the atmosphere as the proximity of lightning gathered closer and closer to the rider and her mount. Rumbles and flashes pelted the terrain as massive wind gusts and sheets of rain threatened her stability. She began to lose her grip on Blaze's mane and felt as though she were slipping away. As she regained her hold, an enormous bolt of cloud to ground lightning struck the turf before them. The two were instantly illuminated by the shard of light that seemed to come directly from the heavens to strike them down. Stunned, Alexandra fell from her mount as Blaze, fatally injured, collapsed to the earth. Both lay without motion. All within Alexandra was eerily still. Her venom, her lust for life, her heartbeat, and that of the tiny soul within had seemingly succumbed to an undoing at her own hands. It appeared she had taken her last ride and it had taken her. As her body settled on the ground, a mighty gust of wind caught her last words as they slipped from her lips into the open air, "I love you always and forever." Amid the final assault of the cleansing storm, the only enduring sound was the reverberating echo of silence.

Beyond the Rose
A Novel
Copyright © 2017 Sharon Allen Gilder

Oatmeal Crisps Cookies
prepared by Emma's Cook at Chestnut Heights
Makes 3 ½ dozen cookies

½ cup butter, room temperature
½ cup brown sugar, packed
½ cup granulated sugar
1 egg
1 tsp. vanilla extract
¾ cup PLUS 2 Tablespoons flour
½ tsp. salt
½ tsp. baking soda
1 ¼ cups slow cooking oats

With electric mixer, cream butter, then add sugars, egg and vanilla extract. Sift together the dry ingredients and add to creamed mixture. Stir in the oats with a wooden spoon. Drop the batter by teaspoonfuls, placing 2 inches apart, onto an ungreased cookie sheet. Bake at 350 degrees for 9 to 10 minutes. (Note: oven temperatures vary, check your oven temperature). Let rest 1 minute. If some edges run together, gently separate with a blunt table knife. Loosen from cookie sheet with a pancake turner or metal spatula, then gently transfer to paper towel topped metal cooling racks. Let cool. Store in airtight container. May be frozen – if there are any cookies remaining after sampling! Cook hopes you enjoy!

Beyond the Rose
A Novel
A Warren Press Readers Club Guide
Copyright © 2017 Sharon Allen Gilder

1. Is Alexandra truly in love with William or is hers an infatuation with someone she can never have?
2. If *Beyond the Rose* were made into a movie, whom would you want to play William? Arielle? Alexandra? Ian? Elsbeth? Emma? Alistair? Morgan? Simon? Thomas? Fiona? Arianna? Sully?
3. Which parts of the novel made you cry? Laugh?
4. Which character in *Beyond The Rose* is most like you? Which character would you most like to hang around with?
5. Who is your favorite character? Who is your least favorite?
6. What attributes do you like to see in a woman? In a man?
7. How does Sir Ian Hargrove change during the course of the novel…or does he?
8. What is your interpretation of the book's ending?
9. Do you believe Alistair and Alexandra's account about Calvin Layton?
10. What element or role does Peepers play in the story?

warren press

Maryland

Photo: Stone Photography

Sharon Allen Gilder is a native Washingtonian. She resides in
Maryland and South Carolina with her husband. Her debut novel
was *The Rose Beyond*. Her road map for a happy life includes time
with family and friends, writing, reading, walking, relaxing on
the beach, and singing her original Irish drinking song "Oh the
Whiskey" at neighborhood restaurants and wine bars.

For more information, please visit:
www.sharonallengilder.com